…Eventually, Sean broke the ice by asking, "…too well during my interrogation?"

After pausing for what seemed like several eons to Sean, Jolene replied simply, "Very well. You give good answers."

Sean retorted, "You ask good questions."

After another long pause, Jolene very softly asked Sean, "Am I too young for you?"

He replied, "That all depends on whether I'm too old for you."

GOOD WILL WIN IN THE END

Rory R. Olsen

John —
With all y best wishes.

Rory

To J.E.S., my friend and mentor…

Acknowledgements

The author gratefully acknowledges the valuable assistance given to him by his friends and readers, who read each chapter as it was produced and shared their valuable thoughts and insights: the Hon. Georgia Akers, Ms. Deanise Jagnanan, Ms. Kathi Perkins and James Wyckoff, Esq. Without their assistance and encouragement, this novel would not have been completed.

Many other friends, each in some way, contributed technical knowledge and advice that assisted in the writing of this book. Thanks are owed to all of them: Ms. Pat Armatta; Ms. Cindy Arrington; Karen Blakeman, A.I.A; Michael Cenatiempo, Esq.; Mrs. Judith Jones; Pat Manson, Esq.; Ms. Helen Morris; Carmen Petzold, Ph.D.; Ms. Connie Pollet, C.S.R.; Douglas Samuels, M.D.; Darlene Payne Smith, Esq.; Deputy Jerry Suntych; Ms. Margie Trevino and Robin Wosje, Esq.

Special thanks are owed to Ryan, at JetNetwork™, for technical advice concerning the costs of renting a LearJet™ 31A.

Genuine thanks are owed to Deborah Long, M.A., for her final editing, formatting and professional writing advice.

My deepest and most sincere thanks are owed to my wife, Trish, for her invaluable help in editing and revising my manuscript, as well as for putting up with me while I disappeared for hours at a time to toil at the keyboard.

Prologue

A short entry appeared in the back of the second section of the *University City Bugle* on Wednesday, March 10, 1999. It read:

"Yesterday Administrative Law Judge Cheryl Nieman Riley died in an automobile accident when her car skidded off of County 191 into Flatboat River. She is survived by her husband, Probate Judge Sean Riley, and two twin daughters, Maureen and Patricia. Funeral details are pending."

BOOK I: THE ROMANCE

Chapter One

"Hi Sugar!" the shapely blonde said, as she planted a wet kiss on Sean's cheek. Sensing her boss's embarrassment, his dark-haired receptionist, Miriam, smiled and asked with a big grin, "Should I hold your calls?"

Judge Sean Riley, sensing that he was outgunned and outnumbered, smiled weakly and told Miriam to hold his calls. As Sean shut the door and ushered Kyra Townsend into his office, he thought about giving Kyra his usual lecture about not being so informal and friendly with him around his staff. Sensing that Kyra was trying to get a rise out of him today, he said nothing. Since Kyra practiced exclusively criminal law as a prosecutor, Sean didn't have to keep her at arms length as he did with lawyers who practiced before him.

As the blonde prosecutor made herself comfortable on the sofa, having already kicked off her black high heels, Sean asked her if she wanted something to drink. Smiling, Kyra answered, "Diet Coke™ will be fine."

When Sean returned from the refrigerator with the Diet Coke, he couldn't help but notice that Kyra had settled comfortably on the sofa, sitting width-wise so that her legs took up most of the sofa. He also couldn't help but notice that although Kyra had thickened a bit in the middle, her legs were still long, tan and awfully shapely. Since she was wearing nude hose, he also noticed that her toes were freshly polished a bright red. Kyra was one attractive woman from head to toe.

"Sean, darlin', you're lookin' at my legs again," Kyra said, with a hint of a tease in her voice and a sparkle in her brown eyes.

"If I didn't look, you'd be even more worried about me than you are now, wouldn't you?" Sean asked, without any affect in his voice.

Not answering him directly, Kyra said sweetly, "Sean, no matter how long you live here, you still act like what you are—a Damned Yankee!"

"Kyra, you just figured that out now? I'm proud of you!"

"Well if you were a gentleman, you wouldn't be so obvious about lookin' at my legs!"

"If you weren't such an obvious flirt with such great legs, I probably could be more discreet!"

"Do you look at the legs of the lady lawyers in your courtroom like that?"

1

Smiling, Sean said, "Heavens, No!" But, Sean was lying. As he spoke, he thought of the reddish-brown-haired lawyer named Kim Brownlee, who while waiting for her case to be called this morning, had positioned herself on the front row of the pews and very obviously flirted with him by crossing and re-crossing her legs and dangling her shoe. Every time he looked up from his papers, there she was. Every time he made eye contact with her, she gave him a friendly smile.

"Sugar, the fact that you are noticin' my legs is a good sign. I think that you may recover!" Kyra said emphatically.

Kyra and her husband, Max, were two of Sean's oldest and dearest friends. They both worried about him because ever since Cheryl's death, he had kept his grief bottled up inside. Sean really appreciated their concern, but wasn't ready to open up yet. After Cheryl's death, Sean directed his psychic energies toward the Twins and buried himself in his judicial and academic duties.

"Why do you say that I may recover?" Sean asked distractedly.

"Darlin', we well know that if a happily married man loses his wife, odds are he will remarry fairly quick. Since you were very happily married, it's 'bout time for you to start showin' some interest in the opposite sex!"

"Kyra, you know that Cheryl has been dead little more than a year! How can you talk about me getting married again so soon?"

"Sean, before you can get married, you have to start datin'. You haven't started, have you?"

Kyra, whether she knew it or not, had scored a hit, a very palpable hit. Being a judge is about the worst job to have if you are middle-aged and trying to meet the opposite sex. The only women that Sean saw on a daily basis were his staff, the ladies in the clerk's office, the widows (and other litigants) in the court and female lawyers.

If a judge were to get involved with one of his staff members, the door would be wide open to a sexual harassment suit. At age fifty, the prospect of being a defendant in this sort of suit was not something that was very appealing, so Sean never seriously considered that option—Miriam's great legs notwithstanding.

The clerks were ruled out because the ladies over there love to talk and talk. The widows on his docket and the female lawyers presented a less clear-cut problem. If Sean met a widow, he could conceivably ask her out after her case was over and done with for good. But, if someone were to file an ethics complaint, Sean would have to justify his actions to an inquiry of the Judicial Ethics Committee. This was not a very appetizing idea since the

2

committee was well known for being rude and abusive to judges, even if there was no evidence to support a complaint.

Similarly, if a woman lawyer only handled uncontested decedent's estates before him, getting involved with her would not necessarily be unethical. But, since most of the women lawyers that practiced before Sean also handled contested matters before him regularly, they were out of bounds. God help a judge accused of sleeping with a lawyer who had a case pending before him! That would be a real bad idea for both of them.

Sean also taught two courses at night at the law school of Southern University,[1] where he met many women. However, with the university's draconian policies regarding sexual harassment, Sean long ago realized that the women he met there were strictly off limits—more so than his employees, the clerks, widows and other litigants and female lawyers appearing before him.

Since the loss of Cheryl was still too fresh and this was an election year, Sean had let the subject of dating go for now, telling himself that he would think about it later. Little did he recognize it then, but destiny—acting through Kyra—had just taken a hand in this game.

"Kyra, we both well know that my chances of meeting anyone that I would and could go out with are pretty slim. If and when I find someone to date, I'll let you know!" said Sean, hoping that Kyra would get off of the uncomfortable subject.

"Sean, would you like Max and me to fix you up with someone?" That did it! Sean sensed that he was cornered. Kyra had played him perfectly.

"By any chance, do you have someone in mind?" Sean asked. He could see what was coming as clearly as someone standing at a railroad crossing could see a smoke-belching steam locomotive coming down a railroad track on a sunny day on a Kansas prairie. Sean asked the question on purpose, hoping that he could find an objection to any specific person that Kyra proposed.

"I don't think that you know her. She's a sergeant on Sheriff Walker's staff," said Kyra, exploiting her advantage.

Damn! He was trapped. "Can I give you an answer in a couple of days?" Sean asked out of desperation.

"Sean, you're a judge. You make many, many decisions daily. We both know that if you wait a day or so, you won't be any smarter. Why not just get it over with and agree?"

Very tentatively, Sean asked, "What did you have in mind?"

"A double dinner date on Friday about six over at The Palm Tree™."

3

"This is Wednesday. Will you and Max have time to arrange a sitter for your kids?"

"My mother is gonna pick the kids up from school. It's all set."

"Errr... What is this sergeant's name?"

"Jolene. Jolene Scruggs."

"Are you going to tell me anything about her?"

"You'll like her. She reminds me of what I would have been a few years ago if I hadn't gone to law school. She all piss n' vinegar on the outside, but a real special lady once you get to know her."

Sean surrendered meekly by orally confirming the time and place, and then writing it down in his bulky calendar. Then, the conversation wandered off for a moment into the required references to the health of Max and the Twins. When this was done, Kyra stood up and put her shoes back on.

"Jury ready to come back?" Sean asked, knowing by Kyra's hairdo, tasteful but expensive black dress, black high heels and pearls that she had been in a jury trial. Normally, when not in front of a jury, she wore a blue suit, little or no jewelry and had her hair in a ponytail.

"Yes Sugar, I've got a rookie waitin' on the jury. Since my cell phone hasn't gone off, they must still be out. I'd best go over there before the poor lad dies of worry."

After a passionate and very sincere hug, Kyra left, having reassured Sean that, as his friend, she was looking out for him and that all would go well on Friday. As Kyra left his office, leaving behind the strong but delightful scent of her perfume, Sean sighed. He realized that it was good to have friends like Kyra and Max to look out for him. But, he wasn't ready to date!

Thinking further, Sean realized that he probably had been a real dud at being single when he was younger, never having actually initiated the relationship with the four women with whom he had been seriously involved. The last time he had begun a new relationship, Richard Nixon was still president. The rules for dating, which he understood poorly back then, had all changed. He started feeling like a time traveler, who had gone too far into the future to understand the new world into which he had ventured.

What really bothered Sean was the prospect of becoming intimate with someone new. Cheryl and he had been together for over a quarter century. The thought of going through all of the adjustments and pain of a new relationship was rather daunting. Sadly, Sean, being a man, had no one to ask for help.

****

On the way home, Sean pulled his F-150™ off to the side of County 191. After looking carefully both ways, he ran across the road and stopped at a simple, wooden, white cross that stood a few feet off of the road, between the edge of the road and the bank of Flatboat River. He crossed himself, said a short prayer and then glumly, after looking carefully both ways, went back to his F-150 and resumed his ride home. The cross marked the approximate spot where Cheryl's Explorer™ had veered off the road and into the river after hitting a patch of ice on that cold March morning last year. In a typically mindless bureaucratic way, the county had also placed a memorial marker there, as well. A few days after the accident, large, yellow signs had appeared on both sides of the short hill that was between the site of the accident and Sean's home, cautioning drivers that the roadway was slippery when icy. While the signs were posted too late to have done anything for Cheryl, Sean hoped that maybe they had been posted in time to save some other poor soul.

When Sean entered the house, he was greeted immediately by two loud sounds, best described as "Mrrrrrw!" Law and Equity, his two Siamese princesses, were there to welcome their human sugar daddy home. Petting them for at least five minutes, Sean was repeatedly nuzzled, rubbed with cold, wet cat noses and told that he had been missed and that he shouldn't have left.

After the furry love-in, Sean looked over his mail. There wasn't much today. Just a few bills, a legal magazine, today's issue of *The Wall Street Journal*,™ a few bits of junk mail and one white envelope, the size and stiffness of an invitation. Opening the invitation, he noticed that it was for the bar association's annual Spring Fling on a Saturday in early May, which, as he reckoned, was only six weeks from now.

Sean choked up for a second. Then his eyes grew moist. Cheryl and he had always enjoyed the Spring Fling, which was one of the few fun formal events that they used to attend. This would be the second one that he would miss. He knew that he would miss it because he had no one to take. If he went alone, he would feel even more alone than he did now. Plus, if he did go alone, that would be an open invitation to every single female lawyer to pounce on him. Even worse, the married women present would start trying to fix him up with their widowed, divorced and single friends and relatives. After Cheryl died, he had offers from ladies to cook and clean for him. He politely and firmly brushed aside the invitations and eventually they slowed down, but had not totally stopped.

As Law purred in his lap, he petted Equity. Suddenly, an intriguing idea came to mind. He thought, *If this Sergeant Jolene isn't too bad, maybe I should ask her to the Spring Fling, just so the word would get out that I have a girlfriend.*

Sean realized that even the rumor that he had a girlfriend had possibilities. It wouldn't stop his few close friends, like Kyra and Max, but it would certainly discourage many of the predatory females he had met and their co-conspirators. With this somewhat useful thought in his head, Sean changed into his workout clothes and hit his home treadmill. After the treadmill, he worked out on his weight machine. As he was doing his last set of reps for the night, something that Cheryl had said to him popped into his brain.

One night, several years ago, when they were experiencing the early joys of having an almost empty nest—which began as soon as the Twins had friends old enough to drive—Sean and Cheryl watched a chick flick on cable. This sort of entertainment wasn't necessarily his thing. But, since Cheryl really liked them, he watched with her from time to time. She had a predictable routine for such occasions. She liked to watch her chick flicks wearing a thin T-shirt with no bra, tight blue jeans and barefoot. She would always stuff herself on microwaved popcorn during the early part of the flick, and then want to sit close to Sean during the rest of it. Invariably, after the movie ended, they would wind up in the bedroom. Sean really missed those chick flick evenings now.

This particular night, after the sex was over, Cheryl snuggled up next to Sean and said, quite out of the blue, "You know that plot was silly. In real life, widowers rarely have to choose between two women like the doctor did in that movie. In real life, if the widower was happily married, the first woman to bed the widower usually weds him." Sean asked himself why he had to remember this conversation less than two days before his first date post-Cheryl.

After his workout, Sean, following his usual custom, grabbed a quick salad. As he was eating under the watchful eyes of Law and Equity, another thought popped into his brain. The name "Jolene Scruggs" rang a bell in the back of his mind. He had heard or read that name somewhere else. Not being able to place the name any better, he took a quick shower and prepared for bed.

Just as Law and Equity started leading him into the bedroom, the idea that he had heard or seen the name "Jolene Scruggs" popped into his brain again. Rather than tossing and turning all night, Sean decided to go online to

6

check the name out. Searching the website of the *Bugle* yielded a link to a brief story, with a headline that simply said, "Deputies receive awards." The article was very short. All it said was that the sheriff had presented medals that morning to a number of deputies, who had distinguished themselves above and beyond the call of duty. Seven names were listed, including Sergeant Jolene Scruggs.

What really caught Sean's eye was the photo that appeared below the text of the story. In the group photo, were the sheriff, of course, five male deputies and two female deputies, both of who appeared to be brass. One of the female deputies was heavy set, mean looking and not at all attractive. The other one, as best Sean could tell from the small Internet photo, appeared to be a dark-haired beauty. Assuming the worst, Sean logged off and went to bed, much to the relief of Law and Equity, who scolded him for not having obeyed their bedtime command previously. Ten minutes later, one tired, lonely, scared judge and his two furry, purring mistresses were all curled up together in a deep sleep.

****

On Thursday morning, while sipping his morning tea, Judge Riley had a chance to chat with his trusty bailiff, Bubba, before going out on the bench. Deputy Weston Claxton "Bubba" Connors looked as if Central Casting had picked him to play the part of a southern lawman. He was about 5'10", mostly bald with gray fringes and had a bit of a potbelly. He had a deep, resonant voice and brown eyes that could pierce you all the way down to your soul. But, what was most noticeable about Bubba was his manner of speaking. He talked so slowly that people said you could plant and harvest a crop while he was still speaking the same sentence.

Actually, there was a lot more to Bubba than the stereotype. He had been a Marine non-com, last serving as a D.I. After doing his twenty, he retired from the Corps and joined the sheriff's department right before the merger with the University City Police Department into the current system, in which the sheriff headed the entire law enforcement operation for the county.

Bubba, notwithstanding his occupational choices, was a very kind, gentle man. He hadn't married while in the Corps because of his concerns that marriage and long overseas deployments did not mix well. Two years after joining the sheriff's department, Bubba married the widow of another deputy, who had died in a vehicular mishap while chasing a fleeing felon. His bride, Shirley, was a fetching, young, buxom brunette who had been left with three teenage boys. They were a great match because she loved to talk and he didn't talk much. The joke was that he talked so slowly because he had few opportunities to speak at home.

Sean asked Bubba, "What do you know about a sergeant named Jolene Scruggs?"

Bubba replied slowly, "Well Judge, from what I hear, she is one damn fine peace officer—even though she's a woman. If'n I remember rightly, couple of years ago she stopped a couple of bank robbers by herself. Brass, in their typical dumb-assed way, thanked her for being so good at her job that she got kicked upstairs to headquarters."

Sean always suspected that Bubba's true calling was to be one of the loafers that sat in rural filling stations, whitlin', spittin', sippin' Dr. Pepper™ and adding local color to an otherwise boring community. After a lengthy pause, Sean concluded that Bubba had finished his thought.

So, Sean then asked, "What does she look like?"

Bubba, after pausing a bit and mulling over his delivery, finally said, "Well Judge, as I recall, she's a real looker!"

Sean, his curiosity piqued, waited for more. It didn't come. Finally, he asked with a bit more speed and loudness than he intended, "Know anything else about her?"

After waiting for what seemed like several eons, Bubba finally said very, very slowly, "Well Judge, any place like the Marine Corps or the department, where there's a whole lot more men than women, the men do talk and talk about the women, 'specially the lookers. With respect to Sergeant Scruggs, seems as if there is what you lawyer types call a *divergence of opinion*. A few deputies say that she isn't the sort that likes men, if you know what I mean."

Pausing for effect, Bubba continued, "Personally, I never put much stock into them sort of comments. Seems like when a man says that 'bout a woman, it's mostly 'cause she had the good sense to stay away from a feller like that."

After a long, slow sip of coffee and a bite on his donut, Bubba continued, "Well Judge, the second bunch says that she only likes to date much older, rich men. Personally, I don't have no reason to say whether that's true or not. But if she does, that ain't a bad thing if'n that's what she wants to do. Older men tend to appreciate young women a lot more than young men do. And of course, it's just as easy to love a rich man as a poor man."

Sean started to get a sinking feeling. Was Kyra fixing him up with a woman who preferred her own sex or was just a gold-digger? As Sean began to space out, he was jolted back into reality by Bubba.

"Well Judge, the third and biggest bunch says that she's a bright, smart lady with a good education and sense of humor, who isn't about to hop into bed with some blue-suited, whorin' drunkard just 'cause he starts feedin' her a line of bull***t."

Sean smiled, knowing full well that Bubba didn't think much of men who drank too much and much less of men who cheated on their wives. Glancing at the clock on his computer, Sean reminded Bubba that it was time for Sean to take the bench.

* * * * * * * * * * * *

Sean thought as he made his way onto the bench, *On tap today, we have a nasty guardianship spat.*

As the parties took their turns throwing verbal mud pies at each other, Sean scribbled "Gold-digger?" on his legal pad, circling the word for emphasis. He had reason to be concerned. His late maternal grandfather, a chemist from France, who immigrated to the U.S. after the Great War, had made a substantial fortune from his patents. This money eventually passed in trust to Sean after his mother and grandparents died.

Sean's late mother had been a very successful author of children's books. Her will left the rights to her books to the trust that her father had created. These rights had been a gold mine, greatly increasing the value of his trust. Several years ago, Sean's father died, leaving his estate to the trust also. While not as successful in financial matters as either his wife or his wife's father, Sean's dad, as a medical school professor and practitioner, had amassed an estate worth several million additional dollars.

Last summer, when Sean hit the big 50, the trust had terminated and Sean received the funds in his own name. He placed the money in a management trust for a matter of convenience. But, since he had the right to claim it at any time he wanted, for the first time ever, he would have to report the existence of this large fortune—valued conservatively at over fifty million dollars—on his annual financial disclosure form later this year.

In retrospect, perhaps the smartest thing that Cheryl and he had ever done was to have her write a will directing her trust fund to pass at her death in trust for the benefit of the Twins. The five million dollars that Cheryl passed this way to the Twins meant that whatever happened in life to Sean, the Twins would never be penniless. The financial disclosure requirement

9

had bothered Sean a good bit for the last few months, giving him something unrelated to Cheryl's death to worry about, which may have been a good thing.

After pausing from his introspection for several minutes to overrule an objection, Sean calmed down. Even if Sergeant Jolene was a gold-digger, there was no way that she could know how wealthy he really was. While it had never been a secret that Cheryl and he were well off since they lived in a big house on a multi-acre tract of land, for a while, at least, there was no way that Jolene could possibly know.

After sustaining an objection and chiding counsel to move their mud fest along, Sean realized that if Kyra arranged a date for him, he was probably safe. Kyra had a career prosecutor's jaundiced outlook on human nature. If she was arranging the date with Sergeant Jolene, she had probably vetted her about as well as the Senate Judiciary Committee vets prospective federal judges nominated by a president from the other party.

After a while, the applicant rested. Following a short recess, the other daughter had her chance to blacken the family name even further. On and on it went, until mercifully the second sister ran out of gas and rested.

Looking at the clock on the wall, Sean recessed court until after lunch, promising to announce his decision at that time.

****

Sean made it over to the Joe's Diner™ just in time to meet his friend and campaign consultant, Bob Griswold, for lunch. It would be mostly a social lunch, with enough business worked in to make it deductible for Bob.

Bob, like Kyra and Max, was a former student of Sean's. Bob had been a lineman for State University and, after graduation, played for several unremarkable seasons in the NFL.[2] On a lark, one off-season Bob took the L.S.A.T. and to his great surprise, scored in the top one percentile. Although his grades had been mediocre at State, Bob was admitted to Southern University's law school, mostly based on a really impressive interview he had with the Assistant Dean for Admissions. In the interview, Bob won the dean's confidence and impressed him with his maturity, freely admitting that his grades were the result of a lack of interest at the time. Bob's intense sincerity persuaded the dean to give him a shot, for which Bob repaid him by doing very well in school. After graduating, he went into practice with a small firm in Capitol City.

Bob had been quite content practicing law. One day, however, one of his partners decided to run in a special election to fill a vacancy created when a congressman died in a boating accident. Bob's partner asked him to run his campaign, which he did brilliantly. The consultant that the RNC had sent out to assist on the campaign was so impressed with Bob that after the successful election, the consulting firm offered Bob a job, which he accepted.

After spending several years in Washington, Bob came back to Southern State and opened his own political consulting firm. As things turned out, Sean was appointed to the bench in '91 on the very day that Bob sent out his announcement cards. Sean was Bob's first client. Having gone through two campaigns with Bob, they were close friends.

Sean inquired about Bob's family. Then, Bob reciprocated by inquiring about the Twins. The pleasantries over, Sean and Bob quickly got down to business.

Bob said, "Sean, this year is going to be a lot different than '92 or '94. In '92, you were the new kid on the block. You had no serious opposition from the D's because you didn't have a record to run against."

Sean realized that was true. Since Sean had been on the bench for little more than a year before the '92 general election, his opponent was a semi-retired, alcoholic lawyer, who had never impressed anyone during his many years in practice. His poor reputation, constantly red face and eyes, his somewhat slurred speech and his unruly mop of white hair scared off what little support he might have had. Besides, his opponent was running against a professor who had drafted portions of the Probate Code and was well respected throughout the state as being an expert in probate law. It was a slaughter. Even the very liberal *Bugle* endorsed Sean.

Bob continued, "In '94, Clinton had so alienated our local electorate with his wife's socialized medicine plan that there was no way a Republican could have lost an election that year, even if he was caught in bed with a dead woman **and** a live man."

Sean knew that statement was undoubtedly true. His opponent that year had been well qualified and personable. Unfortunately for his opponent, even the area around the university broke Republican. Considering how many jobs in the area were tied into the huge Southern University Medical Center, the fear of socialized medicine was not taken lightly.

Bob said, "In general, things have been going our way over the last few years. The suburbs of Capitol City, which have spilled into our county, have added over ten thousand Republican-leaning voters to the county's voting rolls since '94. That is in our favor. But, on the other side of the ledger, the local Democratic Party has been getting a lot of funding from the DNC.

They are going to make a **maximum effort** to try and stop us this time, both locally and statewide."

"How do things look in my race?" Sean asked, with a bit of apprehension creeping into his tone. Bob opened his briefcase and, after sorting through some file folders, handed Sean a memorandum entitled, "Opposition Research—Greene, Thomas A."

While nothing to rival Sir Arthur Conan Doyle, the memorandum was gripping reading in its own way. Thomas A. Greene, unlike Sean, was a native of Southern State. Unlike Sean, Greene was a veteran of Viet Nam. Not only had Greene been a top graduate of the United States Military Academy (West Point), he had also served two tours of duty in-country, coming home after each tour with a chest full of medals.

After leaving the Army, Greene graduated near the top of his class at Harvard Law. After spending several years as a federal prosecutor, Greene joined a PI firm. After twenty years, he retired from the firm a very wealthy man, having bankrupted many a doctor and hospital along the way. Nowadays, Greene only took on cases that interested him, usually death penalty appeals cases. Apparently, Greene had success in a number of these cases, earning quite a few new trials.

Needing reassurance, Sean asked Bob, "Okay, how bad is it going to be?"

Bob replied, "Sean, he does have a few things going for him that you don't have going for you. True, he has a military record and you don't, but you've got a proven probate track record to run on and he doesn't. As far as my researchers could find, there is no record anywhere at all in this state of his ever having been involved in any sort of probate case—not even getting a will admitted to probate. Also, there is something else that I should tell you about Greene. Lawyers who know him say that while a very competent lawyer, he is downright nasty when challenged and holds grudges against people who oppose him."

"That's good?" Sean asked in mock seriousness.

Not catching on to Sean's attempt at humor, Bob pontificated, "A man like that racks up enemies for no reason. That's real good!"

Continuing in his solemn mode, Sean asked, "Will that be enough to get me reelected?"

Bob said in his usually blunt way, "I think so! You've got a good record to run on. That should be enough. But, let's not give them any help. Between now and November, try to keep your head down and don't do anything stupid! Promise?"

Sensing that mentioning he had a date tomorrow night would get him lectured or at least a frown of disapproval, Sean looked at his watch and indicated that it was time to return to court. After a hasty goodbye, Sean scurried back to the courthouse.

****

After lunch, Sean quickly replaced his suit coat with his robe and mounted the bench. After taking the bench, he sat quietly and looked over the expectant crowd. Finally, once he had the crowd's full attention, Sean intoned his best authoritative voice and said, "Guardianships are very different than other types of cases. In most other types of civil cases, there is a winner and a loser. Contested guardianship cases aren't like that. In these cases, our focus is purely on the ward and on his or her well being. From what I can tell here, unless there are some very serious attitude readjustments, neither applicant would be a good choice because of the conflict between the two applicants. If there is conflict in the family, it can't help but have an adverse impact on the ward because incapacitated or not, no one likes to see their grown children fighting."

After a pregnant pause, Sean continued, "Fortunately, under the Probate Code, my choices are not limited to just the two applicants. I have a third option. If I find it to be in the ward's best interest, I can appoint a neutral third party, who need not be a family member, to serve as guardian. At this time, I am going to leave the bench. If I do not hear back from the lawyers within an hour that the parties have reached an agreement that is satisfactory to me, I will appoint a neutral third-party guardian. This would be a thing for the parties to consider seriously because a neutral third-party guardian will expect to be paid from the ward's estate."

Exiting the courtroom in a hushed silence, Sean hurried off the bench, leaving the two sisters to stew in their own juices for a while. After he left the bench, Sean used the time to chat with the ladies in his office. Once he got back to his desk, he returned several telephone calls.

The last call that Sean returned was from the head librarian at Southern University's law school, Beth Shelton. She had called to say that she had been able to purchase an original copy of one of Professor Maitland's lesser-known works. She said that she was keeping it in her office, so Sean could see if he wanted any of it copied for his Legal History class. Being a sucker for old books, Sean indicated that he would be by to see her before his next class started.

After hanging up the telephone, Sean glanced at the mail that had come in. While most of it was junk mail, there were a few things that required his careful review. As Sean went through these items, his concentration was interrupted. Looking up, he noticed that Miriam, his loyal, if sometimes annoying, secretary-receptionist, was staring at him.

With a bit of a smirk, Miriam said, "Judge, Kim Brownlee is out in our waiting area. She asked if you could see her for a minute. I told her that you had people in the courtroom and that you had to leave for your class soon, but I'd check, even knowing full well that you're too busy to be interrupted. Should I send her away?"

Sensing that Miriam was being a bit too territorial, Sean smiled and asked that Kim be sent back to his office. By the time that Kim and Miriam reached Judge Sean Riley's office, he had shed his robe in favor of his suit coat, adjusted his tie and sprayed some breath freshener into his mouth and applied fresh cologne. Sean warmly shook Kim's hand and directed her to the sofa in his office.

Standing in the doorway, Miriam inquired, "How soon before you need to go back on the bench?"

Looking at his wristwatch, Sean replied, "Twenty minutes or so will be fine."

"I'll remember to remind you in twenty minutes," Miriam said a trifle too loudly for Sean's taste.

Sean sat in the small chair located perpendicular to the sofa. As he glanced over at Kim, he furtively peeked at her crossed legs. Kim, having a somewhat ruddy complexion, knew that black hose was the perfect color for her shapely legs to be noticed. Being too polite to embarrass the judge by acknowledging his interest in her legs, Kim made several minutes of small talk. While she was talking, Sean noticed that her reddish-brown hair was nicely accented by her pale-green suit. After the small talk ended, Kim rapidly shifted toward what was really on her mind.

Sweetly, Kim asked, "Judge, can I ask you something somewhat personal?"

Sensing a possible attempt at a *verboten* ex parte communication or something even worse, Sean replied, "Possibly."

"Judge, if I'm not being too forward, I was wondering if you had anyone to take to the Spring Fling? If you do, please forget that I asked."

Sean was in a ticklish spot with that question. Kim had obviously mustered up a good deal of social courage to ask him the question. If he declined her invitation, he risked hurting her feelings. Since he had been on the bench, he came to respect her as a lawyer and, now that the question had been raised, he realized that he was also fond of her as a person. He certainly did not want to hurt her feelings. Sean sensed that if he did hurt her feelings, he would probably spend all night thinking about tears coming from her big, green eyes, feeling as guilty as he could be. But, if he said that he would go with her, he might possibly be harming both of them.

Courthouses are full of nasty people, who have way too much time on their hands. If he went to the Spring Fling with Kim, by noon on Monday, half of the lawyers in the county—and all of the non-lawyers working in the courthouse—would have heard some sort of rumor that Kim Brownlee was sleeping with a judge. Even if their relationship never progressed any further than just attending the Spring Fling together, Kim could face some horrible consequences.

For instance, the next time that Kim had a contested matter before him, the opposing side could file a motion to recuse him from the case. If he didn't give in, Kim would be fair game to be grilled on the stand about her relationship with Judge Sean Riley. Sean probably wouldn't be called to testify, but it was a distinct possibility.

Conceivably, someone might file an ethics complaint against him, alleging that he was trading sexual favors for appointments and favorable rulings. Fortunately for Sean, the hearing would be private at the first level, which barring evidence of something more than a social contact would be as far as the matter went. While not likely, the possibility of an ethics complaint was another factor to consider.

Sensing that he was in the position of a law student called upon by a professor on the one day of the year that he was unprepared, Sean did what law students have done ever since the case method was adopted. Sean quickly glanced up for guidance. As he looked up, Sean saw his large, bulky planner sitting on his desk, which reminded him of tomorrow's double blind date. This was proof positive of the old trial lawyer axiom, "It's better to be lucky than smart."

Looking into Kim's eyes, which by now appeared as green as the ocean on a warm summer day, Sean calmly told her that his friend, Kyra Townsend, had fixed him up with a date just yesterday. Now, this was true. He just didn't say that the date was for tomorrow evening. Speaking from the heart, Sean said, "Kim, thank you for being so kind as to ask me to go with you. I really do appreciate your concern for me."

Whatever doubts Sean might have had about his feelings for Kim were dispelled when he realized that he had been holding her hands in his when he declined. Seconds later, the voice of Miriam announced that the lawyers had reached an agreement, so Sean was needed in the courtroom. As he walked Kim toward the door of his office and into the custody of Miriam, who seemed to be very eager to escort Kim away, Kim suddenly turned and hugged him tightly, saying softly so that only Sean could hear, "Take care of yourself. If you ever need anything, please feel free to call me."

As Sean quickly removed his suit coat and put his robe back on, he realized that his life, miserable as it had been since Cheryl died, had suddenly become quite complicated. As he walked by Miriam's desk on his way to the bench, Sean felt a decided chill.

On the bench, he let the lawyers read their settlement into the record and asked them to send a proposed order to him tomorrow. After that, Sean thanked the lawyers for their efforts, congratulated the applicants on their wisdom and maturity in putting their differences aside for the ward's benefit and adjourned court for the day.

* * * * * * * * * * * *

As Sean drove the few short blocks from the courthouse to the campus, a disquieting thought entered his mind. What if his date with Sergeant Jolene didn't pan out? What would he do about Kim? If he didn't go to the Spring Fling, whatever he said afterwards would still make him look like a liar, which was a disquieting thought in and of itself. What bothered Sean even more was the realization that he probably wouldn't be able to stop himself from calling Kim if tomorrow night didn't work out. Sean suspected that Kim had broken down his defenses and he was emotionally vulnerable around her. Evidently, she had his number.

Before Sean was able to upset himself any more, he turned into the law school parking lot, foolishly thinking that he would be safe there.

After checking the mail in his faculty mailbox, Sean went over to the library to visit Beth Shelton. When he knocked on her office door, he was astonished by what he saw inside her office. Beth, who always seemed to have bought her clothes at a second-hand shop and reportedly eschewed all cosmetics more expensive than Ivory Soap™, looked stunning.

Beth was wearing a flowing, gold dress that nicely accented her figure and features. Beth's dark hair, which he had never seen her wear in any way other than a bun, was long, lustrous and had a nice wave in it. Her red lipstick contrasted very favorably with her fair skin and dark hair. Her makeup made her look younger than her forty-four years.

Rising, Beth asked Sean to sit in one of her two guest chairs. Sitting next to him, she gently handed Sean the book that they had discussed earlier. As she handed him Professor Maitland's treatise, he noticed that her usually short and unpolished fingernails were long and red.

As he examined the book, Beth interrupted him and offered to point out something of interest in this obscure, old edition. When she leaned toward him, Sean was doubly surprised. First, he was pleasantly surprised by the very nice scent that she was wearing. And, as she pointed out several interesting features in the book, he noticed two fleshy features peeking out from the top of her dress. Beth, who in all of the years he had known her had never displayed any signs of sexuality, was oozing with it today.

After agreeing to let Sean keep the book in his faculty office for a week, Beth flashed her pearly whites at him and asked if he had received his invitation to the Spring Fling in the mail. Seeing what was coming next, Sean just smiled as Beth said, "I was wondering if you were planning on attending the Spring Fling."

Having had a good chance earlier to develop his story, Sean decided to stick with it. Looking Beth in the eyes, he told her the same thing that he had told Kim less than two hours before. Looking at his watch, Sean pointed out that he was due in class and took his leave. As he left, Beth, with a sexy tone said, "Judge, I enjoyed visiting with you. Feel free to come back whenever you need anything."

Smiling, Sean waved as he left her office. He could not help but notice that the now standing Beth had very nice legs uncovered by hose. That was information Sean really didn't need right then. Knowing that his Legal History class was an all-male refuge, Sean headed for its safety.

****

On Friday morning, Sean shaved more closely and attentively than he had in years. After splashing on several extra doses of after shave and combing and spraying his hair down real well, he ventured into his closet. Therein a problem rapidly developed because he couldn't decide if he should wear a gray or a blue suit. After a fruitless five-minute internal debate, Sean decided to do what Bob always told him to do on the campaign trail, namely, "When in doubt, always go for the red, white and blue." So, a few minutes later, attired in a blue suit fresh from the cleaner's bag and not yet covered in cat hair, a crisply starched, custom–made, white shirt, a solid red silk necktie, a relatively inexpensive Rolex and gold cuff links, Sean left to meet the world.

As he walked by the living room sofa, Law stretched and Equity rolled over. Sean asked both of them, "If tonight doesn't work out, will one of you ladies go with me to the Spring Fling?" Not surprisingly, there were no volunteers.

＊＊＊＊＊＊＊＊＊＊＊＊

This Friday morning, like all the rest of the Fridays since he had gone on the bench, Sean went to the county mental hospital to hear mental health civil commitment cases. Unlike his usual Fridays, today none of the patients wanted to come to court, all of them having waived their right to hearing. Sean thought that might be just as well since, with the way the last two days had been for him, the female patients would probably ask him if he had plans for the Spring Fling.

After grabbing a quick lunch, Sean called the office and told Miriam that he was going to duck into his faculty office for a while. So, if anyone needed him, they should call him there. After spending a peaceful two hours perusing the Maitland book, Sean emailed a request to Beth to have one small chapter copied for him and left in his mail slot.

Hoping to avoid Beth, he darted into the law library and left the book in the care of a junior law librarian. Then, Sean reluctantly left to go back to his chambers and prepare for his blind date.

As Sean drove back downtown from campus, he realized that if things didn't work out on tonight's date, he had really painted himself into a corner. If Sergeant Jolene wouldn't go with him to the Spring Fling, he would have Kim Brownlee and Beth Shelton angry with him. Since he liked both of them, he would feel their displeasure acutely. Trying to think positively, he told himself that everything would work out just fine.

＊＊＊＊＊＊＊＊＊＊＊＊

At 1720 hours, Sean entered his private bathroom and ran an electric razor over his face for the second time since he had returned from campus. After checking his once naturally sandy blonde hair to see if a stray hair had wandered out of place, he applied a generous helping of aftershave to his face. Glancing at his watch, he knew it was time to leave.

As Sean walked by Miriam's now empty desk, he recalled that she had been very maternal all afternoon. He guessed that she knew he had a date—probably from eavesdropping on his conversation with Kyra—and was very scared. Shutting off the lights in his chambers, Sean left bravely to face his doom.

Sean arrived at The Palm Tree at exactly 1740 hours. Two minutes later, having reserved a table for four people at six, he took a seat at the bar near the door. As he sipped his Perrier™ very slowly, he felt his pulse begin to race while, at the same time, his stomach began to twist into knots more convoluted than any he had learned in the Boy Scouts.

At 1748 hours, Max appeared. After greeting Max warmly, Sean asked the lady at the podium to seat Max and him at their table. Max still sported the same short haircut that he had worn as an infantry officer in the Corps. Max looked just as trim and fit as ever. Sean guessed that if he had to, Max could probably still fit in his first dress blues.

By 1755 hours, Sean's nerves were getting to him. Hoping to calm himself, Sean asked Max as off handily as he could, "Have you met my date?"

Max replied in the negative. Sean felt his level of tension rise to an even higher level. Sensing that Sean was jumpy, Max calmed him down by telling him that Kyra must have really used her considerable powers of eloquence on Jolene since the two had gone shopping on both Wednesday and Thursday nights. When Max mentioned that Kyra had returned home empty handed both nights, Max remarked that had been a first for Kyra.

At 1758 hours, Sean instinctively checked the other doors to The Palm Tree, partially to see if Kyra and Sergeant Jolene Scruggs had entered from another door, but mostly to make sure that he had a ready escape path if one was needed.

At exactly 1800 hours, the door opened and a gaggle of people entered The Palm Tree all at once. Standing, Max and Sean both saw Kyra's bobbing blonde mane from across the room. Seeing them, Kyra waved and then led a small parade of people heading for the tables. Since the others were all behind Kyra, the men in the group blocked any view of the approaching women. Feeling his internal organs getting ready to do cartwheels in his body cavity, Sean braced himself.

As Kyra neared their table, she turned to let her companion arrive at the table first. When Sean saw Jolene standing there in the flesh, two thoughts burst into his consciousness all mixed together. His left brain signaled him, **DANGER! DANGER! TOO YOUNG!** At the same time, his right brain signaled, **RESISTANCE IS FUTILE! SURRENDER NOW!**

Fortunately for Sean, the two competing streams of thought cancelled themselves out, leaving him standing there, appearing quite handsome and dapper in Jolene's eyes.

Jolene correctly guessed Sean to be fifty years old, 6'2" or so and reasonably trim. His face was classically handsome. Jolene noticed favorably that Sean had the upper body of a weight lifter. His sandy blonde hair nicely complimented his green eyes. His suit was custom tailored. What impressed her the most about Sean was his aura of kindly strength. Jolene had a feeling that Sean was a decent man with a strong, but warm character.

Kyra handled the introductions. With her most mellifluous tone of voice, Kyra said, "Sean, I'd like you to meet Sergeant Jolene Scruggs."

Not being entirely sure as to what he should do now, Sean lightly shook her hand and told her that he was pleased to make her acquaintance.

When Kyra introduced Sean to Jolene, her response was a simple nod of the head and a "Judge, how you?"

After they took their places at the table, before the wait staff appeared, Jolene looked at Kyra and asked, "Is this the same judge you told me about? He's a lot younger than what I expected!"

Before Kyra could say anything in reply, Sean said that Kyra's description of Jolene was equally defective since Jolene was far lovelier than what Kyra had described to him. Before Jolene could tell Sean that he was full of something brown and malodorous, the waiter appeared. While the ladies were debating their orders, Sean's brain did some rapid, adrenalin-driven calculations. Based on his observation, he guessed that she was 5'10" barefoot.[3] Jolene appeared to have a nice figure, but it was obscured by her dress.

Jolene looked perfectly color coordinated. Her royal-blue dress, which was set off with a lighter blue scarf that had some kind of gold geometric pattern on it, perfectly accented her stunningly beautiful blue eyes. Jolene's face was delicately carved. Her red lips were full and inviting. She was wearing just enough makeup to add color to her cheeks, but not enough to obscure her freckles. The scent that Jolene wore reminded Sean of a warm spring day. Overall, she was stunningly beautiful. The only flaw in her otherwise perfect appearance was her chocolate-brown hair, which while lovely, was teased and sprayed into submission. While her hairstyle screamed out "COUNTRY GIRL!" the rest of her was put together with great skill and taste.[4]

After Sean ordered the poached salmon, the conversation picked up again. Jolene lobbed her first shot right at Sean by asking, "Are you one of those damn cop-hatin' liberal judges that have screwed up this country so bad?"

At this, Kyra intervened, "Say what you will about cop-hatin' judges, but Sean isn't one of them. Sean, tell Jolene about how you nearly gave Professor Rodriguez the vapors."

Relaxing just a bit, Sean told the story about how the buzz in the faculty lounge one day a few years ago had been about allegations of police brutality in a case in another county, where two alleged cop killers had arrived at the county jail with black eyes and bruises. Suit had been filed against the cops, their agency and the city that employed them. Professor Rodriguez had waxed on and on about what "low life" law enforcement people were in general. Finally, she had blurted out, as far as she could tell, the only reason that most of them went into law enforcement was because it offered great opportunities for promiscuous sex, first crack at the best illegal drugs and great power over other people. At this, Sean had sweetly asked her, "Isabel, I'm confused. Are you talking about law enforcement or law professors?" The laughter in the faculty lounge shut her up. Professor Rodriguez avoided Sean like the plague for several months after that, which was probably much better for the both of them.

After their salads arrived, Jolene struck again, asking, "What are you, a Catholic Yankee, doin' here?"

Sean replied sweetly, "If you check your history books, you will see that during the War Between the States, a number of Yankees and a number of Catholics held very high positions in the Confederacy."

"Like who?" Jolene asked out of genuine curiosity.

After telling Jolene abbreviated versions of the stories of the several northern-born men who had handled the business affairs of the Confederacy in Europe, he told her at greater length about Catholic Dick Dowling, who had recaptured Galveston Bay from the federal blockaders. Then, he closed his case by telling her in great detail about one of America's greatest naval heroes, Admiral Raphael Semmes, CSN. Ending with a rhetorical flourish, Sean rested his case, sure of victory.

Mercifully, at this time the entrees arrived. Once Kyra had eaten a few bites, she asked, "Sean, remember teachin' our first class?"

Since he was too tense to eat much, Sean relished the chance to regale another listener with his experiences on his first day teaching in law school. Looking into Jolene's lovely blue eyes, Sean told the story of how, on his first day in his first class—first-year Civil Procedure—he had recounted the facts of an obscure case, in which an innocent victim of federal governmental incompetence had her case barred from recovery because of the vagaries of the federal Tort Claims Act. When he had asked who thought the decision was unjust, Max, who had had plenty of experience with mindless bureaucracy in the Corps, volunteered.

When he then had asked who thought the decision was just, Kyra raised her hand. So, telling the class that a good lawyer should be able to advocate either side of an issue, he directed them to argue the positions opposite to what their personal feelings were. After the class ended, their classroom argument continued for days and days in the student lounge, much to the amusement of their classmates and the professors and staff, who caught bits and pieces of it.

By the end of the semester, it seemed like everyone in the building, except those two, knew that they were destined to be together—either in marriage or in a double homicide—since they were always arguing about something. As Sean finished his story, he felt Kyra's foot nudge his leg under the table. He smiled back at her to indicate that her message had been received loud and clear.

Feeling brave, Sean asked, "Who finally won that argument?"

Kyra just smiled. After a moment, Max grudgingly said, "Kyra did, of course!" Max, unlike many men his age, had learned that the best aphrodisiac ever invented was the phrase, "Yes, dear!"

A few minutes later, when the waiter appeared, Max motioned for the check. After Sean made the obligatory move to pay the check, Max paid and indicated that they had better run off to rescue Kyra's mother from their children.

After Kyra and Max had left, neither Jolene nor Sean said anything for several minutes. Eventually, Sean broke the ice by asking, "Did I hold up well during my interrogation?"

After pausing for what seemed like several eons to Sean, Jolene replied simply, "Very well. You give good answers."

Sean retorted, "You ask good questions."

After another long pause, Jolene very softly asked Sean, "Am I too young for you?"

He replied, "That all depends on whether I'm too old for you."

She said, "No seriously, am I too young for you?"

He replied, "When a man reaches my age, the age of the opposite sex becomes largely irrelevant. I don't have a problem dating you, unless you mind being seen with a man old enough to be your father."

Jolene smiled and said that Sean looked very young for his age.

With that issue off of the table, Jolene asked Sean for a ride home, letting slip how she and Kyra had ridden into downtown together this morning.

On the ride to Jolene's place, they were both quiet. As he pulled up into her driveway, Jolene asked him if he would like to come in for a second. Sensing danger, Sean tried to talk his way out of going into her house. Jolene overruled him by simply and softly saying, "I need to show you something."

Once they entered Jolene's house, she asked him to wait by the door. A few seconds later, Jolene returned with what looked like a photocopy of an invitation to the Spring Fling. Jolene said, "Kyra told me that you would either be too shy or too stressed out to remember to ask me about this, so she made me swear on a stack of Bibles that I shouldn't let you get away without tellin' you that I would be honored to be your companion, if that is your heart's desire."

"Indeed, it would be my heart's desire," he replied.

Jolene said, "Thank you, kind Sir. This simple, country girl will try to make you the most envied man there."

Not wanting to push his luck, Sean thought, but did not say, that if Quasimodo was there with Jolene, every man at the party would think that Quasimodo was in fact very lucky. After exchanging telephone, pager and cell phone numbers, as well as email and snail mail addresses, Sean was about to leave when reality hit him. "Jolene, the Spring Fling is in early May, and this is only the end of March. Could I see you before then?"

Being prepared, Jolene just happened to have the entertainment section of the *Bugle* available in her purse. After reviewing it, Sean suggested that they see a screening of a colorized version of *Casablanca* next Saturday afternoon on campus, and then take it from there. As he paused to leave, Jolene kissed him tenderly on the cheek, hugged him softly and told him that he had made tonight very easy for her. Not having the slightest idea what she was talking about, Sean smiled and told her how much he was looking forward to their next visit.

About the time that Sean fired up his F-150, Kyra and Jolene were on the phone. Kyra spent quite a bit of time telling Jolene that Sean was really as nice and gentlemanly as he seemed. After that, she reassured Jolene that she had impressed Sean, notwithstanding the fact that she was bare legged thanks to a last minute snag in her pantyhose. Jolene almost sounded like she believed Kyra's assurances that Sean didn't think of her as a dumb cop and a white-trash country girl.

About the time that Kyra and Jolene finally hung up their telephones, as Law meowed and Equity tried to block his view of his CRT, Sean ordered two sets of flowers online. The red roses were to be delivered to Jolene's office at the sheriff's department. The note that was to accompany the roses said simply, "Looking forward to our next meeting. Sean." The dozen white carnations were to be delivered to Kyra at the DA's office with a simple note that said, "Thank you for being my friend. S.R."

Next, Sean found the invitation to the Spring Fling and wrote a check to pay for two people, completed the reply card, inserted the check and card into the envelope and stamped the envelope. He then put the envelope into his bulky black calendar, so he would be sure to see it and remember to mail it. A few minutes later, two rather tired and irritated cats purred an already mellow Sean into his first peaceful, deep sleep in months.

Jolene also retired. But, she did not sleep as easily or as deeply as Sean since a bad memory kept tormenting her.

Chapter Two

Sean arrived earlier than usual at the courthouse on Monday morning. Although it was only the third day of April, he sensed that spring had already begun. Buds were on the trees. Birds were singing. Best of all, after the cold, rainy week that had just ended, a constant, gentle—almost warm— breeze blew from the south.

When Sean entered his chambers, Miriam knew from looking at him that his date had gone well. Sean seemed relaxed, confident and optimistic, which was a welcome change of pace from his previous tentativeness and carefully concealed vulnerability. Miriam was so glad to have her old boss back that she momentarily contemplated pulling a practical joke on him. After thinking about it for a second, Miriam decided to wait until she was absolutely sure that his bad moods were gone for good.

Bubba dropped in to chat with Sean while Sean was sipping his morning tea and trying to work up the motivation to read this morning's edition of the *University City Bugle*. After looking like a cross between the Sphinx and the cat that had swallowed the canary, Bubba eventually spoke. "Well Judge, from what I hear, you and Sergeant Scruggs had a nice time on Friday."

Wondering how Bubba had drawn that conclusion, Sean asked, "Why do you say that?"

After chewing on his donut and sipping some of his third cup of coffee in silence to achieve a heightened dramatic effect, Bubba finally said, "Well Judge, any peace officer, no matter if'n he drives around in one of them shiny new patrol cars, or if'n he wears out his shoe leather like them detective fellers, or even if'n he just sits on his behind like I do, has got to be able to assemble facts, organize 'em and draw conclusions from 'em."

After taking another slow sip, Bubba continued, "Well Judge, seein' as to how that blonde prosecutor friend of yours come by to see you on Wednesday afternoon last week, and then on Thursday mornin' you asked me some pretty direct questions for you 'bout the Sergeant, I concluded, using my law enforcement trainin' to its fullest, that you was fixin' to have yourself a date with her."

After another sip, then a chomp and then another sip, Bubba added, "Well Judge, seein' as how on Saturday mornin' a couple of my buddies on patrol said as how they saw you and the pretty sergeant leavin' The Palm Tree together the night before, lookin' like y'all was havin' yourselves one whale of a good time, I put it all together enough to be certain enough to ask you."

"Ask me what?" Sean said, with a hint of irritation in his voice.

"Well Judge, didn't I just ask you if you had a good time with the sergeant?"

Having no desire to engage in a linguistic dispute with a man who spoke as slowly as Bubba, Sean just smiled and said, "I'm sorry. I was so impressed with your analytical skills that I lost track of your question."

"Well Judge, did y'all have a good time or not?"

"Bubba, what do your analytical powers tell you about that?"

"Lessin' you says different, I'm assumin' that y'all had a good time."

After another bite and sip, Bubba got down to what he really had been trying to say all along. "Well Judge, it ain't no good for a man our age to be livin' alone. I hope it goes well for y'all."

After thanking Bubba for his concern—which was certainly genuine—Sean wondered if every bailiff in the courthouse had already told his or her judge that Judge Sean Riley was seeing a sergeant on the sheriff's staff. After thinking for a moment longer, Sean decided that a rumor like that might not be entirely a bad thing, his loss of privacy notwithstanding, since that rumor carried with it evidence that Sean was doing better and wasn't spending his nights home alone with his cats field testing the pride of Lynchburg, Tennessee.

A few minutes later, just as Sean was about to leave his office and take the bench, Angela Carson, his loyal, devoted, charming courtroom clerk, stuck her head into his office to ask him a question. Angela, who was one of the most charming ladies he had ever met, was engaged to a medical student at Southern University. Rumor had it that they had met on the first morning of their first day of orientation at Howard University and had been madly in love ever since. After Sean answered her simple question, Angela mentioned that she heard a rumor that he had a girlfriend. She asked flirtatiously, "Should I be jealous?"

Without missing a beat, Sean replied that since he wasn't jealous of this mythical medical student that she was supposedly engaged to marry, she had no reason to be.

"Judge, you know that I'd bring him over, but medical types try to stay as far away from courthouses as possible."

Smilingly acknowledging the truth of what she said, Sean told her that he would be right out. As he passed down the hallway, Sean stuck his head into an office and said, "Laura, it's awfully nice to see you back."

Rising, the dark-haired woman smiled, approached Sean and gave him a warm hug. "I missed you, too! You look much better today than the last time I saw you."

Giving no hint as to why he may have appeared different to her, Sean merely said, "Lunch today?"

Laura nodded and said, "Don't take too long, I'm hungry already."

After leaving Laura's office, Sean made his way to the door leading to the courtroom. As he placed his hand on the door, Sean heard a loud "Wait for me!" coming from behind him. Without even turning, he knew that Jane, his loyal, if slightly ditzy, blonde court reporter was dashing to catch him. As Jane passed by, she asked with a knowing wink, "Have a good time over the weekend?"

As Bubba announced "All rise!" Sean half wondered if word of his date was going to be somewhere in the unread copy of the *Bugle*.

****

Normally on Monday mornings, Sean heard what he called his "dog and cat" docket, a mixed bag of things. For some reason this morning, Sean guessed all of the dogs must have found cars to chase while the cats were all curled up taking a nap because the only thing that he had to hear was a discovery dispute.

Sean hated discovery disputes because resolving them didn't require the skills of a judge, as much as those of a kindergarten teacher. Today's dispute was no different. In this case, on the day that the defendant had filed its answer to the plaintiff's complaint, the defendant's counsel noticed the plaintiff's deposition by mail. On that same day, counsel for the plaintiff had mailed a set of interrogatories and a request for production of documents and other things to defense counsel. The dispute was real simple. Each side wanted its discovery completed before disclosing what it knew to the other side. As the lawyers droned on and on, Sean kept thinking that as tedious as these hearings can be for all connected with them, the alternative, "trial by ambush," would be far worse.

Around mid-morning, the lawyers finally ran out of steam, having spent over forty minutes each telling him what he already knew from reading their pleadings. Sean made them go into the hallway and work out a mutually agreeable discovery schedule. After denying each side's requests for sanctions, he sent them on their merry way with a strong suggestion to try to cooperate, knowing full well that they would be back in several months about something else.

After leaving the bench, Sean returned to his office and read his copy of the *Bugle*. As usual, it had little non-wire service content. The only interesting article in the entire paper was the weekly column by the new guy, Winfred K. Rudd, who was chastising the governor for some petty failing that Rudd was trying to build up to be a major crime against humanity. Sean remembered reading some place that Rudd had once received a Pulitzer. He had heard that Rudd retired from some paper up north and then moved south to play golf. The rumor was that Rudd had been lured by the *Bugle* to write a weekly column as a way to keep its readership from declining any further. While Rudd always blasted Republicans and conservatives, he did write colorful copy, which was the only reason that Sean ever read his column.

Sean's reading was interrupted by Miriam's voice. "Judge, there is a lady named Jolene on line two. Should I take a message?"

Flustered, Sean replied too strongly, "No!"

After taking a deep breath and trying to regain control of his now raging emotions, Sean picked up the telephone receiver. With as much of his now flagging confidence as he could muster, Sean said, "Hi! Jolene?"

"Sean, you slick talkin' Yankee, the roses are lovely. You're settin' the bar pretty high for yourself, aren't you?"

By now, being nearly incoherent, Sean was barely able to ask, "Why do you say that?"

"Sean, if you send a lady a dozen roses after one date, she'll expect at least that, if not more, after each date. Isn't that what you lawyer types call, **settin' a bad precedent**?"

"Precedent be damned! I've never been interrogated as charmingly in my whole life. It was worth it!"

"Sean, I'm startin' to think that you're the sort who just likes girls in uniform 'cause we have our own handcuffs."

"Time will tell!" said Sean, with a laugh in his voice and a smile on his face.

"I've got to rush to a meetin' in a minute, but I've got to ask you what will you be wearin' Saturday?"

Totally dumbfounded at the question, Sean was able to mumble, "Nothing fancy! Sports jacket, shirt, no tie and chinos. Okay?"

"Sure Precious, that's what I needed to know, so I'll know what to wear. Lookin' forward to seein' you on Saturday. Bye!"

For several minutes after the call, Sean sat in his chair in blissful silence. Had Sean been pumped full of truth serum right then and made to swear on everything that he believed was holy, he would have said that when he heard Jolene's voice, he immediately started smelling her perfume in his drab office. Even though she was no longer on the phone, he still smelled the scent of her perfume.

After several minutes, Sean decided he ought to splash some water on his face. When he looked at himself in the mirror of his private bathroom, he was shocked to notice how red his face and ears were.

Sensing that his powers of concentration were diminished, Sean checked his email and surfed the net until it was time for his lunch with Laura.

✳✳✳✳✳✳✳✳✳✳✳✳

As Sean Riley and his staff attorney, Laura Rizzoto, walked to lunch, Laura knew that Sean had to tell her what was going on with him. Ten days ago, when she had left on vacation to ski with her husband in Colorado, Sean looked sad and depressed like he had every day since the day that Cheryl died. Ten days later, he was almost back to the way he had been as long as she had known him—just a little more absent minded and spaced out. When Laura asked Miriam about the judge's mood this morning, Miriam was no help at all to her, saying nothing of substance while smiling with a knowing smile. Laura knew that something had changed and wanted to know what it was.

As Laura and Sean neared their favorite lunchtime eatery, Joe's Diner, two deputies—bailiffs in other courts—passed them by. The deputies smiled broadly at them. And, right after the deputies had passed by Laura and Sean, one of them said something *sotto voce* to the other. Laura's curiosity was further piqued.

After sitting down and ordering, Laura was about to ask Sean what was going on with him when two of his criminal court colleagues passed by and exchanged pleasantries with them. As they were leaving, the younger of the pair of criminal judges asked, "Did you get a chance to say anything on Friday night?"

Sean inquired, "Why do you ask?"

The criminal court judge replied, "Not that we were staring, but my wife and I had dinner at The Palm Tree on Friday. It looked to us that you were badly outgunned."

"Not outgunned, just outclassed—badly."

Winking as he said, "Right!" the younger judge motioned to his colleague to find a place to sit.

Just as Laura was again going to start her interrogation of Sean, a group of ladies—including Jane, Angela and the tall, willowy, red-headed clerk wearing horn-rimmed glasses—walked by. Jane and Angela just waved and smiled mischievously. In mock sternness, Laura demanded, "What is going on with you?"

"Why do you ask?" Sean questioned, with a totally transparent look of surprise.

"Judge Sean Riley, don't you dare try to play dumb with me!" Laura said, in her best maternal manner. "I know you too well to fall for it."

Sean knew that he couldn't try to pull anything over on Laura since she had known him for too long. Laura and Sean had been law school classmates at Southern University School of Law. Following graduation, Sean had the rare pleasure of trying a will contest against Laura. After Sean became a law professor, they saw each other regularly at bar and political functions. Sean and Cheryl even attended Laura's wedding.

The day that word of Sean's appointment to the bench became public knowledge, Laura was one of the first to call to congratulate Sean. Unlike the other callers, who all seemed to have called to butter him up, Laura offered Sean some important practical advice. She suggested that he was going to need a good staff attorney to work for him. She then recommended herself for the position. After a lunch to discuss the job, Sean offered her the job, which she accepted on the spot.

Sean had never told Laura this, but he often thought that—except for marrying Cheryl—hiring Laura was the smartest thing he had ever done in life. While Laura wasn't empathetic enough to always know exactly what his emotional state might be, she knew him well enough to know when something was going on in his head. Even though she couldn't read his emotions very well, she knew how his mind worked to the point that they could finish each other's sentences. Cheryl had often joked that Laura was Sean's wife at the office and that Kyra was Sean's substitute mother everywhere. Sean never disagreed with either assessment.

Just as their barbeque arrived, Sean 'fessed up, "While you were gone skiing and not here to protect me, Kyra roped me into having a blind date last Friday."

"And?"

"Kyra, Max, my date and I had dinner at The Palm Tree."

"And?" Laura asked again, sensing that Sean was stringing the details out just to make her work for them.

"And what?"

"I can't take it anymore! Your date, tell me about her!"

"Okay, you just had to ask," Sean said, with a playful expression on his face. "Her name is Jolene Scruggs. She's a sergeant in the sheriff's department. What else did you want to know?"

"What's she like? You know, the good stuff."

Sensing that his time for fun had arrived, Sean wondered for a second just how far could he go from the truth and still sound believable. He decided that saying his date had a visible tattoo, false teeth and looked like Bubba's older sister probably wouldn't work. Then, Sean had a stroke of brilliance. He realized that if he told Laura the absolute, unvarnished truth, she probably wouldn't believe him anyway. So, Sean decided to go for it!

"Okay, she's in her late twenties and has lustrous, brown hair, blue eyes, a great figure, really sexy freckles, long legs and the voice of an angel with a drawl. She's also extroverted, graceful and totally unimpressed with judges and lawyers. Enough?"

"Judge Sean Riley, you really don't' expect me to believe that, do you?"

"You know that I'd never lie to you, would I?" Sean said, in his best mock Bill Clinton voice.

After that exchange ended, Laura and Sean finished their barbecue in silence. From the looks that Laura kept shooting at him, Sean knew she didn't believe a word that he said about Jolene. Sean liked it that way.

✳✳✳✳✳✳✳✳✳✳✳

Sean was supposed to have started a jury trial after lunch on Monday, but when he called the case, the parties announced that a settlement had been reached. After thanking the prospective jurors for their service, Sean sent them on their merry way. Sadly, the now dismissed jurors probably went home thinking that the entire court system was run by lunatics. They had been herded all around the courthouse complex since early morning, only to discover that their whole day was wasted.

Sean spent the afternoon putting the final touches on a paper that he was going to deliver at a seminar in May. This extra time was a definite gift from above for Sean. Now it looked like he wasn't going to have to beg and grovel for an extension from the administrator of the seminar, who was well known for being very unhappy about speakers who sought extensions for their overdue papers.

As Sean was preparing to go to the law school to teach his class, he overheard Laura on her telephone saying, "Kyra, you must have planned this practical joke all last week. I'll confess that this is one of the best ones you and he have ever put together, but I'm not going to fall for it! I'll just wait and find out if he even had a date on Friday." Smiling, Sean slipped stealthily toward the door and release from the prying eyes of the courthouse crowd.

Sean sped to the law school in good time. He found a favorable parking spot and planned his surreptitious entrance into the building. Still in stealth mode, he snuck in the side door and strode up the stairway to the second floor. There his students awaited in Probate II, the second semester continuation of Probate I that was offered in the fall.

Nineteen years ago, Sean had been asked to take over the teaching duties of a professor who died suddenly over the summer. When the Dean called Sean to offer the position to him, Sean was promised that after a year, he could ask to teach other courses. Sean had been very lucky in the beginning. He loved the classes that he taught his first year and never asked for a reassignment. So every year in the fall semester, Sean taught Civil Procedure I, Probate I and Jurisprudence. In the spring, he taught Civil Procedure II, Probate II and Legal History. When Sean became a judge, his course load was reduced by a third, as he stopped teaching Civil Procedure. The school had also made these classes evening classes.

That night's class was one of the best ones of the semester. For some reason, tonight the Rule against Perpetuities seemed almost comprehensible. The students seemed better prepared. Sean noticed that in the last hour of the class, he didn't feel tired like he had felt during the last hour of his last few classes. Sean wondered if things were so much better today because of the definite coming of spring-like weather last night. Sean, being only mortal, refused to admit to himself what was obvious to everyone who knew him: *His date with Sergeant Jolene Scruggs had changed him for the better.*

✱✱✱✱✱✱✱✱✱✱✱✱

Tuesday, at the weekly lunch meeting of the University City Rotary Club, Sean was relaxed and jovial. Part of the explanation for his good mood was that he sat next to Lucy Travis, a visiting Rotarian from the Smithville Club. Lucy was one of his favorite people.

Sean and Lucy had met in a very unusual way. The first day that Sean sat on the bench, Lucy's application to have her father's will admitted to probate was on his docket that morning. As things worked out, that meeting was just the start of their relationship. A few months later, her brother objected to her valuation of some of the real estate in the inventory, alleging that she was not valuing it at its fair market value. The objection would not have been in the least bit memorable if her lawyer had not requested a jury view, which Sean granted[5], and if the property in question had not been a resort.

Sean remembered that on the day of the view, the lawyers, Sean and Laura had all arrived at the resort—which was located a few miles up County 191 from his house—wearing polo shirts, shorts and tennis shoes, ready for a day in the country. After giving everyone in the party a visitor's badge to be hung from his or her neck with a fabric cord, Lucy took the party for a tour of the place. Sean remembered that Lucy really stood out that day, wearing a bright green t-shirt and shorts, which was the uniform of the staff of the resort.

As the party walked through the grounds of the resort, which was wooded and hilly for the most part, Sean remained quite relaxed. What made the jury view truly memorable, however, was their visit to the pool area. One of the guests at the resort, a tall, very well-endowed blonde had appointed herself the greeter for visitors to the whirlpool. When Lucy led the group past the gate surrounding the whirlpool, the blonde bounced up and gave the group a warm greeting. Then, without taking a breath, she asked if anyone had questions that Lucy hadn't answered. Finding none, she wished them well and told them she expected to see them again real soon. Sean remembered that when the blonde left the group, Laura eyed the three male members of their group. Sean was cool as a cucumber, unlike the other two men in the group, who had red faces.

Shortly after the jury view, the hearing was held on the objection filed by Lucy's brother. The testimony of Lucy's expert witness demolished the testimony of her brother's expert witness. Sean ruled in Lucy's favor. Sean's ruling was subsequently affirmed on appeal.

Sean next saw Lucy a year or so after the estate was closed, when she appeared at the University City Rotary to make up a meeting. Since the case was over, Sean greeted her warmly. He wasn't her judge anymore, so he was allowed to be human again. As Sean recalled, Lucy embarrassed him at the meeting by saying some kind words about Sean, that he personified grace under pressure.

A year or so later, he and Cheryl ran into Lucy at some social event and the three of them became friends. At a dinner party at their home one evening, Lucy explained to them that her late father had left her quite comfortably off financially, but she had a problem. Since she spent most of her time from late March until late October running the resort, she didn't have time for much of a social life. And, since her resort catered to families, just about all the men she met were married or otherwise involved in a relationship. A few of her female guests had set her up on blind dates, but none of those relationships ever panned out.

Lucy had asked them if they knew any nice men who would like her for herself and not because she was rich. After a few unsuccessful tries, Cheryl fixed her up with a nerdy attorney named Ralph, who worked at a state agency in Capitol City. Despite Sean's skepticism at the beginning of their blind dinner date, the relationship clicked. Lucy actually asked Cheryl to be matron of honor at their wedding. Lucy and Ralph seemed to be a perfectly matched couple.

"Sean, you look different today." Lucy remarked. "Things pickin' up for you?"

Not wanting to divulge too much of his personal life at the meeting, Sean said, "Lucy, between the nice spring weather and your company, how could I fail to be in a good mood?"

Lucy attempted to say something back to Sean, but at that exact moment the meeting commenced.

∗∗∗∗∗∗∗∗∗∗∗∗

That night, as Law sat in Sean's lap and Equity tried to sit right in front of his computer's keyboard, Sean read the following email from Lucy:

> Dear Sean,
>
> Sean, whatever you are doing with yourself, keep doing it!
>
> You looked years younger and very relaxed at the meeting today.
>
> I've been worried about you since Cheryl's death. Today, you seemed to be more of your old self. You looked good.
>
> If either Ralph or I can ever do something for you, please let us know. Also, email me regularly, so I know how things are going.
>
> Lucy

In his terse reply to Lucy, Sean indicated that he appreciated her kind words and promised to keep in touch with her.

****

Late Saturday morning, as Sean was readying himself for his date with Jolene, his cell phone rang. The call was from Jolene.

"Hi Precious, it's me! I heard on my police radio that a water main has broken on University Avenue right by the main entrance to campus. I thought that I'd better call you to give you a heads up about the traffic."

Sean asked, "Will I have any trouble reaching your place?"

"No, but if you don't mind, I think we'd better walk over to campus."

"Okay by me, if the rain won't bother you."

"Sean, if you want to share an umbrella, it could be fun."

"Okay, I'd better get there a little early if we're going to walk over!"

"Around 1320?" Jolene asked.

"Sure thing! Looking forward to seeing you then. Bye!"

****

An hour later, when Jolene opened her front door to him, Sean did a double take. Jolene, even wrapped up in her raincoat, was lovelier than Sean had remembered her being. But, in the daylight, she looked different—a good different, but different.

As they walked toward campus squeezed together under his bright multi-colored umbrella, which was something he and Cheryl had bought years ago in Bermuda, Sean looked at Jolene, trying to see what exactly was different. After a few seconds, it dawned on him—she wasn't wearing much makeup, so her freckles were very visible. But, the most noticeable change to her appearance was her hair. The teased and sprayed look of last week was gone. She had her chocolate brown hair pulled up behind her with a butterfly clamp. Sean guessed that she was dressed to fit in on the campus.

"Jolene, you look very lovely today."

Jolene smiled and said, "For a damn Yankee who hasn't the sense to come in from the rain, you don't look too bad either." They both smiled. As they walked, Jolene noticed that Sean was getting rained on because he was walking just far enough away from her to have some rain hitting him.

"Sean, it's okay if you walk closer to me." Sean squeezed in a bit closer, but not close enough to get fully out of the rain. Putting her arm around his waist, Joelene said, "That's better!" She sensed that when her arm touched him, even through his multiple layers of clothing, he tensed up.

35

Walking almost cheek to cheek, Sean couldn't help smelling Jolene's delightful perfume. He didn't know what it was, but he liked it. As he turned his head toward her to reply to what she said, he noticed her white teeth when she smiled and her many, many freckles. He assumed that she was in a good mood.

As they walked along, Jolene asked, "Sean, have you seen *Casablanca* before?"

Suddenly, Sean felt his years. Of course he'd seen *Casablanca* before. He was a baby boomer, after all.

"I've heard that it's a real sad movie."

Sensing their age difference very acutely now, Sean said, "This one movie has everything—romance, intrigue, bad guys, heroism."

Several nights ago, Jolene had looked up *Casablanca* on the Internet. But, being a true daughter of the south, she played dumb, asking innocently, "Why do they say it's such a great movie?"

In his most pedantic manner, Sean answered, "There are a couple of things that make it a great flick. First, it had several different writers, each of whom added something good to it, so it is very well written. Next, Michael Curtiz, the director, made sure that it moved along very rapidly. You really have to pay attention to be able to follow it. But, the best part of the movie is that the foreign accents are real because most of the actors and actresses in it were foreign."

"Wasn't that expensive?" Jolene asked, while looking up at him with her big, blue eyes.

Well, no. When it was made in 1942, Hollywood was full of refugee actors and actresses. So Jack Warner, knowing a good thing when he saw one, hired them. That was a very smart move on Warner's part."

As Jolene listened attentively, Sean continued, "When the big scene at Rick's happens, you'll get a big emotional charge. Part of the reason the scene works so well is that the emotion is genuine. Many of the tears you will see in that scene were real, coming from people who had fled Hitler and had families and friends still under the Nazi thumb."

"What happens in the big scene?"

"I don't want to spoil it for you. You'll know it's coming when you see a bunch of German officers singing around a piano."

"Okay," Jolene said, not fully understanding what he was talking about since she had only looked at one website that just gave a brief synopsis of the plot of the movie.

When they reached the Cinematic Arts Building, Sean asked, "Jolene, have you been here before?"

"No! It looks brand new."

"It is. One of the alums, who went to Hollywood after graduation, left a big bequest in his will to Southern University to build a state-of-the-art cinematic arts building on campus. The theater is part of it. It's real nice, better than a multiplex."

After obtaining the tickets and entering the building, Sean helped Jolene with her raincoat and then removed his. When they faced each other, they both started laughing. Heaven only knows how they managed to do it, but they were dressed alike in brown tweed jackets, red remony trade tartan shirts, chinos and deck shoes.

"Sean, if someone sees us together, they'll think we're either **cute** or a father and daughter visitin' the campus from Scotland!"

With a bit of blush appearing on his cheek, Sean suggested that maybe they should go into the nice, dark theater where their matching attire would be hidden. Then he said, "I suspect they'll think it's just the uniform of the day." As they found their seats, Sean thought, *I guess our age difference must not be a big issue for her, if she's cracking jokes about it.*

As they plopped down in the theater's large, comfortable chairs, Sean wondered all of a sudden, *Am I supposed to put my arm around her? Do I hold her hand?* As the lights dimmed, Jolene's angelic voice whispered in his ear, "Sean, I'm a bit chilly. Warm me up a little."

After a few seconds of indecision, Jolene took Sean's arm and put it around her. Once his arm was around her, she snuggled up to him. Seconds later, Sean offered Jolene a nicely ironed handkerchief with his free hand.

"What's this for, Precious?" she purred.

"I'm thinking ahead. I know how you country girls behave in movies." Jolene said nothing, but thought that his gesture was both thoughtful and probably unnecessary.

Seconds later, the screen lit up. Max Steiner's magnificent score began to play. Sean and Jolene, unlike the refugees, were not going to have to wait and wait. Their visit with Rick, Ilsa, Victor, Louis and their friends had begun.

Once the scene shifted to Rick's Café Americain, Sean noticed that Jolene was watching the screen very intently. Jolene, actually, was only paying partial attention to *Casablanca*. She felt a wave of tension go through Sean's body when the beautiful, inebriated Yvonne first appeared on screen. She wondered why.

37

Jolene couldn't miss Sean's soft chuckle when Rick told Captain Renault that he had been misinformed about the waters. She sensed that Sean was relaxing.

When Rick came charging up to Sam and then shot Ilsa that venomous look that Bogart was so good at giving, Jolene whispered to Sean, "Why does he hate her so much?"

"She broke his heart." Sean said, sensing tension in Jolene.

When the scenes in Paris before the Germans arrived appeared on screen, Sean, who was already a bit jumpy about physical contact with Jolene, felt her hand grab his. Her hand felt so warm, soft and tender to his touch, he couldn't have moved his hand from hers—even if he had wanted to do so.

Jolene used Sean's handkerchief for the first time when Ilsa gave her speech to Sam before they parted company at *La Belle Aurore*. While Jolene was dabbing her eyes, he thought, *Cop or not, she's a real girl. Cries at the right part of sad movies.*

Sean and Jolene, while not as glamorous—perhaps—as Rick and Ilsa, were just as wrapped up in their problems as Rick and Ilsa had been. Fortunately for Sean and Jolene, they were reading each other much better.

When Sean saw Herr Major Strasser and his cronies at the piano beginning to sing *Die Wacht am Rhein*, he whispered, "Here it comes!" Sean and Jolene both straightened up in their seats, but Sean kept his arm around Jolene. She held on to his hand tightly.

When the band began to play *La Marseillaise*, Sean moved his arm away from Jolene, sat up straight and began to sing the words softly under his breath. While the scene unfolded, Jolene, out of the corner of her eye, noticed that Sean was really into the song. As the chorus began, Sean dropped all pretenses and sang *La Marseillaise* out loud. When Yvonne shouted at the end, Sean echoed her call, only softer.

After that, as surreptitiously as possible, Sean tried to dab away the tears from his eyes and cheeks. Jolene noted Sean's passion, thinking that beneath his stuffy exterior there was a lot more to the man. When Sean's arm returned to Jolene's shoulders, she snuggled close enough to his cheek to feel the warmth. She also noted that Sean was very tightly wrapped into the fabric of the movie.

A few minutes later, when Rick, seeing Ilsa's revolver pointed at him practically begged Ilsa to shoot him, Jolene whispered, "That's true love!" Sean just squeezed her hand in reply.

They were both quite comfortably snuggled after that until the scene at the airport at the end, when Jolene sat up straight and watched the screen intently. Now she was into the movie as much as Sean.

When the closing credits all had disappeared from the screen and the lights came back on, Jolene returned the handkerchief to Sean, who noticed that it was very damp and had makeup stains.

On the walk back to her place after *Casablanca*, Jolene asked Sean, "What did Captain Renault mean when he talked about Unoccupied France?"

Sean, being a born pedant, a History major and a professor, gave Jolene a very good, if unorganized, impromptu lecture on the fall of France in June of 1940. She couldn't help but be impressed with Sean's command of the names and dates involved. When he mentioned how Marshal Philippe Pétain and the Vichy government were regarded by many as traitors, Jolene was really impressed with his knowledge.

"Sean, why did Rick make the wisecrack about coming to Casablanca for the waters?"

Sean said, "Jolene, at the airport at the end of the flick, remember when Captain Renault started to pour a drink from a bottle, then after looking at the bottle, dumped it into the trash and kicked the trash can?"

"Yeah!"

"Could you read the label on the bottle?"

"I'm good, but not that good. No!"

"Well, if you freeze that frame and stare at it, you can see that the label on the bottle is for *Vichy Water*, which was what Vichy was most famous for before World War II. I suspect that Rick's crack to Captain Renault about the waters was really a subtle crack at Vichy, the Captain's employers."

"Do you speak French?" Jolene asked.

"A bit. My mother's parents were from France, so I learned some as a child. I took two years of it in college. I can read it better than I speak. Why do you ask?"

Jolene replied, "You were singing along when the band played and everyone started singing in the big scene."

"Oops!" Sean said, with a hint of embarrassment in his voice.

"I thought it was neat," Jolene said sincerely. "But, while we're talkin' 'bout it, I guess I ought to ask. Have you been to France?"

"Cheryl and I went there for several weeks the year we turned forty."

"Where did you go?" Jolene asked.

"We spent two weeks in South of France."

Jolene, never having been more than three hundred miles from her place of birth, was fascinated with Sean's apparent knowledge of the world. As they neared Jolene's house, she asked, "Sean, are you hungry?"

"Starved! I had a late brunch, so I'm starting to feel a bit hollow right now."

Jolene said, "Great! I laid in a good supply of ribs and the fixin's last night, so I'm ready." As they walked up the driveway to Jolene's place, Sean noticed that the sun had worked its way through the clouds and that the rest of the afternoon was going to be nice.

After stuffing himself on ribs, Sean couldn't help but notice that this was the first time in a long while that he had his old appetite back. Still being in denial, he ascribed the return of his appetite to the long walk. After they finished the meal and loaded the dishes in Jolene's dishwasher, Jolene said, "I've got a couple of chairs out back. Would you like to sit out there for a while?"

Sean readily agreed, so they went to the two wicker chairs with soft cushions that Jolene had near her back door. As they settled in, Jolene, with a bit of mischievousness in her voice said, "For a Yankee, you seem like you've done a good job of tryin' to learn how to be a gentleman. I'm gonna give you an opportunity to prove it, **if** you're willin' to take the chance. If I kick off my shoes, will you promise not to laugh?"

"Of course!" Sean said, wondering what prompted that question. As soon as Jolene heard the answer, she deftly removed the deck shoes from her feet. Sliding her body back to the head of the chair, she placed her feet on the end of the chair and wiggled her bare toes. Sean noticed nothing but bare feet and very carefully trimmed and painted toenails, which were the result of Jolene's pedicure that morning.

"Sean, you really are a gentleman, Yankee or not! You haven't laughed at my ugly feet. I'm impressed!"

"Jolene, your feet look very nice."

"No! They don't! They're too big and my toes are too long and skinny."

"Sergeant Scruggs, I think the movie got to you. Your feet look fine. I'm sure that if Ingrid Bergman had kicked off her shoes on camera, her feet wouldn't have looked any better."

Jolene asked, "Think so?"

After that exchange, they both sat silently for a minute, looking at the late afternoon sunlight and the budding flowers along Jolene's wooden fence. After a while, Jolene asked softly, "Sean, do you think that Rick and Ilsa ever got together again?"

Pausing for a minute, Sean replied thoughtfully, "Cheryl and I debated that question a number of times. I always said that they probably did."

When Jo inquired, "Why?" Sean's considered response was, "Well, my guess is that after Victor and Ilsa reached Lisbon, the Brits whisked them off to London, not America, because London was where the Free French and the other governments in exile were based. I'd guess that Victor and Ilsa spent the war closely guarded by British security and that Victor probably made propaganda broadcasts for the Allies."

"Well, what about Rick?" Jolene asked.

"My guess is that he and Renault made it to Brazzaville in one piece. I'd guess that they were too old to be much good for combat, so they eventually were sent to London, where they were put into intelligence work. Whatever his duty, Rick made it through unscathed because he was a born survivor."

Jolene asked, with a bit of longing in her voice, "Did Rick and Ilsa meet again?"

"My guess is that they did." Sean, in full pedant mode added, "But, in a sense, whether they did or didn't meet again, misses the point. As long as any one of the quartet from the airport that night is alive, the memory of Rick's sacrifice will live. Rick did a noble thing that night and the other three will always know it."

Jolene, sensing the hidden depths of the plot, further questioned Sean, "I just realized that *Casablanca* was full of brave people. Everyone who stood up and sang in the big scene could have gotten in trouble. Isn't that unusual?"

Sean commented, "No one in the film—except Victor—would be regarded as a classic heroic figure. Victor's arrival and Rick's permission to the bandleader gave the opportunity for the people to rise up and show their resistance. All of my reading of history tells me that most heroic acts are committed by ordinary people, who are presented with extra-ordinary circumstances."

Sean started to get misty eyed at this point. Since he and Jolene had left their jackets in the house, Jolene leaned over to him and wiped away his tears with her soft, warm hand. "Sean, did Ilsa remind you of your late wife?"

"No. The actress who reminded me of Cheryl was Yvonne. From what I've read, the actress who played Yvonne, Madeleine LeBeau, was twenty when the movie was made, which was about the age that I first met Cheryl.

We were college classmates, but I didn't get to know her really well until later."

"Is that why the singing scene really got to you?"

"A bunch of things all hit me at once whenever I see it. Being half-French and speaking the language a bit, I can really feel the emotional intensity of the scene. Plus, once Rick nods his assent to play to the bandleader, you know that Rick has broken out of his shell and rejoined life. That is moving. But most of all, Yvonne is just so beautiful and so totally immersed in the action. When the camera pans her face, I just melt at her passionate intensity."

At this, Sean started to cry. When he was done, Jolene told him to scoot to the middle of his chair and turn around with his back facing her. Having been married a long time, Sean was well trained, so he complied. Jolene began to rub his neck and shoulders while saying, "I'll bet that you are tensed up from my leanin' on your arm and shoulder. Let me get you loose."

Sean didn't know how long Jolene rubbed his stiff neck and shoulders because he lost track of everything, except her touch and the relief that her fingers brought to his aches—physical and otherwise. When Jolene finished her impromptu massage, she remarked that they were loosing the light and suggested that they return to the house. At Jolene's command, they carried their shoes in with them.

As they entered the living room, Sean noticed that the furniture was placed so that if you sat in either the big, overstuffed chair with a large footstool or the sofa, which faced the chair, your view would be away from the television. He found this odd. As Sean was about to ask where Jolene wanted him to sit, she said, "Sean, did you like the rub that I gave your neck and shoulders?"

With a big smile on his face, Sean indicated that he did.

"Then, can I ask you to rub my ugly feet?" For the next several minutes, Sean rubbed her feet and toes while extolling their beauty. Jolene, feeling as comfortable as a cat when its pet human rubs it under its chin, practically purred.

After what seemed to be a blissful eternity to Jolene, she bade Sean to stop, saying if he continued any longer, she would be putty in his hands. Her smile and tone of voice contained the hint that if he did not stop, she might not be too angry. Sean, not catching the hint, stopped.

Jolene directed Sean to sit on the sofa with her. As they faced each other, she said, "Sean, this is our second date. Don't you think we should learn something about each other?"

"I think that I probably know the important things about you already. You are drop-dead gorgeous. You cry at sad movies. You give great massages and are very susceptible to foot rubs. What else do I need to know?"

"Probably nuthin' else is that important, but I guess I'd feel better if we talked a little bit about ourselves." Sean didn't know that Jolene had read his biography on his court's website, so that she was really asking these questions not to gain knowledge, but to get him to open up a little.

"Okay, I'll go first if I can put my feet in your lap."

"Done deal!" Sean said, as he changed position and placed Jolene's feet in his lap.

"I was born in October, 1970, to a Marine and his wife," she began.

While thinking that he was applying to law schools at that time, Sean asked, "Is your father still on active duty?"

"He retired a few years later and bought a cotton farm about an hour from Coastal City. They still farm it." Getting back on track, Jolene continued, "My early life was nuthin' remarkable. Bein' a tall tomboy, I found school borin', except for Physical Education and sports. I was a good student, but it bored me. Despite my Daddy's opposition, I went to State on a track scholarship."

"What did you run?"

"I ran the longer distances the best."

"Oh, I ran cross country in high school," Sean said.

"Sean, I can't picture you workin' up a sweat. How long did you run?"

"I ran all four years of high school. I was a walk-on in college, but didn't make the cut. I liked running, but I just wasn't fast enough."

Jolene asked, "Do you still run?"

"I keep in shape in cooler weather on a treadmill. In the warmer weather, I run on a path that I've got on my property." Sensing that they were getting off track, Sean asked, "What was your major?"

Jolene said, "When I got to college, I half-thought about majorin' in Physical Education, but then I thought about what you could do with that major and decided that Criminal Justice would open more doors for me."

"What did you do after college?"

"Well your Honor," Jolene said with a big grin, "there isn't much else to tell. After college, I went to work for the sheriff and I met you. What about you?"

"There isn't much to tell either. I was born in 1949. My dad was a medical school professor and my mom wrote and illustrated children's books. I grew up in Midwestern City. The family moved to the country when I began military high school. My mom died between my second and third year of military school. My dad died several years ago."

"Sean, was your mother born in France?"

"No. She was born here in the U.S. about a year or so after her parents arrived here."

"Is it true that Frenchmen are great lovers?"

In mock horror, Sean said, "I have no knowledge about that subject one way or another!"

"I'd guess not!"

"Seriously, if Frenchmen are great lovers, and I'd suspect that they are great, it is only because their partners are French women, who are very sexy."

"Oh! Sexier than us southern country girls, huh?" Jolene asked playfully.

"No comment! Anyway, as I was saying before this rude interruption, I came to Southern State to go to law school. Cheryl and I married while she was still in law school and I had just taken the bar. After law school, I clerked for a justice of our Supreme Court for two years. After that, I was a litigator with a big firm in Capitol City for five years. In 1981, I began teaching at the law school at Southern University. In 1991, I was appointed to the bench, where I've been ever since."

"Sean, you have daughters, right?"

"We had two daughters, Pat and Maureen, who are in their first year at Southern University. Sergeant, if you ask me any more questions, I'm going to need a lawyer!"

Jolene said, "I just have three more questions, okay?"

"Okay!" Sean said, with obviously fake grumpiness.

"Question one is real simple. Can I take you to see State and Southern University play baseball next Saturday over in Capitol City?"

"Is April 15th a good day to have a date?"

Looking him squarely in the eye, she said, "It certainly is if I'm the date!"

Then it would be my pleasure!" Sean said in all honesty.

"Meet me here around 1100 hours and I'll take it from there. Make sure to bring a change of clothes because the weather could be anything at all this time of year."

"What's your second question?"

"Did you know that my friends are allowed to call me 'Jo'?"

"No! Jolene, why are you telling me that?" Sean said. After Jo stopped beating him playfully about the head and shoulders with a pillow from her sofa, Sean asked, "Jo, what's your last question?"

"Do Damn Yankees try to kiss their lady friends on the second date?"

****

Several hours later, Jo was soaking in a warm, candle-lit tub, listening to a CD of sad country songs, hoping that she hadn't been too pushy with Sean and hoping even more that her ugly, big feet hadn't turned him off too much. As she wiggled her toes over the edge of the tub, she said laughingly, "Maybe Yankees like women with big feet!"

About the same time that Jo was wiggling her toes over the end of her bathtub, Sean sent her this email:

Dear Jo,

Your present for being such a great date, cook, masseuse and kisser is on its way from Sharper Image. Please let me know when you get it. The present isn't as romantic as a dozen roses, but will last much longer!

I really enjoyed your company today. As I reckon it, only one hundred and forty-nine hours stand between us. I hate every one of them! My preference is to look into your big, blue eyes, not at my watch!

SR

Just as he was about to log off and tuck his furry mistresses into their bed, a thought struck him and he sent off another email.

Chapter Three

On Monday afternoon, Sean was slowly making his way toward the door of his chambers, chatting with everyone on his staff as he worked his way down the hallway. When he stuck his head into Laura's office, she said, "They just called from the hospital. Kim Brownlee is representing a patient on your mental health docket this week. The patient is insisting on a jury trial."

"Well Laura, since we have to give this matter our top attention, do you think we can move the hearings that we have set for tomorrow to Thursday afternoon? That way, we can give them all day tomorrow and Wednesday afternoon, if needed."

Laura responded, "After Bubba told me that he can get us a jury panel tomorrow morning, I rearranged your docket. You'll be number nine on the jury pull, so Bubba will probably have a panel to us by 10:00 a.m."

Sean was mildly annoyed that Laura had reset his docket without asking him, but he knew better than to dampen her enthusiasm. Sean felt that he was a very lucky man to have a friend and employee as dedicated, competent and loyal as Laura. So, he overlooked her controlling tendencies—most of the time. "Great job!" Sean said. "Who will be prosecuting the case?"

"The County Attorney's Office[6] is sending us their new hot shot, Tom Ritter."

Sean said, "Kim had better be ready tomorrow. With Tom's trial experience as an assistant D.A., she is going to have her hands full."

Laura replied, "Kim is a better trial lawyer than you think. You're going to have an interesting day tomorrow."

"No doubt!" Sean agreed. "I'm off to class."

****

As Sean drove the short distance to the law school, he couldn't help but notice the rain that had been off and on during the weekend appeared to have taken hold of the area again. For April 10th, the weather was unusually cool, damp and gloomy. It had been a wet few days.

After checking his faculty mailbox and opening his office to see if anything had been slipped under his door, Sean headed for class, knowing that today would start the interesting part of Probate II.

Once the students settled in their chairs and the noise abated, Sean said, "Today we start the interesting part of the course, where we will deal with the softer side of the law, namely, guardianships and mental health commitments. The theory is nowhere near as abstract and convoluted as the Rule Against Perpetuities, nor is it as cut and dried as Trust Law."

As Sean noticed the class relaxing and smiling, he added, "But, for many of you, this part of the course will be challenging for several reasons." Now that he had their attention again, Sean continued, "First, you will have to become comfortable with quite a bit of medical jargon, which is every bit as confusing to outsiders as legal jargon is to first-year law students. To understand this part of the course, you will have to expand your vocabularies a bit. And, I will test you on the vocabulary in the final exam."

Sean added, "Next, you will need to learn a bit about how Psychiatry operates in diagnosing and treating patients. I have no desire to try to persuade you to change your prospective profession. But, I do expect you to learn their basic theories and methodologies, and I may test on these matters as well. Fortunately for you, the last two hours of tonight's class will be taught by a boardcertified Psychiatrist, who will keep you better entertained and teach you better than I ever could about these areas."

"Your final challenge will not be on the exam, mainly because I know of no effective way of testing for this subject matter. But, it is very important that you develop a feel for what is involved with this aspect of thinking."

"I would like to pose a question to all of you in the class who do not have a background in Psychology beyond an introductory course in college. What is the difference between the function of the left half of your brain and the right half?"

After a few seconds of awkward silence, a hand went up. Calling on the blonde female student with the raised hand, Sean asked, "Ms. Cobb, just to make sure that you aren't a ringer, what was your major as an undergraduate?"

With a smile both on her face and in her voice, Ms. Cobb replied, "Accounting."

Smiling in return, Sean said, "You'll do nicely. Thank you for volunteering. So, what is the functional difference between the two halves of the brain?"

Ms. Cobb, who was very fetching in her tight white blouse and blue jeans, removed her gold-rimmed glasses and replied, "If I remember my Psych 101 correctly, the left half of the brain focuses on order, language and reasoning. The right half of the brain deals with emotions, non-verbal forms of expression and creativity."

Sean replied, "Very good. What part of the brain is most used in law school, right or left?"

Ms. Cobb answered quickly, "The left side."

"When a lawyer interviews a client to ascertain whether the client has a good case, which side of the lawyer's brain is being used the most?"

Flicking her honey blonde mane off of her right shoulder, Sandra Cobb replied, "The left side is being used the most."

Sean asked further, "If that same lawyer, later in the day, views the videotaped deposition of a witness to ascertain whether the witness was lying entirely, lying partially or telling the whole truth, which side of that lawyer's brain would be used the most?"

"The right side."

Sean then asked, "If a few years from now, you find yourself comforting a grieving widow in your law office as part of preparing to probate her late husband's will, which part of your brain should you be using?"

She replied, "The right side."

"Ms. Cobb, you've done a great job so far. Let me just ask you several more questions, if I may. When a judge is deciding whether a person's mental problems require either involuntary commitment to a mental hospital or a guardianship, what time period will the judge be concerned with—past, present or future?"

Shaking her long, honey blonde hair off of the same shoulder again, Ms. Cobb replied, "The future."

"Ms. Cobb, is forecasting future behaviors a right or left brain activity?"

After a momentary pause, the blonde replied, "I'm not totally sure, but I think that it would be the right brain."

"Very good! Thank you, Ms. Cobb."

Looking away from Ms. Cobb's tight jeans and flowing, long, honey blonde hair, Sean addressed the entire class and said, "In most other areas of the law, we look at either past or present facts and try to apply the appropriate legal theories to those facts. These are left brain activities. In guardianships and mental health matters, we are really looking forward to see how the proposed ward or patient will behave in the future. Predicting the future requires you to use your right brain, the part that law school mostly neglects. So, if you are to fully understand these areas of the law, you will need to become comfortable using the starboard side of your head again."

After taking a sip of water, Sean went to the board where he wrote the following:

Mentally ill	Incapacitated

None of the students stirred. After looking around the room for a moment, Sean said, "This question is open to anyone who would like to take a crack at it. Legally, can you be mentally ill and at the same time not be incapacitated?"

Immediately, Norman Jones raised his hand. Sean was not surprised by this since Mr. Jones had all the makings of a natural trial lawyer, being always ready to talk, irrespective of his knowledge of the subject matter under discussion. Norman replied, "I don't think that you can because if you are mentally ill, your thinking is impaired. If your thinking is impaired, you can't function properly. So, you must be incapacitated."

"Mr. Jones, let me ask you something. Have you ever known, read or heard about someone who completely fell apart emotionally if there was a rainstorm or lightning or if they saw a dog, a snake, a spider or some other animal that set them off?" Norman Jones replied that he was unfamiliar with those types of behaviors.

Sean replied, "Those behaviors are called *phobias*. Well, I've seen some of those behaviors and they aren't pretty. For instance, my high school Chemistry teacher had the misfortune to leave a window open a bit too wide one windy spring day, allowing a bird to fly into our classroom. Being an all-male class, we thought it was great fun and tried to catch the bird. When the bird flew in, our teacher started screaming loudly and hid under his desk in a fetal position. We had to call another teacher to help him. The other teacher called for an ambulance and they took him off to the local hospital."

After a sip of water, Sean continued, "Several days later, when our very embarrassed teacher returned to class, he told us that a few years before he and a date had been driving down a busy two-lane highway when their car struck a bird, causing the windshield to crack badly. What was worse than that was that the car's heater sucked most of the bird's carcass into their car. Here was this poor college kid trying to control his car in heavy traffic while dealing with a badly cracked windshield, bird blood and feathers on his eye glasses and all over his car, plus a hysterical young lady sitting right next to him. Ever since then, he freaked out if a bird got too near to him. Now Mr.

Jones, when the bird flew in our classroom window and our teacher acted the way he did, was our teacher mentally ill?"

Jones, sensing a trap, tried to avoid it by saying, "He certainly appeared to act like he was mentally ill when he went hyper like that."

Realizing that Jones had failed to remember the definition of mental illness in the readings for the class, Sean asked, "The next day, when our teacher returned to class looking a little worse for wear, but otherwise in complete control of his faculties, was he mentally ill then?"

Jones, sensing the trap had sprung, struggled by saying, "He wasn't acting like it then."

Sean asked the obvious, "Was he mentally ill or not? Or did he just have a case of a twenty-four hour mental illness bug?" After the laughter subsided, Sean said, "Thank you, Mr. Jones. You did a fine job with that question. Unfortunately, you don't have a full set of analytical tools available to you yet. In a week or so, you'll be able to instruct your classmates on the correct answer to my question."

Looking at the wall clock, Sean remarked, "We have a few minutes before we break. Would anyone like to tell me whether my ornithopic Chemistry teacher was incapacitated?

To Sean's surprise, Mr. Wong's hand went up. "Mr. Wong?"

Very slowly, Mr. Wong said, "Under the code definition of incapacity, your teacher was not incapacitated because there is no evidence that he was substantially unable to provide food, clothing or shelter for himself or to provide for his health or to manage his affairs."

Jeff Wong had never volunteered in either Probate I or Probate II until tonight, so Sean felt that he had made a breakthrough with him. Sean said, "Mr. Wong, you seem to have grasped something that some of your classmates have failed to fully comprehend. Much of the law that we deal with in this class is statutory. Consequently, many, but not all, of the terms of art that are used in the code are also defined in the code. If there is a decision that interprets a term, the case will be in the annotations. Good job!"

Sean looked at the clock again and announced a ten-minute break, with the promise that the next two hours would be pure entertainment.

Once the break ended, Sean appeared in front of the classroom with a stunningly beautiful woman, who, although more than a decade older than Sean by the calendar, looked to be in her mid-forties. She was about 5'4" in heels, had raven black hair, green eyes, a Roman nose, high cheek bones and a very curvaceous figure. Her carriage was dignified, but not stiff. She was very well dressed in a classic, dark-blue wool suit, accented nicely by a tasteful strand of pearls. She just looked too well dressed to be American. In fact, she was not an American by birth. By birth, she was British.

Sean's introduction was short and to the point. "Class, it is my great pleasure to introduce Daphne Hollingsworth, M.D., who holds the Stauder Chair in Psychiatry at the medical school. She will tell you everything that you need to know to be able to answer the questions that I posed to you in the first hour. Plus, she will instruct you so gracefully that you will be heartbroken when her time with us is over. Also, just in case anyone in the room is nervous, Dr. Hollingsworth has promised not to share with me any diagnoses that she may make over the next two hours. Please welcome, Dr. Daphne Hollingsworth."

As soon as the applause ended, Dr. Daphne began to talk. Sean sensed that within two minutes, she had the class, particularly the male students, mesmerized. Sean could never tell if Daphne's ability to completely charm men, especially American men, was because of her veddy upper-class English accent, her considerable charm, her dazzling smile, her good looks, her vitality or her personal warmth and sense of humor. Whatever the source of her ability to charm, Sean knew that she had it in spades. Most of the men in the class were younger than twenty-five, yet they were sitting there completely spellbound, only moving to jot an occasional note. As Sean watched Dr. Daphne simultaneously charm his class and explain to them the differences among the various types of mental illnesses and the psychopharmacology used to treat them, he guessed that over half of the male students, many of whom were young enough to be her grandsons, would have either fantasies or dreams that night about the well-spoken, well-dressed British woman.

As Daphne continued to lecture, Sean realized that age had not dulled her charms one bit. Sean and Daphne had been friends for many years. Sean had met her on the jogging path when he first came to S.U. almost three decades before.

After the break, Daphne took questions in her way, which was to turn the questions back on the audience to see what they had learned. When the final period ended, the entire class rose and gave her a standing ovation. Daphne basked in the glow of the admiration of the students for several minutes and then stopped to chat with several of the male students on her way to the door. Sean, observing from a distance, was sure that had Daphne been asked for her autograph, she could have produced several autographed photos from amid her lecture notes for that very purpose. Wow! Daphne hadn't lost a step!

After class, Sean walked Daphne to her Land Rover™ in the parking lot. After she opened the car door, she turned toward Sean and said, "Sean, you seem very different this evening."

Sean replied, "Spring always affects me like this."

Daphne said, "I suspect that something positive has happened in your life."

Sean, knowing that Daphne always could read his emotions like a book, shrugged and said, "I started dating again."

Daphne smiled and said, "Sean, bend over so I can kiss you!"

Bending over, Sean was expecting a little dry, proper British peck on the cheek. He received the peck on the cheek. But, he also received a very warm embrace as well. It was dark by now, so Sean hoped that none of his students saw what had just happened. After they pulled apart, Daphne said, in her best, unruffled British manner, "I am so glad to see that you are getting over Cheryl's death. Please let me know if I can do anything for you." Returning to her unflappable mode, Daphne said quite calmly, "I'm looking forward to hearing you teach my new crop of residents in the fall. Take care!"

As Sean drove home in the rain, necessity forced him to stop thinking about Daphne and to start thinking about the next day's jury trial.

✳✳✳✳✳✳✳✳✳✳✳✳

Shortly before 1000 hours, Bubba called Sean's chambers to let him know that he was on his way with a panel of sixty prospective jurors. As soon as Sean hung up, he went out into the courtroom and took the bench.

Surveying the scene for a second, he noticed a visual contrast between the two counsel tables. At the left-hand table, Kim Brownlee sat with a bearded, heavy-set man, who appeared to be bored. Even if Sean hadn't read the file and learned from the pleadings that the proposed patient was a professor at S.U., Sean could have easily guessed it from his appearance since the man at the table was wearing a brown tweed jacket with dark elbow patches and a blue button-down shirt with no necktie. Kim, on the other hand, was dressed to the nines. Somehow, Kim's gray suit made her green eyes sparkle. Her black hose made her legs look very attractive. Obviously, she and her client had failed to color coordinate for the day.

At the other table, Sean saw another study in contrasts. At one end of the table, there was a civilian, a rather well-endowed lady in her middle forties, who seemed very nervous. At the other end of the table, there was a tall, athletic-looking, African-American man in his late thirties, wearing a very somber and serious navy suit. Sean assumed that he must be Tom Ritter. He looked cool and comfortable and quite at home in a courtroom.

Calling the lawyers up to the bench, he told them that Bubba was on his way with a panel. Then, Sean started this exchange:

COURT: Mr. Ritter, Ms. Brownlee, have either of you ever tried a civil commitment jury trial before?

Mr. RITTER: No, Judge.

Ms. BROWNLEE: No, Judge.

COURT: Well, far be it from me to tell you how to try your cases, but let me give you a bit of practical advice, learned the hard way. I'm sure that none of us wants to bust a panel and have to start from scratch tomorrow, so when you begin your *voir dire,*[7] please be real careful if you decide to ask the panel questions about their attitudes and experiences with mental health professionals, particularly psychiatrists. Have them raise their hands, be recognized and state their numbers. You will have a chance to question anyone who raises their hand at the bench out of the hearing of the other panel members. In my first jury trial, which was a civil commitment case, a lawyer made the mistake of asking a juror about his attitudes on psychiatrists. The juror blurted out that his son had been in and out of mental hospitals for years and hadn't gotten any better. He then called psychiatrists a bunch of crooks, thieves and liars, who all ought to be hung. We had to bust the panel and start over the next day.

COURT: That won't happen here, will it?

Mr. RITTER: No, Judge

Ms. BROWNLEE: No, Judge.

COURT: One other thing, don't be surprised if a third to a half of the panel has had some direct or indirect experience with the mental health system. So many people have gone into rehab for chemical dependency problems that today receiving mental health care is a fairly common experience, much like going to a dentist or an accountant. Remember this when you question a prospective juror: the test for disqualification isn't experience with the mental health field, but bias one way or another. Okay?

Mr. RITTER: Yes, Judge.

Ms. BROWNLEE: Yes, Judge.

Voir dire was completed shortly before noon, with thirty-one members of the panel having been excused either on preemptory challenges or for cause. Five minutes later, the jury was seated and sworn and the rest of the panel dismissed. After a quick lunch at Rotary for Sean, opening statements started at 1320 hours and ended at 1405. Following a short recess, the fun began...

As soon as Sean took the bench, Kim Brownlee asked if counsel could approach the bench. Sean indicated that they could do so. When they approached the bench, Sean noticed that there was something unusually appealing about Kim today. Besides being well groomed and beautiful, there was something glowingly vital about her. Sean had no idea what was causing the change in her demeanor, but she seemed like she was ready to purr. Tom Ritter appeared to be confident and all set to go. Clearly, both lawyers had their game faces on.

Ms. BROWNLEE: Your honor, as you well know, for the state to prove its case, it must prove by clear and convincing evidence that the proposed patient is mentally ill. If it proves that, it must also prove by clear and convincing evidence[8] that the proposed patient is either a threat to himself, a threat to others or both. The law requires that these elements must be proved, at least in part, through the testimony of a psychiatrist. If those elements are proven, then the diagnosis must be corroborated through the testimony of one or more witnesses that the proposed patient has performed a recent overt act, or has had a recent continuing pattern of behavior that would support the psychiatric testimony.

COURT: Mr. Ritter, do you disagree with anything that Ms. Brownlee has said?

Mr. RITTER: No, your honor.

Ms. BROWNLEE: Your honor, based on a disclosure of information that Mr. Ritter made to me last evening, he has indicated that he intends to call Dr. Gerald Franks as his expert witness. Mr. Ritter also disclosed that he believes Dr. Franks will testify that the proposed patient is mentally ill and poses a threat to both himself and others.

Mr. RITTER: That's correct, your honor.

Ms. BROWNLEE: Your honor, in the interest of saving the time of the court and the jurors, we hereby stipulate as follows:

1. Dr. Gerald Franks is licensed to practice medicine in this state, is board certified in Psychiatry and is qualified to testify as an expert witness in the areas of Medicine and Psychiatry.

2. If sworn in and asked to testify today, Dr. Franks would testify that the proposed patient, Dr. Felix Radofsky, is suffering from a mental illness and that as a result of that mental illness, the proposed patient, if released today without further treatment, would pose a threat to himself and others.

COURT: Anything further?

Ms. BROWNLEE: No, your honor.

COURT: Very well, then. Bubba, please bring in the panel.

While waiting for the jurors to enter into their seats, Sean noticed that Tom Ritter now seemed to be a bit unsure of himself and apprehensive. Kim, on the other hand, radiated confidence and serenity.

COURT: Mr. Ritter, please call your first witness.

Mr. RITTER: The State now calls Dr. Gerald Franks.

As soon as Dr. Franks was sworn in, Kim Brownlee arose and asked for permission to approach the bench. As soon as the two lawyers reached the bench, Sean cautioned them to speak softly, so the jurors could not hear the conversation.

Ms. BROWNLEE: (Softly) Your honor, we object to any expert medical or psychiatric testimony from Dr. Franks on the basis that since the proposed patient has already stipulated to those things that an expert psychiatric witness would ordinarily testify about, such testimony would be not material to any issue to be decided by the jury, would be redundant and cumulative and would also be inflammatory and that such testimony's probative value would be far outweighed by the prejudicial nature of such testimony upon my client's case.

Mr. RITTER: Judge, this is ridiculous! She is trying to prevent me from calling a psychiatrist to testify in a mental case!

Ms. BROWNLEE: Your honor, I do believe that Mr. Ritter failed to understand my objection. I have no objection to the good doctor's testimony as a fact witness.

Mr. RITTER: Judge, I renew my objection.

Ms. BROWNLEE: Your honor, I believe that I am the party with the objection before the court at this time.

Mr. RITTER: Well Judge, I still object to her objection.

Ms. BROWNLEE: Judge, you aren't going to allow him to object to my objection, are you?

COURT: Mr. Ritter, do you have any authority that would allow you to object to her objection?

Mr. RITTER: Well your honor, everyone knows that counsel can object to an improper objection.

COURT: I must have missed class that day when the subject was discussed in law school. I'll treat your objection to her objection as a response to her objection. Ms. Brownlee's objection is sustained. Mr. Ritter, feel free to call the doctor as a fact witness.

After counsel returned to their places, Tom Ritter began to question the doctor. Once Tom established that Dr. Franks had first met the proposed patient the preceding Wednesday when the patient was admitted to the hospital, Tom Ritter asked:

Mr. RITTER: What sort of behaviors have you observed from the proposed patient since he was admitted to the hospital?

WITNESS: On the day that he was admitted, the proposed patient advised me that he would only talk to me if his lawyer was present. After that, he said nothing further and stared at me until I terminated the interview.

Mr. RITTER: How many additional times have you visited with him?

WITNESS: Last Thursday, last Friday and yesterday— Monday.

Mr. RITTER: What happened then?

WITNESS: Each time, the patient told me that he had no desire to speak with me and asked me to leave his room so he could prepare his notes for today's trial.

Mr. RITTER: Have you had any other opportunities to talk with him?

WITNESS: No.

When Tom Ritter passed the witness, Kim declined to cross-examine. The witness, looking very confused and full of pent-up testimony, was excused and released by the court. At Tom Ritter's suggestion, the court declared a short recess.

When the recess was over, Sean noticed that Kim's cheeks had a warm, non-cosmetic glow on them. He sensed that she had at least one more rabbit left to pull from her hat. Sean was really impressed with the way that Kim had handled herself so far. His musings were soon interrupted by Tom Ritter's voice calling his next witness, Maria Radofsky.

Mrs. Radofsky smiled a warm smile at Sean as she worked her way into the witness box. Sean smiled back, being polite. She appeared to be in her late forties, tall, dark-haired and buxom. As she was sworn in, Sean thought that the poor woman was wasting her time trying to flirt with him since this was a jury trial. Sean, being Sean, never let it enter his head that the lady might be flirting with him because she found him to be attractive.

Tom Ritter did a very fine job with Mrs. Radofsky, keeping her on the stand for over ninety minutes. The lady kept on track while Tom took her testimony that she had been happily married to the proposed patient for over twenty years. She did fine telling Tom about their two children, who were students at Southern University.

But, when Tom started to ask her about recent changes in her husband's behavior, the tears began. Mrs. Radofsky did not cry excessively, but just enough so that Sean had to hand her one of the several boxes of tissue that he kept below the bench and give her a minute to compose herself. Sean noticed that the jury—particularly the male jurors—seemed to be watching the crying witness very intently. Sean had to declare two short recesses to allow the witness to regain her composure.

Once Mrs. Radofsky resumed her testimony, Tom Ritter elicited that in the last two months, the professor had begun to withdraw from her, accusing her of infidelities and threatening to kill her and himself if she left him. The lady indicated that these irrational beliefs and very believable threats had compelled her to try to have her husband committed.

After that last bit of testimony, Tom Ritter, having just played his ace, passed the witness to Kim Brownlee. Kim, still glowing, pointed out that the hour was growing late. She indicated that she planned a rather long cross-examination of this witness and requested that the court allow her to begin it tomorrow, so that the she could start and end her cross-examination on the same day. Despite Tom Ritter's perfunctory objection, Sean recessed the trial until Wednesday afternoon at 1300 hours.

****

Sean and Laura took an early lunch at Joe's Diner on Wednesday. After their meals had been ordered, but before they arrived, Sean looked up to see the sheriff and several other uniformed people sitting down at a table near them.

Sean very quickly rose and said, "Laura, let's shake some hands." Knowing better than to interfere with him when he was in political mode, Laura complied. After reintroducing Laura to the sheriff and his little group, the sheriff reciprocated the courtesy, introducing two very middle-aged men—a major and a captain—and Sergeant Jolene Scruggs.

After the introductions were completed and a few pleasantries were exchanged, Sean asked the sheriff if he could borrow the company of the sergeant for a moment. After the sheriff graciously indicated that he could spare her for a minute, Sean and Jo left the table and stood just far enough away from everyone to keep them out of hearing range. All Laura could pick up of the conversation was Jo thanking Sean for a present of some kind and something about what to wear on Saturday night.

Watching closely, Laura noticed that the two of them were obviously glad to see each other. They were talking animatedly and freely, their conversation being punctuated only by an occasional laugh. As they talked, Laura noticed that Sean was smiling quite happily, which was something that he had not done much of since Cheryl died. She also noticed that the sergeant was paying rapt attention to Sean's words and seemed to be as happy to see him as he was to see her.

When the conversation ended and Sean and Jo started to return to their respective luncheon companions, Laura noticed that Jo really was stunningly beautiful. Then, it hit her like a lightning bolt out of the blue. Maybe Sean really did have a date with the deputy last week!

Sean and their waitress arrived at the table at the same moment. As Sean was settling in and the food being served, Laura tried to remember how Sean had described his date last week. She remembered Sean saying that she was in her late twenties, had brown hair, blue eyes, a great figure, long legs, freckles and the voice of an angel.

After a moment of food-induced silence, Laura asked, "Sean, what was that sergeant's name?"

"Jolene Scruggs."

"Was she the lady that Kyra fixed you up with when I was gone?"

"One and the same."

Laura, sensing that she was pushing the envelope here, ate silently, giving Sean an opportunity to say something if he wanted to do so. After several minutes, Sean said, "Thank you for not asking what we both know you want to know. Yes, the blind date worked out very well. Last Saturday night, we went to see an old movie on campus. We are going to go to a baseball game this coming Saturday. We have plans to go to the Spring Fling next month. I enjoy her company—a lot!"

After a short, sphinx-like silence, Laura asked, "Are you in love?"

Looking confused, Sean replied, "I'm not sure."

"Well Sean, be real careful with her. Watching you two talking, I sensed that she has fallen for you big time and that she is very vulnerable. Tread softly!"

Laura's comments came out of left field as far as Sean was concerned. He had been so wrapped up in his own pain and his problems that he hadn't really bothered to think that maybe there was some other reason that Kyra had fixed them up. To the extent that Sean had actually thought about why Jo consented to a blind date with him, he had always assumed she was doing Kyra a favor. He never thought that each of them might have needed to be fixed up on a blind date since he always assumed that a beautiful woman as young and vital as Jo would have men at her beck and call. Laura had given him something to think about.

On their way back to the courthouse, Sean and Laura stopped briefly at the sheriff's table, just long enough to say their goodbyes. Watching Jo and Sean interact, Laura noticed how much Sean lit up around Jo. Laura realized that Sean might not know that he was in love, but she certainly did.

When Sean and Laura got back to chambers, Sean prepared to return to the Radofsky commitment hearing. Meanwhile, Laura dialed Kyra's number, being prepared to eat crow just so she could see what information she could get about Sean and Jo from Kyra.

✱✱✱✱✱✱✱✱✱✱✱

Kim Brownlee's cross-examination was a model of simplicity.

> Ms. BROWNLEE: Ma'am, do you understand that you are still under oath and subject to the penalties of perjury, just as you were yesterday?
>
> WITNESS: Yes.
>
> Ms. BROWNLEE: Ma'am, do you love your husband?
>
> WITNESS: Yes.

Ms. BROWNLEE: Have you been faithful to your husband?

WITNESS: Yes, always!

Ms. BROWNLEE: Do you have any plans to leave or divorce your husband?

WITNESS: No.

Ms. BROWNLEE: Please take a second and consider whether there is any element of your testimony that you might want to change.

WITNESS: No, there is not.

BROWNLEE: Your honor, I pass the witness, reserving the right to recall her a later time.

The State did not seek redirect examination of the witness. At this time, the state rested. Ms. Brownlee sought a directed verdict, which was denied.

Ms. Brownlee then indicated that she was going to call her first witness, one Marvin Swanson. After the witness was sworn and seated, the dialogue began...

Ms. BROWNLEE: Please state your name.

WITNESS: Marvin Swanson.

Ms. BROWNLEE: Do you hold any licenses issued to you by this state?

WITNESS: Yes, I hold a driver's license, a peace officer's certificate and am a licensed private investigator.

Ms. BROWNLEE: Are you personally acquainted with the proposed patient in this case, Dr. Isaac Radofsky?

WITNESS: Yes, I am.

Ms. BROWNLEE: When did you first meet Dr. Radofsky?

WITNESS: We met about three months ago when he hired me to conduct what we call "a matrimonial surveillance" on his wife.

Ms BROWNLEE: For the record, is Mrs. Radofsky in the courtroom this afternoon?

WITNESS: She is sitting there at the counsel's table, next to the man in the dark suit.

COURT: Let the record reflect that the witness pointed to Mrs. Radofsky.

Ms. BROWNLEE: How did you conduct this "matrimonial surveillance" on Mrs. Radofsky?

WITNESS: Dr. Radofsky travels out of town occasionally to visit his book editor. On those days and nights when he was out of town, I maintained surveillance on his wife after he left the house.

Mr. RITTER: Objection, your honor!

COURT: Approach the bench.

BUBBA: Judge, would you like the jury to take a short break?

COURT: I think ten minutes would be about right.

After the jury left the courtroom, the Court considered the objection by Mr. Ritter.

Mr. RITTER: Judge, as I was saying several minutes ago, I object to the previous question and any further questions along those lines on the basis of relevance and materiality.

Ms. BROWNLEE: Your honor, when I cross-examined Mrs. Radofsky, I asked her very specific questions about her relationship with her husband. This witness has information that will contradict her testimony. That goes to credibility, which is always at issue.

COURT: Overruled!

Mr. RITTER: Judge, may I take several minutes to confer with Mrs. Radofsky, the applicant in this matter?

Sean looked over at where Mrs. Radofsky was sitting. She seemed very, very pale. She was sweating visibly. Her hands were shaking. She was in tears.

COURT: Take as much time as you need.

Mr. RITTER: Thank you, your honor.

Fifteen minutes later, counsel asked to approach Sean in his office. Jane was with them. Once Jane told Sean that she was ready to proceed, Tom Ritter said, "Your honor, the State moves to dismiss its application."

"No objection, your honor."

Sean said, "I'll have Bubba bring the jury back in a minute, so I can dismiss them."

Looking at Jane, Sean said, "Off the record." Then, looking at Tom Ritter, Sean said, "It was a pleasure to finally meet you. My friends, Kyra and Max, have told me a lot of good things about you."

Appearing embarrassed, Tom said, "Judge, try not to mention today to them. It's not often that I've been beaten up as badly as I was today."

Kim, now appearing more embarrassed than Tom had a moment ago, piped in and said, "You're being too kind. Everyone knows that I was just lucky."

Sean asked softly, "Kim, if you don't mind my asking, why did you make those stipulations this morning?"

Tom added, "Judge, thanks for asking her that. I was wondering, myself."

Kim said, "Your honor, if the private investigator's testimony hadn't forced her to fold, I was ready to call Dr. Radofsky's psychiatrist, Dr. Daphne Hollingsworth, who was ready to testify that he has been a patient of hers for several months and that Dr. Radofsky is only suffering from a mild form of depression known as "dysphoric disorder." She was prepared to further testify that his depression is under control with medication and therapy, and that he poses no threat to anyone at all. By making the stipulation, I hoped to have Dr. Hollingsworth be the only psychiatrist that the jury would hear."

Impressed, Tom Ritter said, "And I thought those criminal defense lawyers were slick! No one warned me that probate lawyers were this good."

As Kim blushed, Sean ended the conversation by saying, "Jane, go get set up in the courtroom and then tell Bubba to let me know when he has the jurors in their places."

Moments later, as Sean thanked the jurors profusely for their service, the thought crossed his mind that Kim had been glowing for a reason earlier today. He guessed that while she probably wasn't much of a poker player, she had done a good job for her client. Sean was also grateful that Daphne hadn't been called to testify because, ethically, he would have been obligated to disclose that they had had a long-standing personal relationship. He would have kept it at that, but, seeing as how Ritter's case was about to crater, Tom would have probably moved for a recusal, which Sean would have granted—for appearances sake, if nothing else.

A few minutes later, Sean was sitting in Laura's office telling her about his weird afternoon. When he finished, knowing what his social obligation to Laura was, Sean said, "I guess that Kim is a better trial lawyer than I thought she was."

Laura, still embarrassed over having to admit to Kyra that she had been wrong about the practical joke she thought had been played on her by Kyra and Sean, felt better hearing Sean's admission of imperfection. People as near perfect as Laura find the whole process of admission of error to be unsettling. Whenever forced to travel that unfamiliar trail, they are overjoyed to have company along the journey, much like the pilgrims on their way to Canterbury had enjoyed company in Chaucer's time.

****

Wednesday evening, after working out and then eating, Sean and his two furry, lady friends had a chance to play their favorite game called, "Block the computer!" Eventually, despite a valiant last-ditch effort by Equity to unplug the CRT from the CPU, Sean managed to send his email to Lucy and Ralph, in which he accepted their kind invitation for Jo and him to dine with them on Saturday night.

After this signal defeat, Law lost heart and curled up in Sean's lap. Equity, not surrendering entirely, curled up on Sean's desk at the edge, within striking distance of both the mouse and the keyboard. Warily, Sean checked his email. When Equity finally dozed off, Sean got down to the business at hand—an email to Jo.

Jo,

My heart almost skipped a beat when I saw you at lunch. I was so glad to see you again.

You looked so beautiful today. I can't even begin to think how you pulled this off, but the blue of your uniform goes perfectly with the blue of your eyes. Your beauty was set off so nicely by the gray surroundings of Joe's Diner and the grayness of your luncheon companions. No offense to the sheriff or his other companions today, but you did a lot to improve the average looks of the people at your table. <g>

I'm glad that you liked the foot massager. Just remember to think about me when you use it! <g> It may not have my charm, but being electric powered, it doesn't tire as easily as I do!

Lucy and Ralph look forward to Saturday night. They are great cooks and don't have much of a chance to have a social life away from their business. Lucy answered your question for me. She said the water in the lake is too cold for you to go swimming.

I'm looking forward to seeing you again. And I know that we won't be wearing identical outfits this Saturday! <g>

SR

Chapter Four

Great day for a ball game, Sean said to himself, as he parked in front of Jo's place. When Jo opened her front door, Sean realized that only the color blind would have any trouble telling which team she was rooting for since she was wearing her red and white State baseball cap, red and white State t-shirt, white shorts with red trim and red sneakers with white trim and laces. Sean looked less partisan, wearing a white polo shirt, tan chinos and brown deck shoes. The only thing on his person that gave away his team loyalty was his dark-blue and white Southern University baseball cap.

"Sean, put your things on the sofa," Jo said, referring to the large hanging bag that he had carried into her home with him.

"Okay. But, before we leave, I have a present for you," Sean said. "As a former Boy Scout, I came prepared for today. Jo, no matter who wins, I want you to have a baseball signed by the winning starting pitcher." As he said that, Sean unzipped one of the pouches of the hanging bag and produced two signed baseballs, each housed in a little plastic holder.

"Sean, how did you get one from both starters?"

"I'll never tell," Sean said, with a mischievous grin on his face.

As they prepared to leave Jo's house, she slipped a small towel and a mini bottle of suntan lotion into her oversized purse.

As the couple drove the interstate toward Capitol City, Sean noticed that the indicator for the outside temperature showed that it was 78° already. Sean sensed that Jo had been wise to wear shorts and that maybe he should have been willing to forsake his dignity and worn shorts as well.

As they drove along in Jo's SUV, Sean noticed that Jo looked very relaxed. Her hair was pulled back so that a ponytail peeked out from the back of her baseball cap. As the drive continued, Sean asked her, "Jo, I'm sorry that I failed to ask you this before, but what do you do on your job?"

"Precious, thanks for askin'. I'm in what we call *community relations.* Most days I either go out and give speeches or write speeches for the sheriff to give. Some days I review awards citations and prepare everythin' for awards ceremonies, includin' the press releases. I also train our people on how to handle the media, as well as teachin' a segment at the academy. When somethin' big happens, I write the statement for the sheriff. I'm also at our press conferences. As of a few weeks ago, I became the fourth person in the department to go on weekend call in case somethin' newsworthy happens and the sheriff isn't immediately available to hold a press conference."

Sean inquired, "Do you like doing press conferences?"

"Yes and no. It's my own fault, really. Back when I was just a deputy, I loved bein' on patrol. Unfortunately, I got the bug to sit for the sergeant's exam, so once you get some sort of rank above deputy, you don't get to do as much fun stuff as you used to do. It serves me right for takin' the sergeant's exam."

Sean asked, "What will you do after this job?"

Turning to Sean for a second, Jo answered, "Sean, I may be in this job for quite a while. Besides the sheriff, the only two people—not countin' me—that he feels comfortable dealin' with the media in this age of politically correct law enforcement are his chief deputy and my boss, the captain in charge of community relations. When I took the job, it was with the understandin' that as soon as I made lieutenant, the captain, my boss, was gonna retire and I would take his place. I've got about a year to go, but already I'm takin' over more and more of the things that my boss used to do. The plan is that I'm gonna be the **face of the department** to the public since no one—includin' the sheriff—likes dealin' with the media. I don't mind it, really! It's important work, just not as excitin' as bein' out on the streets. Heard enough?"

"You know, Jo, dealing with the press and public is important work. That's why Presidents are so careful in their choice of a press secretary."

"The sheriff isn't exactly the President of the U.S., is he?" Jo questioned, with just a bit of an edge in her voice.

"No he's not, but the job of dealing with the media is essentially the same. Reporters are reporters no matter what the beat and what paper, station or channel employs them."

"You sound like you've dealt with the media yourself, Precious," Jo said, with her voice returning to its usual sweet drawl.

"Back when I was a trial lawyer, I had the chance to meet a few reporters on some of the cases that I handled. And of course, running for office, I met quite a few. Most are decent. A few aren't. Those are the ones who can cause you a lot of trouble, even if you've done everything by the book. I know from experience."

****

Before the game started, Jo and Sean grabbed the traditional hot dogs and Cokes™—his diet, hers with sugar. Right before the game started, Jo pulled out the suntan lotion and towel from her bag. After she smeared gooey stuff on her arms, neck and legs, Jo instinctively put some on Sean's arms and the back of his neck. Sean would have objected, but the warm lotion and Jo's fingers on his skin made Sean quickly forget that his personal space had been invaded. As Jo returned the lotion and towel to her bag, the National Anthem was announced.

Jo, with her cop's eye for detail, observed that as soon as the National Anthem was about to begin, Sean rose, removed his cap and placed it over his heart. Jo also noticed that Sean's body became erect and rigid. Listening to Sean sing along, she heard his normally soft voice become strong, as he sang with great gusto. When the music stopped, Sean immediately returned to normal and relaxed as they sat back down. Then, the game began.

When the starters for State were introduced, everyone on their side of the field cheered wildly, except for Sean, who clapped politely. When the starters for Southern were announced, Sean stood and cheered, ignoring the fact that he was the only S.U. fan in a sea of red and white on their side of the ballpark. Jo thought that Sean showed the courage of his convictions, which was pretty unusual these days. She was duly impressed.

Everyone at the ballpark was expecting a pitching duel since both starters had had great seasons the year before and were doing even better this year. The first batter for visiting S.U. was Garland, their shortstop. After taking the count to 3 and 2, Garland managed to foul off six more pitches before finally drawing his walk.

As soon as the first pitch was tossed to the second Southern batter, Garland took off running for second base. The catcher would have nailed him, if the State second baseman had been in position. Since he wasn't, Garland easily took second and made his way to third base before the center fielder for State could throw the ball to their third baseman. The Southern batter flied out, scoring Garland. The next two batters also flied out. So, at the middle of the first inning, the score was one to nothing, with no hits for S. U. and an error charged against State. Southern's pitcher, Wallace, fanned the three batters that he faced in the bottom of the first, beginning a trend.

Since there wasn't much action on the base paths, Jo and Sean talked and talked and talked. She was really impressed with how much he loved baseball. Sean was equally impressed that she was as knowledgeable as he was about the sport. As the game continued, Sean and Jo almost lost track of where they were.

After the last out in the top of the sixth inning, the score of the game was unchanged from the middle of the first inning. Sean was jolted back to reality by a tap on his shoulder, and a familiar voice saying, "Hello, Father.

What brings you to the game?" Sean turned to see both of his daughters, Pat and Maureen, behind him.

Sean warmly hugged the two tall blondes and then, without missing a beat, he turned to Jo and said, "Jo, may I present my daughters, Pat and Maureen?" Since the two girls were identical twins, Sean was very careful to point out who was who to Jo. Sean then said, "Ladies, this is Jo. She invited me to the game."

Maureen and Pat each shook Jo's hand. Maureen's greeting was warm and genuine while Pat's seemed to be a bit more subdued and distant. The difference in the greetings was not in the least bit unexpected by Sean. Sean asked, "What brings you over to this side of the field?"

Giggling, Maureen replied, pointing across the field to the area behind the visitor's dugout, "We're sitting over there. About the third inning, someone noticed this one lone Southern fan sitting over here surrounded by all that red and white. When it was my turn with the binoculars, I looked across the field and thought that it might be you. I couldn't tell for sure because your baseball cap and sunglasses almost hide your face. But, I was sure enough to talk Pat into coming over here to check it out."

After the bottom of the sixth inning concluded, with the scoreboard unchanged, the girls indicated that their friends might wonder what happened to them. So they made their exit, after saying goodbye to Jo and hugging Sean.

A few minutes after the Twins had left, Jo remarked to Sean, "Your daughters look alike, but have different personalities, don't they? Maureen seems to be very personable, much like you. Pat seems to be a bit more reserved and formal."

"You want to guess which one is majoring in Psychology and wants to be a psychiatrist when she grows up and which one is the Chemical Engineering major?" Sean asked.

"I'll bet that I only get one guess, right?"

"Right!"

The game now being in the bottom half of the eighth inning, their conversation was interrupted by the **ping** of a baseball and an aluminum bat coming in contact. For a second, it looked like the game was about to be tied and Southern's no hitter lost, but the Southern left fielder caught the ball about five feet from the fence. The next two batters for State fared no better.

When Southern came up to bat in the top of the ninth, Cameron, State's pitcher, still having good command of his stuff, set the three batsmen from S.U. down in order, using only eleven pitches to garner three strikeouts.

When the bottom of the ninth came, everyone stood. The first batter for State hit a wicked grounder to Garland, which he tossed deftly to first, beating the batter by one step. One down.

The second batter for State hit the first pitch for a pop fly, which Garland also fielded. Two down.

State was down to its last out when their pitcher, Cameron, came to bat. Sean, even if Jo hadn't reminded him of this fact, knew that Cameron came into the game hitting over .300.

Wallace's first pitch to Cameron was a blistering fast ball just over the inside corner of the plate. Count: Strike one.

Cameron wasn't fooled by the next pitch, which missed the inside corner that time by a gnat's eyelash. Count: Ball one. Strike one.

Wallace's next pitch was an outside curveball that fooled Cameron by breaking at just the last nanosecond over the edge of the plate. Count: Ball one. Strike two.

Now, everyone in the ballpark was standing. Having to protect the plate, Cameron fouled off the next four pitches.

On the next pitch, after waving off signals from his catcher, Wallace— either out of tiredness or faith in both his abilities and those of his outfielders—sent a slow curveball over the inside part of the plate.

At the ping of the bat, the red and white wearing part of the crowd starting cheering wildly while the dark blue and white clad other part of the crowd gasped as the ball sailed toward the fence. Sean noticed that the ball was starting to drop as it neared the fence. Just a second before the game would have been tied, the Southern center fielder leapt like a very athletic cat and caught the ball right inside of the fence.

The final totals were:

	Runs	Hits	Errors
Southern	1	0	0
State	0	0	1

As they walked back through the throng to Jo's SUV, Jo and Sean discussed why baseball had that silly rule that even if you pitched a hitless game for a full nine innings, you couldn't claim a no-hitter unless your team won the game. Sean, not wanting to further ruffle Jo's already ruffled red and white feathers, agreed with her that it was a silly rule while thinking to himself that the rule actually made absolute sense. Jo knew perfectly well that Sean was agreeing with her to be nice, but she appreciated it all the same.

By the time they reached Jo's SUV, both of them had worked up quite a sweat. When Jo planted her body in her seat, she kept her door open and looked at Sean. She said, "I'm afraid if I turn the A/C on, considerin' how sweaty we are, we're both gonna catch pneumonia. Okay if we just ride home with the windows down to cool us?" Since Sean voiced no objections, she asked him, with a glint in her eye and a playful tone in her voice, "Mind if I get comfortable?"

Knowing full well that Jo had her mind made up anyway, Sean said, "It's your vehicle. You're driving."

"Okay Precious, I'm gonna undress a bit." Jo quickly untied her sneakers and took them off, followed by her bobby socks—all of which she planted in the back of her SUV. Next, Jo removed her baseball cap, shaking her dark brown mane as it came free.

Sean quickly asked, "Jo, you aren't going to take anything else off, are you?"

Jo just smiled and said, "Okay, it's your loss."

On the ride back to her place, Sean and Jo mostly talked about the very unusual game they had just watched. After a while, Jo asked, "Sean, were you in the military?"

"Jo, why do you ask?"

"Well, when the National Anthem was announced, you snapped to just like someone in the military or law enforcement."

"Chalk that up to four years at a military school and two years of college R.O.T.C."

"Oh! Why did you leave R.O.T.C.?" Jo asked.

"The Army made that choice for me. They said that my eyes were too bad to be in the military. So, I never served."

"Sean, I've never seen you wearin' glasses. Do you wear contacts?"

"No, I had surgery a few years ago. I'm 20/20 now. If they had had laser eye surgery back when I was in R.O.T.C., I'd probably be a colonel in Army J.A.G. about ready to retire by now."

"Sean, you were in college durin' Viet Nam, right? I've heard that just about everyone your age was against the war. Isn't that why we pulled out of Viet Nam?"

"Many were against the war, but I wasn't one of them. My country was at war. I felt it was my duty to get shot at, just like everyone else."

"Sean, you're not soundin' much like a Yankee right about now. How come you're so different?"

"Well Jo, I'm from the mid-West. We're just as conservative and love God and Country as much as people from the South. We just speak differently."

"Sean, did you ever see any peace demonstrators?"

"Lord knows I couldn't avoid them! But, they did their thing and I did mine."

As the conversation drifted back to less painful matters, Jo thought that Sean really didn't at all fit the stereotype of a Yankee law professor. She found that to be a very comforting thought.

As they worked their way back toward University City, Sean noticed that it was now 92°. Pointing to the outside temperature indicator, Sean remarked, "You may get a chance to jump in the lake tonight."

****

When Sean and Jo arrived back at her place, Jo showed Sean to the guest bedroom with its adjoining bathroom. After a quick shower, Sean dressed quickly, wearing the clothes that he had left at Jo's that morning. Sean looked ready for anything that evening in his navy-blue blazer, clean chinos, pale-blue polo shirt and deck shoes *sans* socks.

When Sean left the guest room, he found Jo dressed in a white Turkish robe, sitting on the living room sofa, combing out her freshly shampooed and conditioned hair. As he looked at her, the scene seemed strangely familiar. After watching her attempt to get a tangle out of her hair, he let his mind wander for a second and suddenly blurted out the name of a famous actress. Smiling a big smile, Jo said simply, "I do believe, kind Sir, that you have just paid me a compliment!"

"Indeed!"

When Jo was finally ready, she really caught Sean's eye as she emerged from her bedroom. She had her dark hair up. She was wearing a red sundress with a white floral design, which showed the tan that she had already started to develop. The sundress also showed that she was well endowed, something that Sean had never fully noticed before since he had never seen her in anything that accented her figure. Carrying on the color scheme of the day, Jo was wearing white, dressy sandals, a strand of pearls around her neck and carrying a small, red purse and a white wrap. Jo looked absolutely stunning! Before they left her place, Sean noticed that her freckles seemed not to stop at her neck.

After they left Jo's home, Sean drove them to their dinner engagement in his F-150. To avoid recalling unhappy memories, Sean took a route that bypassed County 191 until several miles beyond the scene of Cheryl's fatal accident. Jo, having patrolled the area, knew it real well. Since she also knew where Sean lived and where the fatal accident had occurred, Jo noticed the detour, but said nothing.

On the way, he told her about how he had first met Lucy in court, about the contested matter with her brother, the "jury view" of her resort and about how Cheryl had fixed up the couple on a blind date. He also mentioned that Lucy and Ralph had had a very interesting wedding reception, mixing country music folks, construction types, resort personnel and lawyers.

For Jo, the best part of what Sean told her about Lucy and Ralph was his collection of war stories about the "jury view," which had Jo in laughter for a good part of the trip. As they neared their destination, Jo asked if the water in the lake would be warm enough to swim in.

"Jo, how warm is it outside right now?"

"The temperature gauge on your truck says 83°."

"Jo, it's about 1830 hours right? By the time we finish our meal, how late do you think it will be?"

"2100 hours, more or less."

"How warm do you think it will be then?"

"Around 70°."

"Jo, will you really want to swim if the air temperature is only 70°?"

Flirting, Jo said, "I'd be fine since I'm hot-blooded. But most people that I know would freeze under those conditions."

Handing Jo his cell phone and a piece of paper, Sean said, "Jo, we're nearing the resort. Please take my cell phone and tell them we should be there in about two minutes. Here's the number to call."

When Sean and Jo turned off of County 191 up a short, gravel road, they saw a sign that was too dark to read. Standing by the sign was a middle-aged man wearing glasses, a sports jacket, a checked shirt, chinos and deck shoes. "Have any trouble finding the place in the dark?" the man called out.

Pulling even with the man, Sean said through his now open window, "Ralph, those were great directions, given with a lawyerly mastery of detail." Sean let the man into the backseat of his F-150 after introducing him to Jo as "Ralph."

Driving down the gravel road for a quarter mile or so, the F-150 came to a large, mostly deserted gravel parking lot. At the end of the lot, there was a building with lights shining through its windows. Sean parked near the building and the three of them headed toward the building. As they walked along, Jo asked, "Mind if I take my sandals off? I'm a little wobbly on gravel in these things."

While walking barefoot in gravel in the dark is not the easiest thing in the world, Jo knew that slipping on loose gravel in high-heeled sandals would be a lot worse. As they walked along, Jo was glad that she had brought a wrap. She suspected that she might need it tonight. Jo also noticed that Sean was carrying something gift wrapped with him.

As soon as they were within a few feet of the illuminated office building for the resort, Sean asked, "Ralph, y'all open now?"

Ralph replied, "Yes and no. This time of year, we stop accepting new guests after 6:00 p.m. But, we try to maintain a presence in the office until midnight from April through October. Plus, since we have some overseas customers, it is good to have someone there to check for incoming reservations received via email. During our busy season in the summer, we'll hire college kids to work the late shift. Tonight, since Lucy and I are busy, her mom is minding the store."

Right before they reached the office, Ralph directed them to a dirt path to their left, which intersected the path to the office. This new path led them up a small, wooded hill. Once the party reached the top of the hill, they came to a very large, two-story house.

When they entered the house, Sean introduced Jo to Lucy. Jo adjudged Lucy to be about her own height, about forty years old and quite buxom. Lucy's long, brown hair, worn straight, hung down to the small of her back. As soon as the four of them entered Lucy and Ralph's spacious living room, Lucy, noticing that Jo had her shoes in her hand, said, "Jo, I'm glad to see that you're barefoot. I'll take off my shoes, as well! Boys, take yours off, too!"

"Yes dear!" Ralph said meekly.

"Lucy, you aren't this bossy all the time, are you?" Sean asked.

Laughing, Lucy said, "No Sean, just around you two."

As the four of them wiggled their toes on the plush red carpet, Sean offered the gift-wrapped bottle of wine that he had carried with him from his truck to Lucy. Lucy said, "Sean, thank you so much. Will you be offended if we don't open it tonight?"

As Sean said that his feelings wouldn't be hurt in the least, both Jo and Sean noticed Lucy and Ralph exchanging glances. After a second, Lucy said, "There are two reasons why we won't be openin' your wine tonight.

The first is that you brought a red wine and we are havin' chicken for dinner."

Pausing for effect, Lucy said, "But, there is a more important reason why we won't have wine tonight. I want you and Jo to be the first of our friends to know our good news. After tryin' for several years, we finally managed to conceive. The doctor confirmed it yesterday. We'll be expectin' an early Christmas present this year."

Jo noticed how warmly Sean received the news and further noticed that Lucy and Ralph were beaming from ear to ear. Somehow, even though she had known Sean for less than a month and Lucy and Ralph for less than an hour, Jo knew that she was with friends and felt very much at home.

After drinking an iced tea toast to the upcoming blessed event, the two couples happily trouped into Lucy and Ralph's dining room. After grace was said and the Almighty was thanked for the good news that Lucy and Ralph had just shared, the couples began to eat.

The first course was an excellent *vichyssoise*. Lucy gave Ralph credit for preparing this dish. Jo and Sean both honestly remarked that it was excellent. Jo wasn't entirely sure what the name of the soup was, but she liked it nonetheless. She made a mental note to get the recipe.

During the salad course, Lucy said, "Sean, it was nice to see you at your Rotary club several weeks ago. For city folks, y'all make us country visitin' Rotarians feel right at home."

"City Folks? Remember where I live? I'm just up the road a piece from you."

"True, but you work in University City. If you'd move your court out here to Smithville, you'd really be one of us."

"I don't think our county fathers want to pay the moving costs, so I guess I'll be stuck commuting for a while longer. But, it's a good idea."

The entrée was Chicken Kiev served with fresh asparagus spears over seasoned brown rice. Lucy once again gave Ralph the credit for this dish. Sean turned to Ralph and asked, "Ralph, how did you learn to cook so well?"

Ralph replied, "I took courses at night when I was a bachelor living in Capitol City. I figured since I'm not the most outgoing man in the world, my only hope of ever finding a lady would be to offer her something unique, like being a good cook."

Smiling, Lucy said, "Is that what did it? I guess it worked, didn't it! "

After the laughter stopped, Sean said, "Jo, on your job, I'm sure that from time to time you have to look at the laws that the legislature passes. If you ever read one that is written beyond any human's ability to comprehend, Ralph probably had something to do with it."

Lucy said to Jo, "Are you a lawyer, too?" with a tone of faux disgust in her voice.

Feeling a bit out of place, Jo said, "No, I'm a sergeant with the sheriff's department. My current assignment is in community relations. "

Lucy, sensing the tension in Jo's voice, replied, "When I was in high school, I saw a TV movie about a woman police officer. I thought that police work must be the neatest job in the world. When my Daddy, who grew up in rural Kentucky, after all, heard that his daughter wanted to enter police work, he told me quite emphatically that police work was too masculine for his daughter."

Jo, rather defensively, asked, "Before you got into this business, what did you do?"

Lucy replied, "Civil engineerin'/construction management." After the laughter subsided, Lucy continued, "Actually, I didn't really choose this business. My parents started it and I inherited it from my Daddy. I'm glad that I got out of construction and all of that rat race."

After a short pause, Lucy continued, "Goin' back to what you asked me before, Daddy told me after I got into construction management that he was sorry I had listened to him and hadn't gone into law enforcement. I would have met a higher class of people in law enforcement."

"Cops?" Jo asked in return.

Lucy said, "The last time Daddy said that to me, I asked him that same question. He said criminals would have been a step up from the types you have to deal with in construction—assumin' that there was any difference at all. As I think back about some of the characters I had to deal with in business, I think he may have been dead-on right."

After the laughter stopped, Jo turned to Ralph and asked, "Ralph, what do you do?"

Ralph replied, "After law school, I went to work for a state agency. I stayed there for about ten years. One day, quite out of the blue, the head of the Office of Legislative Counsel asked me to come to work for his office. I've been there ever since. I have high hopes that he'll recommend me to replace him when he retires in several years."

Lucy piped in, "Is that all you're gonna tell her?"

Ralph replied, after a bite of Chicken Kiev, "You don't' have to be a lawyer to be in the legislature. Lord knows, you don't have to be anything at all to get elected in some places, except breathing. So, if a legislator wants to introduce a bill, he comes to us to put it into the right words. The job involves a lot of research to make sure that a bill refers to all the right sections of existing law, so that if it ever becomes law, there aren't any loose ends or conflicting statutes remaining on the books. Besides doing the research, we draft the actual language used in the bills."

Impressed, Jo said, "That must be tense, demandin' work."

"It is, sometimes, particularly when the legislative session is nearing adjournment. But, it is a job that requires a painstaking attention to detail, which is what I'm good at."

Sean said, "Ralph, you are a verbal master. You should give yourself more credit."

"Sean, that's kind of you to say. Thank you."

"Honey, he's right. You don't' give yourself enough credit," Lucy added.

When the entrée was completed, Lucy directed Sean and Ralph to clear away the dishes and set out the dessert plates and forks. They were then told to sit at their places and wait for their desserts to be served.

When Lucy and Jo were in the kitchen getting the desert ready to serve, Lucy turned to Jo and suddenly started laughing softly. When Jo asked Lucy what was so funny, she whispered to Jo, "I just realized it. I'm barefoot, pregnant and in the kitchen!" Both ladies laughed and laughed.

When Jo and Lucy brought raspberry tarts out to Sean and Ralph, Ralph asked, "What was so funny in the kitchen?"

Barely able to suppress another round of laughter, Lucy said, "Girl talk, honey." Ralph, his curiosity piqued, asked Lucy the same question again. He received the same answer again. When he asked the third time, Lucy, in an assertive tone said, "Honey, you wouldn't really understand it. It's an inside joke."

That did it! Lucy and Jo both lost it. Ralph and Sean sat there in amused silence, not knowing what was going on, but happy that their ladies were happy.

When the meal was over, Lucy suggested that the men folk do some work for a change and clear off the table and load the dishwasher while Jo and Lucy went over to the resort's office to give Lucy's mom a break.

While the ladies were gone, Ralph opened up to Sean about how happy he and Lucy were to receive the good news. After the dishwasher was loaded and running, Ralph and Sean talked shop, mostly gossip about the upcoming election.

Jo and Lucy were gone for about twenty minutes. When they returned, Lucy suggested, "Why don't we go for a walk? The night isn't too cool. Besides, I think Jo would like to wet her feet in our lake."

Sean and Ralph, knowing that resistance would be futile, concurred. A moment later, Lucy came back with two flashlights and a red tote bag with the resort's emblem in white, which she handed to Jo. Lucy also handed Ralph a digital camera in a case with a long strap on it.

On the way down from the house to the lake, the foursome stopped at the resort's office. Once inside of the office, Lucy introduced her mom, who was sitting behind the front counter, to Jo and Sean. Seated, it was hard to tell exactly how tall Lucy's mom really was. But, the mother-daughter resemblance was obvious. Both were tall and big boned. Mrs. Breen, unlike her daughter, had a long, obviously dyed, wavy, blonde mane. She was very attractive, in a country sort of way. She appeared to be in her late fifties and very well preserved.

After chatting with Mrs. Breen for a few minutes, the group indicated that they were going to head off to the lake. Mrs. Breen said to Sean, "Judge, thank you so much for lettin' Lucy keep the resort. I want to give you a hug."

Sean, embarrassed as he could be, said, "Ma'am, you don't have to thank me for doing what the voters of the county pay me to do. I was just doing my job." Ignoring Sean's protestations, Sarah Breen stood and walked from behind the counter, threw her arms around Sean and hugged him tightly.

As the barefoot foursome walked down the dirt path to the lake, Lucy said, "Sean, I hope Momma didn't embarrass you too much. She's just a warm, passionate person. Besides, since she started datin' again, she's been warmer and more ebullient than usual."

Sean mumbled something back to Lucy. Jo, not being sure what else to do under the circumstances, grabbed Sean's hand.

As they started down the dirt path to the lake, Lucy continued, "You know—present company excepted—Momma might be your biggest fan. It's not everyone who can say that they have a gold-record country singer as a big fan!"

Jo asked, "She used to record, too?"

"Momma always used to sing at home for fun. Daddy could never talk her into cuttin' a record with him because she never liked singin' in front of crowds, not even in the church choir. One day, a songwriter friend sent Daddy a duet. Daddy tried to record the duet with a number of different female singers—some big time and some not—but he never liked the result.

One day, out of frustration, he asked Momma to sing the girl's part, just so he could listen to it without any distraction. Momma sang it so well, Daddy persuaded her to go to Nashville with him to put it on his next album. The album and the individual record went gold. She never did make any more records with him."

Jo, sounding slightly confused, said, "Lucy, Sean didn't say anythin' to me about your father. Please tell me more about him."

Lucy said, "When you were a kid, did you ever hear of a country singer called, the *Singin' Soldier*? That was Daddy. That nickname stuck to him like glue, even though he'd been out of the Army for years and years. I reckon that half of his fans never knew his real name was Tommy Breen."

Slightly embarrassed, Jo said, "Sure, I heard his stuff when I was a girl. How'd he get that nickname?"

Lucy said, "Daddy had just finished college in Kentucky when World War II started. He was an infantry officer for four years in that war. After he got out of the service, he began a career in Civil Engineerin'. He was called back to active duty for Korea. After bein' in Korea for several years, he was stationed at Fort Knox. One of his buddies suggested that he go to Nashville on leave to cut a record. Since Daddy had sung in church and for fun for years, he did it on a lark."

Pausing for a second, Lucy said, "His demo disc was picked up by the first record company that he sent it to. Since he was on active duty, some record company flack called him the *Singin' Soldier* and it stuck."

Jo asked, "How did your parents meet?"

"Daddy had an Army buddy who lived a few miles from here. Momma was the buddy's baby sister. Since Momma was only fifteen, she couldn't marry without parental consent. It took a lot of talkin' from both Daddy and Uncle Earle to get my grandparents to sign off on the weddin'."

Lucy continued, "After Daddy made some money, he and Momma bought this place. Well, not all of it, but the first part of it. Since she was pregnant with me, Daddy wanted her to be near her Momma when I was born. Over time, they bought more and more land."

As they neared the beach, Lucy went on with the story, "Daddy gave up recordin' and tourin' in the mid-1970s. When I was in my second year at Southern, Daddy showed me his plans to dig this lake and asked me if I'd like to manage the construction the next summer. Since that would beat anythin' else I was gonna be hired to do that summer, I jumped at it. Diggin' this lake was my first project, so I'll always remember every detail about it."

Genuinely curious, Jo asked, "How did your parents decide to open a resort?"

With a barely suppressed giggle, Lucy said, "It sort of happened like you undress—a little bit at a time. Daddy and Momma built the lake 'cause it'd look pretty and gave us a place to swim."

Lucy continued, "The summer that we dug the lake, we were real lucky, 'cause right after we finished the diggin' and sandin' the bottom, overnight, before we had a chance to drill for water, two springs spontaneously started fillin' up the lake. By the end of the year, there was plenty of water for swimmin' and sailin' small sailboats. That next summer, Daddy and Momma had lots of their old music friends out to see the lake. One of them said that with all the visitors runnin' 'round the place, Daddy might as well be runnin' a resort. That got Daddy to thinkin'."

After a pause to allow her to catch her breath, Lucy said, "That fall and winter, Daddy and Momma visited a bunch of resorts in California and Florida. They got a passel of ideas about how to run and market one. In the winter of my senior year at Southern, the construction of the guest cabins began. The week after I graduated from Southern, Daddy and Momma had their grand openin'."

About that time, the foursome made the last twisting turn on the dirt path leading down to the lake. Jo gasped in wonder when the lake appeared, all shiny in the moonlight. It was truly a lovely sight, a moonlit lake surrounded by a white sandy beach. Somehow, Jo's reaction to the lake pleased Sean since your hard-core cop types aren't known for their aesthetic sensibilities. After Sean thought for a second, he realized that had Bubba been there, his reaction would have been the same—just said a lot slower. Sean made a mental note that Jo, besides being beautiful, also appreciated beauty when she saw it.

As the four of them reached the sandy beach at the edge of the lake, Lucy said, "Boys, Jo and I are gonna play in the water. Go make us a nice big fire over at the fire pit."

Jo said, "Before we break up, I need to see Sean for a second."

Taking Sean aside, Jo said to him, "Sean, since you are a judge, I'm gonna trust you with somethin' that I normally wouldn't trust anyone else in the world with, except a brother peace officer."

Stretching out her right leg, Jo pulled up her dress. Sean noticed the problem immediately—her holster and mini-badge. Deftly as a stripper, Jo removed the holster and mini-badge from her leg and handed them to Sean, who put them inside his coat pocket. When Jo was done disarming, Sean asked, "Are you girls really going to swim in this water?"

Jo replied, "No, but we are gonna go wadin'." Lucy and Jo pulled their dresses up past their knees and had a good time splashing in the lake water.

Afterwards, as Lucy and Jo warmed up their cold legs by the fire, Jo said, "I may be gettin' too old to wade in 63° water."

Lucy said, "Jo, you'll have to wait years until you're old."

Jo said, "I don't think so. I'm close enough as it is."

Being unable to resist the obvious temptation, Lucy asked playfully, "Jo, at what age do you think *old* begins?"

Catching the hint, Jo replied, "Fifty." Ralph, Lucy and Jo, all being younger than Sean, looked at him expecting a reaction.

Sean, feigning a slightly wounded ego, just smiled. Then he said, "Jo, can I see you for a second?"

The two of them walked off a few steps, away from the light of the fire. Sean handed back to Jo her holster and mini-badge. With Sean blocking the view, she slid them back onto her right leg.

Just to make it look good, as they returned to Lucy and Ralph, Jo said plaintively, "Daddy, I promise that I'll be a good little girl for the rest of the night so you won't have to spank me!"

After Lucy and Ralph stopped laughing, the four of them sat by the fire and talked. Or to be more accurate, Jo and Lucy talked while Sean and Ralph provided an audience.

After what seemed like just a few minutes, Jo remarked about how beautiful the moonlight appeared, shimmering on the almost flat surface of the lake. Lucy suggested that they take some pictures, which they did.

After the picture taking was over, Sean looked at his watch and noticed that the time was getting late, remarking that he was long past his bedtime and that as an old codger, he was apt to become quarrelsome if he didn't get his sleep. As they prepared to leave, Lucy said, "Jo, you obviously enjoyed your wadin' in the lake tonight. Why don't you have Sean bring you here in the summer durin' the day when the water is warmer?"

"Lucy, I don't want to scare away your customers. If your guests saw me swimmin' with all of my freckles, they'd mistake me for a cheetah on the loose and all run far away."

All four of them laughed. Sean remembered seeing a documentary on the cheetah some time before on cable. He remembered thinking that the cheetah was an unusually attractive member of the cat family.

Happily, the two couples walked hand-in-hand back to the parking lot. When they reached Sean's F-150, Lucy kissed and hugged both of them goodbye. Sean and Jo congratulated them again.

When they reached the gate, Ralph punched the right set of numbers into the keypad so that they could leave. After bidding Ralph a warm goodbye, Jo and Sean turned back onto County 191. Once the truck was on the road again, Sean finally realized that he was still barefoot. Turning to Jo, he asked, "Did I forget my shoes?"

"Lucy and I, knowin' how you elderly people are, took care to put both your shoes and my sandals in the tote bag along with my purse. Want to put them back on?"

"No. If you were able to drive barefoot this afternoon, I'm sure that I can do it tonight. Actually, it's kind of fun. It reminds me of my youth. But, please do remember to give them back to me when I drop you off."

Uncharacteristically, Jo left unsaid her thought about how Sean would look leaving her house late tomorrow morning all dressed up except for being barefoot. Something told her that wouldn't happen. In some deep part of her psyche, Jo was starting to sense that Sean was serious about her in a way that she hadn't known before.

While Jo was thinking, the sudden realization hit Sean that when he was with Jo, he really did lose track of things. Since Sean had long been told by family and friends alike that he must have O.C.D., he couldn't escape the conclusion that Jo really had gotten to him in some elemental way.

A minute or so later, as they drove back toward University City, Jo asked, "Did Cheryl fix Ralph up with Lucy or the other way around?"

After thinking for a second, Sean said, "Cheryl found Lucy a date. We both knew Lucy. I think that Cheryl only knew Ralph casually from some mutual acquaintance in Capitol City."

Jo said, not really understanding the full import of her statement, "It's amazin' that Lucy needed to be fixed up. She's so intelligent and lively. I'm surprised that she didn't have men linin' up to take her out."

Sean, as unaware as Jo, said, "Lucy had had several bad relationships while she was in construction management. When her father became ill and she took over running the resort, she hoped that her luck with men would change. Unfortunately, it did for the worse."

"Why?" Jo asked.

"I don't know. Maybe she had gotten too old. Whatever the reason, Lucy had just about given up hope of finding a man who would want her for something more than a bed partner when Cheryl introduced her to Ralph."

As Sean was speaking, a metaphorical light bulb went off in Jo's head. She started seeing a parallel between her own situation and Lucy's before she met Ralph. Jo felt a bit dense for not having seen it sooner. After a short pause, Jo said, "Sean, Ralph seems so shy and timid. How did Lucy ever get him to propose?"

Sean said, "I'm not sure that he ever did. Lucy just kept making plans for them for each weekend. After a while, she started talking honeymoon. He didn't resist."

As the conversation paused for a second, Sean realized that he had missed the turn to bypass the place where Cheryl had died. They would be right by it in a second. When they came to the spot, Sean pulled his truck off of the road and turned on his emergency flashers. Pointing to the right toward Flatboat River, Sean said, "That is where Cheryl died."

For the next few seconds, the only sound that either heard was the click-click of the emergency flashers. Finally, Jo said authoritatively, "Please come around to my door and open it."

Sean, having no idea what was up, put his trusty metallic steed into park and turned off the engine. Being a cautious person, he exited the truck and pocketed the keys. When he reached Jo's door, he opened it and helped her out. After Jo stepped down from his F-150, she stood directly in front of him for a second. Then, she put her arms around him and said, "Thank you for sharin' your pain with me."

After she kissed Sean gently on the cheek, Jo wiped his tears away and asked him if she could do anything for him. Sean just held onto her very tightly. He no longer noticed the moon, the breeze, the soft dirt between his toes or anything else at all, except Jo and the unfamiliar feeling that had swept over him. Had Sean been in an analytical frame of mind, he would have been able to discern that for the first time since he learned of Cheryl's fatal accident, he didn't feel alone. His mental universe now had a second person in it.

****

When the light of a passing car broke the mood, Sean and Jo stopped cuddling. Once they had remounted the F-150, they resumed their drive back to University City. In the silence, Jo knew that something had just happened between them. Not knowing what exactly to do, she took the conversation in a safer direction by asking, "Precious, do you think that Ralph and Lucy will be good parents?"

"Jo, I'm not sure, but I think so. Lucy is obviously a warm, caring person. As you could tell from her mother and the stories that she told us about her parents, Lucy had good role models. I don't know a thing about Ralph's background, but I do know that he is so completely smitten with Lucy that he'd walk barefoot on broken glass for her. I suspect that he will learn from her. I can tell by watching him that he'll do anything to make her happy."

Sensing that Sean was still in serious mode, Jo said, "Precious, you're barefoot. Did you mean to tip your hand about the rest of the evenin's entertainment?"

Laughing, Sean said, "Damn! We'll just have to save the broken glass for another weekend!"

Sensing that Sean was relaxing, Jo asked, "Do you remember anythin' about Ralph and Lucy's blind date?"

Sean said, "Since Cheryl set the thing up, I was more of a participant than a player. I remember very clearly that on the way there, Cheryl gave me orders on pain of death—or worse—to avoid the *N* word—nerd. So, I wasn't sure what to expect."

Being very curious, Jo asked, "How did the date go?"

Sean said, "If I wasn't a believer already, that night would have forced me to convert. When Ralph saw Lucy, who back then was a bit heftier and very busty, he started to blush. Lucy jumped right in and asked him if he was an outdoorsman. When Ralph shocked the three of us by saying he was, Lucy asked what his favorite sport was. When Ralph said that he was a bird-watcher, Cheryl kicked me in the leg, like I could do something. Before I could even think of anything to say, Lucy said that she lived out in the country and had lots of birds at her place. That did it. Cheryl and I spent the rest of the evening in fascination as Lucy and Ralph talked about Ornithology."

Jo, never having known of a successful blind date besides the one she had had with Sean, asked, "How long did they go out before they were married?"

Sean said, "As I recall, they were married five months or so after their blind date."

Sensing the moment had come to find out what she had to know, Jo asked, "Who needed to be fixed up more, Lucy or Ralph?"

Sean, oblivious as always, said, "Lucy."

Jo repeated, "Lucy?"

Sean continued, "Back then, Lucy, besides having the social handicap of running an active business, hadn't quite gotten over the world of construction. Not surprisingly, she impressed a lot of people as being bossy and pushy. Plus, she could swear as well as any sailor. So, she had had countless blind dates and first dates, but very few subsequent ones. When Cheryl and I brought the subject of a blind date up to her, she was very unenthused at the prospect of having another miserable dating experience."

Jo was fascinated. She asked, "Was Ralph easier to convince?"

"Heavens, Yes! Ralph, being rather passive around women, was quite used to being fixed up on blind dates. He told me after he was married that he doubted there were very many divorced, widowed or hopelessly single ladies in Capitol City his age that he hadn't been on a blind date with at one time or another. He was very used to being fixed up—just not to having second dates. Unlike Lucy, however, he remained optimistic."

Totally intrigued, Jo asked, "Why?"

"Cheryl told me that as middle-aged, single guys go, Ralph did have a lot of pluses going for him. He was educated, stable, employed and intelligent. He was in good health and had a full head of his own hair and his own teeth. Plus, he didn't have any ex-wives or children making demands on his time or his money. I think that Lucy was the first woman he dated to figure all of those things out."

Jo, now on a roll, decided to ask one more question, a question that a more cautious woman wouldn't have dreamed of asking on a second date. But Jo, being Jo, asked, "Did you like bein' a father?"

Sean, oblivious as usual, said without hesitation, "Yes."

The drive was nearing its conclusion. Jo, now knowing just about everything that her instincts told her she needed to know about Sean to evaluate him as a prospective mate, sensibly changed the subject and told him, "Precious, gettin' together next week may be a little difficult. Since I'm on call, I'll have to stay near home so that I can dash over to headquarters if somethin' big happens."

Sean, not noticing that Jo was assuming that they would be doing something that weekend, said, "Jo, next weekend will be a problem for me, too, since next week is Holy Week."

Jo, not being Catholic, had only the foggiest idea what his problem was. Faking it beautifully, Jo just kept silent. After a second, Sean asked, "Do you think you'll be working on Easter Sunday morning around eight?"

Jo, realizing that the chances she would ever be expected to make a statement to the press at that hour of the morning on a holiday were slightly less than the odds that one of her department's deputies would arrest Elvis and Jimmy Hoffa for running a red light in a stolen pink convertible, said, "Most probably not."

Of course, Jo hadn't a clue what Sean was going to ask her to do. So when Sean said, "May I ask you to go to Easter Mass with me?" Jo was pleasantly surprised.

In response, she asked, "What would I wear?"

Sean, not understanding the complexity of the issues involved with this question, said, "Cheryl would either wear a pale suit or a pastel dress."

Jo, realizing Sean didn't know everything, no matter how smart he was, made a mental note to get Easter fashion advice from a better source and said, "Thank you Sean, I'll keep that in mind."

At this point, Sean pulled his F-150 into Jo's driveway. When he came around to Jo's door to help her down, she said nothing to him. When he walked her to her front door and appeared ready to kiss her, Jo said, "Yankee boy, aren't you forgettin' somethin'?"

Totally flummoxed, Sean was rendered speechless. After a long pause, Jo took mercy—of sorts—on Sean and gave him a hint, "It's red and canvas. And, I want it."

Sean, looking confused, said and did nothing. After what seemed like an eternity, Jo finally said, "Sean, the tote bag, please!"

A humbled Sean fetched the red tote bag from the truck. After he handed the bag to Jo, she stood there motionless and silent. After another long wait, she said, "I do declare, you Yankees have no manners whatsoever. Do you actually think that I would contemplate enterin' my home with my feet in such a filthy condition?"

Now it was Sean who stood there motionless and silent. After a moment, Jo took Sean by the hand and led him to her back door. She stopped Sean by the hose attached to the spigot near the door. She said, in her most gracious voice, "Precious, I'd be most gratified if you would turn the hose on and then bring it to where I will be sittin' in the yard."

A moment later, a dutiful Sean encountered Jo sitting on the edge of one of her wicker chaise lounges. Being able to figure out this part of his task, Sean obediently hosed the dirt off of Jo's feet. When Sean was about to turn away and carry the hose back to where we had taken it from, Jo stood and asked, "Sean, have you ascertained whether I might have some mud on my legs from that nasty old lake that you practically forced me at gunpoint to wade in for your lecherous gratification?"

Before Sean could say a thing, Jo rose and stood, placing her left leg, which was bared way past her knee, onto the cushion of the chaise lounge. Sean, claiming that no dirt was present on Jo's left leg, also noticed that her leg had only a few visible freckles. So, when Jo repeated the drill on the other leg, Sean pointed to a freckle and tried to claim that it was dirt and tried to wash it off of her leg. Jo just smiled.

After Sean shut off the hose, they both stood there in the pale glow of the light from her patio window. They knew their fourteen hours together were about to end. Neither of them wanted the day to end, but neither knew how to prolong the evening without crossing a barrier that each was not ready to cross, albeit for somewhat different reasons.

Bowing to the inevitable, Jo and Sean had one long kiss standing by his F-150. When they reluctantly parted their bodies, Sean and Jo said their goodbyes. As Sean climbed into his seat in the truck, Jo said, "Sean, I predict that you and I will see each other before next Sunday."

Sean said, "Jo, do you read fortunes, too?"

"Sometimes," was Jo's reply.

So, it was hard to tell who was laughing harder when Sean pulled back up Jo's driveway two minutes later. Jo said, "Aren't cell phones great?" as she handed the smiling Sean his shoes, which he had failed to remember were in the red tote bag. Jo's last words to Sean were, "I'll bet you a foot wash and rub that we'll see each other before next weekend."

Sean replied, "You're on!" as he once again began his way home.

✱✱✱✱✱✱✱✱✱✱✱✱

When Sean arrived home, Law and Equity didn't scold him, which was unusual for them. Instead, they both rubbed up against his legs when he stood and then sat in his lap when he sat down. While Sean knew that one can never know for certain about anything with cats, he was as certain as he could be that his two furry friends were telling him that they had missed him and wanted to know why he was so happy. Not wishing to offend his tiny hirsute friends, he gave them a short version of what he had done since he left their care hours before. The two little ladies listened intently to him. When Sean had completed his tale, the two cats left his lap and headed for the bedroom, verbally informing him as they went that his presence was required in the bedroom immediately. Sean, knowing that females only nag when they are fond of you, complied.

After the kitties assumed their usual positions—Law above the covers and on his hip, and Equity under the covers and next to his chest—Sean thought about the first girl that he had ever kissed, Krista. Sean remembered that when he had been around her, he could never say anything without putting his foot in his mouth. He had spent their last summer together being as forgetful and confused as he was tonight. As sleep slowly entered his brain, Sean reflected how he must have looked like a bumbling idiot to Krista the whole entire summer. Tonight, Sean had felt as distracted as he had so long ago whenever he was around Krista. Sean now knew that he had been in love with Krista that summer, even though he didn't know it at the time.

Sean, adding together Laura's comments, his own observation of his behavior tonight and how happy he was whenever he saw Jo, concluded that he was definitely a man in love. Fortunately for both Sean and Jo, Sean fell asleep before his left brain could reassert itself and try to convince him that he was just imagining things.

At her place, Jo and her stuffed animals curled up in their bed. Jo was happy. For the first time in her life, she had been around educated, older people who accepted her for herself. Not being overly analytical, Jo simply accepted reality as reality and feel asleep happy, not wasting time with useless analysis.

Chapter Five

The next morning, Sean awoke very slowly. His first conscious sensation was of a very soft, warm pressure on his cheek. As his brain slowly shifted into gear, he knew that Equity must be telling him that it was time to get up and fill the food bowl. When Sean finally opened his eyes, he was not surprised to see Equity, the alpha cat of their clowder,[9] next to him, gently pawing him back to wakefulness. Once Sean noticed that it was almost 0900 hours, he realized that Equity was just doing her job, as she understood it. He never fully comprehended why Equity took it upon herself to be his back-up alarm clock. But, on mornings when he would have overslept had Equity not pawed him to alertness, he learned to appreciate her devotion to duty.

As soon as Sean refilled their food and water bowls, the cats bellied up to the bowls. Then, as fast as they could move their paws, the two formerly sleepy felines ran off with reckless abandon, their claws clacking noisily on the wooden floor as they scampered.

Sean quietly ate his breakfast, showered, shaved and dressed for Palm Sunday Mass.

* * * * * * * * * * * *

About the time that Equity was waking her pet human, Jo also opened her eyes. Unlike Sean, she had not been roused from her slumber gently. When Jo sat up in her bed, she remembered very clearly the anxiety dream that had caused her to awaken jittery, sweaty and in a very vulnerable mood.

"That's it! I'm gonna do something about this! It's bad enough that bitch insulted me to my face once. I'll be damned if I'll let her do it in my sleep, too!"

A very pensive, but equally resolved, Jo ate her breakfast slowly, spending much of her time staring off into space. Eventually, Jo took her second glass of juice with her out to the patio and enjoyed the morning sunshine while thinking. As she sat there, she pulled her nightgown up way past her knees—hoping to improve her tan as she contemplated a plan. About the time that the juice glass was empty again, Jo said out loud, "That's it! It'll work."

Jo then rushed back inside, turned on her computer and sat down in front of it. Had Jo thought about her appearance as she sat at the computer, she would have said that she looked like something the cat dragged in. But, in reality, she looked more beautiful—in a rumpled way—than she had the night before. Her sheer white nightgown contrasted so well with the brown of her hair and her lightly tanned body that had A.W. Bouguereau been present to paint her right then, the world would have had another masterpiece to delight the eye. Running her bare feet slowly over the carpet, Jo typed away an email to Sean.

****

As Sean pulled into the church's parking lot for the last Mass of the morning, he asked himself the same question that he always asked himself on Palm Sunday. He wondered why the liturgy still called the Sunday before Easter "Palm Sunday," when the Gospel was the Passion. Sean, knowing that the church of his youth was no more, said what he always said in these circumstances, *Vatican II,* in a disgusted tone.

During the course of the Mass, Sean felt lonely. He missed the Latin Mass that he attended most Sundays. Realizing that this would be his second Holy Week without her, Sean missed Cheryl even more than he missed the Tridentine Rite. Remembering what Sister Frances had told him in third grade, Sean offered up this suffering for the Poor Souls in Purgatory and followed the Mass as closely as he could.

After Mass, Sean's gloomy mood picked up considerably when Father Wilson greeted him at the door of the church with, "Oversleep this morning, Sean?" They both laughed since Sean normally attended the early Mass in Latin. Father Wilson always seemed to know what to say to cheer up people who needed cheering. That brief conversation brightened Sean's morning considerably.

On the way home, Sean grabbed an order of his favorite **naughty food**— barbequed ribs with beans and potato salad. He might be spending his Palm Sunday with the cats, but at least he was going to eat well.

****

While Sean was talking to Father Wilson, Jo was completing the fifth draft of her email to Sean. Being finally satisfied with its tone, Jo hit the send button and her email was off into cyberspace. Looking at her wristwatch, Jo decided that she had enough time to send off one more email. So, Jo sent Kyra a fashion S.O.S. about what to wear to Mass with Sean next Sunday. She assumed that being both Catholic and a clothes horse, Kyra would know exactly how Jo should dress for this occasion.

After sending the email to Kyra, Jo decided that the time had come to ready herself for the Spring Fling in a way that she hadn't anticipated a week ago. Last week, Jo and Kyra had found the perfect gown for Jo to wear to the Spring Fling. But, because the gown gave Jo an opportunity to display more of her ample chest than she had anticipated, Jo realized that she would need to work seriously on her tan. So, Jo went outside with her radio, her suntan lotion, a beach towel and a portable alarm clock. Once she had the towel laid out to her satisfaction and the alarm set to go off in thirty minutes, Jo laid down on the towel.

Hearing nothing but the tick of her alarm clock, Jo thought back on the events of the previous day and evening. She had had a blast at the ballgame, even if State did lose. Sean had been both a gentleman and fun to be with, which in her experience, was a rare combination.

The warmth of the sun on Jo's body did wonders to help her shake off the residual effects of the bad dream that had troubled her the night before. She had almost dozed off entirely when the alarm went off. Jo rolled over and repeated the process.

A few minutes later, Jo was completely in dreamland. As she slept, she had a very vivid dream of lying on her stomach on a beach towel, just as she was in reality. But in her dream, she was on a lovely white tropical beach, listening to the sounds of the sea birds and the gently rolling waves. As Jo's sleep grew deeper and deeper, she dreamt that Sean was with her, lovingly massaging her neck, shoulders, back, legs and feet with suntan lotion. Just then, the alarm went off.

When Jo sat up a moment later, her body was very sweaty and oily. Realizing that she needed to clean off, she gathered her things and reentered the house headed for the shower. On the way to the shower, Jo raised the setting on the air conditioning from 74° to a balmy 78°.

✱✱✱✱✱✱✱✱✱✱✱✱

After Sean returned home, he quickly changed into casual clothes. Almost as fast as the cats had gone to their bowls this morning, Sean ate his take-out meal. He did not dine alone, however, because both Law and Equity sat on the opposite end of the dining room table and kept him company. Never demonstrating the slightest interest in Sean's food, the cats presumably just enjoyed watching him gnaw on the ribs. Once the last rib had been defleshed, sensing that the show was over, Law and Equity departed for a sunny windowsill.

Not wanting to settle into his usual afternoon routine just yet, Sean went out to the pool to check the water temperature. He was pleased that the temperature in the pool was up to 76°. After turning on the pool's water heater, Sean went back inside and turned on his computer.

Remembering what he had thought of on the way back home from Mass, Sean searched the Internet for music recorded by Tommy Breen. After just a few clicks of the mouse, once he entered the Amazon.com ™ website, Sean found just what he was looking for—a four-CD collection of the *Singing Soldier's Greatest Hits*. Sean ordered two sets of the collection, one for himself and one for Jo. He, of course, sent her a sweet message to go with the CDs.

After leaving Amazon.com, Sean checked the Drudge Report™ and the Fox News™ websites. Seeing nothing exciting happening, Sean checked his email. Besides the usual SPAM, there were three emails in his Inbox that caught his eye—one from Jo, one from Lucy and one from Maureen.

Jo's email was a hoot. As he read it, he could almost hear her saying the words to him out loud. It read:

Precious,

Thank you so much for yesterday. I had the greatest time. The ballgame was fun, even if State lost on some technicality. Your daughters are both beautiful and charming. Obviously, they favor their mother's side of the family in that regard. <g>

Lucy and Ralph were the most gracious host and hostess that I have ever been blessed to know. I really enjoyed meeting them and was so happy at their good news.

On the ride back, I felt as if I really got to know you quite well. Thank you for sharing your feelings with me as openly and honestly as you did.

Perhaps the most memorable aspect of our long day and evening together was discovering what a great lady's maid you are. I have never had anyone wash my feet and legs as well as you did last night. I am definitely going to be jealous if I hear even a whisper of you performing any similar service for any other female deputies in our department. <g>

Seriously, Sean, when I met you, seeing as how you're a judge and all, I half-expected you to be all stern and serious. You're not at all like that. But, since we haven't known each other real long, down deep I still half-expect that you must have a stern side. So, me being me, I may flirt with you too much just to see if you are really as nice and fun as I think you are. If I went too far with you yesterday, I do apologize. If my flirting was too much, please forgive me. I'm just a simple country girl not always sure how to behave around you.

Finally, I meant to ask you this yesterday, but between the ballgame and the resort and all, I just forgot about it. Anyway, one of my friends in the department had a problem in a relationship with a man a year or so ago. I'm not sure if she's completely over it. She asked me if I knew any shrink types that she could talk to who aren't connected to law enforcement. I don't know anyone like that. Do you?

XOXOX,

Jo

Sean smiled and then laughed at her email. It was so "Jo." He replied back to her:

Dear Jo,

I'm so glad that we **both** had a wonderful time yesterday. Come to think of it, I've never spent any time with you when I didn't have a good time. I hope that the same goes for you, as well.

About your flirting, I have just one comment: **I enjoy it!**

Remember when you were in high school? Everyone gossiped about the teachers, right? And everyone thought that the teachers didn't really have personal lives because only real people have lives. And back in high school, we all knew that teachers weren't really people. Being a judge is a lot like being a high school teacher. Everyone treats you like you are a plaster saint. Everyone also thinks that you must have been born yesterday. So, everyone lies to you. I'm surrounded by people who want something from me. So, it is very rare for me to talk to anyone who treats me like a real person. And if they do, I have to be suspicious about what they are after.

Well, one of the great things about our relationship, from my vantage point, is that you don't treat me like a judge. You treat me like a man. Since you don't have anything to get from me, except for the usual male-female stuff—I can relax and be myself. Don't ever stop. And please don't start behaving around me. That wouldn't be fun. That wouldn't be you.

One of the great things about you is that you are spontaneous. You say and do what pops into your head without calculation. After spending my week surrounded by people who very cunningly contrive and plot their words and actions to persuade me to do something for them, I feel so at home with you because with you, I see a real person. So, I can be a real person in return. One last thing, if you are afraid that you'll embarrass me if you flirt too hard, don't worry! I'm not a prude. I was married for over a quarter century. I have two daughters. I work in an office full of women. Women lawyers nowadays are quite willing to smile, laugh, wink, show some leg, etc. to get a judge to favor their side in a case. At this stage in my life, I have no illusions about the opposite sex. I seriously doubt that any degree of flirtation will embarrass me.

But, if you do embarrass me, I won't get angry. I promise.

Finally, I'd suggest that you tell your friend to call my good friend, Dr. Daphne Hollingsworth. She is a professor of Psychiatry at the Medical Center and also maintains a private practice. I understand that she is quite busy, so tell your friend to drop my name. I doubt that it will do any good, but you never know. If she is too busy, she will be glad to refer your friend to newer doctor.

I can't believe that I'm not going to see you for almost a week.

SR

Holding Maureen's email for last, Sean opened Lucy's email next.

Dear Sean,

You know me well enough by now to know that I still think like an engineer. So, let me answer your questions in the order that you asked them:

1. Yes. You are definitely in love with Jo.

2. Yes. She is definitely in love with you.

3. No. You aren't too old for her.

4. No. She isn't too young for you.

5. No. This isn't too soon for you to be getting involved with someone after Cheryl died. She loved you and wanted you to be happy.

I hope that these answers to your questions were long enough. If you want me to write more, just ask.

Lucy

When Sean read Lucy's email, he stood up and cheered, much to the confusion of his furry *catpanions*, who had left their sunny perch just to be with him. Sean's email reply to Lucy read:

Dear Lucy,

After reading the long-winded, redundant and verbose memoranda and briefs that the lawyers throw at me and expect me to digest in too short of a time, I really appreciate your short, concise answers. Thank you. You are a true friend.

SR

Maureen's email to Sean read:

Father,

It was nice to see you and Jo at the game yesterday. Your daughters have been worried about you ever since Mother died. Pat and I were both happy to see you out of the house and out of the office for a change. You looked like you were enjoying yourself. Please keep being happy!

I'm sorry that Pat and I didn't get much of a chance to visit with Jo. She seems real nice. Is she a lawyer? Forgive me for asking this, but how did you meet her? Have you been dating long? Email me back when you have a chance. Gotta run!

Mo

Knowing that Mo could read him like an open book, Sean read and reread Maureen's email several times to analyze what she might be trying to say between the lines. He concluded that the references to both Mo and her sister meant that they both were happy that he was doing better. He concluded that Maureen's questions were her own and that Pat may not have been quite as enthused about his relationship with Jo as was Maureen. Sean replied to the email:

Dear Mo,

Thank you for your thoughts. I know how stressful and time consuming your first year in college can be, so I'm flattered by your quick email to me.

Jo is real nice. And no, she isn't a lawyer. As you probably already guessed, she graduated from State a number of years ago and joined the sheriff's department out of college.

She is a sergeant in their Community Relations department. Before receiving her current assignment, she was a patrol deputy and was decorated for valor. (See the attached link to the story in the *University City Bugle*.)

Remember Kyra Townsend? (Like anyone who ever met her could ever forget her!) Well, last month she waltzed into my office and practically twisted my arm to go on a blind date with a sergeant that she knew in the sheriff's department. I really tried my best to talk my way out of it, but—well you've met Kyra. You understand.

I went on the blind date, expecting to meet some fat, ugly, blonde jailer in the women's side of the county jail. I was very pleasantly surprised. We've had several dates on our own after the blind date and everything is going along fine.

I hope that this answers your questions about Jo.

How did Pat react to seeing me on a date? Is she okay with it? When you get a chance—no big rush—please let me know.

Love, Daddy

After reading his emails, Sean was in an irrepressibly good mood. He quickly changed into his workout clothes. Today, since the weather was nice, he hit the jogging track (actually an unimproved trail) that went around the edges of his property. Since it was warm and sunny, Sean ran without his t-shirt. After twice around the one-mile trail, Sean came home and hit the free weights. After pushing all of his muscle groups harder than he had in the last few weeks, Sean decided to check to see if the pool was warm enough for a swim.

Sadly, the pool thermometer read only 84° degrees, so Sean elected to turn on the whirlpool and soak away some of the stress from his sore muscles. Returning to the house to change, Sean reemerged moments later wearing only a towel and a pair of flip-flops. As soon as Sean inserted his body in the bubbling water, he relaxed and let the warm water and the sunshine relax his bare skin. As he soaked, Sean thought about how less than a month before, his mood had been dark and gloomy. Ever since Kyra twisted his arm into the blind date with Jo, his world had changed. He actually had something to look forward to again. He didn't know exactly how Kyra had managed to pull this one off, but she picked out a good date for Sean. Sean realized that he owed Kyra, big time.

Shortly before Sean's body was close to turning into a prune, he left the whirlpool, turned off the pool heater and headed into the house, where he feel into a deep sleep, surrounded by his furry friends.

After his nap, the rest of Sean's day and evening were routine, except that right before he was ready to turn in for the night, he had an urge to check his email. The only thing of note was one message from Jo:

Precious,

I guess because you grew up in Yankeeland, where the weather is cold for eight or nine months of the year, you probably know more about hot and cold stuff than I ever will. Remembering what you said about the weather being too cold to swim last night, you were right.

Jo

Sean replied:

Dear Jo,

I'll try not to make a habit of being right. I know how women hate that. <g>

SR

P.S. I miss you.

****

Sean and Jo each had an interesting morning on Wednesday, April 19th. Sean heard his will docket—as usual—that morning. Most Wednesday mornings, the docket usually moved along fairly smoothly, thanks to both the efficiency of Sean's staff in reviewing the wills beforehand to red flag potential problems and the professionalism of the lawyers, who had their paperwork in order and were ready to go. On those Wednesdays, Sean was able to listen very intently to the routine questions and give the grieving relatives (widows, mostly) a few words of sympathy and kindness. Normally, this was Sean's favorite part of his job.

That Wednesday, however, almost everything that could go wrong did go wrong. When Sean took the bench, before he could even call the first case, the relative tranquility of the courtroom was shattered by two ambulance attendants wheeling in a frail, elderly man on a gurney. Guessing that they were lost, Sean sent Bubba to direct them to Judge Schwarz down the hall, where guardianships are heard on Wednesday mornings.

Once the attendants and the man on the gurney left the courtroom, Sean surveyed the audience. They looked grim. Sean thought that the last thing a room full of grieving relatives needed was a very tangible reminder of human frailty and death. Something told Sean that this was going to be a very atypical will docket.

Several cases into the docket, an elderly lawyer, whose hearing aid wasn't working very well, appeared with his equally elderly widow client in tow. She appeared to be hard of hearing, as well. When Sean opened the file, he saw a big, yellow note attached to the inside cover. The note told Sean that the lawyer had failed to plead properly and was going to have to replead before Sean could hear the matter. Since the lawyer was hard of hearing, Sean tried to tell him several times what the problem was. Unfortunately, the poor man's hearing was too far gone to allow Sean to communicate with him successfully. Sean, wanting to preserve some of the elderly lawyer's dignity, finally wrote the man a note explaining the problem and asking him to replead before returning to court. The lawyer, once he understood the problem, thanked the judge profusely and turned to leave the courtroom with his now very confused client.

As lawyer and client neared the door, she screamed at her lawyer, "What's the matter?" The lawyer, forgetting where he was for a minute, screamed back at her, "The s*n***b***t wants me to replead the case!" After the laughter inside the courtroom subsided, Sean knew that this Wednesday would be one to remember.

A few cases later, a *pro-se* litigant appeared in front of Sean. Knowing how people who represent themselves can be a problem, Sean gingerly examined the file. The decedent had left an estate valued at over $500,000, apparently all to one relative—a nephew. Sean, although not shocked, was always a bit surprised at how some people will try to save a few dollars by not hiring a lawyer, even when large sums of money are at stake.

After the *pro-se* was sworn in, Sean asked him for his proposed order, which was the same question that Sean asked all of the lawyers. The *pro-se* looked as confused as a deer caught in a driver's headlights seconds before the inevitable collision occurred. After waiting a bit, the *pro-se* attempted to hand Sean a copy of his application. When Sean told the man that the application was not an order, the *pro-se* thought for a second and then said, "The clerk's office didn't give me one!"

When Sean told the man that it was his responsibility—not anyone else's—to appear in court with the proper documents, the man said very loudly, "Hey, Judge! I'm not a lawyer. Cut me some slack here."

Sean, noticing that Bubba was already on his feet, said, "Sir, if you wish to represent yourself, that is your right under the law. If you appear as your own lawyer, I am obligated under the law to treat you the same as I would treat a lawyer. If you don't have an order with you, I cannot go any further today. Please come back another day when you are ready to proceed."

Before the *pro-se* could utter more than a preliminary curse word, he felt Bubba's firm grip on his arm. As soon as Bubba asked him if he would like help leaving the courtroom, the *pro-se*, who, although not the brightest bulb in the lamp, wasn't that stupid, indicated that he would be glad to leave unassisted. He did leave, slamming the door as he went. After that, things slowly degenerated into a mass of under-prepared lawyers, missing files, lawyers waiting on clients and clients waiting on lawyers in other courts.

✳✳✳✳✳✳✳✳✳✳✳✳

While Sean was suffering through his painful docket, Jo visited Dr. Emerson. While shaking hands with Jo, Dr. Emerson introduced herself. Then, she asked Jo how she preferred to be addressed. After that, Dr. Emerson looked at Jo's paperwork and started off the interview by asking, "Jo, tell me about these dreams that you have been having."

Jo's response was obviously well thought out and prepared since she described her reoccurring nightmare in detail. She was also able to pinpoint when the dreams began.

Dr. Emerson asked, "What do you think the dream means?"

Jo's response was direct, "It doesn't mean anythin'. It really happened to me."

As if Dr. Emerson had opened a spigot, Jo poured out the traumatic events of the preceding year in detail. The doctor was impressed by Jo's organization and control over her emotions. Although obviously agitated, Jo never lost control as she told her story.

When Jo was done, Dr. Emerson asked, "Have the dreams been constant in their frequency?"

Jo replied, "Right after it happened, I had the dream almost every night. After a month or so, it started to be less often and less strong. By the beginnin' of this March, I was only havin' it once a week or so."

"When did this pattern change?" the doctor wanted to know.

Jo replied, "At the end of last month."

"Why do you think that they started becoming more frequent and stronger?" Dr. Emerson asked.

Smiling, Jo said, "A friend introduced me to a wonderful man."

The doctor asked, "Why would meeting a wonderful man make you have bad dreams?"

Jo paused for a second and then said, "I'm afraid that down deep, the woman in the dream might be tellin' the truth."

Dr. Emerson immediately asked, "What do you think? Is the woman's statement accurate?"

Pausing for a nanosecond, at most, Jo said, "Hell, no! I'm not at all unsure about myself. I know who I am and that I'm damn good at what I do!"

Dr. Emerson asked, "Then, why are you having these dreams?"

Jo blurted out, "I'm afraid he may think that it's true!"

Pausing for a second, Dr. Emerson asked, "How serious are you with your new boyfriend?"

Jo replied, "The way things are goin', I suspect that he's gonna propose in a month or so."

Logically, the doctor asked, "Why do you think that?"

Jo's response was direct and immediate, "He asked me to go to church with him on Easter. Have you ever known of a man askin' a woman to go to church with him if it wasn't serious?"

Dr. Emerson's response shot back, "If you are that serious, why don't you tell him about it and see how he reacts?"

Jo replied quickly and harshly, "What if he says he wants nuthin' further to do with me?"

Dr. Emerson's cold, logical reply was, "Then, in the long run, you'll save yourself a lot of heartache and a lot of money on psychotherapy." After pausing long enough for Jo to use a facial tissue to dab her tearful eyes, the doctor added, "Jo, in law enforcement, you have to make life and death, split-second decisions sometimes, right?"

After Jo's *pro forma* assent, Dr. Emerson continued, "If you are in one of those situations and you don't have time to think everything through coldly and logically as to what is the best course of action, what do you do?"

Having learned this lesson thousands of times over, both at the academy and on the job, Jo said, "You've got to go with your gut."

Dr. Emerson inquired, "Jo, what does your gut tell you here?"

Jo replied quickly, "He won't give a damn one way or another."

The doctor said, "Jo, in the past, you've trusted your instincts and reactions to make life and death decisions involving both yourself and others, right? Why don't you do the same thing here?"

After what seemed like an eternity to Jo, she finally said softly, "You're right. When should I tell him?"

Dr. Emerson, returning to her nurturing mode, said, "Why don't you give yourself as much time as you can to observe him and to get more data? There is no reason to hurry the disclosure, is there? If and when he proposes, that is when you'll have to tell him."

Jo, nodding her head in agreement, said, "Thank you so much for your help and advice."

Looking at the clock, Dr. Emerson told Jo that their session was about over. She wrote Jo a script for an anti-anxiety agent to be taken at bedtime.

When the doctor suggested that, if she wished, she could refer Jo to a Ph.D. psychologist, who could explore with her in greater depth the issues that confronted her, Jo declined, saying, "Doc, I'll bet that there ain't a person alive who don't feel inferior to somebody. That's just part of livin'. My problem is my fear that my man might feel that way. The only way to get past that is for me to tell him at the right time. Thanks so much, you've been so gracious and kind to see me on such short notice. Thank you kindly, again."

As Dr. Emerson walked Jo to the receptionist for payment, she said, "I'd like to see you again in six weeks. Please have the receptionist set a time. Meanwhile, if you have a problem, feel free to call me. Here is my card. During regular business hours, call my office. After hours, I'll give you my pager number to call."

****

Just as Jo was leaving Dr. Emerson's office, Bubba took a phone call at his desk. Whispering, so as to not interfere with the hearing going on, Bubba said, "Well Sarge, I think that I can handle that. I'll call you later." Paying no attention to Bubba's telephone call, Sean finally finished the first of his two will dockets for the morning. As Sean exited the bench, Bubba motioned to Jane to come by and talk to him for a second.

A few minutes later, when a decidedly beaten down and unenthusiastic Judge Riley was preparing to take the bench again, Jane turned to him and smiled her big smile. Something in the back of his brain told Sean that Jane must be up to something because Jane only smiled that really big smile when she was about to manipulate him. Sean had no idea what she could possibly be up to, but he had an inkling that she was up to something.

Mercifully for Sean, the second docket moved smoothly and quickly with no problems. As Sean had his hand on the handle of the door leading out of the courtroom, two things happened almost simultaneously. The first, which Sean did not notice at all, was that Bubba picked up his telephone and had a short, whispered telephone conversation. While Bubba was on the phone, Jane, using her most coquettish tone, said, "Judge, do you have a minute before lunch to talk to me?"

Knowing that Jane rarely ever asked to talk to him, Sean felt obligated to say that he could spare her a moment. So, when they entered Sean's office, Jane asked, "Judge, can you give me some travel advice for our honeymoon?"

Sean, never being shocked at anything Jane asked, said, "What would you like to know?"

Jane questioned, "If we are going to get married in late September or early October, where should we go for our honeymoon?"

Sean, not knowing that he was being conned, gave her a somewhat confused look before saying, "Besides the traditional activities, what else would you like to do on your honeymoon?"

After making her usual girlish giggle, Jane said, "Well, we probably would like to go to someplace where we can be casual and swim a lot."

Now being totally confused, Sean asked, "Jane, have you considered going to a beach resort?"

"But, September is hurricane season!"

Still not knowing that he was being set up, Sean asked, "Then, have you considered a resort in the desert?"

"Like where?"

Sean, relieved to be getting down to specifics, said, "Southern California around Palm Springs has plenty of resorts. Also, take a look at Southern Arizona."

Jane, now smiling from ear to ear, said, "Thanks Judge, you know everything!" Just as Sean was about to stand up and take Laura to lunch, Jane asked, "How do I find those resorts?"

Sensing that he might finally get a chance to escape, Sean said, "Jane, go to Google™ and type in *Palm Springs* to find resorts in and around Palm Springs. For resorts in Arizona, type in *Arizona + resort*. If that doesn't work, let me know tomorrow and I'll help you. By the way, Jane, have you talked to a travel agent? You know, a good one could help you a lot."

"Wow! Judge, thanks! Do you know a good one?" Sean wrote down a name and number for Jane. She was ebullient as she left his office.

✱✱✱✱✱✱✱✱✱✱✱✱

When Sean and Laura entered Joe's Diner, Sean saw that attractive, green-eyed, red-headed sergeant, Bubba's supervisor, seated at a table near the door facing him. Sean couldn't have missed seeing her if he had been blindfolded since Sergeant Maggie Anderson was a real eyeful. Sean guessed that she was in her mid-thirties, about as tall as Jo, but much larger in build and measurements.

Sean and Laura stopped to say hello to her. Just as they were about done with their brief conversation, Jo appeared suddenly from the back of the restaurant, saying, "Maggie, did he ask to wash your feet yet?"

A blushing Sean said, "Oh, hi Jo!"

Maggie said quickly, "Judge, we're at a table for four. Would you and Laura like to join us?" Very quickly, Laura and Jo said that they thought it would be a great idea. Already outvoted, Sean pulled up a chair and sat down.

Before the waitress could get to their table, Jo blurted out, "Sean, remember our bet? Wanna guess who won?"

Smiling, Sean said, "Yes, dear!"

Seconds later, the waitress appeared, saying to Jo, "Hon, now that your guests are all here, would y'all like menus?" A blushing Jo indicated that they would.

After looking at Jo and then at Laura and then back at Jo, Sean asked, "How many people were in on this conspiracy today?"

Maggie Anderson, who looked like a maple tree in Vermont with its fall foliage at its reddest, blushed when she said, "I'm not sure if the D-Day landings were better coordinated than our little plan to meet you today, so it took a lot of people."

Thinking for a second, Sean said, "I'm assuming that, from their guilty looks, Jo and Laura were involved in this with you, Sergeant Anderson."

"Judge, I'll confess, but only if you call me Maggie."

"Off the bench, I'm Sean, okay?"

"Okay Sean, the three of us were in on it," Maggie said.

Thinking for a second, Sean said, "Good heavens, Jane must have been in on it also!" Pausing, Sean said, "Okay, if Jane was in on it, Bubba must have been in on it, too, because Jane looks up to Bubba like a father figure. Am I right?"

After a second, the busty redhead said, "Judge, why didn't you become a detective? You're a natural."

Sean replied, "When I was young, there weren't attractive female officers like there are now."

As Sean recovered from Jo's gentle, barefooted kick to his shins, Jo said, "Sean, I don't remember if I told you this before, but Maggie and I were roomies at the academy. We've been best friends ever since. What started our little conspiracy was Maggie's call yesterday to me."

After taking a second to rub—not kick—Sean's shin with her bare foot, Jo continued, "Back when we were in the academy, six of us female cadets bonded and all became close friends. Once a year, we have a party someplace. It's Maggie's turn this year. It's gonna be a week from this Saturday at her place on Plum Lake. Wanna go?"

Sean asked, "Are men invited?"

Maggie said, "Since it's at my place and I couldn't talk my husband into golfing that afternoon, I guess that I'll have to let the other girls bring some guys to keep my husband occupied and out of trouble."

Sensing an opening here, Sean said, "If Jo would like to go, I'd love to go. I know how Jo likes lake water."

Maggie, who wasn't in on the joke said, "We've got a sand volleyball court and a heated pool, too. So, if the lake isn't warm enough to swim in, Jo can still get wet."

Jo just smiled a knowing grin at Sean. With a completely angelic look on his face, Sean said, "It sounds like fun. I wouldn't miss it for the world."

Finally, the waitress took their orders. From that time forward, right until the meal ended, the three ladies chatted, giving Sean a good deal of time to look at Jo. There was something slightly different about her, but he couldn't immediately put his finger on it. Just as the meal was about over, Sean concluded that Jo seemed to be just a bit more hyper than usual. He couldn't figure out why.

When they left the restaurant, Laura and Maggie tactfully walked together, just out of hearing range, in front of Sean and Jo. As Sean and Jo followed behind, Jo said, "Precious, I'm glad that we had this chance to get together today."

"Me, too!" Sean said.

"Sean, I hope that you didn't mind our little conspiracy."

"Jo, I loved it!"

"Great! Besides wantin' to show you off to Maggie, I was havin' a bad day. Just seein' you made me feel better."

As they neared where their paths would part, Jo looked at Sean and said, "Laura told me that since she has lunch with you several other days a week, she'd be willin' if you and I had lunch on Wednesdays. Is that okay with you, or wouldn't you be able to work after bein' 'round me?"

Finally understanding why Laura and Jo had been communicating, Sean said, "I'd love to make you my standing Wednesday lunch partner, our schedules permitting, of course.

Jo returned Sean's smile. Then, looking as deeply into his eyes as she could, Jo asked softly, "Sean, do you trust me?"

Knowing that something was up, Sean took her two hands into his. Completely ignoring the passersby, Sean asked, "Jo, do you think I cry in front of women that I don't trust?"

At his response, Jo stood as tall as she could and threw her arms around Sean, kissing him on the cheek saying, "Thanks, Precious, I needed that reminder."

Seconds later, Jo was on her way back to work, blowing kisses at Sean as she walked. Sean, although a bit confused, felt warm inside, sensing Jo's need for him and her vulnerability. In some strange way, Sean felt happy—confused, but happy!

****

Thursday was a very light day for Sean. Since the long, three-day Easter weekend was going to start the next day, very few lawyers wanted to set anything and take the chance that some follow-up action might ruin their holiday. So, Sean spent the day signing orders and doing the things that he had put off doing until he had a slow day.

Since Laura had taken the day off, Sean went to lunch by himself. He wasn't too terribly hungry, so Sean dropped in to a local take-out sandwich shop. As he was standing in line, lost in thought, he felt a tap on the shoulder.

Before he could even turn around, he heard Max's greeting, "Sean, if it weren't Holy Week, and if I hadn't given up using foul language for Lent, I'd probably say something to you right now."

Facing Max, Sean said, "Okay Max, what'd I do now?"

A grinning Max said, "You invited Jo to church with you on Easter. This meant that she called Kyra for fashion advice. So, Kyra and Jo went shopping. You know that Kyra can't go into a clothing store and not buy something. Your relationship with Jo is starting to cost me, big time!"

A smiling Sean said, "You can relax for a week or so. The weekend after this one, we're going to a party out at Plum Lake. I'm sure that Jo has a good supply of casual wear already."

Max smiled and said, "That's a much better plan, my man."

After they had paid for their orders, Max and Sean walked back to the courthouse complex. When they were about to split up, Max said to Sean, "You'll probably never know how happy Kyra is with you right now. She had a gut feeling that despite the obvious differences between you and Jo, the relationship would click. From what Kyra tells me, you have completely swept Jo off of her feet. Kyra is so grateful to you!"

Seeing that Max was speaking seriously, Sean replied, "It didn't take much effort on my part to be overwhelmed by Jo. She's quite a lady."

Looking Sean square in the eye, Max said, "Kyra knew that you were smart enough to see through Jo's façade and understand just what a special person Jo is. Kyra admires you more than she did before, which I didn't think was possible." A moment later, Max and Sean parted company after shaking hands.

As Sean ate his tuna melt alone in his office, he thought about his conversation with Max and then about his conversation with Jo the day before. He wondered why Jo had asked him if he trusted her. After a few seconds, his subconscious brain sent Sean a message. The idea that hit him was *maybe Jo didn't have a doubt in the world about his trust in her. Maybe she raised the subject because she had a concern if she could trust him.* As he thought about it, Sean remembered back to his days as a trial lawyer. People often would let things slip in depositions that indirectly raised issues that were in their own heads.

Letting his mind go blank for a second, Sean stared out the window. After a bit, his subconscious sent another message to his conscious brain. He remembered his conversation with Jo on the ride back from Lucy and

Ralph's place. He remembered Jo asking about Cheryl's fixing up Ralph and Lucy, and how interested Jo had been in Lucy's dating problems.

After a few seconds, Sean finally got the full picture. He had always assumed that Kyra arranged his blind date with Jo because, as an old friend, she was worried about him. This he knew was true. But, a slightly embarrassed Sean finally realized that the fixing up might have been a two-way street. Maybe Jo needed to be introduced to someone, too.

At first blush, the idea seemed insane to Sean. Why would a woman as beautiful, intelligent and lively as Jo ever need to be fixed up on a date? As Sean turned to the piled up files for him to review and orders to sign, the answer to his question hit him. When it did, he felt like a blue-ribbon winning fool.

Being as logical as he could, Sean reasoned that a woman as beautiful as Jo must have had men in her life before him. If Jo had been on the market when Sean met her and had trust issues, the most logical hypothesis was that her previous man had been a low-down, dirty rat who betrayed her somehow. Kyra had paired him with Jo because he was honest and trustworthy. This made too much sense to not be true.

Then, the big one hit Sean with the force of a twelve-gauge shotgun at close range—Kyra had paired them off because they were two damaged people, who had what the other needed. Sean, being a lonely widower, needed a warm, caring female. Jo was that and a lot more. Jo needed someone who would treat her well and not betray her. Sean hoped that he was all that and more—a lot more.

Alone in his office, Sean broke down and cried. After a few moments, he started to regain his composure. He realized that his tears weren't tears of sorrow or pain, like the many he had shed in the first few months after Cheryl died. No, these tears were something entirely different. Sean felt loved. He knew that God loved him. He knew that Kyra loved him and trusted him enough to introduce him to Jo, who, like all people, needed to be loved. And he suspected very strongly that Jo loved him.

After saying a silent prayer to thank his Creator for His love, Sean moved on to thanking Kyra. He sent her a short email that read:

Kyra,

You are simply magnificent.

Tell Max that he is awfully lucky to have you, no matter
how much you spend on clothes. Thanks for everything!

SR

Knowing that his next task would require him to have a clear, firm voice, Sean paused to go to the office refrigerator and swig down a Diet Coke. Then, he cleared his throat and went into his bathroom, shut the door and practiced speaking until he was sure that his voice would display no hint of his recent tears. Once Sean was confident that his voice was steady, he dialed Jo's personal cell phone number from his personal cell phone.

When Jo answered, she asked, "Precious, how are you?"

Sean said, "I hate caller I.D. I wanted to surprise you."

"Sean, you shouldn't try to surprise me at work. I carry a gun and might go and shoot someone from the fright."

"Sorry, I'm still learning about you. Am I catching you at a bad time?"

Jo replied, "The sheriff just left town. The first deputy took this week off. My immediate boss, the captain, just waved to me on his way out. From now until Monday at 0800, I'm in charge of dealin' with the media. So, with no one lookin' over my shoulder, I can take a minute. Of course, I've got a ton of stuff piled on my desk, but I have time to talk to you, Precious. What's up?"

After drinking another swig of Diet Coke, Sean said, "I just felt an urge to call you and tell you that I really enjoyed seeing you yesterday."

With the hint of a tease in her voice, Jo asked, "That's all you wanted to say?"

"Well, to be totally frank, I really called to say that I think you are totally magnificent!"

After pausing for a second, Jo said, "I'm so glad that I didn't let you stop when you wanted to stop. You responded well to my interrogation. Well, I think that you're magnificent, too, for a Yankee and all!"

Now coming from left field, Sean asked, "Jo, did I give you what you needed when we walked back from lunch yesterday?"

A now surprised Jo responded with a question, "Why do you ask?"

Sean replied, "Well, being a man and out to lunch quite often, I've learned that sometimes I don't always pick up on the subtleties in conversations. Did I give you what you needed then?"

Jo, surprised at Sean's analysis of her emotional needs yesterday, replied, "Precious, I was havin' a bad day yesterday. You gave me what I needed most of all—you."

"Jo, will you promise me something, please?"

"Yes, Precious, whatever it is, I'll give it to you."

Ignoring the emotional blank check that Jo had just handed to him, Sean said, "Jo, if I ever don't catch on to what you need from me, please don't give up on me. Stick with me until I can understand what you need, okay?"

Jo replied, "I promise, if you'll truthfully answer one question for me. Deal?"

Sean replied, "Deal."

"Precious, have you been watchin' movies on Lifetime™? I've never heard a man sayin' anythin' as sweet and concerned as what you said, except in a chick flick."

Sean replied, "No, I haven't been watching Lifetime recently. I just wanted you to know that I really want to be there for you if you need me."

Jo asked, "Sure?"

Sean answered, "I'm sure."

Jo said, "You're the one that's magnificent." Jo's reply was met by silence. Before Sean could say something lame in return, Jo asked, "Precious, may we assume that you have watched chick flicks on Lifetime?"

"Well, I used to watch them with Cheryl from time to time."

"Did you like them?"

"Jo, the main thing that I remember about those movies was that all the actresses were stunningly beautiful, middle-aged women—like you'll be in three decades or so."

"Judge Sean Riley, you are the sweetest, most silver-tongued flirt that I have ever met—Yankee or not! You're just wonderful."

Sensing that he was about to loose control of the conversation entirely, Sean said, "Jo, we need to discuss logistics for Sunday. Can you be ready at 0730 sharp?"

Jo replied, "Of course, I'll be ready." After a second, Jo added an afterthought, "Precious, I'll be on call then. Could I ask you to wear my pager on your belt? I'll set it on vibrate. But, that won't work if it's in my purse. Okay?"

"Jo, if that is what you need, I'll do it for you gladly. But, you've got to promise me something in return, okay?"

Jo asked, "What do you want me to promise to do?"

A somewhat embarrassed Sean said, "Remember to ask for it back when we leave church. Otherwise, this absent-minded, old professor might forget to give it back to you. You remember how bad my memory was last Saturday night?"

Jo said, "I promise. But, only if you'll admit that you might have been a bit distracted that night."

Sensing what was coming, Sean played dumb and asked, "How was I distracted that night?"

"Precious, before last weekend, when was the last time that a woman pulled her dress up to her panties and asked you to wash her bare feet and legs?"

"Too long!"

"See my point?"

Before Sean could reply, Jo asked, "After church, do you want to have breakfast at my place?"

Sean said, "Jo, if you'd like to we can. But, I've already made reservations for us at the Horizon Club. And, being the thoughtful person that I am, I even checked the menu. Grits will be available on the buffet."

With a giggle in her voice, Jo said, "Sean, you think of everythin'! I'll even be ready a few minutes early, just for you."

Sean said, "Jo, you're wonderful."

Jo responded, "No, you are! Gotta run! Bye!"

✱✱✱✱✱✱✱✱✱✱✱✱

When a somewhat sleepy Sean rang Jo's doorbell at 0725 hours on Easter morning, a peppy Jo opened the door a crack and said more loudly than necessary, "Precious, cover your eyes until I tell you to look."

Once Sean indicated his compliance, he heard the door open. Then, he heard Jo say, "Okay, you can look now!"

The big smile on Sean's face said all that Jo needed to hear at that moment. She did look magnificent. She was wearing a very sedate, short-sleeved, French Blue silk dress. The top of the dress almost went to her neck. Around the waist of the dress, there was a belt also of French Blue silk, ostensibly secured by a bow at her navel. The hem went down to almost her knees. Her tan legs were bare. What really impressed Sean the most was not the dress, which was lovely in a Donna Reed sort of way. The accessories were what really impressed him the most. Somehow, Jo had found a pair of open-toed pumps in the same color, a matching bag and a white hat, which was similar to one of the ones that Ilsa wore in

Casablanca. Sean knew that Jo had worked hard to impress him. And she had succeeded splendidly.

If it would not have made them late for church, Sean would have picked Jo up in his arms and kissed her. She was a sight to see. Fortunately for all concerned, Jo asked Sean to take several shots of her with her new digital camera while she stood on her doorstep. When that task was completed, Jo deposited the camera inside and grabbed a white wrap.

After Sean had fired up his F-150, but before he put it in gear, Jo reached into her bag and produced her pager, which, after she turned it to vibrate mode, she had Sean place on his belt. And then, they were off to Mass.

The weather, although somewhat cloudy, showed every possibility of clearing into a nice, warm, sunny spring day. The temperature was already at 68°, which suggested to Sean that the day would be warm. As they journeyed the two miles to Holy Angels Church, Jo turned to Sean and said, "I've been to a Catholic church before. I was at the one in Smithville when Maggie got married. The whole time that I was there, I wasn't exactly sure about what I was supposed to do. I hope that I didn't do anythin' I wasn't supposed to do. You'll help me today, right?"

Sean said, "Just do what I do, except when I get up to go to communion, stay in your seat." After a second, Sean added, "Now that I think of it, there is something that you might find a little different about this service. Except for the sermon, it will be in Latin."

With a confused look on her face, Jo said, "I thought that Catholics don't use Latin any more."

Sighing, Sean said, "Talking about this subject irritates me to no end, so let me be brief and forget about it. A long time ago, there was a meeting of the bishops in Rome called *Vatican II*. Now, there was no need for this meeting since everything was going along well. But, they had it anyway and managed to screw the church up in ways that it may take generations to recover from fully.[10]

One of the loopier ideas that came out of *Vatican II* was that the Latin Mass is somehow inferior to the Mass in English. Many bishops won't allow Mass to be said in Latin at all in their diocese, at least not publicly. Fortunately, our bishop allows Father Wilson to say one Latin Mass a Sunday, but makes him say it at 0800 hours to cut down attendance. Enough old timers—as well as us rebellious baby boomers—go every Sunday, filling the Church, much to the annoyance of the bishop."

Jo asked, "Will I know what's goin' on?"

"Pretty much. In the pews, there will be books with Latin on one side and English on the other. Follow along as best as you can. I'll help you find the right pages. Just watch me."

As Sean pulled into the slowly filling parking lot, Jo said, "Forgive me for asking, but why do you and the other people get up so early to go to services in a foreign language?"

As they walked toward the entrance of the church, Sean smiled and said, "I'll remember to remind you of your question when Mass is over. By then, you'll know why."

When they entered the church, Sean found a pew near the front and off to the right side by an aisle. He told Jo that they needed to sit there just in case her pager went off. By the 8:00 a.m. starting time, the church had filled up nicely. Looking around, Sean noticed that the building was unusually beautiful with its Easter flowers. Jo noticed that she seemed to be the only woman wearing exactly what she was wearing, which made her feel good.

They stood when the music started. When the procession reached the altar, Father Wilson intoned, *"In nomine Patris, et Filii, et Spiritus Sancti."* As the Prayers at the Foot of the Altar proceeded, Jo looked at Sean. She noticed a peaceful, almost sublime, look on his face. Jo was fascinated. She had never seen Sean look this way before. Jo followed along quite well with Sean's help. After a few minutes, Father Wilson sang out, *"Gloria in excelsis Deo."*

Then, the chorus responded mightily with the body of the Gloria. Jo was very impressed with the beauty and the grandeur of the moment. Looking over at Sean, she noticed that, although he was physically there, his head was somewhere else entirely. He looked very happy.

Father Wilson's homily was excellent. He addressed the multiple meanings of Easter. Easter certainly marked the Resurrection, the triumph of life over death, good over evil. But, it also marked the coming of spring, a time of hope, a time of rebirth. Father Wilson pointed out that just as winter was a trial for those living through cold, harsh times, spring marked a time of rebirth, a new flowering of life and vitality. Father Wilson urged the congregants to seize the opportunity to overcome the past winter's cold and to let life, warmth and love back into their hearts. Jo felt as if Father Wilson was speaking directly to her, even though he had never met her, because Jo had just finished the coldest, cruelest winter of her life. His words made her feel hopeful again, deeply hopeful.

When Jo looked at Sean, she noticed that he was dabbing his watering eyes with a handkerchief. Jo felt his pain. Not knowing what else to do, she squeezed Sean's hand. Sean turned to her and smiled in response.

After the homily was over, the beauty of the choir singing the Credo almost overwhelmed Jo. She sat quietly, taking in the majesty of the moment. Sean also appreciated the moment. But, he also thought that the loss of inspiring moments like this was one of the greatest evils of *Vatican II*. Sadly, most Catholics would never again hear the Mass in Latin, which, until *Vatican II*, was their birthright. The Mass of the Faithful proceeded without incident.

As they were leaving after the Mass, Sean leaned over to Jo and whispered, "When I introduce you to Father Wilson, do I use your rank?"

Jo said, "I earned it, why not?"

When Sean introduced Sergeant Jolene Scruggs to Father Wilson, the good Father shook her hand warmly. Jo sensed that he really was glad to meet her. From the brief conversation that they had on the steps of the church, Jo also sensed that Father Wilson was glad to see Sean at Mass with a date. Father Wilson's final words brought a smile to all three of them. Looking at Jo, he said, "You look lovely. Your hat looks like something that Ingrid Bergman wore in *Casablanca*."

As they walked out, Sean told Jo a bit about Father Wilson's background. He was a local man. When he had been at Southern, he earned an N.R.O.T.C. commission and was stationed in San Diego. One day, when his commitment to the U.S. Navy was almost over, he and some brother officers toured a motion picture studio. Quite by accident, they met the casting director for a movie that was going to start filming about the time that he was due to muster out. The casting director said that he was looking for some experienced naval officers to be in his big movie, so he handed them his business cards and asked them to call him.

Father Wilson was the only one who did call. His reward for making the telephone call was to spend a glorious six weeks filming a movie in Hawaii. After his time in Hawaii, he was offered a part for another movie, which led to a career in acting. His last role was playing a priest, who was hiding from the Loyalists during the Spanish Civil War. Father Wilson's role must have opened his eyes to something inside of him because after the movie was over, he applied to the seminary serving their diocese. Since ordination, he had been a parish priest in the local diocese. He was loved and respected by his parishioners, who admired both his deep spirituality and his sense of humor.

As Jo and Sean negotiated their way through the chaotic church parking lot, Sean noticed that the next Mass looked to be full to overflowing. Sean was glad to see so many students from Southern University entering the church. While they were working their way very slowly out of the parking lot, Sean asked Jo, "Do you understand why so many of us get up early to attend the Latin Mass?"

Jo replied, "Precious, I certainly do. It was beautiful and awe inspiring. If you ask me to go again, I'll gladly go."

"Jo, would you like to go with me next Sunday?"

"Why Sean, I thought you'd never ask. I'd love to go, again."

✱✱✱✱✱✱✱✱✱✱✱✱

Jo was as impressed with the view from the Horizon Club as Sean knew she would be. Located at the top floor of the tallest building in town, it boasted a panoramic view of the Southern University campus from two directions, Holy Angels Church from a third of the way around and University City's downtown skyline from the other side. It was a truly magnificent view on a sunny day like this Easter Sunday. Although a long-standing member, Sean rarely went to the Horizon Club anymore since, except for holidays, it was only open for lunch. Thinking about it for a second, Sean realized that this was his first time at the Horizon Club since Cheryl had died.

Sean and Jo were both hungry. Jo had a traditional Southern breakfast from the buffet—country ham, scrambled eggs, grits with gravy, toast and coffee. Sean stuck to his low-carb menu of scrambled eggs, wheat toast and two thin slices of bacon. Jo gently teased him about drinking hot tea with milk instead of coffee.

Over breakfast, Jo mentioned that right after they got off the phone on Thursday, his present had arrived. She said, "I haven't played all the CDs through entirely, but what I have played was wonderful. There is this beautiful duet on the first CD called, *Good Will Win in the End*. Is that the one that the Singin' Soldier made with Mrs. Breen?"

Sean replied, "I emailed Lucy that very question on Thursday after I received my set. She said that it was."

"Sean, that's just about the loveliest harmony I've ever heard."

Before Sean could reply, he smelled the scent of a particular perfume that could mean only one thing. Turning rapidly, Sean caught a glimpse of Kyra, just as she said, "Sugar, I hope you don't get in trouble with Father Wilson for bringin' such a lovely distraction to the Latin Mass. How any man would be able to pray next to such a beautiful woman in that lovely dress is beyond me!"

As he rose, Kyra planted a big, wet kiss on his turned cheek. Max just smiled and waved at him. Kyra continued, "Jo, that's the loveliest Easter outfit that I've ever seen! Where did you get it?"

As Jo said something about a sale at a thrift shop, Max winked at Sean. No sooner than Jo finished answering, Kyra said, "We'd better go back to the kids. No tellin' what they might be doin' just to get back at us for forcin' them to be all dressed up this mornin'."

The rest of their brunch was peaceful. Just as Sean and Jo were standing up to leave, Sean was startled to feel the pager on his belt begin to vibrate. Giggling, Jo asked him to hand it over, much like a first-grade teacher asked for contraband from a misbehaving student. Looking at the pager for a second, Jo took her cell phone from her purse and made a call. After a conversation lasting several minutes, Jo looked at Sean and said, "Duty calls. Can you drop me off at headquarters? Somethin' big has happened and I've gotta hold a press conference in about an hour."

As they rode down in the elevator, Sean asked, "Will you be tied up all day?"

Jo said, "The sheriff is flyin' back from the coast. I'll do the initial conference at noon and then prepare his statement for later in the day. I figure that I'll be off duty by 1400 hours or so since he'll want to do the big conference later on. We could go someplace when I'm done, if there would be an email connection, in case he needs me to revise his statement."

Sean replied, "As you know by now, I've got email. Would you like to swim at my place? If the sheriff needs you, I've got all of the modern conveniences at home."

"Sean, that sounds great! Should I just call you when I'm done?"

"Jo, could I watch the press conference? I've never seen one live."

"Precious, you sure that you won't get bored watchin' me write a statement?"

"Jo, I wouldn't get bored watching you floss your teeth. If I'm with you, I'm happy."

"Okay, I'd love to have your company."

Chapter Six

As Sean pulled his F-150 into Jo's parking place at the sheriff's department, Jo looked at him and said, "Precious, I'm in a bit of a hurry, so to avoid any hassles when I check you in, please ditch your piece and any spare clips that you might have with you."

Sean asked, "Jo, how did you know?"

"I didn't for sure, but since judges are allowed to carry concealed weapons, I always assumed that you're armed."

Sean said, "Cool!" as he ditched his spare clip and Glock™ nine millimeter in the panel on the driver's side door of his F-150.

As they neared the doorway to the building, Jo pointed to the newspaper vending machine and suggested to Sean that he might as well buy one to keep himself occupied while she was busy. Sean obeyed.

As they walked into the headquarters, Jo showed the deputy at the desk her I.D. Sean produced his judicial I.D. from his pocket. When Jo said that he was with her, the deputy handed Sean a clip-on I.D. badge and had him sign for it. Seconds later, Jo led Sean into an elevator going up to the top floor, which Sean guessed must be where the big chief and his support staff work.

When they exited the elevator, the first thing that Sean noticed was the entrance to the sheriff's office. He couldn't have missed it if he tried because there was a large replica of a badge on the door, right next to the large letters that had the sheriff's name and title spelled out for the world to see. Turning away from the sheriff's office, which was obviously at a corner of the building, Jo led Sean down the hallway. Jo's office was eight doors down from the sheriff's office. Sean took this as a sign that Jo was well regarded in the organization.

When they entered Jo's office, Sean noticed that it was much larger and nicer than a cubicle. She had a window that looked out on the county complex. Jo had a large, dark wood desk. The side panel of her desk held her computer monitor. Her matching dark wood credenza was stacked with papers and files, neatly ordered. Sean's quick visual tour of the premises was interrupted when Jo said, "Precious, go lock the door. When you're done doing that, please give me the hanging bag from the back of the door."

After locking the door, Sean took the hanging bag and turned to Jo. She was fumbling in her desk for something, which she eventually found and took out of one of her desk drawers. Sean noticed that the object she had taken from her drawer was a package of nude pantyhose, which she opened quickly. Standing, Jo kicked off her open-toed pumps and pushed them under her desk. Very quickly, she turned to Sean and said, "Precious, please unzip me."

Having learned long ago that needing help with zippers on the back of dresses is one of the main reasons that women put up with men, Sean undid the snap at the top of the dress, and then pulled the zipper down a few inches. Jo said, "Precious, pull it down all the way. I don't have time to waste fooling with that damn thing."

Sean obeyed without protest. As he unzipped her, he was very careful, so as to not catch Jo's skin in the zipper. When he had finished, Jo said, "Sean, when you're done with that, please open the hanging bag, take out my white uniform shirt and hand it to me." When Sean was ready with the white uniform shirt, Jo walked over to him to put it on. At that moment, Jo had on only a very lacy set of panties and a matching bra. Her dress and half-slip were piled on the top of the desk. As she put on the uniform shirt, Jo said, "I hope that I haven't embarrassed you by undressin' in front of you like this, but I figured that you'll see at least this much when we go swimmin'. Besides, you've been married, so I doubt that seein' me in my underwear will shock you too much. And, at least now you know that I wear underwear—at least some of the time."

As Jo put on her pantyhose and pulled up and zipped her skirt, Sean knew that she was right. He hadn't been in the least bit embarrassed. If anything, he felt very comfortable. In Sean's experience, when a woman feels comfortable enough to undress in front of a man, she must trust him. Sean was experiencing a feeling of intimacy—something absent from his life since Cheryl died.

As Jo was putting her uniform jacket on, she said, "Sean, if you would be so kind, please put my dress on a hanger and then hang it inside the bag. Then, put my slip in the bag, zip it up and hang the bag on the back of the door."

When Sean completed his assigned duties, Jo was standing, brushing her hair. After Jo had her hair fixed the way that she wanted it, she lightly sprayed it. Then, after putting on red lipstick, she searched under her desk for a pair of black, closed-toe flats. After putting her purse inside her desk, Jo announced to Sean, **"Ready!"**

A moment later, Jo had the door unlocked and told Sean that he might as well start reading the *University City Bugle* because she had to start getting her statement ready. Sean couldn't get much reading done. Eventually, he gave up trying to read. Watching Jo was a lot more interesting than anything in the *Bugle*. Jo was a study in controlled chaos. One minute, she was charging down the hall. A minute later she was banging something out on her computer. Then, she was off again, returning a minute later with some official form in hand. Then, she was back to computer banging. Finally, just about the time that Sean thought Jo was about ready to scream, he heard the sound of her laser printer at work. A moment later, she handed several pieces of paper to Sean and asked him what he thought.

After reviewing the proffered document, Sean said, "You write well. The statement is clear and concise. If I can understand it, I imagine most crime reporters will, as well."

Smiling at Sean's comment, Jo said confidently, **"It's show time!"** As they walked down the hall, Jo said, "When we get to the Media Center, you go in ahead of me and find a chair. I'll come in a moment later from the other door."

When Sean entered the Media Center, he noticed a group of reporters all seated near the front of the room. Behind them in the aisles, a group of TV cameras were all set up. Sean also noticed that at the front of the room there was a light-brown, wooden podium with a bunch of microphones placed at the top. It took Sean a bit to adjust his eyes to the brightness of the room, which was the result of the TV lights that were being tested. Sean observed that the wall behind the podium was a very appealing color of blue. After a second, Sean smiled, realizing that the wall was the color of Jo's eyes.

As Sean sat in the back, several reporters looked at him. He did not recognize them. Apparently none of them recognized him either, so they ignored him. A few seconds later, a door opened at the front of the room. Jo entered, looking serenely calm. After walking slowly to the podium, Jo took a moment to look around the room. Sean thought that this was for dramatic effect, but as he found out later, this was to give the cameramen a chance to make last minute adjustments. After a bit, Jo began reading from her prepared statement:

"This morning at approximately 0500 hours, a deputy on a routine patrol on Foster Avenue noticed a westbound, blue, two-door Chevrolet with Pennsylvania tags, moving at a slow rate of speed. When the deputy pulled closer to the vehicle, the vehicle accelerated rapidly to a speed forty miles in excess of the posted speed limit. Turning his flashing lights on, the deputy pursued the vehicle. When the vehicle failed to pull over, the deputy called in for back up. After a ten-mile chase, involving six patrol units, the suspect vehicle crashed into the median strip, thereby disabling the vehicle."

Pausing for a second, Jo continued:

"After the crash, the two occupants of the vehicle surrendered to the deputies at the scene, offering no resistance. Upon booking, it was ascertained that the two occupants of the vehicle—James Hannah, 22, and Thomas Franklin, 24, both from Pittsburgh, Pennsylvania—were both wanted by Pennsylvania and federal authorities for a series of bank robberies in the Pittsburgh area. Our department is in contact with both Pennsylvania and federal authorities. The sheriff will have a further statement later, when more details are available. At the present time, the two suspects are being held in the county jail, pending further legal proceedings."

Now that Jo had finished her prepared statement, she opened the floor up to questions. Having seen presidential news conferences on television many times before, Sean knew that when the media person opens the briefing up to questions, the reporters tend to get a bit out of control. Still, he was surprised by the kindergarten atmosphere in the room.

The first question that Jo took was from the crime reporter for the *Bugle*, a rumpled, overweight, balding man. "Sergeant, are any local charges going to be filed against these two?" he asked.

Jo replied, "The two suspects are currently in custody on a number of charges relatin' to the chase."

The *Bugle* reporter blurted out a follow-up question, "Are they wanted for any other crimes locally?"

Very coolly, Jo replied, "The matter is currently under review. The sheriff will provide y'all with more details when he makes his statement."

Next, a middle-aged, male television reporter from the local NBC™ channel asked, "Will they waive extradition?"

Jo replied, "That will be up to the suspects and their lawyers. I have no information about that at this time."

A young, female television reporter from the local Fox™ affiliate asked, "What was in their car?"

Jo replied, "The contents of the vehicle are currently bein' inventoried, so I'm unable to give you a complete listin'. But, I can tell you that a large amount of cash, a number of firearms and a large supply of ammunition were found in the vehicle when the suspects were apprehended."

A blonde, female television reporter from CNN™ asked, "Is it true that their vehicle was full of racist, neo-Nazi literature?"

Jo replied, "I have no information to that effect. When the sheriff makes his statement after the vehicular inventory is completed, he will have more details available as to the contents of the vehicle."

Sensing that the questions were degenerating, Jo said, "I'll take one more question."

Another television reporter, this one a middle-aged male, blow-dried, talking head from the local CBS™ affiliate asked, "Is there any truth to the rumor that they were headin' to the airport to catch a small plane to the Caribbean?"

Giving the reporter a quizzical look, Jo said, "Sam, they were headin' westbound on Foster Avenue. The airport is miles east of there. If they were goin' to the airport, they were sure goin' about it the wrong way!" Jo's response to the reporter brought hoots of derision and laughter from the other reporters in the room. After the laughter had stopped, Jo said, "We'll let y'all know when more details are available."

Jo exited from the same door from which she had entered. Sean watched quietly as the throng packed up and noisily left the room. When the room had almost emptied out, a deputy entered the room and whispered something into Sean's ear. A moment later, Sean and the deputy were in the hallway, walking away from the throng, which was now gathered at the elevator.

The deputy escorted Sean into the sheriff's waiting room, where Jo was seated with the sheriff watching a closed-circuit television monitor. As the door closed and the deputy pointed to a seat, Sheriff Walker said to Jo in his deep bass voice, "I got here just in time to see your press conference. Jo, you did a darn good job. If I didn't know better, I'd swear that you've been doin' this for years. You done good, real good!"

Turning to Sean, the sheriff rose to his full height of 6'6" and offered his hand to Sean, saying, "What did you think of Jo's performance, Judge?"

Smiling, Sean said, "Sheriff, I'm too biased to give an objective evaluation. From what I can tell, Jo managed to give them enough sound bites to make their editors happy."

"Judge, I think that you hit the nail square on the head. Jo managed to end the briefin' with a good use of humor, which will make future conferences easier. Now that the reporters know that Jo has a sense of humor and a sharp tongue, they may be a little more careful about the questions that they ask, not wantin' to be laughed at like Sam was. It served Sam right. He has the brains of a goose."

Turning to Jo, the sheriff said, "Jo, while you were in there, I was on the phone with the D.A. It's gonna take him until at least tomorrow to work the details out with the D.A. in Pittsburgh and the feds to see who gets these miscreants first, so I won't be doin' a statement until tomorrow. If you want, go ahead and take the rest of the day off. Just keep your cell phone on, in case I need you."

Sean and Jo both said in unison, "Thank you, sheriff."

The sheriff leaned back and laughed, saying, "Are you two datin' or workin' on a country act? You've got your harmony down real good!" After all three finished laughing at the sheriff's witticism, Jo took Sean's hand and practically dragged him back to her office.

As soon as they entered her office, Jo quickly took off her black shoes and put them back under her desk. Then, she pinned Sean against her locked office door and kissed him passionately. After a second, Jo said, "Tell me the truth, did I do okay?"

Sean, answering honestly, said, "The sheriff may be a politician, but he was telling you the truth. You handled the reporters just fine. I overheard comments from a couple of them as they were leaving. They said that they hoped you start doing more briefings because you told them what they needed to know and were highly telegenic, so that their segments would get the okay for airtime from their producers."

Pushing Sean back against the door again, Jo said, "Even though I learned from my Momma's Momma years ago that no one, least of all a lady, should ever believe anythin' that comes out of a Yankee's mouth, I believe what you said. Precious, I was scared goin' out there today. I was glad to see you in the back of the room."

Jo gave Sean a very passionate kiss, pressing him very firmly against the door once again. Sean said, "Jo, if I hadn't known that you'd never done a briefing by yourself before today, I wouldn't have believed it. You were very calm, controlled and in charge. You were great."

"Sean, what time is it?"

"Jo, it's about 1330 hours, in military time."

"Precious, let's hurry up, so we can get into the pool before the sun goes away."

Knowing what was expected of him, Sean took the hanging bag from the door. Reaching inside, he pulled out Jo's half-slip and dress and the hangers. As Jo removed items of clothing, Sean hung them on the hangers. A minute later, Jo was back in her Easter outfit and ready to go out the door.

∗∗∗∗∗∗∗∗∗∗∗∗

On the way to Sean's place, Jo stopped off at home to change into casual clothes. Ready in less than five minutes, Jo left her place with the same oversized bag that she had brought to the ballgame the week before.

On the way to his place, Sean asked, "Jo, do you get time and a half for working today?"

"No Precious, it doesn't work that way. Today, I've racked up four more hours of comp time. I've got enough logged in that I could take off six weeks and still have time left over, not to mention my vacation time. If you work hard, by the time you retire, you can build up a year or more of accrued comp time, which they pay off when you retire. It's like a second pension."

As they drove along, Sean said, "Jo, I just realized something. My cats are going to be surprised when I bring another female into their house. My suggestion is to just ignore them until they come up and introduce themselves to you."

Jo asked, "How long have you had the cats?"

"I got them right after the Twins left for their dormitory last August. Except for visits from the Twins, they've had me all to themselves. They may be a bit possessive."

"What do you call them?" Jo asked.

"*Law* is one cat's name. The other is named *Equity*."

Giggling, Jo asked, "How did you come up with those awful names for your cats?"

"Just blame it on the academic in me. Since Law and Equity are the two strands of judge-made law in our system, I figured that the names were perfect for two female cats from the same litter, living in the house of a judge."

Jo inquired, "Will they be hostile?"

"No, but they will probably stare at you a lot. They're awfully good at that. Just don't get too physically close to me at first since they might perceive you as a threat to their social status in the household."

"Precious, do you have somethin' goin' on with your cats that I should know about?" Jo asked playfully.

"Jo, I feed them. I play with them. I sleep with them. I don't think they would like that to change."

"Sean, if you tell me that you wash their paws for them, I'm going to demand that you take me home this instant!" Jo said, with mock seriousness.

Sean said, "No. As spoiled as they are, there are some things that they prefer to do for themselves. I do clip their claws, but no paw washing. Besides, you only told me not to wash the feet of other female deputies!"

"Okay, I'll be cool with them," Jo said, with a toothsome grin.

At 1405 hours, Jo and Sean were at the gate to his house. After Sean placed his magnetic card next to the sensor panel, the gate automatically opened. As they drove up the wooded hill toward Sean's house, Jo couldn't see much of the house until they made the last turn in the driveway. Jo was really impressed at both the size and simple elegance of the exterior of the house.

Pointing at the house, Sean said, "The house is in the style of Frank Lloyd Wright. Since the side of the house away from County 191 is built on the gentle slope of a hill, our architect adopted some of Wright's techniques. I really love living here."

When they entered the house, Sean said, "Jo, I'll give you the full tour later. Let me show you to a guest bedroom, where you can change."

About three minutes later, Jo emerged from the guest bedroom wearing a blue pastel bikini. The bottom part was a thong. The top part was neither very large, nor very small, being tied around Jo's back by a very thin strap. Besides the bikini and her flip-flops, Jo was wearing a pair of dark sunglasses and carrying a towel and her oversized bag.

While waiting for Sean, Jo looked at his very large library, which was divided into sections, much like the books in a public library. While Jo looked at the books, Law and Equity stared at her from their concealed vantage points. Jo noticed that many of the volumes were not law books since Sean was a man of catholic reading tastes. Several minutes later, Sean emerged from the bedroom wearing flip-flops, a t-shirt and a pair of swimming trunks that were the size and shape of physical education shorts.

Looking at Jo in her bikini, the first thing Sean observed was that Jo's tan mostly hid her freckles. The next thing Sean noticed was that Jo had very long, tan, well-muscled, athletic-looking legs. Her bottom appeared to be small and tight. Her waist, he guessed, might be less than twenty-four inches. But, what really caught Sean's attention was Jo's very ample, very tan bosom, which was incongruous for a woman as slim as Jo.

As soon as they walked out to the pool, Jo began putting her gooey suntan lotion all over the front of her body. While Jo was greasing herself, Sean turned on the pool heater and then checked the water temperature, which he read to be 88°. As he walked back to the chair where Jo was stretched out, Sean removed his t-shirt. Jo, glancing surreptitiously from under her sunglasses, noticed immediately that Sean had an athletic build. While not bulging, Sean's upper body muscle groups—shoulders, biceps, triceps and pecs—all showed that he worked out regularly. Sean's legs were firm and muscular, definitely the result of running. Jo guessed that hidden inside his baggy swimming trunks, Sean probably had an equally firm behind. Jo also noticed that, although Sean didn't have a set of "washboard abs," he obviously was not overweight and worked his abdominal muscles regularly. Sean's exposed skin had a mild bronze tinge to it. While his tan was not as dark as Jo's, Jo observed that Sean must have spent some time outdoors recently.

Sean's hairless chest was fascinating to Jo. She wondered if he just had no chest hairs, or if he shaved his chest. She liked the look of his smooth, muscular chest.

When Sean sat in the pool chair next to Jo, she asked him if he wanted to share her suntan lotion. As soon as he replied in the affirmative, Jo's fingers generously applied the gooey stuff to the exposed portion of his front side, starting with his toes and working her way up slowly. When Jo's fingers applied the lotion to Sean's chest, she felt his pectoral muscles slowly relax at her touch. Honoring Sean's request to apply the lotion to his face, Jo applied it to Sean's face very delicately and lovingly, in stark contrast to the massage that she had just given his chest moments before.

When she finished oiling Sean's body, Jo wiped her fingers on the edge of her towel. Next, she set her alarm clock for thirty minutes later. And then she took her cell phone out of her bag and placed it near her chair for easy access. Finally, she relaxed in her chair. Jo grabbed Sean's hand and held onto it until the alarm went off.

While Jo jumped into the pool to cool off, Sean went into the house to bring them some sweetened ice tea. When Sean returned, Jo was lying on her stomach. After sipping a bit of the tea through her straw, Jo asked Sean to put some lotion on her back and legs. When he was done, Jo said, "Lay down and I'll oil you up." Jo applied the oil starting at the back of his neck and worked down to his ankles.

As they lay there basking in the warmth of the sun, both relaxed and unwound. After ten minutes or so, Sean, without forethought or calculation, blurted out, "Jo, do you know why I haven't made a pass at you?"

Without a moment's hesitation, Jo said, "Sure. I'm not just a casual fling for you. You're serious about me."

A shocked Sean sipped his sweetened iced tea for a second, and then said, "Jo, how long have you known how I felt about you?"

Jo replied, "By the end of our date last week, I was absolutely sure of it."

Curious, Sean asked, "How could you tell?"

Jo replied, "I was 90% certain when you asked me to go to church with you today."

"What removed the other 10% of doubt?" Sean asked, genuinely curious as to how Jo was able to read him as well as she could.

Jo said, "Remember last weekend when I was bein' a bitch and made you wash my feet and legs? The way that you did it removed whatever doubts I might have had."

Now confused, Sean asked, "What did I do that was so special?"

Jo said, "You Yankees are so dumb. Here I was being a prize bitch and you complied with my demand. You were sweet and gentle. That removed any doubts that I had about your intentions."

Sean asked, "Jo, you didn't plan the foot washing as a test, did you?"

Jo replied, "Precious, I'm too darned spontaneous to plan ahead. I do things and analyze them afterwards. Don't worry. I don't test people. Besides, I love you."

After Jo's statement, she and Sean just looked deeply into each other's eyes while holding hands. Eventually, their lovely moment was shattered by the ringing of Jo's alarm clock. Just as Jo had it turned off, a second rude noise interrupted them.

Picking up her cell phone, Jo answered and listened to the voice on the other end. After thanking her caller, Jo sat up. Turning toward a somewhat startled Sean, Jo said, "Precious, let's go into the house real quick. The sheriff says that I'm gonna be on national TV in the next few minutes."

As Jo started to walk to the house, she heard Sean say, "Jo, wait a second." When Sean reached her, he covered her with her towel, saying, "You'll freeze to death dressed like that in the house. Wrap yourself in the towel until I can kick up the A/C." Before Jo could say anything to Sean, he said in a steady, firm voice, "Jo, calm down just a second. You'll need to take your cell phone and bag in with you. And, you better wear your flip-flops if you don't want to slip on the floor."

In the few seconds that it took Jo to slide into her flip-flops and pick up her cell phone, Sean had moved closer to the door into the house. As Jo moved toward him, Sean asked, "Beautiful, what channel are you going to be on?"

Jo replied, "Sheriff said on Fox News™ at the breaks at the top and bottom of the hour and CNN Headline News.™"

When they walked into the house, Sean looked at his wristwatch and said, "It's ten to four. We've got enough time to record everything." A second later, Sean's big screen TV was tuned to Fox News.

When Jo saw Sean fiddling with the remote control, she asked, "What are you doin'? Don't you think you should be puttin' a tape in the VCR, so I can record my bein' on TV?"

Sean said, "Beautiful, never fear! I'm here! I've got this new technology called TiVO.™ It lets you record shows directly from the TV to a hard drive, without having to fool with tapes. If you want to record to a tape, you can do it later. You can even record two different shows at the same time. Right now, I've got it set to record both Fox News and CNN Headline News for an hour, starting at four."

Jo was duly impressed, not being familiar with the technology. A few second later, Sean said, "I'll be right back!" When Sean returned, he had a red and white checked flannel shirt on over his swimsuit. He was also carrying a blue denim shirt, which he handed to Jo. After Jo put on the denim shirt, Sean said, "I turned up the thermostat to 78° degrees, so you'll be comfortable in a few minutes. If you get uncomfortable in the meantime, let me know so I can get you a blanket."

As they sat on their towels on the edge of Sean's large, green modular sofa waiting for the four p.m. update on Fox News, Jo thanked Sean for covering her up, so she didn't look like a hooker in his living room. Seconds later, the top of the hour newscast on Fox News carried a thirty-second story about the apprehension of the two fugitives earlier today in University City. For about ten seconds, the broadcast cut away from the blonde info babe on Fox News and showed Jo speaking at the briefing. Then, it was over.

As Sean rose to switch to CNN Headline News, Jo jumped up and asked, "What did you think?"

Sean said, "I'm starting to get afraid that I'm going to lose you to Hollywood. Jo, you were absolutely stunning!"

Before Jo could kiss him, Sean switched the television to CNN Headline News. Just as Jo was about to say something, there she was on the huge television screen, much larger than life. Jo was on camera for at least twenty seconds on this broadcast. When her time on CNN Headline News was over, Jo reached over and kissed Sean on the cheek. Then, she said, "I know that you were kiddin' about Hollywood. But, in case you weren't, if I go to Hollywood, you're gonna go as my agent. Deal?"

Laughingly, Sean replied, "Deal!"

Sean then rose and set his TiVO to record the local news on the area's four network TV channels. Once he explained that TiVO would record all four of the local news shows, which luckily were staggered in time, Jo seemed to be quite happy. Sean then asked, "Jo, are you as hungry as I am?"

When Jo said she was starving, Sean told her that he had a baked ham in his refrigerator and side orders of potato salad and baked beans. Minutes later, the couple was sitting down to eat at the round table in Sean's breakfast nook. As they ate, Sean said, "A few minutes ago, you said something about hookers. Did you ever work vice?"

"Well Precious, I was a decoy for a prostitution sting once when I was in my first year with the department. We had staked out this industrial area, where on weekends johns were goin' to meet hookers. They got me all tarted up real good with a Dolly Parton blonde wig, short shorts, a real tight shirt tied around me to show my belly and most of my boobs and a pair of shoes with real high heels. That was the most miserable day of my life. It was hot. I was in the sun. I was sweatin' like a pig under that wig and the damned adhesive that held my wire in place itched and itched so bad, I jus' about wanted to scream."

Sean asked, "Did you catch anybody?"

"Well Precious, the first three hours, I had a couple of men stop me. I told them to drive around the corner where I'd make them real happy. Of course, when they turned the corner and pulled into the parkin' lot, they got busted."

After taking a sip of her iced tea, Jo continued, "After I took a break, the weather got hotter. The sun was pourin' down and I felt like I was gonna melt. That's when I noticed that men would drive by me and not stop. Sean, you don't know how bad that makes a woman feel when she is lookin' as trashy as she can and men just drive by. At the end of the shift, I found out that I had been the least productive decoy in the sting that day. Vice never wanted me back again."

Sean said, "Thanks! Jo, I'm going to have trouble going to sleep tonight thinking about you dressed up like a hooker."

Before Jo could kick Sean in the shins, she jumped up in her seat a bit and had a startled look on her face. Immediately looking down at the floor, Sean said, "I see that you and Miss Equity have become acquainted. Congratulations, she just *marked* you."

Looking a bit confused, Jo asked, "Sean, do I want to know how she marked me?"

Laughing, Sean said, "Cats have these little scent glands in their cheeks. When they rub up against someone, they leave a bit of their scent behind. This way, you don't' smell like a stranger. That is a good sign."

Jo said, "Sean, when I felt that fur on my bare leg, it really startled me in a very erotic way. Sorry, if I overreacted!"

"Jo, I fully understand your reaction, which must have been a third as strong as my reaction was when you changed clothes in front of me today."

"Ouch!" Jo replied. Once they finished laughing, Sean and Jo cleaned up after their meal. When they had the dishwasher fully loaded, Sean looked at his watch and said that they could either try to catch the local news or go out and play in the pool and review the broadcasts later. Jo said that she'd like to go outside and play in the pool some more.

When Sean joined Jo outside, Jo had a big smile on her face. As Sean came up to her, she kissed him tenderly and said, "Sean, you're wonderful."

Being confused, Sean suggested that they go and sit in the whirlpool and look at the beginning of the sunset from the unique prism of his pool. Standing at the edge of the pool, Sean said, "Jo, in a while you are going to see a unique light show. As you noticed earlier, the west wall of the pool is made of a very strong, clear translucent plastic. As the sun begins to set, the light from the sun will start to change the color of the water in the pool. Right at sunset, the pool will appear to be full of orange or red water. As the twilight sets in, the pool will take on a purplish hue. We've got a little time left, so let's soak in the whirlpool."

Ten minutes later, Sean and Jo were quite mellow, stretched out in the warm, swirling waters of the whirlpool. As Sean relaxed, he felt Jo's foot tapping his leg. Looking at him, she asked, "Sean, will you rub my big feet for me?"

After telling Jo that her feet were dainty and delicate for her frame, Sean did as he was requested and rubbed her feet. As Sean rubbed, Jo had a look of peaceful contentment on her face, similar to the looks that cats have when they are rubbed under their chins.

As Sean continued to rub away, Jo said, "Sean, thanks for not being offended when I changed clothes at the office. I really am sorry that I was almost runnin' 'round half nekid. I was just focused on the press conference."

"Beautiful, just let it go! You aren't the first woman that I've seen in my life." Pausing for a second, Sean added, "But, you are definitely the most beautiful woman that I've ever seen in her undies in her office. And, by far, you're the liveliest and the most impetuous to boot!"

Jo said, "*Moi*?"

Laughing gently, Sean said, "*Moi*? I thought you wanted me to believe that you are just this poor, little, unsophisticated country girl. While I haven't known too many daughters of cotton farmers, the few I knew didn't respond with *Moi*? when I asked them a question."

A giggling Jo said, "Sean, I don't know how it is up North and all, but down here, most cotton farmers are able to send their daughters to school. Some of our schools even teach French."

After kicking Sean very gently in the leg, Jo continued, "You aren't the first person to call me *impetuous*. One of my coaches in high school used the same word to describe me. Of course, back then, I had to look it up to see what she meant."

Changing the topic, Jo said very seriously, "Precious, I really am sorry about bein' half-dressed 'round you. It's Easter Sunday. I shouldn't be actin' like I'm tryin' to seduce you."

Straightening up and sliding near to Jo, Sean said, "Jo, you seduced me the first night that we met."

Looking confused, Jo asked, "You mean, by being a bitch and all?"

Snuggling up to Jo, Sean said, "I am a man that appreciates complexity. I guess that explains why I took up the law. That probably also explains why I have cats rather than dogs as pets. On our first date, I sensed that you are one very complex person, full of life, energy and needs to be met. Looking back, I realized that you seduced me with your personality."

With just the hint of a giggle in her voice, Jo asked, "You mean I seduced you with my shoes on? Wow!"

Sean said professorially, "Not exactly! Didn't you have your shoes off most of the time that we were at The Palm Tree?"

Jo asked, "Precious, how did you know that?"

"While you were speaking to Kyra, my napkin fell off my lap. When I bent over to pick it up, I noticed that you had your shoes off."

With a teasing hint in her voice, Jo said, "May I ask what else you noticed when you were pokin' 'round down there?"

"Beautiful, I noticed that you had no hose and long, sexy toes with toenails painted the sexiest shade of red that I ever observed."

With a now playful tone in her voice, Jo asked, "And what else did you notice?"

Pausing for a second, Sean asked, "Should I start at your ankles and work my way up?"

Jo's response was direct. She stood up and said, "Go right ahead, if you don't mind me taking my top off right now." As Jo said that, she made a half-hearted motion to undo her bikini top. Sean's response was equally direct. He stood up and kissed her passionately on the lips. After a minute, Jo suggested that they go back into the heated water since the air was starting to cool.

After a second, Sean said, "If you look in the dictionary, the verb *to seduce* has many meanings. One of the meanings is to entice, beguile or win over. That first day, in retrospect, you totally enticed, beguiled and won me over. It has just taken me a few weeks to fully realize it."

"Precious, did you just tell me that you love me in a lawyer kind of way?" When Sean conceded the point, they both laughed.

Noticing that the sun was beginning to set, Sean suggested they turn and watch the natural light show that was beginning. As they knelt in the whirlpool, Sean put his arm around Jo's smooth, taut waist. As the sun set, Sean thought that being with Jo was far more beautiful than any sunset he had ever seen. When the light had almost totally gone away, Jo turned to Sean and whispered in his ear, "I love you, too."

Then, as fast as the sun sets at the equator, Jo was out of the whirlpool and drying herself off. Several minutes later, the happy couple was back inside Sean's now 78° house.

After changing clothes, turning down the A/C a bit and making themselves a set of ham and cheese sandwiches, Jo and Sean retired to the big screen TV to see if Jo had appeared on any of the local TV news broadcasts. Jo was impressed with how fast Sean was able to fast-forward through the local news broadcasts to check for any story in which Jo appeared. Sean's observation was that if you speed through the commercials, you've cut out 40% of the broadcast time right there.

As Sean and Jo sat watching the screen intently, they didn't notice that they had company. Suddenly, Jo discovered that she had two furry companions sitting on her lap. Very slowly and motionlessly, Jo asked Sean, "What do I do now?"

Sean told Jo to pet them, showing her where Law and Equity liked to be petted. Apparently, Law and Equity had really taken a shine to Jo since, by the time the last local TV show had been run through TiVO, both cats were purring noticeably. Sean told Jo that she should be impressed because cats are very good judges of character—better than most people.

Jo's face had made it onto the broadcasts of the local ABC™, Fox and NBC affiliates. Since Jo was mothering Law and Equity, she had to sit motionlessly as she saw herself on the tube, which was a real test of Jo's willpower. When the last broadcast was over, Sean promised Jo that he would copy the broadcasts from TiVO to a videotape and give it to her on Wednesday. She smiled at that and asked Sean if he could run a second tape, so she could send one home to her parents. Sean agreed to do so since he had the technology available to him.

Once Sean and Jo were done watching the local news broadcasts, Sean very gently removed the two sleeping lumps of fur from Jo's lap. He told Jo, "You've made two new friends today. I don't know what you did, but whatever it was, they liked it. Cats are very quirky little creatures. No one has ever figured out their likes and dislikes entirely. But, if you and a cat bond, you've got a very loyal friend. Congratulations!"

❋❋❋❋❋❋❋❋❋❋❋❋

On the ride back to Jo's place in University City, Jo reached into her bag and extracted the CD set that Sean had bought for her. Taking out the top CD, Jo asked Sean to play the fourth song on it, the duet that Tommy and Sarah Breen had recorded long ago, entitled "Good Will Win in the End." After the duet ended, Sean played it over again several times. When he was done replaying, he said, "Jo, that song is pure poetry set to music. That is as good as any poetry that I've ever come across. I doubt that William Shakespeare would disagree."

Jo asked, "Precious, want to sing the chorus with me?" When Sean professed reluctance, Jo reminded him that she had heard him sing the

National Anthem, so she knew that he had a great singing voice. A moment later, an enthusiastic Jo and a reluctant Sean, *a cappella*, belted out:

> No matter what hardships flow,
>
> We won't break or bend.
>
> 'Cause deep in our hearts we know
>
> That good will win in the end.

When they had finished singing the chorus, each remarked on what a fine singing voice the other had. Jo asked, "Precious, have you sung much? You sounded real comfortable singing with me. Our harmony was perfect!"

Sean replied, "Beautiful, the good Sisters taught all of us to sing in grade school. I was in the choir until my voice changed. How about you?"

Jo answered, "Well, we always sang at home. When I was in high school, a couple of friends and I put together a country group. We sang at school functions and around the local area. Since I knew my Daddy wouldn't think of his daughter runnin' off to Nashville, I never pursued singin' beyond that."

Sean said, "Maybe you should think about it. Think the world is ready for the *Singing Sergeant*?"

After they both laughed, they sang the chorus once more, this time more slowly and with more feeling. When they were done singing, Jo suggested that they learn all of the words, so they could sing the whole song. Sean agreed, just as long as Jo promised that this wouldn't lead him to running around in a sequined, aquamarine, western-cut suit with a bunch of electric guitars playing in the background. Jo laughed at the thought.

As they pulled into Jo's driveway, Sean and Jo went over their schedule for the next week. They were going to have lunch on Wednesday. They were going to go to the party at Plum Lake on Saturday. On Sunday, they'd go to Mass and then back to his house to swim. Sean also promised to give Jo a full tour of his place. Neither one of them noticed the obvious—a month ago they had been strangers. Now, they were planning on seeing each other three times in one week.

****

The next morning, Jo woke in a happy, if slightly confused, mood. For the first time since she had started taking the medication that Dr. Emerson prescribed for her, the dream had come back. Actually, not the same dream—rather, Jo had experienced a humorous variation of that dream.

Usually in Jo's nightmares, she was seated in the dining room of a stately, old house, surrounded by old, expensive furnishings. The mean, hateful things that were said to her were said face-to-face. In last night's dream, Jo was working undercover vice again—all tarted up. She was walking up and down Dexter Avenue, waving at men driving by in an attempt to lure them to stop. As Jo was shaking her arms at the passing traffic, the woman who had so insulted her drove by on the opposite side of the street in her shiny, black limousine. After driving by Jo, the limousine made a sharp u-turn and approached her slowly. Just before the limousine reached her, a good-looking young man in a bright yellow Porsche pulled up beside Jo and said something to her. The Porsche then quickly turned the corner into the parking lot that Jo had pointed out to him. Just as the limousine reached Jo, police sirens went off and the limousine went speeding away. As Jo stretched, she said to herself laughingly, *Maybe I should check to see if I've gotten too old to work another vice sting.*

Chapter Seven

After Sean had handwritten the date—April 26th—and signed the order, he looked up at the teary-eyed widow standing before him and said, "Ma'am, I've signed the order admitting your late husband's will to probate. I'm sorry about your loss. Please step over to the clerk to take your oath."

The widow said, "Thank you, Judge Riley. I really appreciate your compassion."

Just as Sean was about to call the next case, Angela handed him a note from Miriam, who was standing nearby. The note said that Jo had called to say she had real good news that she wanted to share with him at lunch. Would he take her to the Horizon Club? Sean nodded to Miriam, who silently mouthed the words, *I'll reserve a table for you for 12:15 and call Jo back.* As Sean resumed his docket, he wondered what the good news was that Jo had to share.

****

Sean arrived at the Horizon Club, carrying a tote bag full of gifts for Jo. Less than a minute later, the elevator dinged its arrival. The doors slid open and out of the elevator emerged Jo, beaming from ear to ear. She was wearing her dress uniform, just as she had on Sunday for the press briefing. After kissing Sean warmly on the cheek, an irrepressibly happy Jo and a curious—but happy—Sean were led to their table by the hostess, a charming, little, dark-haired beauty with a thick Scottish burr.

After Sean and Jo had made their pass through the buffet line, Sean opened the tote bag and presented Jo with a videotape, which contained recordings of her appearances on both the local and the national news channels. After Jo received the tape, Sean pulled out a large, sealed, legal-sized, manila envelope. On the front of the envelope, Sean had written, "To my favorite celebrity."

Jo opened the envelope with the help of Sean's pocketknife. She was awe-struck for a second when she saw what was in the envelope—two copies of the very same photograph of Jo that had appeared on the cover of Monday's edition of the *University City Bugle*. One of the copies had a little, sticky, yellow note attached to it that read, *Please autograph and return same to me. SR*

A wide-eyed Jo remarked, "You never cease to surprise me. Precious, how did you get these?"

"Jo, a friend of mine in the Communications department of S.U. hunts with one of the editors at the *Bugle*. It took me a few seconds to email him my request on Monday evening after class. Last night, I found the photo emailed to me as an attachment. Then, I printed it on my color printer."

"Precious, could you run me another one to send to my parents?"

"Beautiful, your wish is my command. Now, what is your good news?"

"Before I tell you, I need to ask you somethin' first. Would your schedule allow you to be at the sheriff department's Media Center at 1630 hours today?" Sean indicated that he was sure his afternoon hearings would be done by then. Jo replied, "Great, let me call the sheriff right now." Quickly, Jo phoned the sheriff on her cell phone.

After her called ended, Jo said, "Precious, this won't be official until this afternoon, but you are no longer speakin' to Sergeant Jolene Scruggs. I am now Lieutenant Jolene Scruggs. Because I'm a bit shy of havin' enough time in grade, I wasn't expectin' a promotion until later this year. But, since I've already passed the exam, and since the captain and the sheriff decided that after Sunday I was ready to take on the duties of my boss, the captain has put in for retirement effective the end of the month. Under our regulations, if the sheriff certifies that no one else in the department has the needed skills to replace a retirin' deputy, the sheriff can make a temporary promotion. He is going to do that in my case. The promotion will become permanent later in the year, when I've got sufficient time in grade. I want you to be there when my promotion is announced, so I had to call the sheriff to let him know that everythin' is set for this afternoon."

"Jo, I need to ask you an etiquette question. In the military, the first person to salute a new ensign or lieutenant is entitled to a dollar. Does your department have a similar custom?"

"Sean, do you need change for a five?" Jo asked laughingly.

"No, I was just checking," Sean said.

"No, we don't. And since you're not in uniform, you can't salute me. But, go ahead and say it, so I can start getting used to the idea."

Rising and holding his water glass aloft, Sean said, "To Lieutenant Jolene Scruggs." Sean wasn't sure if it was the looks from the other diners or the toast, but Jo's cheeks were turning red.

After the toast, Jo remembered to autograph one of the photos, which she returned to a smiling Sean. Sean promised her that the next time she saw that photo, it would be framed and hanging in a very visible place in his home office.

Before leaving, Sean and Jo discussed the mechanics of Saturday's date to attend Maggie's party at Plum Lake. By the time they had their weekend details worked out, Jo's face had almost returned to its normal color. Sean decided that it would be tactful of him not to tell her how lovely she was when she blushed.

After lunch, Sean walked Jo to her SUV. When they reached the vehicle, Jo gave Sean a very wet, passionate kiss. As she slid behind the driver's seat, Sean noticed that somehow, her skirt had risen way up. When Jo noticed Sean's eyes on her thigh, she smiled and said, "I figure that the wet one and the flash of skin have got to be worth a lot more than a dollar."

Sean grinned in reply.

****

After his docket was over at 1500 hours, Sean took one last long, hard glance at his financial disclosure form. Hoping that letting the world know how wealthy he was wouldn't lead to problems, Sean took a short walk to the clerk's office and filed the blasted thing, trying to appear as nonchalant as possible. Fortunately for Sean, right after he filed the form, the clerk put the document into the tray of documents to be scanned. Moments later, another clerk took that form and many other filings directly to the scanner. Sean thought to himself, *Well, maybe no one will notice.*

****

Sean arrived at the Media Center at the sheriff's department a few minutes early. When he entered the room, he saw a gaggle of reporters and cameramen getting ready. The noise and the lights somehow seemed to be less hostile and foreign than they had been just three days ago.

At precisely 1630, the back entrance to the Media Center opened. Jolene stepped into the room first, followed by her boss, Captain Morris. Behind them strode the sheriff a few seconds later.

Every time that Sean saw the sheriff, he couldn't help but think that Sheriff Walker looked like Hollywood's version of a good, non-corrupt Southern lawman. At 6'6", the sheriff towered over everyone else in the room. Although gray haired, he still looked quite trim and athletic, much like he had looked more than three decades ago when he was a linebacker for State and an Army infantry officer in 'Nam. As the sheriff started speaking, Sean felt his *basso profundo* voice shake the room.

The first part of the sheriff's remarks concerned the retirement of Captain Morris. After making a brief statement announcing that Captain

Morris would retire effective the end of the month, the sheriff then proceeded to praise the captain in lavish terms, extolling both his long years of service to the department and his professionalism and dedication to duty. Sean realized that most eulogies did not sound this impressive. Sean was duly impressed—both with the record of Captain Morris and by the sheriff's eloquence.

After lauding Captain Morris, the sheriff segued smoothly into the announcement of Jolene's promotion and her assignment as the replacement for Captain Morris. While the sheriff did not lavish as much praise upon Jo as he had her predecessor, he did a fine job of letting those assembled know that as a decorated and skilled and professional deputy, he had no doubt she would carry on the fine tradition of Captain Morris and build on the solid foundation that Morris had laid. Seconds later, the sheriff produced a small box containing a set of lieutenant's bars, which he then handed to Jo.

The sheriff surprised Sean to no end when he said, "In our department, we have a long standing tradition that a newly promoted deputy has his or her new insignia of rank pinned on by someone near and dear to them. In keeping with this fine, old tradition, Judge Riley, would you please come front and center to pin the new bars on the new lieutenant?"

As the lights of the TV cameras shone in his face and the digital cameras clicked, Sean made his way to the podium. Despite being surprised at being called forward—and suffering from a congenital case of "fumble fingers"— Sean somehow managed to pin the new bars on Jo's collar and uniform epaulettes without drawing blood or embarrassing himself.

After saluting the sheriff and Captain Morris, Jo went to the podium and said a few words about what great mentors Captain Morris and the sheriff had been and about how she would try to uphold the high standards that they had set. Jo also indicated that she was looking forward to working with the reporters assembled in the room.

After Jo spoke, the sheriff concluded the briefing. Very rapidly, the sheriff, the captain and the new lieutenant exited the room. After they were gone, Sean found himself suddenly surrounded by reporters, inquiring as to why he had been asked to pin the new bars on Jo's collar. Sean smiled and told them that he had to be the one to do it because he was the only person in the room without an assigned duty.

Smiling, he added, "Besides, if she had asked one of you to do it, all of the rest of you reporters would have had your feelings hurt." Sean's comment drew a big laugh from the reporters. Seconds later, the reporters were scurrying out the door.

****

An hour later, Lieutenant Jo and Judge Sean were comfortably seated in a quiet, out-of-the-way booth at The Palm Tree. As they ate and talked, Sean asked Jo if she meant what she had said about Captain Morris and the sheriff being great mentors.

"Sean, I guess you don't know about the sheriff's background. He and the captain played football together at State. They both were infantry officers in the Army in the same unit. When they left the service, they both joined the department. They are real close."

After nibbling a bit, Jo continued, "When the sheriff was a trainin' officer, he and one of his rookies were ambushed by three drug dealers durin' a routine traffic stop. The rookie took a round to the shoulder, so he wasn't much good durin' the ensuin' fire fight. A female deputy was the first backup to arrive at the scene. Comin' up unannounced from the rear, her marksmanship took out two of the bad guys. The sheriff took out the other one."

After eating a bit more, Jo said, "Before that day, the sheriff thought that female cops should only ride desks and handle juvenile cases. After having a female deputy save his life, the sheriff's attitude about women in law enforcement turned 180°. Since that time, he has been as fair as anyone could ever be to women and minorities servin' under him. Captain Morris adopted the sheriff's attitude. A fairer pair you'll never find anywhere."

A bit later in the meal, Sean asked Jo about her decorations. Looking uncomfortable, all she said was that she apprehended a fleeing felon with a karate side kick to his gut. This gave Jo and the two other officers in pursuit a chance to disarm him. All she said about the second decoration was that she had stopped a bank robbery. She looked really uncomfortable talking about the subject, so Sean let the topic slide. Jo's tone for the rest of the meal was happily pensive.

****

An hour later, Jo and Sean were back at her place, seated at her kitchen table. After making small talk for a bit, Jo took Sean's hands into hers, looked deeply into his eyes and said, "Precious, since you came into my life, just about a month ago, every part of my life has improved in ways that I can't even begin to describe. I owe my promotion to you because if you hadn't been there last Sunday, I'm not sure that I could have handled my nerves. Seein' you there made me feel strong and confident. Thank you for bein' there. I love you."

Sean replied, "Jo, I feel the same way about you. Having you in my life has made a lonely, unhappy man smile again. I love you, too."

After the two kissed passionately, Jo sat down and said to Sean, "Precious, I know there is somethin' that you want to say. Here, hold my hands. I won't let anythin' bad happen to you."

For a minute or so, Sean said nothing. He just held her hands and looked into her lovely blue eyes. Jo noticed that his face had reddened and little beads of perspiration were visible on this forehead. Eventually, Sean managed to control the emotions welling up from deep within him. After taking several deep breaths, Sean straightened up and said very calmly, "Jo, will you marry me?"

Jo's instant reply was, "Yes. But, here is how I think we should handle the situation. Let's not tell anyone just yet. Do you have any plans for the weekend other than bein' with me on Saturday afternoon and Sunday mornin'?"

When Sean said that his calendar was clear, Jo told him she was going to spend Friday and Saturday evening bunked out at his place, so that they would be able to be together for two entire days. After hastening to add that she was going to sleep in a spare bedroom, she proposed they spend their time talking because they really didn't know each other that well. If, after their weekend together, neither one of them came down with a case of cold feet, then they could shop for a ring and tell their families and the world about their engagement.

Sean agreed that the plan was sensible. After that, they discussed logistics. A little while later, they parted after a very long, passionate kiss.

✳✳✳✳✳✳✳✳✳✳✳✳

That night, Sean slept like a log, much to the joy of Law and Equity, who never had learned to accept his tossing and turning. In the last hour of his sleep, he had a dream in which he and Cheryl were driving home from playing tennis. Cheryl mentioned she had heard that a mutual friend, whose wife had died a year before, had just gotten engaged. Cheryl blurted out to Sean, "If anything ever happens to me, remember, I want you to be happy. If you'd be happier alone, stay alone. If you'd be happier remarried, then please remarry. I love you and want you to be happy."

Sean awoke after the dream. He couldn't remember if he and Cheryl had ever had that actual conversation. But, Sean was astute enough to know that whether he and Cheryl had had that conversation was beside the point. He reasoned that his subconscious mind was giving him permission to go forward with his relationship with Jo.

Jo went to bed happy, too. She slept soundly until about an hour before her usual wakeup time, when the recurring dream came back again with its full force and fury. Jo awoke sweaty and jittery. After looking around her bedroom for a second, Jo remarked out loud to herself, *Well bitch, in a few days, we'll know if you were right or not*!

Chapter Eight

On Friday morning, just as Sean's F-150 had turned onto County 191, his cell phone went off. "Griswold, what is so exciting that a night owl like you is calling me before eight in the morning?"

"Sean, I was calling to say two things. First, let me offer my congratulations. You're the first client of mine to ever have his photograph make it into *Julie's Jewels*, the gossip column in the *University City Bugle*."

"Me? I'm not the gossip column type, you know that Bob."

"Sean, my mind isn't that warped to come up with something like this just to pull your leg. I guess that you haven't yet read today's issue of the *Bugle*, have you?"

Sean said, "No, I always read it about mid-morning."

Bob continued, "Well, when you get a chance to read it, you'll see your picture pinning bars onto a new female lieutenant in the sheriff's department. In her column, Julie Sharpe asks if wedding bells are in the offing for the most eligible man in the courthouse and the beautiful young pressie for the sheriff's department." After pausing for a second, Griswold said, "Sean, this leads me to my question. Are they?"

Sean asked, "Bob, why do you ask?"

"Sean, you're in a tough race for reelection. The last thing you need right now are rumors about your personal life. Are you serious about her?"

Sean, pausing for a second, said, "Yes, Bob, we are very serious and very much in love."

Griswold added, "Sean, as both your friend and your consultant, I need to tell you that the best thing, politically speaking, would be for you two to get married before Labor Day. If you don't, every move that you and she make come the fall will be fair game for your opponent."

A surprised Sean said, "Bob, can I get back to you in a few days about this?"

Bob continued by saying, "Okay, but don't wait too long. If you two don't get hitched, the door is open for both of you to have your reputations thoroughly trashed. I hate to be blunt, but falling in love during an election year wasn't a wise political move. Since the world now knows about you two, your options are limited."

"Thanks, Bob. I promise that I'll get back to you by Monday evening, at the latest."

Bob said, "Sean, if you do propose, I can just about promise that you'll get great press coverage."

Sean replied, "Bob, you're too kind. By the way, her friends call her Jo."

Bob answered, "Sean, please let me know. With a little advanced planning, we can even stage an announcement party at The Palm Tree, which I hear is Julie's favorite restaurant."

Sean's reply was "Thanks, Bob. I guess I needed that reality check."

"Sean, one more thing. From her picture, it's obvious that she is a very lovely lady. From what I've heard about her, she is very bright, a good cop and madly in love with you. You could have done a lot worse. You're a lucky man."

"Thanks. Bob, I'll be back with you real soon."

As he drove along, Sean guessed that before Bob called him this morning, he probably called one of his other clients—the sheriff, himself. After mulling over Bob's comments for a while, Sean smiled and said to himself, *He is right. I am a lucky man.*

****

As Sean and Jo were preparing to leave her place late on Friday afternoon, Sean said, "Beautiful, I have an apology to make. I know that we promised we wouldn't say anything about our engagement until after we talked this weekend. Well, I called Father Wilson to check out possible wedding dates. Let me tell you why I did it."

A very apologetic Sean told Jo about his call from Bob Griswold. He told her that a little bell went off in his head warning him that there might be a problem because the bishop normally makes engaged couples attend six months of preparation classes before marriage. Sean mentioned that the first thing he did was to call her, but wasn't able to reach her. Jo explained that she had been teaching a class at the academy.

Sean, after apologizing again, said that after he couldn't reach Jo, he decided to go ahead and call Father Wilson on his own. Jo concurred, with a laugh in her voice, "Sean, after the paper came out today, there wasn't much of a secret left, was there? What did Father Wilson say?"

"Jo, his comment floored me. He said that he was amazed that something that Julie Sharpe had written was accurate. He said that he would check with the bishop, but in light of the circumstances, Father Wilson anticipated that it could be done in August. I tentatively reserved a date—August 12th. He wants to see us next Wednesday evening to discuss the details and begin our classes. He said that if August 12th didn't work for us, there would be a problem since the church is reserved for the rest of the month. Jo, you aren't angry, are you?"

"Precious, do you think that I could be angry with you for actin' spontaneous? That would be the highest form of hypocrisy, wouldn't it? Of course, I'm not angry. You were jus' bein' practical."

****

Later that evening, after Jo and Sean had finished their take-out Chinese meal, Sean suggested that he give Jo the grand tour of the place before they sat down to talk. Jo agreed.

Starting with the pool, Sean showed Jo the grounds, including his jogging path and his target shooting range. Since Jo both ran and used firearms, the presence of these two things made her feel very comfortable.

After touring the grounds, Sean moved the tour inside, showing Jo the house, room by room. Not far into the tour of the house, Jo said, "Sean, forgive me for sounding like a cop, but I'm a little concerned about you livin' so far out in the country. Do you have a portable generator?"

"Jo, do you think that I might need one?"

Jo responded, "Sean, have you ever ticked off anyone in your time on the bench?" Sean nodded.

Jo inquired, "If someone were to cut off your power, would your home security system work?" Sean agreed that it would not.

"So, if someone wanted to do you harm, if they were to cut off your power one night, or if a big storm blew out your power, you'd be left out here in the country with no way of gettin' help, except for your cell phone, which may or may not work, dependin' on atmospheric conditions."

Sean said, "Jo, thanks for the tip. I've written down in my planner to check them out next week."

Jo added, "Precious, while you're at it, check out gettin' a safe place to store extra gasoline, just in case you have to rely on your generator for a while. Also, you really need to think about gettin' a satellite phone. They aren't cheap, but they're a lot more reliable than either a land line or a cell phone."

Putting his arm around her waist, Sean said, "Jo, thanks for looking out for me."

Pulling away from Sean, Jo said, "What makes you think that I'm lookin' out for your hide, Yankee Boy? If you haven't noticed, I seem to be spendin' a fair bit of time here recently."

"Yes, Ma'am," Sean said, in faux submission.

Sean's home office was the last stop on the tour of the house. As soon as Jo entered the room, she noticed that Sean had framed the photograph she autographed for him at lunch on Wednesday. It was hanging with a number of other photos.

"Sean, I'm gonna guess that this is your father, right?" Jo said, pointing to four photos. In the first one, his dad was wearing his WWII uniform. The rest, which were taken later, showed him dressed casually. Jo said, "Precious, I see exactly which parent you favor. You're a spittin' image of your father."

"Well, not exactly," Sean corrected. "If you look real closely, you can see that his hair is darker than mine and he is a bit taller."

"Precious, if you say so. But, you two look an awful lot alike to me."

Looking at his many photos of Maureen and Pat, Jo pointed out what lovely young ladies they were, even in early childhood. Sean gave Cheryl all of the credit for their good looks.

Moving on, Jo pointed to a faded black and white photo of a middle-aged couple, very attractive, but a bit foreign looking. Sean remarked, "Those are my mother's parents. This one was taken on the day that the Allies liberated Paris from the Nazis. You can tell that they were very, very happy that day. Their only regret was that they weren't in Paris at that time for the celebration. Once the war was over, they did go back for a long visit."

The next photo really caught Jo off guard. It appeared to be a ferrotype of a Renoir-type, full-figured model in a low-cut, peasant blouse and skirt, sitting barefoot on a low, stone fence. The woman in the photograph appeared to be a redhead with freckles. She also seemed to have been blessed with a full set of curves and a sunny disposition. Jo inquired, "Sean, is that your mother?"

"One and the same. My dad took that photo using a regular camera and then did something to it to give it a Victorian look."

"Sean, your mother was a very beautiful woman."

"Her parents were both born in France. Why would you be expectin' anything else?"

After they shared their laugh, Jo took a deep breath and commented about the two remaining photographs. "Sean, I'm going to guess that the beautiful blonde in the tennis dress is Cheryl. But, the other one—isn't that Madeleine LeBeau, who played Yvonne in *Casablanca*? "

Smiling, Sean said, "Those are both Cheryl. A number of years ago, we went to a costume party as Captain Renault and Yvonne. Somewhere, she found a dress and earrings that matched exactly what Yvonne wore in the big scene in *Casablanca*. When she had her hair done the same way, Cheryl really did look just like Yvonne. Of course, I looked nothing like Claude Rains, but with her on my arm, I doubt that anyone noticed."

As they walked from the office back toward the kitchen, Jo hit Sean with a hard question. "Sean, do you want any more children?"

Sean said, "Any man with half of a brain in his head involved with a woman your age without children has to face that question at some point in the relationship. I've thought about it. Yes, if you want to have children, I'm game."

As Sean tried to kiss her, Jo pushed him away saying, "I wasn't planning on starting a family nine months from today. So, be good!"

Once seated in the kitchen, Jo took Sean's hands in hers and said, "Sean, for us to work, I need to tell you some things about me. I'm a little bit scared right now. Would I be prying if I asked you to tell me about the women in your life before Cheryl? It would make it easier for me to tell you about myself if you went first. Okay?"

Sean, sensing tension in Jo's voice, agreed. Sean began his tale. "My mother died after my second year of military school. I didn't realize it then, but I guess that after she died, I went into a mild, but long-lasting depression. After she died, I stopped doing things for fun. I threw myself totally into school, which was my job at that time."

Sipping on his Diet Coke, Sean continued, "The summer after my third year of military school and the summer after I graduated, I worked at a commercial sod farm. A local insurance agent owned the land and left his daughter in charge of getting the sod ready for shipment. The owner's daughter, Krista, was a year older than me. She was about 5'5". She was solidly built—very muscular. She had black hair, a bit shorter than yours. Krista and I could have had a lot of fun those two summers, except for two things. Her younger brother and sister worked on the job with us, for starters. The other thing was that I was so into my job that I didn't pick up on her flirtations. I know this because the week before I started college, she asked me to take her to a movie. On the way home, she told me about how she had tried for two years to catch my eye. I felt embarrassed. Suffice it to say, we both got home late that night. I'm sure that when I dropped her off, she understood the problem was with me and not her."

"Sean, did you sleep with her?"

"Krista? Before that night, I had never even kissed a girl. I wasn't ready for anything as involved as that."

A slightly embarrassed Jo said, "Oops! Did you ever see her again?"

Sean said, in a tone with no emotion, "I did see her a couple of times more. She started a junior college a year before me. So the next summer, she was totally focused on her upcoming transfer to a four-year institution. Besides, by that time, I sort of had a girlfriend. I think."

Laughingly, Jo asked, "You think you had a girlfriend? You aren't sure after all of these years?"

"Jo, honestly, I'm not. Her name was Connie Klausman. She was from a small town in Wisconsin, where her family was the richest family in the county. Actually, the little town near where she and her parents lived was named *Klausman*."

After taking another sip of Diet Coke, Sean added, "Connie and I were in the same speech class during the first semester of our freshman year. One day, at the beginning of the semester, I gave an informative speech on *How to grow grass for fun and profit*. The class liked the topic until they found out that marijuana wasn't involved. Then, they all tuned me out, except for Connie. After class, Connie sort of invited me to invite her to have a Coke at the campus snack shop. Over the Coke, Connie peppered me with questions about my attitudes concerning farming. I told her that I liked it, which was certainly true since my experience with farming was all out of doors in the summer, with no foul smells or animals to butcher or anything unpleasant like that. I must have given her the right answers because, after that, I found myself with a steady date all year."

"Precious, what did she look like?"

Smiling for a second, Sean said, "She was about 5'3", blonde, blue eyed, very fair and had a lot of nice, round curves. No Jo, we didn't do anything more than kiss—and little of that—our first year."

"At the beginning of our second year at Midwestern University, Connie seemed different," Sean continued. "She became quite serious about me and about our relationship. I don't mean *serious* as a euphemism for *passionate* or *sexual*. No, I mean that she seemed to be throwing her entire Teutonic self into us. I can't say that she was either pushy or manipulative. It just seemed that she was intensely dedicated to making the relationship work."

Jo asked, "Did it?"

Sean replied, "Depends on your vantage point, I guess." After taking a deep breath, Sean said, "Connie invited me to spend the week between Christmas and New Year's with her family up in Wisconsin. She and I had a great time snow skiing and tobogganing. Her parents and I really seemed to have hit it off, as well."

"Precious, you don't expect me to engage in those pastimes do you?" asked Jo. "They all seem to involve things that I do not find appealing, such as snow, cold weather and possible frostbite."

"Jo, I've learned from experience that snow is best observed in a paperweight, not in person." After stretching for a second, Sean resumed, "When school started up in January, I received a very nice letter from Mr. and Mrs. Klausman, thanking me for visiting with them up there near the North Pole and telling me that I was a fine young man, who was going to *make his mark on the world* and was *going places*. Being the fool that I was, I took their comments as being positive."

Jo asked, in all seriousness, "They didn't like you?"

"You're asking me? Like I'd know? Catching his breath, Sean continued, "Anyway, that fourth semester Connie seemed different."

"So, what happened?" Jo asked.

"We parted at the end of the semester. Connie and I had half-made some plans about getting together for the Fourth of July weekend, but nothing definite. About two weeks later, I received a totally shocking letter from Connie. For the first time in our entire relationship, she was actually truthful with me."

Jo, now into the story fully, asked, "What'd she say?"

"Well, in the letter, she told me that being an only child, her father had sent her to Midwestern University to find someone who would be a suitable mate for her and could take over the family's various businesses in due course. After her first three weeks on campus, Connie concluded that no one she had met there—male or female—had the slightest interest in farming or small town life. Then, she heard me give my speech. It was like a sign from on high. That was why she stuck to me like glue all first year."

After another sip of Diet Coke, Sean said, "When she went home at the end of our freshman year, her parents were particularly disappointed in her lack of progress in finding a potential mate and successor to their business empire since she was dating a city kid. Connie said that she had insisted that they would find me suitable if they met me. So, that is why I had been invited to meet them over Christmas vacation. And I failed the test miserably. They didn't want their daughter to bring home someone who was *going places*. They wanted her to bring home someone who would be content to live in rural Wisconsin. So, her parents told her that at the end of the school year, she was going to transfer to a smaller school, much closer to home, where they hoped that she would find a more suitable potential mate."

"Sean, I'm going to guess that you never saw her again."

"There wouldn't have been any point to it," Sean explained to Jo.

"Sean, knowing you, I'm going to guess that you weren't deprived of female companionship for too long, were you?"

"Jo, I need to take a break. When I come back, I would be most obliged if you had a glass with about three fingers of Jack in it, a couple of ice cubes and just a splash of branch water. I don't think that I can handle telling you about Alicia while stone cold sober."

"Sean, just when I thought you were a teetotaler, you've done surprised me again."

"With my last name bein' Riley, you'd be surprised that I'd be havin' a wee nip?" Sean said in a perfect brogue. After Jo stopped laughing, Sean bellowed, "Hell, bring the bottle and a second glass. If you don't use it, I might!"

When Sean returned to the table several minutes later, Jo noticed that his mood had changed. He seemed to be very animated. Jo was really expecting a story about this Alicia character. Sean started out by saying, "In Italy during World War II, an American Army officer named O'Connor, a big bruiser of a man, met a lovely, young school teacher in a small town near Rome. Nature took its course and after the war they married and moved to the States. Eventually, they had a daughter named Alicia. Alicia inherited her size and her fair skin from her father. From her mother, she inherited her black hair, her dark, flashing eyes and her great figure. Alicia just exuded sensuality. Wherever she went, Alicia turned heads. If she said a few words to a male of the species, he was completely under her control."

After sipping his B&B, Sean continued, "She and I were in the same class at M.U. Two weeks into the first semester of my junior year, we sat next to each other at an Honor's Convocation. Since the seats were placed tightly together in the auditorium, our bodies rubbed up against each other for the ninety minutes of the program. Being male, I couldn't but like the feel of her warm, fleshy thighs pressing firmly against mine. After Alicia and I, as well as Connie and a few other students, received our certificates for having maintained a perfect 4.0 G.P.A. during our first four semesters of work at M.U., the dean began an oration that was longer than anything that Cicero ever dreamed of giving. As the dean droned on and on, Alicia slipped me a note. The note read something like: *I understand that you and Connie broke up. I'm not seeing anyone right now, either. Where do you want to take me on Saturday night?* Just in case I was a little slow on the uptake, I felt her foot massaging my leg. Surprise! I asked her out."

Jo asked, "Did your first date with Alicia go well."

Sean replied, "In retrospect, too well."

Jo asked, "What do you mean?"

"I was about twenty years old when I met Alicia. She was every young man's dream. I learned the hard way that getting what you've dreamed of doesn't always lead to happiness."

"Sean, would you describe her in greater detail?"

"I'll have no trouble there. Alicia had a very pretty round face with a short nose and a mouthful of bright white teeth. She was 5'10" barefoot. Her long, dark black hair went down almost to her backside. Her hair contrasted perfectly with her skin, which was almos. cream colored. She was probably fifteen pounds overweight, but had curves in all the right places. She was stunningly beautiful."

"Sean, somethin' tells me that your relationship with her had its problems."

Sean asked, with a wry smile, "Jo, what gave that away?"

"Precious, you know how intuitive we ladies are," Jo said, with a gentle laugh.

"Besides all of those wonderful attributes, I discovered slowly over time that Alicia had a very mercurial personality. Depending on the hour of the day, she was either madly in love or very angry with me. Whatever her mood was, it was passionate."

Sensing that Sean was relaxing a bit, Jo asked, "I'll bet you were head over heels in love, weren't you?"

Sean replied, "I certainly was. Alicia was very beautiful, intelligent, intuitive, passionate, emotionally demanding and very affectionate. I was completely enraptured by her."

Sipping his drink, Sean continued, "I learned an awful lot of good about life and love from Alicia. If I didn't please her, she never played mind games with me. After she chewed me out, she told me why she was upset and let me know what to do better in the future. After secretive, dishonest Connie, Alicia was a welcome change of pace. By the time that I graduated, we had the relationship pretty well down pat and were talking about getting married after I finished my first year in law school and she received her Masters."

Jo asked, "What was her major?"

Sean replied, with a perplexed look on his face, "Go figure this one out. She was a Math major."

"I always thought that female Math majors were all nerds with no interest in people or fun," Jo said.

Sean added, "Her area of interest was Statistics, rather than pure Math, if that changes anything."

Jo stood for a second and stretched in a very feline manner. When she finished stretching, Jo asked, "Did the physical separation break you two apart?"

Sean replied, "No, it didn't. We had that first semester divided up so that one weekend each month, one of us would fly in to see the other. It was expensive, but student discount fares made it possible. The last one of our rendezvous weekends was in the beginning of December. When I dropped her off at the airport, we agreed that my first evening back from S.U., we would get together and discuss where to buy an engagement ring. We spoke a number of times on the phone after that and everything seemed really great. She had even begun checking out job possibilities in the University City area for the next academic year."

"Precious, what happened?" Jo asked, with wide-eyed curiosity.

After finishing his first round, Sean poured himself another. After taking a deep drink from the second round, he continued, "The drive back home from S.U. was a long day and a half trek. I drove long and hard on the first day after exams, wanting so much to see Alicia again. That night, I called Alicia from my motel. I told her that if a snowstorm hadn't been forecast for the night, I would have tried to drive straight through to her because I missed her so much. I was surprised when Alicia told me very calmly that I had acted wisely in getting a motel room for the night. I didn't notice then because of my exhaustion, but looking back, there was something odd in Alicia's tone of voice. Her voice was calm and flat, displaying none of her usual earthy passion."

"Anyway, I remember that the conversation ended with me telling Alicia that I was going to get a good night's sleep and leave around mid-morning the next day, once the snow storm had passed and the main roads were clear again. Anticipating that I had about a five-hour drive ahead of me, we planned that I would meet her at her place at 4:00 p.m. We decided to have an early supper at our favorite Italian place. She told me that she would call ahead for reservations for us. That is how the call ended. I remember that night in the motel vividly. All night I kept waking up, wishing that Alicia were there with me. I missed her so much."

Leaning forward, Jo asked, "What happened the next day?"

With a sad tone in his voice and a sadder expression on his face, Sean said, "When I knocked on her apartment door, her roomie opened the door and said that Alicia hadn't told her anything about a visitor coming by. She was just about to turn me away, when she recognized me. Her roomie, Cheryl Nieman, and I had been in the Honors Program together. She invited me in and told me that Alicia wasn't there right then. She kept me company while we waited for Alicia."

Jo interrupted by asking, "Was this Cheryl, your future wife?"

"Yes, my dear, it was. After pouring me a drink and one for herself, Cheryl and I chatted. As we chatted, I recall noticing that she was very attractive in a way unlike Alicia. Cheryl was 5'8," slim, very athletic looking and leggy. I remember when we were sitting at the table in their apartment, Cheryl was a bit embarrassed because she was wearing ratty old sweat clothes and no make up. I remember that night she looked really good with her hair wrapped up around her head casually. I also remember that she had bare feet with very long toes and a fresh coat of polish on her toe nails. It's funny how some things just stick in your memory."

After another deep draft of his drink, Sean continued, "I remember that we talked for a bit about law schools because Cheryl was thinking about going to law school after she finished her M.A. in Economics in the spring of the next year. I remember her asking me about the law school at S.U. in some detail because she said that it looked to her like a good school."

Looking Jo squarely in the eye, Sean said, "This is where my memory starts to get a bit fuzzy. I sort of remember finishing my first drink with Cheryl and her pouring me another one. I think that I remember it was sometime after 5:00 p.m. when I finished the rest of my second drink. Then, I remember her saying something about Alicia probably wouldn't be coming back to the apartment that night. I think I can remember Cheryl telling me that right before Alicia had received my telephone call, she had gotten a call from a previous boyfriend. Cheryl said that she was pretty sure Alicia and the old boyfriend were back together because right after Alicia ended her conversation with me the previous night, she packed a suitcase and left. Alicia hadn't been back since then."

"Precious, what happened?' Jo asked, with obvious concern in her voice.

"Beautiful, I have no clear recollection. From what Cheryl told me later, when she had mentioned that Alicia was back with her previous boyfriend, I passed out cold on the floor. Cheryl said that she was able to rouse me just enough to get me to lie down on her bed with a lot of help from her. She told me that when the shock of Alicia's abandonment finally hit me, I cried inconsolably for a while. She said that she then managed to get enough booze into me to allow her to put my head on her chest and rock me to sleep like a baby. Cheryl told me that she wouldn't let me leave the next morning until she had fed me and was sure that I could safely drive to where my dad and stepmother lived out in the country."

After drinking a bit more, Sean said, "I do remember Cheryl calling me that afternoon to see if I had made it home okay."

Jo asked, "Did you ever hear from Alicia again?"

Sean said, "Alicia called me several days later to apologize for standing me up like she had. I told her that if she had been at her apartment and told me there she was leaving me to go back to a previous boyfriend, I probably wouldn't have taken it any better. I remember her asking if we could get together so she could explain the situation to me. I remember telling her that the next time I wanted to see her would be in **HELL!** I remember hanging up the phone and going into my room to cry my eyes out. I never saw her again! And I've never regretted my decision to not see her for one last time."

Sensing that Sean needed a minute to regain his control, Jo took a break. When she came back to the table, Sean looked much better. Jo asked, "Are you thinking about Cheryl?"

Sean replied, "No, I'm thinking about the lady before Cheryl, a lady who never treated me any way but good and is still my friend."

After waiting for a second, Jo said, "I'm all ears!"

Sean began, "You know the jogging course that runs around the edge of the Southern campus?"

"Sure. I've jogged on it many times."

Sean continued, "Well, once I arrived on campus, I jogged that course early in the morning before class on weekdays. On Saturdays, I jogged it in the middle of the morning. When you jog at a set time, you get to know the regulars who jog at the same time that you do. After a few Saturdays, I had made the acquaintance of a very lovely British lady doctor. The Saturday before the change from Daylight Savings Time to Standard Time, she asked me if I would change my routine and jog with her in the late afternoons during the week, so she wouldn't have to run alone in the dark. I agreed. By the end of November, we knew a good deal about each other. One Saturday, after we jogged, she invited me to her place for something to eat. We talked and talked and had a really good time."

Jo asked, "Are you talking about Dr. Daphne Hollingsworth?"

Sean said slowly, "Yes." After a second's pause, he said, "That's right, I gave you her name for your friend a few weeks ago." Sean continued, "After Alicia and I went our separate ways, I left my dad and stepmother's place a few days after Christmas, much to my dad's displeasure. I just had to get away—far away. I figured my apartment and the S.U. campus wouldn't remind me of Alicia like the Midwestern City area did. When I arrived here, I called Dr. Daphne to let her know that I was back in town, in case she needed a jogging partner. I suspect that the first time she saw me after my hasty return, she saw right through me—but, said nothing. After our Friday jog on the week that I returned, she asked me if I had lunch plans for Saturday. Since classes hadn't started up again, I was free as a bird, so I accepted her invitation to lunch."

Jo inquired, "Did she get you to open up?"

"No, she didn't play shrink with me. She asked me while we were eating if I considered her to be my friend or my doctor because she couldn't be both to me. When I told her that I considered her to be my friend, I remember that she gave me a dazzling smile. After lunch was over, we had a few ales. Afterwards, she gave me a great neck, shoulder and back massage. It must have done some good because that night, I had my first good night's sleep since Alicia abandoned me. The next week, I asked Daphne if I could reciprocate the luncheon invitation. She accepted. I prepared some French dishes that my mother had taught me to make. We had a great time."

Jo inquired, "Sean, you can cook, too?"

Sean replied, "Not as well as your average French housewife, but I do know my way around a kitchen." As Sean said this, Jo made a mental note that she was going to need to buy a couple of cookbooks since cooking wasn't something that had interested her much. Jo could cook enough to get by, but couldn't cook anything fancy.

Sean continued, "The next week, I asked Daphne for a real, honest to God, boy-girl date. I was afraid that she was going to laugh at me and tell me I was so young that she had had her first kiss before I learned to read. Mercifully, she graciously accepted. After that, we saw each other fairly regularly. We became close friends, the age difference notwithstanding."

Jo asked, "Was the age difference as big as the one between you and me?"

Sean, being serious, said, "I was barely twenty-three. She was more than ten years older. At the age I was then, the age difference seemed huge. I suspect that if I had been a few years older, I wouldn't have been bothered by it at all. You're at that stage now, I hope."

Jo said sweetly, "If I wasn't, do you think we'd be sittin' here right now?"

Sean added, "Never hurts to check. When classes started, I found out that I had aced every exam and ranked first in my class. I was amazed. I was even more amazed when my Civil Procedure professor talked to me after class a week or so after the new semester began. He told me that some lawyer friends of his were about to file a case in which they were going to challenge the constitutionality of a municipal ordinance. Professor Cornish told me that he was assisting them on the trial level, but would handle the appeal himself. He asked me to be his research assistant that summer, helping him work on his brief. Seeing an opportunity to avoid spending a painfully long summer in Midwestern City doing meaningless grunt work for some large law firm, I jumped at the opportunity. Of course, it also gave me a chance to be with Daphne for the summer."

Jo said, "Sean, I'll bet that you had a great summer."

"Jo, that summer was the first truly happy summer that I'd had since my mother died. My summers with Alicia were fun and exciting, but for some reason—probably self-preservation—I never truly relaxed. Every weekend, Daphne and I either traveled to the beach or to the mountains. By the end of the summer, I had half-way convinced myself that I should propose, even though that meant fatherhood in the relatively near future."

Very hesitantly, Jo asked, "What happened?"

"Destiny took a hand. When school started at the end of August, each second-year student was assigned a first-year student to mentor. They tried to match students by home states and undergraduate schools, so I drew a 1L named Cheryl Nieman as my mentee. We were both surprised."

"Sean, did this cause problems for you and Daphne?"

"No, it didn't since Cheryl and I kept the relationship very professional for the first semester. Actually, this was pretty easy to do. Cheryl was scared to death because she actually believed the stuff that they threw at her during orientation."

Pausing for a second, Sean continued, "After her first semester grades were posted at the beginning of the second semester, Cheryl was in the same spot that I had been a year before—first in her class. After that, she relaxed. One day, we had a long talk and discussed our feelings for each other. I told her that I was seeing someone else and needed some time to think. After a few days, I told Cheryl that I was going to end the other relationship on the chance that ours would work out."

Looking deeply into Jo's eyes, Sean said, "I was so afraid that I was going to hurt Daphne when I told her that I wanted to end our relationship. I was really relieved when she told me that she had always known our relationship was doomed, but that she had hoped against hope that she was wrong. We parted very amicably. She and I guest teach for each other and get together for lunch several times a year. She is still one of my closest friends. It just wouldn't have worked. I was just starting out in life and lacked the maturity to juggle the long hours and stresses of being a law student or a young lawyer with fatherhood. I know that I did the right thing, painful though it may have been for both of us."

As Sean took a tissue to his eyes, which were tearing, Jo noticed that talking about Alicia hadn't brought tears to his eyes, but talking about Daphne did. Jo observed to herself that Sean obviously needed more in a woman than a great body. He apparently needed depth and tenderness.

After Sean recovered, he continued his story. When Sean started talking about Cheryl, Jo was more than a bit nervous as to what Sean's mood would be. He said, "Jo, once again, the law school seemed to play Cupid for Cheryl and me. I had accepted a clerkship with a firm in Capitol City for the summer, so I knew where I was going to be. As soon as the class rankings were released, Cheryl received an offer from our Con Law professor to be his research assistant that summer for a book he was writing. Thanks to her summer job, we had two months together."

Jo asked, "How was it?"

Sean replied, "It was truly wonderful. We were young and very much in love."

Jo asked, "When you went back to class, did things continue?"

Sean answered, "Very much so. Since she and I were both on the law review, we were practically inseparable."

Jo asked, "When did you two tie the knot?"

Sean answered, "After the bar exam, which was at the end of July, I planned to veg out. Cheryl's summer internship in Capitol City ended in the middle of August. So, we decided to take a couple of weeks off since my clerkship with Justice Brown at the Supreme Court wouldn't start until the beginning of September. A few days after the bar exam, after I had caught up on my sleep, Cheryl proposed. I offered no resistance since I loved her with all my heart. We had a JP marry us one evening with no fanfare."

Jo remarked, "Sean, I'm a little surprised that you didn't get married in church."

Sean said, "You aren't nearly as surprised as our parents were. We had the Devil to pay with them and with Holy Mother Church. But, eventually, everything worked out."

At that, Jo stood up and refilled both of their glasses with Diet Coke. When she came back to the table, she asked, "Was your marriage happy?"

Sean said, "Jo, that isn't really a fair question to ask someone who was married for nearly twenty-five years. Marriage is a big part of anyone's life, if he or she is serious about it. Have you ever known anyone who was consistently happy for twenty-five years—married or single? I never have. Did we have problems, issues, disagreements and arguments? Of course we did. But, were we happy overall? Definitely! I am not sorry that we married. I miss her and always will."

Jo said, "I'm sorry if I've made you think about your loss."

"Jo, I've got to learn to deal with it. Life goes on, which is why we are sitting here together tonight."

After a few minutes of hand holding, Jo noticed the time. A minute later, they went off to sleep in their separate rooms. Sean slept very deeply. Jo was tormented by her recurring dream.

✳✳✳✳✳✳✳✳✳✳✳✳

On Saturday evening, a tired and tan Jo and Sean were sitting around his kitchen table eating take-out Mexican food. Sean said, "Your friend Maggie certainly throws a good party, doesn't she?"

Jo said, "She's thrown me a challenge for next year."

Sean asked, "What?"

"Well, she took me aside after the volleyball game and said that once we were married, I needed to host the next get together out here as a pool party."

With a mock scowl on his face, Sean asked, "Did you talk out of turn?"

"No Sean, but Maggie and I are best friends. She can put two and two together as well as anyone."

Sean asked, "Am I that obvious?"

"Precious, you're a man. You can't help it. Besides, once I told Maggie how we went to church together on Easter, she drew the obvious conclusion."

Sean inquired, with a tone of confusion in his voice, "Obvious conclusion?"

"Precious, proper and respectable men don't ask women to go to church with them if they aren't serious. Trust me on that one." Jo added, "That

160

reminds me, I've talked to Father Wilson about convertin'. He gave me a book to read on the subject. Religion won't be an issue for us."

"Oops! I guess that I should have mentioned the subject earlier."

Jo replied, "That was equally my fault. Talkin' about church made me think about it."

"No problem," Sean said.

"Sean, did you have a good time today?"

"Jo, any day that a busty, redhead like Maggie pops out of her bikini top while scoring the winning point in a volleyball game is a good day in my book. Ouch! That hurt!"

"Sean, a gentleman, which bein' a Yankee you can never hope to aspire to become, wouldn't have noticed!"

"I noticed that the local boys at the party noticed, too!" Sean retorted.

"But, they were more circumspect," Jo said, giggling.

Sean changed the subject by saying, "Until today, I didn't realize that Maggie was married to a doctor. How did they meet?"

"Back when Maggie was a sergeant in the patrol division, she visited one of her deputies in the hospital after bein' in a wreck in a high-speed pursuit. Her future husband was a resident on the case."

"You know, he's a great guy for a doctor!"

Jo responded, "That's funny! Maggie said that he told her you were okay for a lawyer." After the laughter stopped, Jo said, "You were a real big hit with my friends. They said that you weren't stuffy at all."

"Is that all they said?" Sean asked.

"Okay, a couple of them thought that you had a great sense of humor. And Darla, the trashy blonde, said you were awfully cute. Happy?"

Sean said, "Now I feel better. Having a group of attractive women praising you by saying that you aren't stuffy doesn't do a lot for a man's ego. I guess praise like that is the equivalent to saying a girl makes all of her own clothes."

"Okay. Darla told me that she thought you were a keeper."

"I'm much happier now. You know, you were the most attractive woman there. But, you had a lot of competition."

"You noticed?" Jo asked, with a hint of mock jealousy in her voice.

"Jo, I spent four hours with a bunch of women in skimpy bikinis and you expect me to not to notice? Besides, I think that I've learned I have a weakness for female cops, thanks to you."

Jo said, "It serves me right for openin' your eyes to those possibilities."

"Beautiful, you do remember me saying that you were the best looking one of the bunch, don't you?"

While playfully hitting Sean's leg with her bare foot, Jo said, "Just say that to yourself twenty times before you go to sleep tonight."

Sean said, "Speaking of sleep, we'd best turn in now. Normally, I'm up at six on Sunday mornings. What time do you want me to get you up?"

Jo said, "Six will be fine for me, too."

Just as they were about to turn in, Jo suddenly asked Sean, "Did you really have a good time today?"

Sean said, "I had a great time. Why do you ask?"

Jo, looking a trifle anxious, said, "I was afraid that ropin' you into singin' *Good Will Win in the End* with me was a bit much. I hope that I didn't embarrass you too bad."

Looking deeply into Jo's hauntingly beautiful blue eyes, Sean said, "Give me credit for having at least half of a brain. By the time our second date was over, I figured out that being with you will never be dull. With you, spontaneity is part of the package. I've learned to accept that."

Just as they were about to go their separate ways, Sean said, "I guess that we had better learn all the lyrics of *Good Will Win in the End*, so you don't have to lug two copies of the song with you in your purse, just in case someone asks us to sing the song again. Did I do okay?"

"Precious, in song—like in life—our harmony is perfect."

After a rather long goodnight kiss, they both went off to sleep in their respective bedrooms.

After turning in, Sean did what he had been told to do and said to himself over and over that Jo had been the most attractive woman at the party. He never made it past the fourteenth repetition because he fell into a deep sleep. Law stayed with him the entire night.

In the guest bedroom, things were a bit different. Jo tossed and turned. Despite the pills prescribed for her by Dr. Emerson, Jo could not fall asleep. Finally, around 0100 hours, Equity jumped on her bed and laid down right next to Jo, purring very loudly. As millions of humans have learned over the centuries, purring has a very calming effect on troubled psyches. Jo fell asleep next to Equity. Jo didn't sleep long enough to fall into the deep dreams associated with REM sleep, so she avoided her bad dream for once.

****

162

On the ride back from Mass, Sean asked Jo if she was feeling okay because she hadn't said much all day. Jo replied that she just hadn't slept very well.

Once they were back at Sean's place, Sean took out two steaks from the freezer. After they changed into their swimwear, Sean suggested that they sit out by the pool for a while until lunch. Jo agreed, but asked Sean to make a pitcher of Bloody Marys. Sensing that something big was up with Jo, Sean complied. Just as they were about to go out the door to the pool, Jo said, "Silly me! Sean, wait here for a second."

A moment later, Jo returned with a flat, rectangular-shaped object, wrapped up in very expensive looking gift wrap, with a big red bow on top of it. Jo said, "Precious, do you know what today is?"

Without missing a beat, Sean replied, "Do you mean Sunday or do you mean our one month anniversary? In case you mean the latter, wait a second for me."

A minute later, Sean returned from his office carrying a smaller, thicker rectangle, also wrapped up in wrapping paper, but without a bow. After they had exchanged gifts, Sean suggested that Jo should go first in opening hers.

Jo seemed to be really pleased with her gift, a nicely illustrated, hardback anthology of love poems. Jo opened the book and saw that Sean had written a dedication to her. She looked really pleased with what he had written. After she finished gushing about her present, Jo, looking a little bashful, said to Sean, "Precious, if I remember correctly, many of those poets who wrote love poems seemed to think of their loves—true and otherwise—in rather earthy, fleshy ways. Think of my present to you as being along those lines, just in a visual medium."

As Sean began to unwrap the gift, he had no idea what to expect. When the ribbon was peeled away, Jo strongly suggested that he turn the package around 180° degrees. Knowing that a suggestion from one's love, just like one from a flag officer, is an order, Sean complied. When he finished unwrapping the present, Jo said, "Let's see just how good your damn Yankee memory is!"

Sean looked and looked at the present, which was a framed photograph about the width and length of a piece of legal-sized paper. Jo grew concerned by Sean's silence. She hoped that he was trying to place the image, but was afraid that she had crossed over some line and had insulted him.

Just as Jo was about to say something to him, Sean said, "You didn't stop many cars dressed like that? Where were you, out in front of an erectile dysfunction clinic? Jo, in a sleazy sort of way, you were gorgeous dressed like that! How did you learn to wrap your blouse that way? You showed as much skin as you do when you are wearing a tiny bikini top."

Throwing her arms around him, Jo said, "Sean, I'm flattered that you remembered what I said last week. That is one of the nicest compliments you could pay me."

As they went out to the pool with the pitcher of Bloody Marys, glasses and ice bucket in tow, Sean said, "Jo, would it be better for me to display your gift in my office at home or my office in the courthouse?"

"Precious, just how crowded do you want your chambers to be? If you display my present downtown, I'll bet you'll very quickly get to meet all of Bubba's friends and the friends of Bubba's friends, until eventually Bubba would need to request backup to handle crowd control. If you're a good Yankee and put that photo someplace safe—like on the dresser in your bedroom—in a year or so, I might just let you see the shot that had both Darla and me in it."

A smiling Sean asked, "Do you think that I could handle it?"

Jo said, "I'll need a note from your doctor first. By the way, want to guess who stopped the most johns that day?"

Wisely avoiding the trap, Sean just looked blankly at Jo. After a second, he asked, "Jo, just out of curiosity, after all these years, how did you manage to come up with this photo?"

Smiling a big smile, Jo said, "'Cause I had the foresight to bring a disposable camera to work that day. After we got all tarted up, but before the male deputies saw us, we took pictures so we would have somethin' to laugh at in our old age. I gave everyone copies, but I saved the negatives."

"Oh, I see!" Sean said, as he led the way out to the pool.

Since the air temperature hadn't really warmed up enough to allow Jo and Sean to get into the pool, they sat on the edge of the whirlpool with their legs in the water. Sean was wearing a navy-blue and white S.U. sweatshirt over his swimsuit. Jo wore a light State t-shirt over her bright yellow bikini. Once they sat down at the pool, Jo became very quiet. A silent ten minutes passed.

Finally, Jo, crossing her fingers, told herself that it was time to begin. "Precious, do you know what a *mustang* is in the Marine Corps?"

"Jo, that's a former enlisted man who obtains a commission as an officer, right?"

"Right! Daddy joined the Corps right after he finished high school back in '48. He took to the Corps like a duck takes to water. In '52, he was a corporal in Korea. One day, his platoon was ordered to guard a pass. That night, the Chinacoms hit them with everything they had. By the time they were relieved at 1200 hours the next day, he was in command of what was left of the platoon since he was the only non-com still able to fight. After his lieutenant recovered from his wounds, he recommended Daddy for a medal. Right after the Armistice was signed, Daddy received a Medal of Honor."

"Jo, I'm impressed."

"Well, Daddy, being a country boy, would have just as soon have gotten some extra leave instead. But being a good Marine, he did as he was told. After the war, he was stationed in Washington, D.C. His CO took a shine to him and told him that he ought to use his spare time to get an education. So, after five years of night school, Daddy received a degree. His CO recommended Daddy for OCS. So, Daddy spent the rest of his years in the Corps as an officer. Being a country boy, he always felt a bit out of place. But, he must have done something right because he retired as a Colonel."

Sean asked, "How did he meet your mother?"

"My Momma was a Navy nurse in 'Nam. They got married right as her commitment for active duty was about to end. A few months later, her rather eccentric, old-maid aunt—a retired school teacher, who reportedly never spent a dime that she didn't have to spend—died and left her life savin's to Momma. Momma bought our farm with the money. When Daddy retired from the Corps, we already had been livin' on the farm for a bunch of years."

Sean asked, "Did you like growing up in the country?"

"I loved it. I was the oldest child. My brothers arrived several years later. I went to school in a little country schoolhouse. Everyone was just plain folks. No one put on any airs. Unfortunately, my life went downhill when I started high school."

Sean, not wanting to interrupt the flow, simply asked, "Why?"

"Well, our high school had kids from both the country and from the small town nearby. Most of the kids from the small town had fathers who were doctors, lawyers, bankers, business owners or big landowners, so they looked down on us country kids. Since I was an athlete, I had to hang around with the jocks, which was social death."

Sean asked, "Any boyfriends back then?"

Jo answered, "Not really anythin' serious. The problem was that the jocks weren't real bright. They were a lot of fun, but didn't have much ambition or interest in school."

Sean said, "Jo, as I recall, you said that your father didn't want you to go to college at State. Why?"

"Well, he rightly sensed that a country girl like me wouldn't like bein' with all the city types at State. He wanted me to go to a smaller school near home. But, being my Daddy's daughter, I ignored him and went to State."

"Jo, I gather that you didn't like State."

"Precious, I hated my first two years. Since I was on the track team, the only guys that I met were jocks. They were as dumb and unambitious as the jocks back in high school. Plus, all they wanted was to get in my pants. I didn't let them. So, the word got out that I was gay."

"You?" Sean asked, with a big laugh.

"Well, majorin' in Criminal Justice didn't help any. The rumor on campus was that all of the girls who majored in it were either sluts or gay. Since I wasn't a slut, a lot of guys assumed that I must be gay."

Sean said, "Something tells me that a man must have entered your life about this time."

Chapter Nine

"Precious, I'm gonna start watchin' you real close. You know me too well. Anyway, it all started innocently enough. The first semester of my junior year, I fulfilled a Humanities requirement by takin' an Art History course. I loved the course. The professor was distinguished and handsome."

At this point in the conversation, Sean noticed that Jo's glass was empty. After asking her if she wanted a refill, he poured half a glass for both of them. He also made a mental note that when they had finished this round, it would be time to begin cooking the steaks and the baked potatoes.

Jo continued, "Sean, remember that cute teacher that I'd mentioned?"

"How could I forget?"

"Well, his name was Antoine Mercier. I didn't know then that he was a famous art historian. I found out later that State paid big bucks to lure him there. All I knew back then was that he was French and charming. The entire semester, even though he was perfectly professional with me, I sensed that he found me attractive. Toward the end of the semester, he asked me to have dinner with him. I jumped at the offer. But, I kept asking myself over and over, *Why would a sophisticated, cultured Frenchman be interested in a dumb ol' country girl like me?*"

Hearing that question, Sean involuntarily started to laugh in mid-swallow, nearly choking on what was left of his Bloody Mary. Recovering, Sean blurted out, "You mean beyond the fact that you were young and beautiful?"

After laughing both at Sean's reaction and her naivety, Jo continued, "Well, I didn't know as much then as I do now."

Sean, now gripped with curiosity, asked, "What happened?"

Jo replied, "The dinner led to a serious relationship with him."

Looking for an escape, Sean suggested that they start cooking. Once the steaks were on the grill and the potatoes in the microwave, Jo continued her narrative by saying, "In April of my senior year, he proposed to me."

Sean asked, "What happened?"

Jo replied, "When he proposed, I was taken aback. I was just twenty-two. I asked for a few days to clear my head. I was full of questions. Not knowin' what else to do, I did what everyone else does when they need to do research. I went to the library and looked up everythin' that I could find about him. What I saw convinced me that it would never work."

Curious, Sean asked, "What did you find?"

"Well, I found out that back when he was in France, he was active in protestin' various American policies. He was quoted as sayin' some really vile and nasty things about America."

Sean asked, "Is that what broke you two up—politics?"

As they started to eat their salads, Jo said laughingly, but with a hint of bitterness, "What really did it for me was learnin' that he had two ex-wives and three children. In all of our time together, he never mentioned any of them even once. I started to figure that in five or ten years, I'd be his third ex-wife, probably stuck in France with a couple of kids, surrounded by anti-American Frenchmen. That just didn't cut it for me."

Sean and Jo ate their steaks and baked potatoes in silence. After the meal was over, Jo asked, "Wanna go to the whirlpool?"

After about five minutes of basking in the sunshine and the warm water, Jo said, "Tony—he hated that name!—was my first love. I still have mixed feelin's about him. My next love was about as different as could be from Tony."

Sensing that Jo was in deep thought, Sean said, "Okay. I'm here for you."

After a minute or two, out of left field, Jo said, "I'll bet that sometime after you passed the bar you bought life insurance."

Genuinely surprised, Sean said, "Sure."

Jo said, "And I'll bet that you bought it from Abe Goldberg, right?" Sean said, "Right, again. How did you know that?"

Jo said, "Wives just naturally know these things." Now that Jo had Sean's complete attention, she continued, "After I broke up with Tony, I directed all my efforts to gettin' in shape for the academy. I guess that I prepared well enough because I finished at the top of my class. After graduation, I was a probationary deputy for six months, workin' with a T.O. After that time, I was assigned to patrol in the First Precinct—the area around downtown and the S.U. campus. After a few months on patrol, I started to realize that I didn't have much of a personal life. Except for my friends from the academy and the few that I'd made on the job, I really didn't know anybody in University City. One day, that changed in the strangest way."

Sean inquired, "What happened?"

Jo responded, "I answered a routine call at an insurance agency located in one of those converted warehouses at the north end of downtown. A young lady, who worked at the agency, had just bought her first new car. On the same day that she took delivery, someone knocked out her front window and stole the radio from the car. My job was to write up the incident, so she would have a report to file with her insurance company. When I arrived, she was in tears, so her boss—Abe—helped her through the situation and acted as host to me. I was really impressed with how protective he was of her. A few days later, I received a very nice, handwritten thank you card from him, tellin' me that my assistance and professionalism had been appreciated by both of them. Sean, you know how rarely anyone in law enforcement is ever thanked or appreciated? I was flattered."

Sean replied, "I'll bet you were. I know how I appreciate the few thank you cards that I've received from jurors and litigants."

Jo continued, "So, a few weeks later, when Abe called to invite me to lunch on my next weekday off duty, I wasn't totally surprised. When I told him that I wasn't in the market to buy life insurance, his reply surprised me."

Smiling, Sean said, "I'll bet Abe had a good response ready."

Jo said, "He asked me if I arrested or investigated everyone that I met. When I told him that I didn't, Abe said that he didn't try to sell a policy to everyone that he met either. Intrigued, I took him up on lunch."

Sean said, "Let me guess, he was charming to no end."

"You're right on that one. We had a great time. When the lunch ended, he asked me to go out to dinner a week or so later. Since I had been so charmed, I accepted his invitation. The dinner was even more fun. Abe kept me in stitches, telling me stories about the big adjustments that he—a boy from New York City—had to make when he arrived at S.U. on his scholarship. What really surprised me the most were his stories about his time as an Army officer in Korea. Sean, did you know that he was decorated twice for valor?"

Sean replied, "Even though I knew Abe fairly well for twenty years, I never knew that."

"After the war, he had no desire to go back to New York. He surprised his family when he came back to University City and started in the insurance business here."

Changing the topic slightly, Sean asked, "I gather that you kept on seeing him?"

"Definitely! We'd go to a movie, a play, the symphony or an art exhibit twice a month for about a year or so. We were friends. I really enjoyed bein' with him. My intuition told me that he surely enjoyed my company, as well. One night over dinner, Abe surprised me by talkin' about his personal life. He told me about his late, first wife slowly wastin' away a few years before.

He told me about bein' childless because of her ill health. I felt really sorry for him. When he proposed to me, I was surprised."

Sean remarked, "You were still naïve, weren't you?"

Jo replied, "I guess so. Abe told me that if we got married and anyone found out about it, everyone would think that I was a gold-digger. He asked how I would feel about keepin' our marriage a secret, not tellin' anyone who didn't have a legal right to know about it. After thinkin' about it for a week or so, I agreed to his condition. We slipped north—just across the state line—on my next weekday off and got married. He only told his life insurance company and his lawyer about it. I only notified the department's personnel office about my marriage, as I was required to do under departmental regulations. Abe told me a couple of weeks later that he had made the right moves, so that if somethin' happened to him, I would be taken care of for life."

Sean asked, "Did you talk about having a family?"

Jo replied, "Abe couldn't have children. Because of his first wife's health, he had had a vasectomy years before. Besides, when you are in your mid-sixties, the idea of startin' a family doesn't really sound very smart, does it?"

Sean nodded his head and asked, "How long were you two married?"

Jo replied, "A bit over three years. He bought me the house that I live in now. He figured that if I had my own place and kept my own name, people would be thrown off the track. It was a bit of a hassle livin' a double life, but we were happy."

Sean asked, "How did Abe die?"

Jo said, without any affect, "Two days after my promotion to sergeant was announced, Abe was on his way to a business meetin'. A drunk broadsided his Lincoln™. Abe died instantly. The drunk only did five years for his crime."

Pausing for a second, Jo stated, "Sean, I think that another Bloody Mary would be a good idea 'bout now. In case you're wonderin', I brought a change of clothes for tomorrow, so don't worry about havin' to drive me back home tonight."

A moment later, Sean appeared with a tray holding a pitcher of Bloody Marys, two fresh glasses, an ice bucket and some munchies. After Jo decided that she wanted to sit out in the sun, they stretched out on Sean's poolside recliners.

After taking a deep drink from her glass, Jo continued by saying, "Sean, this is when my life really started gettin' complicated. A secret marriage to an older man brought me complications enough for one lifetime, but things got worse. A few days after Abe died, his lawyer contacted me. Abe had left me the house free and clear of any debt. I was overwhelmed by his kindness. But, what really surprised me was that Abe, who left the bulk of his estate to Southern University, also left me some money in what you lawyers call a *marital deduction trust* with Southern State Bank as the trustee."

Sean's professional curiosity was piqued. He knew that Southern State Bank normally only agreed to serve as trustee for estates of seven figures or more.

Jo continued, "Sean, he left me **seven million dollars**. Do you know what a shock that was? My entire life, I grew up feelin' poor—or at least not comfortable. All of a sudden, I had money. I had to make choices about my life that I never had to make before. You know what a responsibility that is?"

Smiling a knowing smile, Sean nodded his head. After taking another sip, Jo said, "Under the terms of the trust, I receive the income quarterly. The trustee can dip into the body of the trust if I need the money for some reason, like I'm sick or somethin'. I get to decide who gets the money when I die. The bank directed me to a lawyer, who drew me up a nice will."

Sean asked gingerly, "Do you let the bank handle the income that you don't spend?"

Jo continued, "Well, when I received my first quarterly check from the bank, I damn nearly fainted. Just to be sure that they hadn't made some sort of math mistake, I called them. They said that it was right. So, once I had deposited that first check in the bank, I realized that I needed to learn about investments. I guess I could have taken the bank up on its offer to handle that money, too. But bein' my father's daughter, I wanted to handle it on my own. So, I spent all of my off-duty time for about two months readin' up on investin'."

Jo continued, "When I finally felt comfortable with handlin' my money, I called up Abe's friend, Norman, a stockbroker. We've got me in a money market account, a bond fund and four different stock funds. I've learned a lot about asset allocation since then. Since I started gettin' the checks, I've invested most of what the bank sends me. It's added up nicely. My own investin' has been better than the bank's."

After Jo stopped talking, she noticed that Sean had a pensive look on his face. When Jo asked him what he was thinking about, Sean said, "I'd never really thought about this, but since you trusted me to discuss your finances, I guess now would be a good time to say something about mine."

Jo blurted out, "Sean, you don't' have to tell me anythin' if you don't want to."

Sean said, "No, I guess that I have nothing to hide since it is all in the public record."

Protesting, Jo said, "Sean, I've always assumed that you aren't worried about your next meal. You don't have to talk about it, really. My not bein' a poor ol' country girl doesn't bother you, does it?"

Sean said, "No dear, I love you for who you are, not your money. But, I don't want to go into marriage with any secrets. Later on, I'll show you my disclosure form. Suffice it to say that I picked my ancestors well. I'm considerably wealthier than you."

After a second, Jo started laughing and said, "Okay. I guess that both of our mothers told us you can love a rich person just as well as a poor one. Sean, I'm guessin' that you never seriously considered retirin' for the same reason that I never thought about leavin' the department. We both want to be useful and have somethin' meanin'ful to do with our lives." Sean nodded.

Jo told Sean that she wanted to swim for a bit. After her swim, she asked Sean if he minded if she just lay on her stomach for a bit and caught the rays silently. Sean agreed. Once she had rolled over, she asked Sean to let her know when thirty minutes were up. Jo also asked Sean to undo her top and to rub suntan lotion on her back and legs. As Sean rubbed the lotion on her shoulders, he felt the tension in her body, particularly the neck and back muscles. Sean said nothing.

Thirty minutes later, Sean told her that her time was up and silently helped Jo put her top back on. Saying nothing, Jo jumped in the pool and swam several laps. When Jo emerged from the pool, she asked Sean if it would be agreeable if they went in the house and sat on the sofa.

They reentered the house together, with Sean carrying the tray. Once they were back in the house, Jo asked Sean if she could have a blanket to wrap herself up in. Moments later, Sean complied by bringing Jo a large blanket. Sean, after turning the setting on the air conditioning way up, returned in a long, white cotton robe.

After Sean returned, they sat in silence for ten minutes or so. The entire time that they were sitting there, Jo just looked out the window, avoiding eye contact with Sean. Suddenly, Jo said, "My TO told me this a long time ago. He said that when you are about to go chargin' into a suspect's place, fear is normal. He told me that if I ever felt myself freezin' up, I should just ask myself if I thought that I was gonna live forever. Here goes nuthin'."

Sean, not knowing what to do or say, just looked supportively at Jo, who said, "After Abe died, one of the books that I read about investin' told me that one of the important things in investin' is to read business publications. So, I probably became the only person in our department to take out a subscription to *The Wall Street Journal*. The book also said that it would be helpful to take a course in investin'. So I signed up for a class at S.U. in their continuin' education division. Our teacher was a Harvard M.B.A. and president of an investment company. He was also a man with a famous last name in these parts, Covington McReynolds."

Sean said, "He's the great grandson of one of the Founders,[11] right?"

Jo added, "He is the only livin' descendant of his great grandfather."

Sean said, "If I remember right, the McReynolds family made their money in timber and railroads."

"I think you're right about that, too. Anyway, because I came to class in uniform—I was workin' graveyard back then—I sort of stood out. Also, since I was the only person in the class on the sunny side of forty-five, Covey couldn't help but notice me. Back then, he was in his late thirties. After our last class was over, he asked me out. I had doubts about goin' out with him since I still hadn't totally gotten over Abe's death. But, I figured that I had never been out with a man who cut as fine a figure as Covey did, so I agreed to a date. I guess the combination of bein' 6'4", handsome, impeccably well dressed and havin' all the right credentials and family connections was just too much for a little ol' country girl to resist."

Jo continued after a deep sip of her drink, her voice still emotionless, "Our date worked out just fine. He was charmin'. Even though my research of the *University City Bugle's* gossip column—you know, the one we were in—suggested that he changed women about as often as my Daddy changes oil in his pick-up truck, I sensed that there was somethin' deeper to him."

Jo shifted position on the sofa, uncrossing and recrossing her long, tan legs, which kept coming out of the blanket. Sean never noticed, his gaze never moving from Jo's eyes.

"We dated for over a year. During that whole time, Covey was a complete gentleman with me. Although he put his arm around me in movies and kissed me good night, he never once made any sexual moves on me. I was quite unclear if he lacked interest or what. After a while, I decided that his reputation for bein' a skirt chaser may have been over stated."

After a sip of her drink, Jo added, "Just about the time that I was starting to wonder if our relationship was gonna lead to anythin', Covey invited me to spend a Saturday at his cabin in the woods. He spent the afternoon tellin' me his life story. It was really sad."

Sean asked, "How so?"

Jo said, "His father's parents arranged his father's marriage to his mother, who was a Richmond Belle of impeccable lineage, but short on cash. Apparently, the relationship never clicked. They only had one child—Covey. When Covey was fourteen, his father died when his small plane crashed into a mountainside. The death was ruled an accident, but Covey suspected that his father, who was a very experienced flyer—a decorated former naval aviator—had flown too low deliberately. His father's will, which was part of some sort of contract that their families had insisted they sign before they got married, left half of the estate to his mother. The other half went to Covey in trust, but his mother had control over it until he turned fifty."

Jo continued, "Poor Covey, his mother rode him ragged. He told me about several women that he had brought home to meet his mother. She had always found something wrong with them. She insisted that Covey needed to do like his father had done and marry someone that his mother picked. He refused. He was miserable."

Sean added, "Are you familiar with Edward Arlington Robinson's poem, *Richard Corey*?"

Jo said, "I am. It really applied to his life." After setting down her empty glass, Jo continued, "Covey really shocked me with what he said next. He told me that I was the first woman that he ever met who was strong enough to stand up to his mother. He asked me if I was willin' to marry him under those circumstances. When I told him that I was, we started plannin' how he was gonna introduce me to her."

Sean asked, "Did your plan work?"

Jo said, "Surprisingly, it worked really well. There was gonna be a party in a few weeks at the home of one of the other descendants of one of the Founders. I came as Covey's date. He bought me my first pearls to wear to the event. It went really well because no one knew anythin' about me or had read anythin' about me in *Julie's Jewels*. Somehow, I hit it off with his friends. The hostess was most gracious to me. When his mother arrived, she was quite pleasantly surprised that Covey was there with a popular date."

Sean interrupted Jo by asking, "What did you do that made you so popular at the party?"

Jo replied, "I was myself. Since I was wearin' somethin' fairly low cut, I was an immediate hit with the men. I charmed the ladies by tellin' war stories about women cops bustin' bad guys. Somehow, those society types found that to be fascinatin'."

After standing up and stretching for a bit, Jo continued, "A few days later, I received a handwritten invitation from his mother, asking me to lunch with her and Covey the next Saturday. It took me some effort to rearrange my schedule, but I was able to have lunch with them at the McReynolds' mansion."

Spellbound, Sean asked, "How did it go?"

Jo continued, "It went better than I expected. Mrs. McReynolds started off by tellin' me that while she had long hoped Covey would marry within his class, she had come to the conclusion that that was not to be. She told me that she wanted her son to be happy. If marriage to me would make him happy, she was gonna accept it because he was at the age that if he didn't marry soon, he might never give her any grandchildren. At the end of the evenin', she asked me if I would agree to a formal announcement party to be given in about six weeks. Of course, I agreed. She said that she'd work out the details with the University City Country Club. I thought that everythin' went really well."

Sean asked, "I gather that things didn't go according to plan. What happened?"

Jo replied, "The next Monday, right after I came off of graveyard shift, I stopped off at a branch of my bank to use the ATM. It was just a few minutes after the bank opened. When I pulled into the almost deserted parkin' lot, somethin' caught my eye. There was a car sittin' there with its motor runnin' and someone behind the wheel. That was suspicious, by itself. When I glanced at the license plate on the idlin' car, I knew that somethin' was up. I remembered that at the start of my shift the night before, I'd seen paperwork on a stolen car whose license plate was a combination of my birthday and my initials—1005JS. The car in the lot matched the description of the stolen car. For some reason, I remembered the details about that stolen car very well."

A totally captivated Sean asked, "What did you do next?"

Jo replied very calmly, "I parked my SUV a few spaces away, so that I was on the passenger's side of the stolen car. Then, I called in a possible bank robbery in progress on my cell phone. Then, I drew my Glock. After that, I slid down in the passenger's seat and reached around and grabbed my police jacket and put it on. Before I left the SUV, I remembered to put my spare clips and cuffs in the jacket pockets."

Jo paused and asked Sean for a glass of water. After he gave her the water, Jo continued. "Then, I slipped out of the passenger side of my SUV and waited for back up. I didn't have to wait more than a few seconds before all hell broke loose. All at once, two perps came runnin' out the front door of the bank. The one closest to me was holdin' a revolver in his right hand and a large green duffel bag in the other. The one farther away from me—who was in front of the other one by about two paces—was holdin' a 12-gauge with his right hand and was holdin' onto a very frightened young teller with the other. Just then, a patrol car pulled into the entrance to the parkin' lot. Real quick, the perp with the 12-gauge pushed the teller into the flowerbed and fired off one round at the patrol car, shatterin' its front window. Just as he was about to chamber another round—without thinkin'—I double-tapped him. The other perp—the one with the revolver—got one round off at me. Fortunately, he missed badly, firin' way over my head. I fired and hit him in his right shoulder. As soon as he was hit, he dropped his revolver and fell to his knees in howlin' agony, clutchin' his bleedin' shoulder with his left hand."

After taking another sip of water, Jo said, "Durin' the gunfire, the getaway driver tried to escape from the parkin' lot. His bad luck was to try to pull out at the same instant that a second squad car was pullin' into the lot. The deputy in that second squad car disarmed and cuffed him while I approached the two perps in the doorway of the bank. When I approached, I yelled at them to freeze. Neither one of them moved."

Sean, not knowing what exactly to say, asked, "What happened then?"

Jo continued, "Very quickly, actin' on instinct, I kicked the two weapons away from the perps in the doorway while keepin' my Glock pointed at them. Somehow, the deputy from the shot-up patrol car came up to me and covered the two perps while I tried to cuff them. The perp who had been carryin' the money and the revolver had a bad shoulder wound on his right side. He was in too much pain to offer any resistance. When I turned to the other perp, I realized that we didn't need cuffs for him—just a body bag. I then entered the bank to look for any other bad guys that might be hangin' 'round. There weren't any more."

After taking a long sip, Jo resumed, "A few seconds later, it seemed like all of the patrol cars and ambulances in the county arrived at the same time. The parameds said that the perp, who had carried the shotgun, appeared to have taken one round to the heart and one to the carotid artery. They guessed that he was dead by the time his body hit the ground. The other perp survived and lived to be convicted and given twenty years to life. The deputy in the first squad car had wounds to his arm and shoulder, but recovered. The teller was badly shaken, but physically okay."

A very concerned Sean asked, "How were you?"

Jo replied, "Sean, I'm not sure. Physically, I was okay. But, I have only a vague recollection of surrenderin' my Glock to the supervisor on the scene or of talkin' to the detectives. I do remember talkin' to the teller when the detectives were through with us. She was just a little ol' country girl tryin' to get by in the city. I felt so sorry for her."

A very visibly concerned Sean said, "That must have been horrible for her! What did you do then?"

Jo said, "Precious, I'm really not entirely sure. I think that after the detectives were done with me, I went straight home, but I'm not sure. Maybe I got somethin' to eat. I don't remember. I do remember that when I got home, I had so much adrenalin in my system right then that I was 'bout bouncin' off of the walls."

Jo recalled, "First thing that I remember for sure doin' was callin' Covey. He offered to come right over. I told him that I needed some sleep, but asked him to come over that night. I do remember that a few minutes later, just about the time that I was gonna soak in a hot tub with a large B&B, my captain called. He told me that I was on administrative leave until further notice. I had orders to report to the departmental shrink the next mornin'—Tuesday—at 0900 hours. On Thursday mornin' at 0900, I was to go before the shootin' review board."

After pausing for a second, Jo said, "Covey gave me a lot of moral support durin' that horrible week. I'm not sure that I would have made it through the shootin' review board without him. Fortunately, the board ruled that everythin' I had done was righteous. They recommended that I return to duty."

Sean said, "Jo, can I interrupt for a second? I've got a couple of questions for you. First, back before our first date, I looked up your name on the *Bugle's* website. I saw the story where you received a commendation. How come I didn't come across a story about the bank robbery?"

"Sean, I guess it was because you looked me up under *Jolene*. If you would have searched under *Joe Scruggs (with an "e")*, you would have found me. The problem is that you can spell my name, but the idiots at the *Bugle* couldn't."

Sean said, "Okay. How did your meeting with the shrink go? You didn't say anything about it."

Jo replied, "I don't know. I thought it went okay, but I'm not sure because a couple of weeks later, after I returned to duty, I had orders to report to the sheriff. When I arrived, I was offered my current assignment by the sheriff. I suspect that the shrink had some doubts about my mental health."

Looking a bit uneasy, Sean said, "If you don't feel comfortable talking about your session with the shrink, please don't say any more."

Jo said to Sean, "The shrink never said that he was going to give me a bad report. But, since I didn't get to see the report, I'll never know. I suspect that he might have had his doubts about me 'cause he kept pressin' me about if I had any guilt from killin' the one perp and woundin' the other. The more I told him that I was doin' my job as I had been trained to do, the more he acted like he didn't believe me. Then, he started talkin' about repression of bad memories."

Jo explained further, "Sean, it's been eight months. I haven't thought about it for months. I did what I had to do. There was a civilian in danger. An officer was in danger. I did what I was supposed to do. Why should I feel any guilt?"

Looking squarely at her, Sean said, "You did the right thing. Unfortunately, sometimes doing the right thing leaves emotional scars. I don't know. I'm not a shrink. My guess is that if your mind needs to deal with it, it will in its own sweet time."

Rising from the sofa, Jo said, "I see that it's almost 1600 hours. Let's take a break and then go back out to the pool. By now, the sun should be far enough down that we won't have to worry too much about burnin'. Be warned, the bad part is yet to come."

A few minutes, later back at the pool, Sean felt a tight knot in his stomach. He knew that poor Jo had had a rough day. He had doubts that either one of them could handle much more.

But, Jo continued on, "Covey was really supportive through the whole ordeal. I was a little surprised when, right after my first shift once my leave was over—a Friday night/Saturday mornin'—I received a page from Covey at a number that I didn't recognize. As soon as a maid answered the phone, I guessed that he was callin' from his mother's house. He asked me if I could come by to see him there. I suspected that trouble was brewin'. Lord, was I right!"

After shifting a bit in the shallow end of the pool where she was with Sean, Jo said, "Thinkin' back, if I hadn't just been through the week from hell, I would have told him that I was exhausted and needed some sleep. Unfortunately, my judgment wasn't workin' too well right then."

Jo asked Sean to hand her water glass to her. After she took a drink, she said, "When I arrived at his mother's mansion, I must have looked as tired as I felt. His mother offered me breakfast, which I gratefully accepted. While I was eatin', Mrs. McReynolds praised me for my courage and fidelity to duty. I didn't see what was comin' next."

After another sip of water, Jo continued, "After I'd finished breakfast, she invited me and Covey to sit with her in her drawin' room. After a minute or so of small talk, Mrs. McReynolds asked me if I planned to continue to work after Covey and I married. When I said that Covey and I hadn't really talked about it—which was true—Mrs. McReynolds told me that my continued employment might present a problem because, as the wife of a prominent member of the community, I would be expected to engage in a rather gruelin' schedule of charity functions. She indicated to me that she just couldn't see how I could possibly expect to fulfill my spousal duties if I was gonna stay in law enforcement. When I told her that my career was my decision, subject to Covey's input, her response was that I did not seem to sense the difficulties that my continuin' in law enforcement might cause."

Smiling, Sean said, "Beautiful, I guess that she didn't know you well enough to understand that subtlety isn't your strong suit."

Smiling for the first time in several hours, Jo said, "Damn right!"

Then, Jo continued, "Mrs. McReynolds said that she understood the dilemma that her request might be causin' me. She indicated that she understood my reluctance to give up my livelihood, in case the engagement did not work out. She indicated that to relieve any financial pressures that might be botherin' me, she had arranged a solution to my problem. She told me that Mr. Wharton at University City Bank was prepared to offer me a position in their trust department. It would be a good opportunity for me to meet many of the right families in town. And as a further inducement, she handed me a cashier's check for $250,000 made out to me. She said that the only condition attached to the check was that I had to resign from the department at least one week before when our engagement was to be announced."

Sean had a completely blank look on his face when he said, "Jo, just when I thought that I'd heard everything, you go and surprise me with this one. Did she understand what country and century she was living in?"

"Precious, I guess not. After Mrs. McReynolds said that, I told her in no uncertain terms that my life and my career were subjects that only Covey and I would deal with. In response, she told me that Covey was in full agreement with her. At this point, Covey, who so far hadn't said much of anythin', tried to interject somethin' into the conversation. I'll never know what he would have said because as soon as he tried to speak, his mother turned to him and shrieked, *Covey, if you interrupt mother again, you'll have to leave the room. Do you understand?* "

Sean said, "Dare I ask what happened next?"

Jo said, "I told her in no uncertain terms that I would not tolerate her treatin' her son—or anyone else—like that in front of me."

Sipping some more water, Jo said, "I must have hit her hot button because at that she turned to me and said, *Jolene, you'd be wise to remember that my son is a child, a very naughty boy who likes to play with trashy girls with big breasts. He is no more a man than his weaklin' father ever was.*"

A wide-eyed Sean asked very softly, "What did Covey do?"

Jo said very calmly, "He left the room, obviously upset."

Sean pressed, "What happened then?"

Jo said, "This is the **really** weird part. Mrs. McReynolds turned to me and apologized for the unseemly display that I'd just witnessed. She told me that she was sure I would make some nice man very happy, but not her Covey. When I asked her why, she told me there were two reasons why she was certain that I was not suitable for Covey. She said the first reason was that I was too maternal for Covey. A weaklin' like her son needed a strong woman to make him live up to his potential."

Sean said, "I shudder to think what you said back to her."

Jo said, "I very calmly asked if drivin' a man to crash his airplane into a mountainside was an example of how a good wife helped her husband reach his potential."

Sean asked, "How did she react to that?"

"Surprisingly well," responded Jo. "All she said was that in this life, only the strong survive and prosper. If a man is weak, he is better off dead. Then, she told me her other reason. She said I had the spirit and intelligence needed to be a successful wife for Covey. But, sadly, I lacked the social standin' to ever fit in their world. Then, she hit me between the eyes when she said, *Of all the girls from the wrong side of the tracks that Covey has seduced, you are the best by far. I'm so sorry, but whatever you do, you'll just never fit in polite society.*"

Pausing for a second, Jo added, "When I tried to reason with her, Mrs. McReynolds said, *Jolene, America is a great country. If you work hard enough and are smart and lucky enough, someone from a humble background like yours can achieve great things. Sadly, there are some things in life that take more than one generation to achieve. Jolene, I hate to be so blunt, but a girl who was born on a military base and who grew up skinny dippin' in a creek runnin' by a cotton farm will never be accepted in polite society. If you marry well, maybe your daughter can hope to achieve what you can't. I'm terribly sorry to tell you this, but you will never be accepted in our world."*

Sean inquired, "What happened next?"

Jo recounted her final moments in the McReynolds' mansion by saying, "Well, Mrs. McReynolds and I were certainly done speakin'. When I told her that I wanted to see Covey, she sent the maid to fetch him. When Covey arrived—what was left of him—Mrs. McReynolds suggested that if we would be more comfortable, we could visit in their garden. I took her up on her offer."

Sean inquired, "Why did she let you visit with him?"

Jo said, "My guess is that she knew she had already won. She wanted me to see it for myself."

After standing up and stretching, Jo asked if she could have a neck and shoulder massage while she finished up her story. Sean, ever the gentleman, agreed.

Jo continued by saying, "When Covey and I went out into the garden, he'd regained his composure. After he apologized for both his mother's boorishness and his weakness, I told him that his mother was dead set against our marryin'. I asked him whether he still wanted to marry me. When he started pointin' out that his mother held the purse strings of his trust, I surprised the hell out of him by tellin' him about Abe and the money that he had left me. I tried to convince him that with his name and social connections and my money, we could turn his small investment firm into somethin' really big if he immersed himself in it. He was almost persuaded, when his mood changed and he pulled back. When he asked me if he could think about it, I knew it was over. I told him that I would give him until the end of the year. I told him that all he had to do was send me a one-word message saying, *Yes*! He never did. The only communication that I've had with him since that day was a Christmas card with a note apologizin' for the grief that he had put me through. He wished me well and enclosed a clippin' of a book review of a new book on investin' that he thought I might enjoy."

Taking one more sip of water, Jo said, "I'm almost done. After I began at my new position, I threw myself—body and soul—into my new duties.

When Kyra started to try to talk me into meetin' you in early February, I told her that I wasn't interested. It took her six weeks to convince me."

Sean asked, "You resisted Kyra's arm-twisting for six weeks? How did you manage it?"

"Precious, it wasn't easy. My head wasn't in a good place right then. I was afraid that I would say somethin' out of anger and embarrass Kyra and myself."

With a look of recognition, Sean said, "That was why you were the way you were on our first date!"

Jolene said, "Well, I guess I was testin' you. The last thin' I wanted was to get involved with another wimp. The real problem was teasin' the hell out of my hair like that. Darla was a real help there. Sean, are you ready for the whirlpool? I am."

Five minutes later, Sean was sitting in the swirling waters with Jo, gently massaging her feet. Jo finally got the courage to ask Sean, "Did anythin' that I said today change your opinion of me?"

Sean's reply was short and simple. He told her, "Yes, but only for the better. You are one mighty wonderful lady. I'm awful lucky to have you."

Jo asked, "You sure that my relationship with the Frenchman won't bother you?"

Sean retorted, "You sure that my relationship with wild and crazy Alicia won't bother you?"

Jo said, "No."

Sean said, "Same for me."

Sensing that her burden was about to be lifted from her mind and soul, Jo asked Sean the **BIG QUESTION**, "Precious, was Mrs. McReynolds right about me not fittin' into polite society?"

Sean asked, "Do you want the long version?"

With a twinkle in her eyes, Jo said, "I've learned to love your long, ramblin' answers. Please, let me hear the long version."

Smiling at her, Sean said, "The answer to her question really depends on how you define the term, *polite society*. If you define the term narrowly, meaning old money snobs like Mrs. McReynolds, then the answer is in the affirmative. If you include the term to include successful business people, professionals, university professors, military officers and government officials, then you get another answer. Frankly, I can't imagine why anyone ever would want to be friends with Mrs. McReynolds, can you?"

Jo's response was, "No, I can't either."

Sean added, "Jo, let me loan you a copy of a book written by a former History graduate student at S.U. In the book, he explores in depth the family trees of the Founders. You'll find it very interesting. It seems as if the Founders had some rather dubious characters in their backgrounds, including slave traders, corrupt lawmen and people who made their money off of the backs of convict labor. It will help you put the matter in better perspective."

Jo asked, "Want to go in? I'm startin' to shrivel up."

Five minutes later, Jo was sitting on the sofa, wrapped in the blanket again, thumbing through the book that Sean had loaned her. Sean interrupted her by asking, "If it is okay with you, I'm going to email Father Wilson that Wednesday is a go and that we want to keep that wedding date in August."

Jo said, "If you don't mind marryin' a killer, I'm on."

Sean said, "I live with two professional killers now. One more will make it all the more interesting." As soon as Sean had finished speaking, Equity and Law came charging into the room very loudly, their claws clacking noisily on the wooden floor. While Sean was at his computer, Jo began looking in the refrigerator to see if she could fix something to eat.

A few minutes later, over a meal of leftovers, Sean said, "I need to call Griswold and the Twins. Which call should I make first?"

Jo suggested Griswold. Ten minutes later, Sean said, "I can't believe that Bob already had the party room at The Palm Tree reserved for Friday. I guess that we should start inviting people right now. Jo, I've already called Kyra and Max. Who do you want to invite?"

"I'd like to invite Maggie and her husband. Now that I think of it, I'd better contact all of my friends from Maggie's party. I'm curious to see who Darla will bring with her."

Sean said, "Will she have any trouble getting a date on short notice?"

Giggling, Jo responded, "Darla? I doubt it."

A few minutes later, after Sean returned from his office, Jo said, "Maggie and her husband confirmed. Everyone else from Maggie's party who isn't workin' that evenin' will be comin'. Darla told me that she was gonna bring an *A- list* date, whatever that means. Precious, who did you get confirmations from?"

Sean, feeling rather proud of his efforts, said, "Kyra and Max. Bob and his wife, of course. Laura and her husband. Lucy and Ralph. And, believe it or not, Bubba and Shirley. Miriam sends her regrets, as do Jane and her fiancée and Angela and her fiancée. It looks like we are going to have a nice party."

After they had the table cleared off, Jo asked Sean if she could borrow his computer to send herself a reminder email. When she returned a minute later, she said, "While I was typin', I saw a quarter on the floor. It gave me an idea. Let's flip to see which one of our families we call first."

Jo won the coin toss, so she elected to go last. Standing in the library next to Sean's speaker phone, Sean punched in the number for Maureen's cell phone. A second later, Mo answered. Before Sean could say anything, Mo blurted out, "Father, Pat is with me. Can I put you on speaker?"

"Sure. I've got Jo with me on my end, okay?"

After a nanosecond, Pat inquired, "When will the wedding be?"

Sean, totally flummoxed, asked, "Why do you ask that?"

After the Twins stopped giggling, Mo said, "Father, you taught your daughters to be logical. Pat and I go to the 10:00 a.m. Mass at Holy Angels. We've seen you and Jo leaving about the time that we arrived the last two Sundays. So, we've known that you two must be serious."

A baffled Sean asked, "Why do you say that?"

Pat, barely suppressing a giggle, said, "If a man takes a lady to church with him, particularly a lady as beautiful as Jo, the logical deduction is that he must be serious about her."

Sean said, "Okay, I guess."

A now giggling Mo added, "And when the man is written up in the paper with a picture showing him pinning a woman's bars on her uniform, you know that he's got to be serious about her."

A now very confused Sean said, "Okay, I understand your reasoning. How did you reach the conclusion that we are getting married?"

Now, Sean had three women giggling. After a second, Mo said, "You're calling on the phone. You only do that when something big is up. When's the date?"

Sean, sensing that further resistance was futile, said meekly, "Saturday, August 12th at eleven in the morning."

Now that Sean had done his part, Jo and the Twins chatted about wedding plans. After a few minutes, Jo promised to have dinner with the Twins on Thursday evening. The Twins and Jo parted a few minutes later in great spirits. After the ladies were finished speaking, a still somewhat confused Sean asked Jo, "I thought that girls always get weird when their widowed fathers remarry. What happened?"

Jo said, "I'm not sure, but here's my guess. I'm closer in age to the Twins than I am to your age, right? My guess is that I'm still young enough, so that the Twins don't see me as a threat to their mother's memory since they can relate to me better. If I was your age, they wouldn't see me as a person very clearly."

Sean, now resigned to never understanding his daughters, just smiled. A moment later, Jo called home on her cell phone. Jo lit up when her mother answered. After a moment's conversation, Sean heard Jo say, "Who is that man pinning the bars onto my uniform in that picture? Well, Momma that's why I'm callin'. As of a little while ago, he became my fiancé. Can I bring him down to see y'all over Memorial Day? Do you want to break the news to Daddy, or should I call back later when he's back in the house? Okay, I'll let you tell him. His name? Judge Sean Riley. I'll call you back tomorrow night after you've told Daddy. Love you, too, Momma. Bye."

Looking at Sean, Jo said **non-stop**, "We've had ourselves one weekend, haven't we? There is something else—small—that I still need to tell you. I've never had any memories or dreams or anythin' like that about that day at the bank. But, I've had reoccurrin' dreams about Mrs. McReynolds and what she said to me. Well, a few weeks ago, right after our first date, the dreams started comin' back stronger and stronger. Remember when I asked you for a referral to a shrink for a friend? Well, that was for me. In my one session with Dr. Daphne's colleague, Dr. Emerson, she convinced me that the only way that I could ever put my fears to rest about whether I'll ever belong would be to tell you about them. She was fairly brutal about it, but she convinced me that if you loved me as much as I thought you did, you'd understand. She was right. I'm gonna call her tomorrow to thank her and set a time to talk to her about the shootin'."

Sean, amazed at how many words Jo could utter in between breaths, just smiled and told her that it was okay by him.

Jo added, "One more thing. Tomorrow is my first day reportin' directly to the sheriff. I'm gonna ask him straight up if I'm eligible to go back out in the field. As a lieutenant, I doubt that will ever come up again. But, I've got to know. Think that will be okay?" When Sean agreed that would be just fine, Jo threw her arms around him and hugged him in a tight bear hug.

Sean said, "As long as we are at it, mind if I discuss a mundane detail? Would you have your lawyer call me, so we can coordinate our estate planning? At our level, taxes become a very big issue."

Jo replied, "I'll call him tomorrow."

Sean asked, "What time do I need to drop you off tomorrow morning?" When Jo told him, he told her what time he would be getting up. Jo thought that was a great idea. Sean said that he was totally exhausted and really needed some sleep. Jo agreed.

Before they retired, Sean said, "Jo, this has been one long, emotion-filled weekend for both of us. I can think of only one way to end it. Go pull those lyrics out of your purse. A moment later, a very puzzled Law and Equity watched Jo and Sean sing the entire long version of *Good Will Win in the End*. After that, two drained, but happy people wandered off to sleep in their respective rooms. For some reason, Equity chose to tuck in Sean, while Law tucked in Jo.

****

The next morning over breakfast, neither Sean nor Jo was inclined to talk much. On the ride to Jo's place, the only thing that Jo said to Sean was that she loved him. Sean told her that he loved her, as well.

****

Mid-morning, Sean checked his personal email account. There was an email from Jo that made his day:

Precious,

I love you with all of my heart.

Dr. Emerson asked me to send her congratulations to you.

The sheriff let me look at the report from the shrink. All that the report said when you translate it into English was that I was dealing with the trauma well. He said that he anticipated I would fully recover and recommended my return to active service immediately. Precious, you know what that means? I wasn't kicked upstairs! I'm not riding a desk because I'm a head case. The sheriff always trusted me. My transfer really was a reward. It's just hitting me now. WOW!

I'm looking forward to ring shopping tomorrow. I really don't care about the ring, as long as it comes from you.

XOXOXOXO, Jo

P.S. I didn't take a sleeping pill last night. I slept well all night and didn't see Mrs. McReynolds in my dreams. Dr. Emerson was right. I had to trust you enough to tell you. God Bless both of you!

Chapter Ten

As they rode in the darkness, Sean realized that today was Friday, May 12th. If all went as planned, three months to the day, he and Jo would be on their honeymoon. Just as Sean began to think of all the things that could go wrong, his gloomy thoughts were interrupted when Jo asked him, "Precious, do you really like how I look?"

Suppressing a strong urge to laugh, Sean said, "Beautiful, after all of my years using the English language as a tool to communicate my meaning with precision and clarity, this evening my command of the language has failed me completely. You are as stunningly beautiful as any actress in Hollywood at the Academy Awards."

"Precious, you're too kind. Does the ring look okay?"

"Beautiful, on your hand tonight, anything would look good. But yes, the engagement ring looks beautiful."

Discovering a new worry, Jo asked, "Are my earrings and choker too much with the engagement ring?"

Smiling a very patient smile, Sean said, "Jo, the gold and the emeralds in both of them go perfectly well with the honey color of your gown and the brown in your hair. You are a study in earth tones this evening. The matching wrap adds a touch of mystery to your appearance."

Jo's honey gold gown was pure silk, held up by two thin straps. The exposed tan skin of Jo's back and bosom went perfectly with the gold of the gown. The gown was quite tight around Jo's body, down to the long slit just below her left hip, which gave her freedom of movement. Sean guessed that both Jo and Kyra had spent quite a bit of time shopping to get this gown, which was perfect.

"Beautiful, if I didn't think that you looked incredibly lovely, do you think that I would have taken over thirty digital photographs of you this evening?"

Laughing, Jo said, "I guess not."

Sean, sensing an opening to calm Jo, said, "Jo, you are a natural model. I didn't have to pose you at all. You and the camera were made for each other."

Jo had worked very hard to look beautiful that evening. She had taken the day off from work to get herself ready. After a trip to the beauty shop, she had made a side trip to the bank, where she took the jewelry that Abe had given her as an anniversary present out of her safe deposit box. After leaving the bank, Jo posed for a portrait photographer. Since she planned to give Sean the portrait as a wedding present, she was very glad to hear that he really appreciated her efforts to make herself look as good as she could for him that evening.

After a short pause, Jo took Sean's hand in hers and said, "Sean, if you ever want to give up law, you ought to consider becomin' a dance teacher. While I'm worried about a lot of things tonight, makin' a fool of myself on the dancer floor isn't one of them. Thank you so much for teachin' me how to dance last weekend. You were very patient. If I hadn't fallen in love with you a long time ago, the way that you gently and patiently showed me how to dance, while ignorin' my mistakes, would be enough to charm any woman."

As they approached the University City Country Club, Sean felt happy and proud to have such a beautiful lady with him. Jo felt unsure of herself, not quite scared, but unsure and anxious. When they turned down the long, broad street leading to the country club, Jo said, "Sean, what on earth possessed you to rent a limousine for us? It's got to be expensive."

Sean replied, "I've been to quite a few events here over the years. I've noticed that if you wait for the valet parking attendants to bring your vehicle after the event is over, you'll wind up waiting a long time. The limousine will keep us from having to wait in the cold and damp."

A few seconds later, an attendant opened the door to the limousine. Sean exited first, so he could assist his lovely fiancé out the vehicle's door. After climbing up the long, elegant, white marble staircase, passing through the white Georgian columns that flanked the entrance into the building and then taking a short walk through the ornate marble lobby of the building, Sean and Jo arrived at the threshold of the Holy of Holies of the old money of the area—the Grand Ballroom of the University City Country Club.

As the couple approached the entrance to the ballroom, a uniformed attendant asked Sean their names, which the attendant wrote on a small, off-white card that the first attendant carefully handed to the attendant at the microphone. When Sean and Jo entered the ballroom, the second attendant announced them, saying, "Judge Sean Riley and Lieutenant Jolene Scruggs."

As they were announced, Sean felt a malevolent presence behind him. Assuming that he was just suffering from a case of nerves, Sean put the feeling out of his mind. Had Sean given in to his instincts and looked behind him, Sean would have seen nothing out of the ordinary—just other people coming into the Spring Fling and a few other people connected with other events at the club passing through the ornate lobby. Since he had only seen

Mrs. McReynolds once before, he would not have noticed her. But, there she was, staring at Jo and Sean as they entered the grand ballroom.

Descending the ornate, marble staircase into the grand ballroom, Jo and Sean both felt that everyone in the room was looking at them. A moment later, Jo and Sean were surrounded by a sea of friendly, smiling people, all of whom greeted them warmly. The happy couple truly was the center of attention of the 2000 Spring Fling.

****

As the rain pounded against the breakfast nook window, Jo slowly sipped her coffee. After a minute, she looked at Sean and said, "Do you think that all cops eat donuts?"

Not wanting to enter into a rather boring discussion concerning the limits of induction as a way of understanding the universe, Sean smiled as he said, "I figured that we probably weren't going to be up at the crack of dawn this morning and have a good breakfast, so I bought some yesterday. I guess you had more important things on your mind than what I carried into the house last night, so you probably didn't notice the donuts."

Looking serious for a second, Jo asked, "Sean, will you treat me this well after we've been married for a few years?"

Sean responded seriously, as well, "Jo, I'm the domestic type. I learned a long time ago that I do better if I have a woman in my life. I've always been very grateful to the woman in my life. Also, I learned long ago that if a man goes along with his woman on most things, they both live happier lives."

"Precious, will we fight after we are married?"

Smiling, Sean said, "It comes with the territory. But, I doubt that we'll fight very much because of our ages."

"Why, Precious?" Jo asked sincerely.

"When people are younger, they are more demanding of their partners than mature people are. We've both loved and lost, so we are both grateful to have someone to love in our lives."

Changing perspective, Sean added, "You, being vibrant, sexy, young and madly in love with me, makes me appreciate you that much more. Being human, I'm sure that we'll have disagreements. But, knowing how horribly lonely I was before I met you, I can put things in context very easily."

With a mischievous expression on her face, Jo said, "Precious, if I say somethin' critical about your behavior after we came back here early this mornin', would you be too offended?"

"Lieutenant, whatever I did, I apologize!"

A now laughing Jo said, "Not so fast, Yankee Boy! You need to hear how you failed me."

Sean, feigning meekness, said, "Yes, Ma'am."

"Precious, as I remember, I was very sleepy in the limousine when we were fixin' to leave the Spring Fling. What time did we actually leave?"

"0230. You fell sound asleep on the ride home."

Pretending to be serious, Jo inquired, "How did you get me into the house?"

Sean replied, "I carried you since you were dead to the world."

Sounding serious, Jo asked, "Yankee Boy, tell me what you did after we entered my home."

Now wondering a tad if he had done something wrong, Sean said, "Well, after I shut the front door with my foot, I carried you into the bedroom. Then, I took your gown off you and tucked you in. Did I do something wrong?"

"Sean Riley! For weeks and months I've labored to teach you how to function as a proper manservant. I guess that in my instructions, I neglected to inform you that proper ladies do not sleep in their undergarments. I trust that if this situation occurs after we are married, you will remember that the only proper attire for a lady to sleep in is either a nightgown, a long t-shirt or Nature's Own Garb. Undergarments are not appropriate sleep wear."

Now knowing that he was being teased, Sean fell to his knees and looking up at Jo said, "Please forgive me. Under the circumstances, had I undressed you any more, I would not have been able to sleep at all. As it was, between the rainstorm and the excitement of the evening, I slept very little."

"Alright, I'll forgive you!" Jo said, as she kissed his cheek tenderly.

✻✻✻✻✻✻✻✻✻✻✻✻

Several hours later, Jo and Sean were at Chez Riley, sitting under an awing that overhung part of the deck. They had a great view of the rain falling on the Lesniak's dairy farm to the west. The movement of the clouds suggested that the storm might pass that night. Far in the distance, little hints of daylight occasionally poked through the clouds. Although the weather was damp, the day had warmed pleasantly.

As she wiggled her bare toes, Jo turned to Sean and said, "Precious, when we walked into the Spring Fling last night, I knew how Ilsa must have felt when she first walked into Rick's place. I sensed that everyone there was lookin' at me."

"Did that make you feel uncomfortable?" Sean asked.

Jo replied, "No, not really. I just wasn't expectin' it. I guess after all the press coverage that we've had recently, I should've. In any case, I was glad when Kyra and Max came up to greet us. I felt better seein' folks I knew."

"Beautiful, I sensed that once they came by, you started to relax," Sean assured her.

Jo asked, "Sean, I guess that you didn't exaggerate a bit about women askin' you 'bout the Spring Fling. How many were there?"

"Well, only two asked me directly. But, a few others hinted at the subject. I really didn't want to go with any of them for professional reasons. Once I had agreed to the blind date, I used you as an excuse. If our date hadn't worked out, I probably would have had to check myself into the hospital or have hired someone to go as my date."

"Sean, you don't mean what I think you mean?" Jo asked, with a decided giggle to her voice.

Sean played along, "No, but I'm sure that I could have found a half-way presentable lady, who would have gone with me in return for a nice evening gown, the pleasure of my company and a few dollars."

Jo said, "I'm so glad that it didn't come to that."

Sean agreed, "Me too! Of course, knowing my luck, I probably would have asked some off-duty lady cop and gotten busted."

Jo said, "You could have asked Ralph for help. As I remember, he knew lots of ladies over in Capitol City." After they stopped laughing, Jo asked, "Just so it isn't hangin' over us, do you want to talk about Kim Brownlee? She was the first one to ask you, wasn't she?"

Sean said, "Yes, she was. Did seeing her date bother you?"

Turning to Sean, Jo said, "I've had a lot of time to think about whether I was wrong for Covey. As much as I hate to admit it, his mother was probably right, but for the wrong reasons. Covey's a very uncertain man in his personal life. While he is good at what he does professionally and confident about his work—thanks to his mother—he is very scared about makin' personal decisions. If you're like that, it probably isn't good to get involved with a strong woman. If Covey would have married me, I'm afraid that he would have just substituted one strong woman in his life for the one he left behind. I think that he needs to be with someone warm and nurturin', who won't overpower him like I probably would have. What's Kim like?"

Sean said, "Kim is very nice, warm and nurturing. She is bright, industrious and tenacious. But, as lawyers go, she isn't a really strong, overpowering personality. Did seeing Covey upset you?"

Jo replied with considered, measured words, "Precious, I've always known that I'd see Covey again. I feel no anger toward him. I'm glad to see that he is lookin' well and goin' out again. From what I could tell, Kim seems to be smitten by Covey. I suspect that she'll have to use her charms on him for a while, though, since he is real cautious about women. But, I'm sure that if she sticks with him long enough, he'll reciprocate her feelin's. I hope that everythin' works out for both of them. I really do!"

Asking about Beth Shelton, Jo declared, "Sean, I can't picture you ever feelin' comfortable with her. She's awfully serious and intense."

Sean responded, "Jo, I couldn't either. That's probably why I didn't let you intimidate me on our blind date. When you consider the alternatives I would have faced, I was determined to make our date work."

Jo said, "Precious, you aren't gonna try to convince me that you didn't notice her cleavage last night, are you?"

Looking slightly guilty, Sean asked, "If I plead guilty, will I get a lighter sentence?"

Jo replied, "The only punishment that would fit that crime would be life."

Smiling, Sean said, "Jo, I don't know what is going on with her. Until the end of March, I'd never seen her looking dressed up, attractive or pretty. As long as I've known her, she always looked like she bought her clothes at a rummage sale and didn't believe in cosmetics. Now look at her!"

Jo said, "Her date seemed to be quite taken with her. What was his name?"

Sean replied, "I think it was Dr. Meadows. If I heard him rightly, he is a professor of Chemical Engineering at S.U. I know he was looking at her curves with great interest."

At Jo's suggestion, Sean went inside the house to bring out two Diet Cokes. When Sean returned with the drinks, he noticed that Jo was very slowly sliding her bare feet back and forth on the cool concrete. Sean decided to ignore the obvious clue as to Jo's physical and emotional condition.

"Precious, what was the name of Sarah Breen's date? I caught that he was a judge? Do you know him?" asked Jo.

Sean replied, "Jo, remember a couple of weeks ago I told you that I had clerked for a justice of our state supreme court when I graduated from law school? Sarah Breen's date was the justice that I clerked for over in Capitol City, the Honorable Sam Brown."

"Precious, don't take this the wrong way, but he doesn't look much older than you. Are you a lot younger than you seem or was he a child judge?" asked Jo.

Sean said, "He was close to being a child judge."

A puzzled Jo said, "Seriously?"

Sean explained, "When Sam Brown started grade school in the mountains, he was promoted to third grade by the end of the first week since he could already read and do simple arithmetic. Back then, the idea was to not waste time and money on kids who already knew what the teacher was going to teach in that grade. So, he was almost sixteen when he finished high school. He went to S.U. on an academic scholarship and graduated first in his class after being there only three years. So, when he started law school, he was almost nineteen. When he graduated from law school and passed the bar, he had just turned twenty-two."

Sean continued, "After working for the District Attorney in his county up in the mountains for six years, the governor appointed him to a district court bench at age twenty-eight. After serving a few years in district court, the next governor, being very irritated with the old buzzards on the bench, decided to appoint someone young to the Supreme Court in the hopes that he could get them to realize what century they were living in. So, when I first went to work for him, he was only about thirty-five or so."

Jo said, "Okay. Now I understand. How did he and Sarah Breen meet?"

Leaning toward Jo, Sean said, with a slightly conspiratorial tone in his voice, "It's not quite public knowledge yet, but Sam is planning on retiring later this year. Since his kids have all flown the coup and he's been alone for the last few years since his wife died, he decided to look for a place in the country, someplace around Smithville. As luck with have it, somewhere he came across the name of Sarah Breen, who works as a real estate broker when she isn't helping Ralph and Lucy. I'm not sure if he has found any real estate to buy. However, I think that he's found something else more valuable. Did you notice how they looked at each other?"

Jo said, "How could I miss it? Did you notice that they both looked very tan?"

Sean said, "I guess that Justice Sam Brown and I both like women with good tans."

Jo giggled, "If you expect me to comment on any peekin' that you might have done last night when I was under your control, Yankee Boy, keep on dreamin'!"

Sean said, "Jo, Justice Brown told me that after he goes off the bench at the end of August, he and Sarah would like to get together with us. It seems as if while they were looking at properties, Sarah let slip what she thought of me. She was surprised to learn that clerking for Sam had been my first job after law school. From what they both said, if I may be so bold as to count you into the number, my fan club probably has at least three members, who aren't related to me by blood and don't eat out of food bowls on the floor."

After discussing Laura's doctor husband's obvious discomfort being surrounded by lawyers at some length, Jo said, "Sean, while you were away from our table, you'll never guess who I saw havin' a grand ol' time with Laura's husband—Julie Sharp. If he hadn't grabbed Laura and practically dragged her by her hair out onto the dance floor, Julie probably would have had her photographer take his picture. I guess that the last thin' a doctor wants is his picture in the newspaper havin' a good time at a lawyer event. My guess is that doctors may forgive each other for sleepin' with the enemy, but I'm not sure if they would accept one of their own partyin' with a bunch of lawyers."

Jo then asked, "What sort of doctor is Dr. Rizzoto?"

Without thinking, Sean said, "He's a plastic surgeon." Jo and Sean both agreed that one mystery had just been solved since Julie easily could pass for being at least ten years younger than her chronological age.

A minute later, Jo snuggled up next to Sean and asked, "Did I fit in last night?"

Knowing that Jo needed a serious answer, Sean looked into her eyes and said, "As far as I could tell, every man there—except **maybe** Justice Sam Brown—envied me. You were your usual self—charming, funny and the center of attention. The fact that you also can dance with the best of them didn't hurt either."

"Sean, I didn't embarrass you when I took my shoes off, did I?"

"Jo, you are hardly the first woman to dance without her shoes. Considering how pretty your feet are, I doubt that anyone was offended in the least."

"Sean, I thought that I fit in. I'm glad that my instincts were right."

Now snuggling up real close to Sean, Jo said, "Sean, I imagine that bein' around me, particularly out at the pool, has been difficult for you these last few weeks. If it will make you feel any better, last night I had a dream that you carried me to bed and then undressed me and made passionate love to me. It was a very strong dream. When I woke up, I realized that part of it hadn't been a dream. I also felt very happy to know that you trusted me enough to know I wouldn't be offended if you got me ready for bed."

Seconds later, Jo told Sean, "I am awfully lucky to have you in my life." After that, she smothered Sean with a big wet kiss.

✱✱✱✱✱✱✱✱✱✱✱✱

Six weeks ago Jo and Sean were two lonely strangers. Now, on that rainy afternoon in May, they were two people deeply in love. They were, indeed, both very lucky.

BOOK II: THE CAMPAIGN

Chapter Eleven

"Sean, I never hiked as a girl. Back on Daddy's cotton farm, we did enough walkin' as it was just to git where we needed to be. I didn't think that I'd like today. But, it was fun!"

"Beautiful, I'm glad that you liked it. I hiked a lot when I was a Boy Scout. Hiking is good exercise, as well as a way of seeing the countryside up close."

While Sean was speaking, Jo had been sitting on the edge of the double bed, removing her hiking boots and socks. When Sean finished talking, Jo rose and pulled her very wet t-shirt from her body. Without Jo needing to say a word, Sean immediately stood behind Jo and unsnapped her bra, which Jo let fall to the floor next to her boots, socks and t-shirt. As Jo wiggled out of her shorts, she said with a girlish-sounding giggle, "Since I'm gettin' nekid, should I pull back the covers on the bed?"

Laughing, Sean said, "Jo, if we play in the bed again, we won't get to the restaurant on time. Let's wait until this evening."

With mock petulance, Jo said, "A gentleman, which, with my assistance, you just might someday hope to aspire to become, wouldn't have declined such a request."

Sean replied, "Jo, I suspect that a very hungry Southern gentleman, who has been nearly worn out by the constant demands of his beautiful lady, might need to eat occasionally, his fine and gracious manners notwithstanding."

Before Jo could reply, she saw that Sean was starting to fill up the large, black marble tub. When Jo saw Sean adding drops of bubble bath into the water, she asked, "May I assume that you would like my company in the tub?"

Sean replied, "Indeed, I would!" A moment later, Sean, who now was also naked, stood in the rapidly filling tub and offered his hand to Jo, who gracefully climbed into the warm, bubbling waters. As Jo joined him in the tub, Sean realized that he was a very lucky man, indeed. Jo's tan, freckled, leggy body was as beautiful as a woman's body could ever be. As Jo settled into the sudsy, warm water, Sean pressed the button that turned on the flow of water from the multiple jets located in the sides of the tub.

Stretching out, side-by-side for a few minutes, they both relaxed, their sore, tired muscles giving way to the warm healing of the jets of water gently massing them from all directions. After a few minutes, Sean said, "It doesn't get any better than this, does it?"

Jo said, "I can think of only one thing that would make it better." As she said that, Sean felt Jo's fingernails slowly moving down his chest, past his nipples toward his navel. As her fingers worked their way down his torso, Sean said, "When we're done, please remind me to call to see if we can get a later table."

✱✱✱✱✱✱✱✱✱✱✱✱

A few hours later, as their baby blue Mustang convertible left the parking lot of the Station Grill™ restaurant, Jo said, "The meal was magnificent. I never would have believed that we'd find food this good in a strip shoppin' center located out here in the middle of nowhere. How did you find this place?"

A smiling Sean looked over at Jo, as the wind spilling over the open top of the convertible blew her now nearly long, brown hair almost straight back and said, "I normally come to the area at least once a year to take a class at the National Judicial College in Reno. Since the classes run pretty much straight through from eight to four every day, it's impossible to make up a Rotary Club meeting during the day. There's a club that meets here in Carson City in the evenings at this restaurant. So, I learned about this place purely by accident."

After pausing for a second, Sean added a few thoughts to set the imaginary record straight, "Actually, Carson City isn't really *nowhere*. It is a booming, very nice little city and is also the state capitol of Nevada. If you want nowhere, drive east on U.S. 50 for a while. After a few miles, all you will see is desert. The locals say it's the loneliest highway in the country. I can't argue with them about that."

As their convertible turned off of I-395 onto westbound U.S. 50 toward Lake Tahoe, Jo said, "Speakin' of Rotary, are you gonna need to go to a meetin' this week?"

"Well, we have a number of choices," said Sean. "If you'd like, we could drive to Carson City on Thursday afternoon and tour the Nevada State History Museum before the evening meeting."

"Precious, I'd love to do that! Could we go for a drive afterward on that lonely highway? I just love the desert at night."

Sean replied, "Beautiful, if that is what you'd like to do, we will do that. Your wish is my command. Just remember to bring a jacket. The desert can cool off rapidly at night."

"Precious, did you have any other ideas for the week?" asked Jo.

Sean explained, "Well, Lake Tahoe should keep us pretty busy most of the time that we are here. But, if you'd be interested, I'd like to show you Virginia City, which was once an incredibly wealthy mining town and now caters to tourists. It is also full of cutesy stores. Besides, the view on the ride there is magnificent."

Giggling, Jo said, "I guess that we have to give the maids a chance to clean up the condo sometime. And now that I think of it, I guess that I should give my elderly husband a chance to catch his breath."

"Jo, you just realized the age difference?"

Laughing, Jo said, "Precious, in case you're worried, you aren't showin' any signs of age where it matters."

Sean replied, "The week is still young. By the time that we get home, I may be a shadow of my former self."

"Precious, is that a complaint or a request?"

"You'll find out in about a twenty minutes."

Jo felt the convertible speed up as Sean spoke.

∗∗∗∗∗∗∗∗∗∗∗

Several hours later, Jo snuggled up closely to Sean and said softly, "Precious, can I ask you a question?"

"Sure."

"Precious, what have you been doin' when you've been typin' on your laptop?"

Somewhat startled by Jo's question, Sean replied, "Back in college, one of my English professors required us to keep a journal for one semester. I enjoyed it so much that I kept doing it after the semester was over. Once computers came around, I transcribed my written notes into my computer. Someday, when I'm old and feeble, I'm going to use those notes to help me write an autobiography. I'll have my notes all ready to go."

Jo said, with a very breathy tone in her voice, "I don't want to intrude, but could you tell me what you said about the weddin'?"

"Yes, Beautiful, I'd be glad to read it to you, if you don't mind my not reading the entire entry to you."

Once Jo agreed to his request, Sean, naked as he could be, went to fetch the laptop from the other room. As he left, Jo smiled appreciatively at his well-muscled physique, particularly his posterior.

A moment later, Sean sat on the edge of the bed—totally unaware of his lack of attire—and turned on the laptop. Jo, sitting upright in the bed, let the covers drop. After Sean put on his horn-rimmed reading glasses, he read out loud to her:

August 12, 2000.

As I readied myself this morning, I realized that the reason men my age marry women Jo's age is that only younger women have the physical strength and fortitude to endure a big church wedding.

Had I gotten involved with a woman my own age, when she realized the ordeal facing her to get married in church, she probably would have either had a nervous breakdown, dumped me for a boy-toy, demanded that we elope or suggested that we just move in together.

Fortunately, as the groom, all I have to do is stand around and do as I'm told and speak when spoken to. Since I'm an experienced husband, the entire drill seems like old hat to me now—except that my line is "I do!" instead of "Yes, dear!"

The wedding ceremony itself went by so fast that I can only remember bits and pieces of it. I remember that when Jo's father, the Colonel, walked her down the aisle, he looked very relieved.

Jo looked like a very radiant goddess. Her long, brown hair contrasted very well with the white of her wedding gown.

She obviously had taken my advice and not covered her freckles with a bunch of makeup. The blue in her eyes sparkled as brightly as the Milky Way on a cool, clear desert night. She was as beautiful a bride as there ever was.

Jo's four bridesmaids and matrons—Kyra, Lucy, Maggie and Darla, especially Darla—all looked real good, too. Max did a fine job as best man. Ralph, Justice Brown and Bubba added a touch of maturity and seriousness to the male side of the ceremony.

The wedding reception must've been one of the strangest ones that the Horizon Club has hosted in years and years. The groom's side consisted of my daughters, lawyers, courthouse types, church friends and academics. The bride's side was full of cops and her country relatives. While I had some doubts about how they would all mix, somehow it worked very well. Since the reception started a little after noon, everyone stayed sober—at least until we left! I remember dancing with a number of the ladies present there.

Angela, Jo's mom, was a real hoot! I suspect that Jo didn't get all of her strong will from her father! If Jo looks as good as Angela does near sixty, I'm hoping that I live for a long, long time!

Kyra, unlike the way she normally is, was really sentimental when we danced. She cried on my shoulder while wishing

Jo and I all the happiness that she and Max have had. She is a special lady.

Sarah Breen can really cut a rug. While we were doing a sixties dance, she told me that she and Justice Brown were very much in love. She said that she hoped something would push him to propose. Little did she know that a conspiracy was in the works!

Lucy was as charming as she could be, dancing as best she could, considering how pregnant she was. She told me that Ralph was pampering her so much that she might just keep getting pregnant to keep the attention coming!

Daphne also danced with me. I was a little surprised since she and I had never danced. But, back when we were an item in the early seventies, dancing was more a display of athleticism than dancing ability. She told me that she and her husband had taken up competitive ballroom dancing several years ago. She wished us well. I could tell from her expression that she meant it very deeply.

Perhaps the second weirdest moment that I experienced at the reception was dancing with Professor Rodriguez. She gushed about how sad she had been when Cheryl died and was overjoyed when she learned that I was getting married again. I was even more shocked when she told me that our disputes had always been purely political and that she never meant anything personal by them. She told me that for a damn right-winger, I was a decent man. She told me that if she or her husband could do anything for us, I was to let her know. When I suggested that the four of us dine together some evening, she accepted. What can I say? I wonder if when she told her husband about it he was as shocked as I was? Probably!

Sean recounted an edited version of the following paragraph to Jo:

Kim Brownlee came stag. While we were dancing, she told me that Covey's psychiatrist ordered him not to come to the wedding or the reception. The shrink had concerns that with all Covey had going on in his life at the moment, the stress would be too much. Kim asked me to send Covey's best wishes to Jo. When the dance was over, Kim had me bend down, so she could kiss me on the cheek. A second later, she left the reception, but did wave a tearful goodbye. Mercifully, Jo didn't see it.

Sean merely told her that Kim had expressed Covey's regrets at being unable to attend the wedding because he was needed in New York to meet with the producer of the Saturday morning investment show on Fox News, on which Covey was a regular panelist. Thinking about it for second, Sean added that Covey had wished them both his best. After observing that Jo showed no emotion at his mention of Covey, Sean continued reading from his journal:

The funniest part of the reception was my dance with Darla. Darla looked country yummy—as always. Darla's ruddy complexion really stood out during the reception, highlighted as it was by her long, silver-blonde hair. While we were dancing—and I was struggling very hard to maintain eye contact—I innocently remarked that I noticed that her date, my colleague, Professor Boyington Sims, III, had also been her date at the engagement party. That did it!

Darla stood as straight and tall as her 5'6" frame would allow her to stand. When I realized that she wanted my ear, I bent over a bit. Darla told me that she had decided a few months ago that he was a keeper. I didn't tell her that I thought she was out of her mind because Sims had always struck me as a completely asocial nerd, whose entire life revolved around the law. As a former U.S. Supreme Court law clerk and an appellate lawyer for the Justice Department, he was a natural to teach Constitutional Law. But, as a good Con Law professor, he spends most of his time thinking deep thoughts. I doubted that he was much of a catch. But, what do I know?

After the socializing was over, we had several last ritualistic ordeals to endure. Jo and Darla must have threatened all of the single women in the audience with death if they caught the bouquet because when Jo tossed it, no one moved toward the arc of the bouquet except Darla. I've seen Major League center fielders with less fielding skill than Darla. She caught it easily.

Then came the garter toss! This was a very weird moment. I was a bit apprehensive about the whole idea of Jo pulling up her wedding gown and showing a lot of leg to the crowd, but Jo kept me distracted—big time.

First, when we got on stage, Jo put her foot on a small stool. Then, she ordered me to remove her shoe. As I very meekly bent down and complied with her request, I noticed that she wasn't wearing hose. After I had her shoe off, Jo motioned to me with her finger that I was supposed to let her whisper something in my ear. When I presented my ear to Jo, in her deepest, sexiest and most country drawl, she said, "Precious, with all the excitement this mornin' gettin' ready for church and all, I'm not sure if I remembered to put on my panties. So, do be careful!"

I know that I must have turned as red as the reddest rose in full bloom because I could feel my face, neck and ears burning. As Jo slowly worked her gown up past her knee, I started to sweat because I wasn't seeing a garter. Finally, just before the whole world would see if she was wearing panties, Jo stopped and said in her best Scarlett O'Hara imitation, "Why silly me! The garter must be on the other leg!"

After the laughter stopped, Jo slowly lowered her gown. Then, I had to bend down to take off her other shoe. When she pulled up the other side of the wedding gown, mercifully, the garter was there, just a few inches above her knee. I was so relieved.

Justice Brown did a fine job of catching the garter. I guess Sarah must have guessed that we had a conspiracy going, too because, as soon as Sam caught the garter, Sarah rushed up and kissed him very passionately on the lips—right in the middle of the dance floor!

According to the plan, we were supposed to do one last dance and then leave. The dance, with Jo barefoot—of course—was really wonderful. I felt Jo's warmth and love radiating to me. When the dance was over, Jo totally surprised me when she whispered a request in my ear. After I agreed, a moment later, Jo and I were back on the stage.

I believe the memory of what happened next was indelibly chiseled into my brain for all time. Jo picked up the microphone and said, "Sean and I, like a lot of other couples, have a favorite song. Unlike most other couples, we have had the great pleasure of knowin' one of the artists who first recorded our song. Our song was first recorded years ago by Tommy Breen, the *Singin' Soldier*, and his lovely bride, Sarah, who's a guest here today. Sarah, with your permission, Sean and I would like to sing it now to let everyone here know just how important love and faith are to us."

Once Sarah shouted a very loud assent, the band started playing and Jo and I sang *Good Will Win in the End*. I hope that it wasn't my singing, but at the end of the number, I saw a lot of people holding handkerchiefs and tissues to running eyes. We actually heard resounding applause and a few cries of *Encore! Encore!*

Jo solved that problem by telling the crowd we'd love to sing another number, but if we did, we'd miss our plane and have to have our honeymoon at the Horizon Club, which the management probably would prefer not happen. So, we went out the door.

Sometimes, the ball bounces your way. Instead of having to leave early next morning to catch a plane to Hartsfield to connect to Reno-Tahoe, we had lucked out. A few days ago, I was able to make arrangements for us to fly to the Reno-Tahoe Airport on a commercial air-taxi Bombardier LearJet 31A that was going to be deadheading on Saturday afternoon from Hartsfield to Lambert-St. Louis, where they were going to pick up a party going to Reno-Tahoe. They were very happy to come to the U.C. airport to pick us up. Since we would not have any other passengers on board until we arrived in St. Louis, we were going to be able to have the flight from the U.C. airport to St. Louis all to ourselves, except for one hostess and the flight crew. We were able to get the plane relatively cheaply—only $5,500.00. Ouch! But, looking back, it was worth every penny of it!

We boarded the LearJet right at four thirty in the afternoon. Jo and I were both dressed casually. I was wearing my usual polo shirt, chinos and navy sports jacket. Jo, bless her heart, wore a red knit top and the shortest blue denim skirt that I have seen since the late sixties. Fortunately, since Jo wasn't born until 1970, she had the legs to wear that skirt to very good effect.

As we boarded the plane, I noticed a very mischievous twinkle in Jo's big, blue eyes. Knowing Jo as well as I did, I didn't even bother to try to guess what she was up to, knowing that whatever it was, I would know soon enough.

Once we boarded the plane, the hostess directed us to the two seats furthest aft. Unlike all of the other seats on the LearJet, these two were physically together, while the other seats were separated by the aisle. The passengers in those two seats can actually touch each other, like you could in cars, before bucket seats came along.

The hostess was real nice. She gave us a bunch of extra pillows and enough blankets to sleep through a long winter in the High Sierras. After we reached cruising altitude, the hostess came back to us with a bottle of champagne, several glasses and a tray of caviar, crackers and a few other munchies. She winked at us and said, "I understand that you two love birds are on your honeymoon. Well, if you want anything, there's the buzzer. I'm going to kick my shoes off and take a nice, long nap. I won't be back for several hours if you don't buzz. Have a nice afternoon."

As the hostess went forward, she pulled down the shades in the entire cabin. So, in practical terms, Jo and I were alone in the dark, sipping our bubbly and enjoying being alone.

Thirty minutes later, Jo and I were both feeling no pain. The caviar and bubbly had been just what we needed to relax us. About halfway through the bottle, Jo had both kicked off her sandals and wiggled her sexy toes at me. In response, I kicked off both my loafers and socks and also actually took off my sports jacket!!!

After the bubbly was gone, Jo vetoed my idea of buzzing the hostess for another bottle. Instead, she told me to move the tray forward to one of the unoccupied seats. When I returned to our nice double seat a few seconds later, Jo had a big grin on her face.

Suffice it to say that Jo and I really enjoyed our time alone together. We were both glad that the hostess gave us ample warning time before the descent into Lambert-St. Louis. When the hostess checked on us before the landing, Jo and I were dressed—except for shoes—and cuddling again.

When the hostess asked us if we had enjoyed our time alone, Jo giggled. It is hard to believe just how easily and freely this hard-bitten peace officer can giggle. Jo is truly magnificent!

We picked up a bunch of golfers in St. Louis. I don't know what they were told about us before boarding because they all looked at us with friendly smiles and gave us a few winks. Other than that, they respected our privacy.

I don't know where she got them, but the hostess gave us the greatest prime rib sandwiches after we took off in St. Louis. Jo and I both drifted off to sleep after eating the sandwiches.

When the LearJet landed at the Reno-Tahoe Airport, the hostess and flight crew asked us if we would stay on board for a few seconds after the other passengers—the ones we had picked up in St. Louis—deplaned. When we were the only passengers left on board, the pilot presented us with an 8-½" by 11" manila envelope. The captain then extended his hand and welcomed us to the Mile High Club. The co-pilot and hostess did the same as we exited the plane. I guess that I should have been embarrassed, but Jo and I were laughing too hard. The envelope held two certificates—one made out to Sean Riley and the other to Jolene Riley. When Jo saw her married name written there for the first time, she started crying big, wet, happy tears. Like all women, she's crazy, but I love her too much to care.

When Sean finished the reading of his journal excerpt, he half-expected Jo to hit him over the head with a pillow. Uncharacteristically for Jo, she just sat there in the bed, looking at Sean with a smile on her face. Not knowing what to do, Sean got up and put his laptop away in the other room. When he came back to the bed, Jo suggested another soak in the whirlpool.

As they soaked, Jo inquired, "Sean, do you know what would make me very happy right now?" Without speaking, Sean grabbed Jo's left foot and began massaging it while Jo purred. After doing the same to Jo's right foot, Sean half-expected Jo to slide under the surface of the water in the tub, considering how relaxed she looked. Several minutes later, Jo crooked her finger at Sean, who leaned close to her mouth. Jo whispered something in his ear.

Sean looked at Jo and asked, "Are you sure that you want me to do that? We've been married less than sixty hours."

Jo said, "Please! Please! Please!"

Sean said, "Okay, here goes!"

Taking Jo's hands into his while looking into her eyes, Sean very softly said, "I love you, Mrs. Riley."

They both cried.

****

The morning of Wednesday, August 16th, was the first cloudy morning that Jo and Sean experienced since they had arrived at Lake Tahoe. Abandoning their usual morning routine of having a leisurely breakfast, sunbathing in their enclosed patio and soaking in the marble tub, they grabbed a quick breakfast and were on the road to Virginia City as the sun started to warm the area and burn away the light fog that still remained from the night before.

As they turned east on U.S. 50, Sean said, "Beautiful, think we ought to check and see how the Twins are doing on the big move?"

Jo agreed. So, she called the Twins on Sean's satellite phone. Poor Sean barely got a chance to talk to the Twins since they and Jo went on and on about where Jo's stuff was supposed to be put at Sean's house and what, if anything else, of Jo's stuff was to remain. Sean gathered that Pat had enlisted the aid of several young men to do the heavy lifting, while Mo gave moral support and Pat supervised everyone. Sean was amazed at how fully Pat had taken over the entire move.

Jo decided that after the Twins had graduated, she would sell her place. But, she was in no rush since real estate prices in the area were moving up rapidly.

As their Mustang convertible went through Carson City, Jo felt warm enough in the sun to take off her red and white State jacket, which she had on over her sundress. As she applied suntan lotion onto her exposed skin,

Sean asked if he should force himself to call the office. Jo giggled and said that it would probably be safer, for several reasons, if she did the talking.

The conversation, as Sean heard it, went like this: "Hi! Miriam, this is Jo. Sean, against my wishes, insisted that I call."

After Sean heard Jo giggle at Miriam, Jo said, "Just barely. I'm practically force feedin' him oysters and raw meat. But, he's not strong enough yet to be able to hold onto the phone. Does he have any messages that won't keep until we get back?"

After Jo and Miriam went back and forth on the phone for a minute, Jo turned to Sean and said, "Miriam said that she has two things to tell you. First one is that Justice Brown has invited us to have dinner with him and Sarah at his new place on the evenin' of Saturday, the 26th."

After discussing the invitation with Sean, Jo told Miriam that she should call Justice Brown back and tell him that they would love to dine with him and Sarah. With a raised eyebrow, Sean said to Jo, "Ask her what she did now."

A moment later, Jo, barely suppressing a giggle, said, "Miriam wants to know if she'd be in trouble if you heard that she went skinny dippin' after the reception."

Sean said to Jo, "Tell her she'd be in big trouble."

Jo repeated the answer to Miriam. Giggling, Jo said, "Miriam said that she's glad you don't listen to rumors."

Now smiling, Sean said to Jo, "Ask her if the lake at Lucy's place was warm enough for her."

Jo finished the call with Miriam and then said to Sean, "Miriam was so disappointed. She was so sure that she had pulled one over on you. What gave it away?"

Sean just smiled. As the convertible left U.S. 50 and turned onto Nevada 341, he said, "Jo, welcome to Virginia City, Nevada. You are now in one of the most famous mining towns in history."

*　*　*　*　*　*　*　*　*　*　*

Hours later, as their convertible began to take them from Virginia City back to Lake Tahoe, Jo and Sean discussed the day's trip. Jo said, "Precious, no matter how long I live, I'll always remember that miners in Virginia City were paid $4.00 per day, which was at least double what other workin' men in the U.S. were paid at that time. When you consider they got paid that princely sum for workin' half-nekid in the heat while some goon swung a big sledge hammer at a huge spike that was perched on their shoulder just

212

inches from their head, with only one candle to light up their work, it doesn't sound like much, does it?"

After agreeing that the wage wasn't worth the danger involved, Sean's additional comment was that he suspected many of the miners were probably in the mines just to earn a grubstake to go prospecting. He reminded her that the life expectancy of miners—according to the tour guides—was measured in months, not years.

Jo and Sean talked about the sights they'd seen in greater detail. As they discussed the beautiful vestments and other religious objects that they saw in the display cases at St. Mary's in the Mountains, the satellite phone buzzed. Since Sean was quite occupied with a switch back, Jo answered the phone.

That was just as well since the call was for her, anyway. After chatting for several minutes, Jo ended the call. She said to Sean, "Precious that was Darla. She started off by scoldin' me for not replyin' to the email she sent me on Sunday evenin'. When I reminded her that I'd been kinda busy, I think I embarrassed her. After I said that to her, Darla paused and said that she sort of assumed since you were a judge, we weren't that busy. I think that she understands now that you are a man first and a judge second."

After Sean gave Jo a quizzical look, Jo continued, "The big news from Darla is that Professor Sims proposed."

A very surprised Sean inquired, "How did she manage that?"

Jo replied, "Sunday afternoon, they went out to Plum Lake to Maggie's place. Maggie mentioned somethin' about the time that Darla and I had been decoys in a prostitution sting. On the ride back to her place, Darla mentioned that she had a some photos that were taken that day. When they got back to her place, she showed him a few of them. Darla said that Sims was really surprised at how tarty I looked. I guess I fooled him!"

After they both laughed, Jo continued, "When he saw the pictures of Darla, she said his eyes got all big and very round. His face got all red. And he started sweatin'. Darla said that he didn't say anythin', he just looked at her. Darla moved him off center by askin' him if he wanted to see the pictures of her undercover as a topless dancer. When he said he didn't think he could handle it, Darla said that she was just kiddin'."

Sean said, "I am sure that he was close to fainting by that point."

Jo added, "Sims really floored her then when he asked her if she and I had arranged for her to catch my bouquet. When he heard that the whole thing was planned in advance, he asked her why we had planned it."

Sean laughed and said, "And I thought that I was dense! What happened next?"

Jo said, "He got down on one knee and proposed, just like they show men doin' in old, old movies."

Sean said, "Beautiful, can I ask you a question? What does Darla see in him? He always struck me as being one of those people who confuses real life with what goes on in law books."

Jo replied, with a very serene look on her face, "Even though Darla is very country, a bit wild and often crude, he treats her like a lady. As I can tell you from **very personal** experience, that really impresses a woman. I was really impressed by you on our first date when you treated me that way. You had my heart by the end of that date. I guess you and Boyington Sims, III have something in common besides teachin' at the same law school."

After discussing the scenery for a moment, Jo asked, "Precious, can you keep a secret?"

Stifling the urge to say, *Better than you, apparently!* Sean promised to keep mum.

Jo giggled and then said, "Darla has a pet name for Sims—BS. She said that the first time she tried it out on him, he doubled over with laughter. He told her that she was one of the first people he'd ever met who figured that out about him. He loved it!"

Sean's comment was, "Love may be blind, but not stupid!"

Jo liked that comment a lot!

****

On Thursday evening, when they left the Rotary meeting, there was still some daylight left. About the time they had driven a good forty miles east of Carson City on U.S. 50, the sun began to finally set. Noticing that the sunset was absolutely breathtaking, Sean pulled the convertible off the side of the road, so they could take some pictures with the digital camera. After Sean had filled up one memory card, he came back to the convertible and changed out cards. As he was fumbling around with the memory cards in the fading light, Jo asked, "Precious, think it would be okay if I sat on the hood and you took a few sexy shots of me?"

After looking both ways on the deserted highway, Sean inquired, "How sexy?"

After Jo assured him that she wouldn't do anything to get them arrested, Sean said, "Okay, but cover up if anyone comes."

In the five minutes of their very impromptu photo shoot, Jo had a chance to live out one of her deepest fantasies. She had always wanted to have her picture taken looking sexy, sitting on the hood of a car like Faye Dunaway in *Bonny and Clyde*.

Before any traffic came along to disturb them, Jo had her jacket back on, her blouse buttoned back up and her skirt pulled down again. The biggest problem they had was finding her sandals, which she had kicked off a little too enthusiastically. Jo repaid the trouble and effort that Sean took to find her sandals by not wearing them on the ride back to the lake. Instead, Jo squished around in her seat and managed to wiggle her bare toes at Sean. Sean liked that, although he pretended to not notice at first.

As they headed west again in the convertible, Jo asked Sean, "Precious, did the flash give us enough light?"

Sean told her to check out the camera for herself. Jo giggled a lot and finally said, "Precious, you've got another career possibility. If you don't want to be a judge or law professor any more, besides bein' a dance teacher, you could always become a boudoir photographer. Damn, I look sexy!"

Pulling off of the highway for a minute, Sean demanded a chance to look. He was also impressed—just not as much with the photography as with the model. As they drove along, Jo said, "Precious, I want to ask you somethin'."

Sean, not knowing what was going on in Jo's mind, said, "Yes, dear."

"Precious, how long until we're back at our place? I've got to use the bedroom." The convertible sped rapidly through the dark of the desert. Sean had to struggle valiantly to keep his mind on his driving.

* * * * * * * * * * * *

As Jo and Sean looked out the window at the garish glow of the neon lights, Jo said, "Precious, I'm really glad that you came up with the idea of spendin' a few days here in Reno at the Peppermill.™ I didn't guess when you suggested the idea that we would have such a great time. Between havin' dinner with your ol' friend, Keith, and his wife, stuffin' ourselves silly at Bavarian World™ and your luck in the casino, we've had quite a great second part of our honeymoon."

As Sean refilled Jo's champagne glass, Jo continued, "You and Keith were in school together. How come Keith's older than you?"

Sean, said, "If I told you that keeping a younger bride happy tends to tire yet rejuvenate an older man, you wouldn't believe me, would you?"

Jo, shaking her head, indicated that she wouldn't. Sean continued by saying, "Actually, Keith **is** older than I am. Although he and I began law school together, he was in his late twenties when we started. After college, he served as a naval aviator. He didn't start law school until after he got out of the service."

Jo said, "Whatever his age, he seems to be a really nice man. He and Joan look very happy together."

After Sean agreed, Jo changed the subject, "Precious, what possessed you to want to play over at the Big Dollar slot area?"

Sean, returning to form, said, "Actually, I think they call it the *High Dollar Slots*. Whatever it's called, with you on my arm, I was feeling really lucky."

Jo said, "I suppose it must be that famous Irish luck. I never would have guessed you would hit the big jackpot after only puttin' five twenties into that video poker machine. How much did you win?"

Sean, turning pensive for a second, said, "Let's see. If I had just one royal flush at the five-dollar level, that would have been $20,000. But, since I was playing a five-play machine, you multiply that figure by five. If you would have looked at the check they gave me, it was for $100,000.00, less withholding."

"Precious, I was too excited to pay attention to that. All I knew was that you'd won something big. I was just so excited."

Sean said, "When I hit the button to play the hand and it came up in sequence, Ace, King, Queen, Jack and Ten—all in spades—I was totally shocked. Fortunately, my legal training made me obsessive-compulsive, so I managed to hit the 'hold' button for each card and then check and recheck them. I don't think you really noticed that I had a sequential royal flush until after the lights started going off."

Jo looked at Sean and said, "Precious, will I ever be able to read you? I was lookin' at your face when you drew the royal flush. I couldn't tell that you had somethin' really big from your expression."

Sean apologized for his old, bad habit of repressing his emotions too much. After he apologized, Jo promised she would perform her spousal duty of nagging him if he didn't let her know what was going on in his head. After that, Sean and Jo turned and looked out their other window, where they could see a deep wine-red sunset slowly turning into royal purple on Mt. Rose in the distance. This display of colors made the neon of the sign at the entrance to the Peppermill pale in comparison. As the light slowly faded in the room, Jo held Sean tenderly to her very ample bosom and cuddled him while telling him how happy she was.

****

216

Several hours later, Sean and Jo were sound asleep, close together as two spoons in a kitchen drawer. Jo felt Sean shudder and shake violently in his sleep. Jo, not knowing what was wrong, gently massaged his back until Sean woke up. Once Sean was awake, he turned to Jo and said, "Beautiful, I just had this horrible dream. In the dream, we were blissfully happy here in Nevada. When the scene changed to back home, it seemed like bad things were waiting for us everywhere we went. When you woke me up in the dream, you were drifting away from me like a helium-filled balloon, shouting at me, *Precious, I'll always love you!* It was **so** intense that my hands are shaking. Look!"

Jo, putting her experience with bad dreams to work, jumped out of bed and came back to Sean a minute later with a miniature bottle of Jack Daniels that she had extracted from the mini-bar and a glass half-full of ice and water. Between the alcohol, Jo's massage and the TLC that Jo gave Sean that night, Sean was able to fall asleep again. But, before sleep came to Jo, she wondered what was bothering him. Eventually, Jo slept...but not well.

Chapter Twelve

As Jo admired Sarah's engagement ring, Sarah said, "We bought it the Monday after y'all got hitched." Jo noticed that the stone was the same size as hers, but thought that it looked smaller on Sarah's larger hand.

Somehow, despite the large meal Sean and Jo had eaten, they managed to find room for the peach cobbler that Sarah offered them. As they ate, Justice Brown said, "While y'all were off on your honeymoon, I was real busy. The Monday after the weddin', I actually took a half-day off to shop for a ring with Sarah. That afternoon, I went back to chambers and turned in my resignation to the Chief Justice. The effective date will be September 1st, which will give me thirty-two years to the day on the bench."

Jo asked, "Justice Brown, what are you gonna do after you retire?"

Grinning, he said, "Probably, I'm gonna spend a lot of time tellin' people to call me *Sam*."

After all four of them laughed, Sam Brown continued, "Jo, that was a fair question. I'm plannin' on doin' what I'd originally wanted to do when I was a law student. I want to help people solve their problems."

Sean said, "You certainly helped people your entire professional life."

Sam continued, "Lawyers were respected in the small town that I grew up in. It's true that most of them made more money than the average person and got to dress up nice. But, that wasn't why they were respected. Forty years ago, lawyers always seemed to have the time to listen to people's problems. If they could help, they would. If the troubled person needed to be referred to someone else—maybe a preacher or an accountant—they'd make the referral. But, if they couldn't do anythin', they'd at least listen and offer their sympathy, if nothin' else. That's why they were respected. They put people first and money second. Unfortunately, I lived a different life than that of a small-town lawyer."

"What happened?" Jo asked.

Sam continued, with a wry smile, "Like most things in life, there was a lady involved."

After the four of them shared a laugh, Sam went on explaining, "Toward the end of my second year of law school, I met an undergraduate lady at S.U. Since I had started law school so young, she and I were the same age. We really hit it off. The idea crossed my mind about marriage. Then, it dawned on me that if I followed my plan of hangin' up a shingle, I wouldn't have anythin' to offer her. So, when the District Attorney in my home county offered me a job with his small office, I jumped at the offer. My plan was to stay there long enough to save up some money to tide us over when I finally hung up a shingle. Unfortunately, about that time, the governor asked me to accept a district court bench. You know the rest."

Sean asked, "Why are you retiring now?"

Sam replied, "Sean, two things happened at once to point me in that direction. First thing was at the beginnin' of the year, the retirement people sent me one of their computer generated mailin's that showed me how much money I'd get if I retired at age sixty. 'Cause I've been on the bench since I was twenty-eight, when I retire, I'll make about as much as I do right now. So, from a purely economic standpoint, I'm just about workin' for free. That makes no sense to me."

Jo, Sarah and Sean all agreed with Sam on that point.

"The other thing was meetin' Sarah," claimed Sam. "She and I really enjoy each other's company. I'd rather not have to get up every mornin' and drive to Capitol City, when she's right here. So, if I open a law office here in Smithville, I can be closer to her."

Turning to Sean, Sam asked, "Sean, what are your career plans?"

Sean, looking a mite confused, said simply, "Getting reelected."

Sam laughed and said, "Are you interested in becomin' an appellate judge?"

Sean indicated that he'd never thought about the matter one way or another. Then, he asked, "Why do you ask?"

Sam indicated, "Sean, back when I was a trial judge, trials were slow things. Most trial judges heard pleas and motions in the mornin' and often didn't start the trials 'til after lunch. Trial judges weren't under the pressures that they are now. Nowadays, with the big dockets that trial judges face, they have to act fast to keep dockets movin'. For instance, there's a district court judge in Queen City, who tried over one hundred felony jury trials last year. Can you imagine the strain that poor man is under day in and day out? Bein' under that much pressure is a young person's game. You're still pretty young, Sean. But, someday you won't be. You should plan to get out while you're still doin' a good job. Nuthin' makes the legal system look bad as much as a trial judge who hung on to the job too long."

Sean said, "I understand very well. Why did you mention becoming an appellate judge?"

Sam said, "I had a couple of reasons. Appellate judges have less stress in their lives than trial judges do. I figured that Jo might appreciate seein' a bit more of you, particularly in a good mood, than she would if you stay a trial judge. My other reason is that I think you'd be a good appellate judge."

Sean's reply was a simple, "Thank you."

Sam continued, "In a few days, there's gonna be an appellate bench comin' up. Want me to put in a good word with the governor? Knowin' how slowly these things move, I doubt that he'd name anyone 'til after the November general election."

Sean looked at Jo for guidance. Jo, not being cursed with an overly introspective mind, nodded her head. Sean said, "I doubt that the governor even remembers meeting me. Feel free to pass on my name, for what it's worth."

After some small talk, Sam obtained permission from the ladies to take Sean outside for a short walk. As they walked in the balmy, late summer evening, Sam said, "When Sarah and I discussed my settin' up a law practice, we agreed that I need to have a younger lawyer to work with me. You know, I haven't tried a case as a lawyer in over thirty years. I suspect that once I send my announcements out, I'll have more business than I can say grace over. At your weddin' reception, I talked to a young lawyer, who said that he's tried cases in front of you. What do you think of Tom Ritter?"

Sean said, "He's got a great reputation. First time he was in my court, he was beaten up pretty badly by a lawyer, who knew the tricks of mental health law better than he did. Since then, he's been back in my court many times. He's done a real fine job those times. I think that he's got a good grasp of civil practice. I think you'd be real happy with him."

Sam smiled and said, "That settles it for me. If you think that he's good, that's good enough for me. I'll call him at home tomorrow and offer him a partnership. Between September 1st and when he can leave the county, I'll be a solo practitioner. Look for an announcement of our new firm sometime in mid-September. I've got an option on some office space in Smithville. The space will hold two lawyers real easy. There'd be room for a third lawyer if you decide to retire someday."

Sean just smiled.

✳✳✳✳✳✳✳✳✳✳✳✳

As Sean and Jo made the short drive home, Jo asked, "Precious, did you say nice things about Tom Ritter?"

Sean, being curious, wanted to know, "Why do you ask?"

"When you and Sam were walkin', Sarah guessed that's why Sam took you outside."

Laughing, Sean said, "I told the truth. He's a fine lawyer. What else did Sarah say?"

"She said that you'd be a good successor to Sam."

Sean asked, "What else were you two up to?"

Jo replied, "She asked if she had embarrassed you too much that night she hugged you at the resort."

"What did you say?" Sean asked.

"I told her that I was workin' real hard to get you over bein' quite so easily embarrassed. I told her that livin' with me, you're gettin' a chance to stop bein' so stuffy."

Sean said, "We're home. Just in time, I think!"

＊＊＊＊＊＊＊＊＊＊＊＊

As Jo stepped off of the elevator with Sean at the Horizon Club, she immediately noticed the very large sign in the middle of the lobby that read:

> ## JUDGE RILEY RECEPTION
> Main Dining Room
> August 30, 2000
> 5 – 7 pm

The sign was surrounded by two large clusters of red, white and blue balloons. As Jo and Sean walked into the room, Sean said, "If you can't read someone's name tag, squeeze my hand, so I can introduce the guest to you."

As soon as Sean was done speaking, Bob and Roxanne Griswold appeared, warmly greeting Jo and Sean. After the greetings were over, Bob said, "Sean, I hope that you're in good voice today. We've received over one hundred RSVPs in the mail as of noon. So, you can probably expect another hundred to show up with checks in hand."

As Bob walked Jo and Sean to the table at the entrance to the room, which was manned by two very pretty young ladies, Jo asked Sean, "Do you really know two hundred lawyers by name?"

Sean replied, "By face, I know a lot more than that. The problem is sometimes I have trouble putting the name and face together. That's why we give them very nice, large name tags. Unfortunately, that doesn't always solve the problem. Last time I ran, I made a complete fool of myself at my fundraiser. A lawyer showed up with a very pretty, little redhead. I made the mistake of assuming that his lady was his wife, who I knew was a very pretty, little redhead. It turned out that the lady he was with was the reason

221

that he was getting divorced. I guess that he has a thing for pretty, little redheads. I hope I've learned from that experience."

Jo said, "Should I ask who the two sweet, young things were at the reception table?"

"Beautiful, nowadays, most Political Science professors require that their students put in some time getting involved in actual politics. I'm sure that those young ladies are students fulfilling their course requirement."

Being playful, Jo asked, "Seein' them, are you sorry that you rushed into marriage like you did?"

Sean, more alert than usual, said, "No! The only mistake I made was waiting so long. I should have proposed on our blind date. Besides, those sweet, young things are about the age of my daughters. A wise man never gets involved with a woman the same age as any of his daughters. Doing that tends to make holidays a little too exciting."

As Sean finished speaking, Roxanne appeared and placed very large, plastic-encased name tags on their lapels. No sooner had she finished, when the elevator dinged in the distance as the first of the guests started to arrive.

Jo, being a stranger to the world of day-to-day politics, found the fundraiser to be fascinating in a strange way. It seemed to her, **if** all the lawyers who spoke to them were telling the truth—something that she very much doubted—Sean must have at least one hundred and fifty close friends that he had never told her about.

As they greeted their guests, Jo noticed that all of the conversations seemed to share the same theme. Either the speaker was telling Sean that it was a darned shame someone was running against him, that he needn't worry because everyone loved him or that he was doing a great job and shouldn't worry about the election.

Jo noticed that she seemed to have caught the eye of most of the male lawyers. The female lawyers also gave her the eye, but much more critically. Since Jo was wearing a conservative, navy-blue suit with an expensive white blouse, a small string of pearls, moderate black heels and nude hose, she knew that none of the women lawyers could find fault with her attire. Jo was wearing her hair up, which accented her face and blue eyes.

Jo was surprised by how many of the guests at the fundraiser had seen her on television. She managed to entertain a number of the guests by telling them a bit about how reporters behave when off camera. She was a big hit with both sexes.

Jo's biggest surprise of the evening came later, when Kim and Covey appeared near the end of the reception. Kim told Jo that she and Covey had gone out of state the week before and had gotten married. Jo handled the situation well, chatting with Kim for a few minutes before wishing her the best. Covey looked a bit sheepish when his time to speak to Jo came. Jo took his hand and wished them both the best. Then, Kim and Covey moved on, their places in the line being replaced by other well-wishers. (Jo found out later that their check, drawn on a new checking account with the names Kimberly and Covington McReynolds III, was in the maximum allowable amount of $5,000.00.)

On the ride home that evening, Jo asked Sean about why people gave money to judicial candidates. Sean told her that originally he thought the idea of taking money from lawyers smelled a bit funny. He told her that he had gotten over his initial revulsion after he figured out that big-time lawyers all gave about the same to all the candidates—incumbent judges and their challengers. So, it sort of cancelled itself out. Sean said that what had pleasantly surprised him was the large numbers of lawyer donors, who might only appear once a year in his court on something uncontested. They were doing it out of public spiritedness and a chance to hobnob with all of their lawyer friends.

As they drove along, Sean wondered if he should say anything to Jo about Covey and Kim. Fortunately, just as Sean was caught in the midst of indecision, Jo said, "I'll bet that Covey and Kim went out of state to get married to avoid hassles with his mother. I guess that he learned from our engagement that he shouldn't give her time to react."

Sean asked, "Think she and Kim will hit it off?"

Jo surprised Sean when she said, "I doubt it very seriously. From what I've heard about Kim, she's really scrappy—in a nice, polite way. Sean, did you know that she was an Army nurse before she went to law school? In my experience, women with military nursin' experience tend to handle pressure pretty well and don't take kindly to bein' bossed around."

Remembering that Jo's mother had been a Navy nurse, Sean smiled at Jo.

Then, Jo added, "Kim's a JAG major in the reserves. From what she told me, she has a good shot at changin' the color of her oak leaves in the next few months."

Sean said that he never knew that about Kim. Although Sean thought the matter was closed, Jo added, after a minute's silence, "Precious, I was still in my twenties when Covey and I faced his mother. Kim's got to be a decade older and a lot more mature and sure of her place in the world. I doubt that Mrs. McReynolds will get to her like she got to me."

As soon as they got home, Jo led Sean into the bedroom. Sean knew exactly what she wanted and gave it to her. Afterward, Jo held Sean very close to her and whispered in his ear several times, "I love you."

Sean held her tightly and told her that he loved her, too. If Law and Equity hadn't demanded that their food bowl be restocked right then, Jo and Sean would have just drifted off to sleep in each other's arms. When they finally turned in for the night, both slept very well.

****

The main parking lot of the Ransom County Fairground was starting to fill up when Jo and Sean arrived for the big September 4th Labor Day Campaign Rally. Since the morning was almost over when they arrived, Sean and Jo were dressed for the heat, knowing that the rally would be outside. As they walked from the parking lot to the reception area where they would sign in, Sean said, "Labor Day has traditionally always been the start of the *official* campaign season for the two parties. For many years, we have always had our rally at the fairgrounds. The opposition has its rally in the central city. Both sides battle for better media coverage. My guess is that we are going to win the battle of the rallies this year because we are going to have the governor and one senator at ours."

As soon as they had checked in and received their name tags, Roxanne Griswold appeared and greeted them both warmly. A moment later, Bob appeared. After explaining the schedule to Sean, he told them to grab some barbeque before the line got too long and then to work the crowd. As Bob and Roxanne were about to greet someone else, Bob turned and asked Jo if he could take Sean aside for a second.

When they were by themselves, Bob said, "Sean, I sent you an email just before I left home this morning. The governor's office called me earlier today and asked if you would be interested in the opening on the Supreme Court. Are you interested?"

Sean said, "I hadn't really thought about it."

Bob replied, "They're interested in you. My email tells you what to do, which is basically to email a letter along with your biography to the appointments secretary. I don't know what you did, but they called me, which has got to be a good sign."

A few minutes later, Sean whispered to Jo what Bob had said as they worked their way through the food line. Jo smiled and said, "I'll give you one guess who suggested your name." They both laughed.

The part of the rally before the speeches was a lot of fun. Jo was surprised at how easily her usual shy and self-effacing husband slipped into the role of politician. She smiled at the thought that Sean was a lot like her, in that both of them easily adapted to their surroundings. Jo noticed that Sean, who normally found being with people to be a drain on his energy, seemed to draw strength and energy from the many well-wishers that he spoke with at the rally. She couldn't help but be impressed with how Sean was pumped up and ready for reelection. Jo was sure that the festive surroundings, the music, the smell of the excellent barbeque and the prevailing red, white and blue color scheme had worked their spell on Sean, just as they had on her. She was also energized.

At precisely 1345 hours, as it was scheduled, the master of ceremonies requested that the candidates and their companions go to the side door of one of the buildings, off a way from the main pavilion of the fairgrounds. Once they were in the building, the candidates were given the numbers of their seats on the big stage. After they were numbered, the candidates and their companions went through a receiving line to meet the guests of honor—the senator and the governor.

Since Sean and the senator didn't know each other, Sean and Jo just exchanged the usual remarks with the senator and his wife. When they got to the governor and first lady, they were very pleasantly surprised. The governor greeted Sean very warmly and told Sean that he had heard good things about him from a number of different people, including the dean of the S.U. law school. The governor knew enough about Sean's biography to convince Sean that he was definitely under consideration for the S.C. opening. The first lady surprised Jo when she greeted her by her law enforcement rank. She knew enough of Jo's background to impress Jo. When the first lady quoted the sheriff, saying that he had mentioned she was on her way to higher positions, Jo was pleasantly surprised.

After the candidates and their companions had completed their treks through the receiving line, the candidates were led out the door to their seats on the stage. The companions of the candidates were led to their reserved seats at the front of the crowd. Jo had guessed correctly that the companions of the candidates—wives mostly, but certainly not entirely—were going to be seated up front. Obviously, they would know when to cheer and would cheer loudly. But, Jo also deduced that the companions acted as a shield for the people on stage since, if there was anyone in the audience intent on causing harm, they would be another ten to fifteen feet further back from the stage than they were in the first row. (Jo knew that, at distance, very few people could hit much of anything with a handgun.)

The crowd was lucky that afternoon. Both of their illustrious speakers were committed to fly to other parts of the state after their speeches were over at the fairgrounds, so they gave short speeches. At the end of the program, each and every one of the local candidates on the upcoming November ballot was introduced. Jo was very proud and happy when Sean got a big cheer. Sean suspected that he got the big cheer because his name was the last one of the candidates, but didn't say anything like that to Jo, who was beaming with pride.

After the program ended, Sean was glad to be back with Jo. She was very happy to see him, planting a big, wet kiss on his cheek as soon as he was within range. Sadly, their embrace was interrupted by a voice coming from behind Sean. Turning to the sound of the voice, Sean said, "Jo, may I introduce our illustrious County Chairman, Bill Morrow."

As he shook her hand, Jo noticed that Bill's eyes kept darting back to her chest. Although most women would find Bill's handsome, square face offset by dark, earnest eyes; his dark hair; his tall, athletic physique; and his toothy smile attractive, Jo did not. He struck her as very insincere and a born back-stabber.

Sean and Bill talked for several minutes about Bill's plans for the upcoming campaign. Bill went on and on about the great television ad that the county party was going to prepare for wall-to-wall advertising during the last ten days before the election. When Bill turned to Jo and said that after talking to her, maybe he should revise the ad format to allow camera time for judicial spouses, Jo wanted to gag. But, in spite of her revulsion, she said, "Bill, that would be very nice. But, I think that the voters would probably want to see the judges, not their families."

Feigning a reluctant retreat, Bill agreed with Jo. Then, Bill surprised Jo when he asked, "Jo, have you ever considered running for office? You have a great presence. The voters would take to you very readily. You ought to think about it for 2002."

Jo replied, "I'm flattered that you'd even think about me runnin' for office. I'm not a lawyer, so what could I run for?"

Bill, sensing that he was making some progress, said, without hesitation, "Ransom County is going to pick up one or two seats when the Leg redistricts next time. You'd love being a legislator."

Jo, being intrigued with the idea, said, "I'd have to quit the department, wouldn't I?"

Morrow, knowing that Jo had caught the bug, said, "I'm not a lawyer, but I don't think so. State law doesn't let governmental agencies fire, demote or reassign employees for service in the Leg. Besides, by then, wouldn't you be vested in the pension plan? If you did leave the department, I'm sure that you could find some other business venture to keep you occupied. Or, you could divide your time between being a homemaker and a legislator. Think about it."

After exchanging a few further pleasantries, Bill departed. Looking at his watch, Sean said to Jo, "I guess that we'd better be leaving. I've got to get ready for class tonight."

As they rode home, Jo asked, "Precious, do you think that Bill was serious?"

Sean said, "Bill is always serious about politics. He eats, sleeps and drinks politics."

Jo inquired further, "If I ran, would I have to leave the department?"

Sean replied, "I have no idea. Why don't you wait until after the Leg completes its redistricting plan next year? If it looks like a seat might be available, talk to the sheriff. In the meantime, you can get your name and face out before the public by working with me on my campaign. After the election, you ought to get involved in a Republican club."

Sensing that Jo was intrigued, Sean decided to change the subject. "Beautiful, what did you think of the rally?"

Jo answered, "Precious, I had a good time. I was really impressed with the energy and enthusiasm of the crowd. The senator and the governor both gave really good speeches. The lady from the Bush campaign was really good, too. But, the best part of the rally was when you were introduced. I got a lump in my throat when I heard everyone cheerin' as your name was called out. I was so proud."

A few second later, Sean's F-150 was at the gate to their home. As they pulled up the driveway, Jo asked Sean if it would be okay with him if she planted flowers alongside their driveway and some trees by the stone fence that separated their property from County 191. Sean agreed that planting flowers and trees there would be a nice touch.

When they entered the house, Sean quickly showered, changed clothes and headed off to class. Sean never liked making the law students go to class on a legal holiday. But, because law school classes had started the week before, the schedule said there would be classes on Labor Day. So, law students had to labor on Labor Day while everyone else got the day off.

****

As Jo and Sean hurried to his truck in the late afternoon sun on a very hot Wednesday, September 6th, Sean said, "I hope this evening with Professor Rodriguez and her husband, Dr. Rodriguez, the Chemistry Professor, won't turn out to be a dud. I was shocked when she extended the invitation at the reception. When I saw her at the beginning of the new semester, I'd hoped that she'd forgotten all about it. I guess not. I have no idea what to expect."

Jo asked, "Precious, what's she like?"

Sean replied, "She's very passionate. I don't know much about him. I guess that we'll just play it by ear."

La Casa Rodriguez was in a very nice, tree-lined area of University Acres, located near the campus. As soon as Jo and Sean rang the bell, the door opened and they were greeted very warmly by the Dr. and Professor Rodriguez. Soon, Sean's misgivings were gone.

Before they sat down to eat, Professor Rodriguez said, "Sean, I imagine that you probably don't remember, but back after you joined the faculty, the few female professors and the wives of the male professors held a tea to welcome Cheryl to our extended family."

Sean said, truthfully, "You're right. I don't remember it."

Looking at Sean, Professor Rodriguez said, "Not announcing your engagement until the very end of the school year and then getting married over the summer created an etiquette problem for us."

Turning to Jo, Professor Rodriguez continued, "Lieutenant, please accept our apologies for not contacting you sooner about the scheduling of the tea, but a number of us were concerned that with Sean's reelection campaign, you might not have any spare time available until after the election. Would you prefer to wait until after that is behind you?"

Jo replied, "Professor, that would be fine."

Professor Rodriguez responded by saying, "I'll write you in a few weeks with several proposed dates. But, please call me Isabel."

Jo replied, "I'll look forward to the tea. But, I'll only call you Isabel if you call me Jo." Isabel agreed.

The diner was fabulous, featuring dishes from both Spain and Cuba. Over the meal, Sean and Jo learned a good deal about their host and hostess. Both of them had stories to tell.

Isabel's family was from Catalonia. They were highly placed in the Loyalist Government. When that government fell, her family escaped to Cuba, as did many other Loyalist families. Isabel was born in Cuba.

Fortunately for her, the family business was export-import, so when Castro came to power, they just transferred their business operations to New York City. She grew up wealthy. She was also an overachiever in school, graduating Summa cum Laude from Vassar and Order of the Coif from Columbia Law. After clerking for a U.S. District Court judge in Manhattan, she was an Assistant U.S. Attorney for several years. After that, she surprised her colleagues by going to work for the federal public defender's office.

Isabel said, "The work load was incredible. We didn't have enough lawyers to handle all the cases that we had. After about three years, I was near burnout. One day, purely out of the blue, I received a call from a law school classmate who told me that she had heard about an opening at Southern University to teach Evidence and Criminal Law. As soon as she told me about the opening, I rushed—actually, I ran—to a pay phone to find out if it was true. Thinking back, I'm surprised that the lady who first took my call didn't just assume I was a mental patient calling from Bellevue and hang up. I must have talked a mile a minute in my rapid Cuban-accented English. A few days later, I was out of the cold and damp of Manhattan and in the sunshine of University City. I probably would have worked for free if the Dean had asked me. I didn't know it until I arrived at Southern University, but I hated the cold and the congestion of New York."

Jo asked, "Is this where you met your husband?"

Dr. Rodriguez now spoke. Befitting his elegant manner, his words were calm and measured. "The first week of the school year, there was a reception in honor of the new faculty. Because I was a junior tenured professor in my department, I was asked to attend the reception. But, since my first wife had been dead for less than a year, I only went out of a sense of duty."

After Jo and Sean both expressed their regrets at hearing of Dr. Rodriguez's first wife's passing, he continued, "Just like your first wife, Judge, my wife died in an automobile accident. She left me very lonely and sad. But unlike you, I had three small children in the house."

After pausing for a second, Dr. Rodriguez continued, "As soon as Isabel spoke, I knew that she had grown up speaking Catalonian-accented Spanish. As a Castilian, I can sense those things. We spent enough time talking at the reception that I was emboldened to ask her for a date. To my surprise, she accepted my offer."

Jo said, "Doctor, did y'all hit it off well on your first date?"

Jo was surprised when both members of the host couple laughed at her question. Dr. Rodriguez first requested that Jo call him Carlos. After that, he continued, "On our first date, I made the mistake of making a political remark. She was not impressed at all with my politics. We argued the entire time. Our first date seemed to be a miniature version of the Civil War, with Isabel telling me just how evil Franco was. When the evening was over, I knew that we would never see each other again."

Isabel added to the narrative by saying, "Carlos was shocked when I delivered a note to him right before the start of one of his classes a few days later."

Carlos continued, "She stole my heart with the note."

Jo said, "May I ask what she said?"

Carlos laughed, "The note, which was written in proper Castilian Spanish, said the war is over. If we agree to never discuss politics again, I would love to see you another time."

Isabel added, "We never, ever discuss politics in this house. I know that he belongs to Opus Dei, but I say nothing. He knows that I am very liberal, but says nothing. Love is more important."

Sean asked Carlos about his area of interest within Chemistry. When Sean seemed to follow along with his explanations, Carlos inquired if Sean had a background in the subject.

Sean said, "Indirectly."

When Carlos asked Sean what he meant, Sean explained that his grandfather had been a chemist. Carlos asked his name.

When Sean replied, "Pierre Le Beque," Carlos smiled and said, "I do not know if you realize just how great a chemist your grandfather was. My work today is based on discoveries that he first wrote about after World War I. He was truly a giant in Chemistry."

Sean was flattered to learn that his grandfather was that well regarded. Jo started to wonder if their children would be too smart for her to understand.

The rest of the evening's conversation was devoted to Isabel's war stories about several criminal cases that she was working on. Jo was a little surprised that Isabel practiced law on the side.

As they drove home that evening, Jo remarked, "Precious, I was surprised to hear that Isabel handles criminal cases. I thought law professors just all taught school and wrote books and stuff."

Sean commented by saying, "Daphne sees patients, doesn't she? Why should law professors be any different? Actually, once you've got tenure, outside of your academic responsibilities, it is really up to you. I have some colleagues that might write an article or two a year, but don't do much else. Some of my colleagues are real scholars, cranking out books and articles year in and year out. I have other colleagues who work part-time for law firms and are well paid for their efforts. Some of my colleagues sit on various boards and committees for the bar and the state. But, one of my colleagues, a guy named Reddick, is into fitness. When he isn't teaching, he is either working out or running someplace. He cranks out an occasional article on Sports Law, but his heart isn't into the law anymore. We all suspect that he likes teaching because he gets to use the university's athletic facilities for free."

Jo was surprised to learn that academics could be so dissimilar. Changing topics, Jo inquired, "Precious, did you know that your grandfather was famous?"

Sean responded, "Sort of. When I was an undergraduate, I had a course that dealt with the Theories of History. There has been an ongoing debate for about a century and a half or so whether great people make history or if ordinary people, being caught up in extraordinary times and events, make things happen."

Jo asked, "What do you think?"

Sean continued, "As part of the class, we had to do a paper about someone we knew personally who was famous. For this assignment, someone was considered famous if they were listed in an Encyclopedia or some other reference book of famous people. Being only twenty, I didn't think that I had ever met any famous persons. But, when I discovered that my grandfather and both of my parents were famous in their fields, I understood the question. To me, they were just regular people who did what they had to do, or needed to do, when the time came."

Jo said, "Sean, until I met you, I don't think that I ever knew anyone famous."

Sean replied, "Are you forgetting your father? I'm sure that if we look in the library, we could find his name in a book of Medal of Honor recipients. What about you? You've been decorated for valor and been on TV. A lot of people recognize you by sight. Doesn't that make you famous?"

Jo, after pausing a minute, replied, "My Daddy just got the Medal of Honor for doin' what he was supposed to do. I was decorated for bein' at the bank at the wrong time and reactin' like any other peace officer would."

Sean said, "You've just made my point. Famous people are just like everyone else. We all have families, get sick, shop for groceries and make love. Famous people are just like everyone else—except that somebody else decides that what they did deserved special recognition."

Jo looked surprised at Sean's comment. Sean, employing his teaching skills to their fullest, said, "Jo, somewhere in my library, I've got a book written about President and Mrs. John Adams. If you read the part that contains the letters between them when he was working on the Declaration of Independence, you can see that in addition to trying to give birth to our country, he also had to deal with all of the problems of normal life, things like running low on funds, the cow stopping giving milk and the like. He was just a human being in extraordinary circumstances. He rose to the circumstances, as the truly great ones always do."

Jo asked Sean to find the book for her when they got home. As they got near home, Sean said, "One of the great things about America is that both the great and the regular people all lead ordinary lives. So, it is hard to tell them apart. When I was in law school, there was a professor there who had been in a number of high positions in government, including a stint as attorney general of the United States. One day, after Cheryl and I were married, we saw him and his wife shopping for groceries. He was a great person, doing an ordinary thing. If he would have lived in another country, he wouldn't have done those things for himself."

Jo pondered what Sean said for the rest of the ride home. Later that evening, as they were snuggling together with Law and Equity in their bed, Jo asked Sean very softly, "Precious, if we found ourselves in extraordinary circumstances, would we rise to the occasion?"

Sean, after thinking for a moment, said, "God willing, may we never find out."

****

Sean was tired and jumpy. First, the wind started making the windows shake and rattle around 0200 hours. At 0315 hours, a thunderclap followed a second later by a bolt of lightning, shocked Sean, Jo, Equity and Law into a groggy state of semi-wakefulness. A minute later, the rains came pouring down. At 0450 hours, Sean gave up and slipped into the kitchen to fix himself breakfast, knowing well from years and years of experience that thunder, lightning, rain and a falling barometer made him edgy, irritable and nervous. As Sean ate, he recalled Durkheim's thesis in Sociology that weather like this was strongly linked to increases in deviant behaviors, such as crime and suicide.

After eating, Sean went back into the bedroom. Jo was still sound asleep. So, he gathered up what he needed to shower and shave, and went to a guest bathroom, hoping that he wouldn't wake her. He didn't.

Jo didn't wake up until the alarm went off at 0615 hours. Sean kissed her on the cheek and told her to drive carefully because this Monday, September 11th promised to be a nasty day.

Sean was at his desk in his chambers by 0700 hours. Normally, court didn't start until 0900 hours, so on most days he would have been way early. But, since he had an emergency guardianship hearing set at 0730 hours and was going to begin picking a jury at 0900 hours, he really wasn't all that early. As he reviewed the file for the guardianship hearing and the research that Laura had done for him, Sean realized that he'd left home without picking up his copy of the *University City Bugle* from the metal delivery box near his front gate. Sean decided that he probably didn't have time to read the *Bugle* this morning, anyway. He hoped that his copy would stay dry until he got home.

The guardianship hearing really was an emergency. An adult child of an elderly ward—the one who had been rejected by Sean as the guardian at a previous hearing just six weeks ago—was being accused by the guardian of planning to abduct the ward. The guardian was seeking an injunction barring the accused child from the premises of the ward's nursing home, except under strict supervision. The behavior of the witnesses was as unruly as the weather that morning. Mercifully, the parties ran out of verbal ammunition just as the lawyers for the jury trial were beginning to arrive at around 0830 hours. Sean granted the injunction and then warned the enjoined child of the very serious potential consequences of violating one of his orders. Sean hoped that the message sank in, but he had his doubts.

After a quick recess, Sean returned to the bench to ask the lawyers if they had any preliminary matters to be addressed while Bubba was waiting for a jury panel. The lawyers surprised everyone present by informing the court that a settlement had been hammered out in the hallway a few minutes ago. After the lawyers read the settlement into the record, the lawyers and litigants left the courtroom. While Angela called Bubba to tell him that they weren't going to need a jury panel that morning after all, Sean talked to Jane about her upcoming wedding.

Angela interrupted the conversation by saying, "Judge, Bubba said that we were really lucky they settled, because it would have been a close call on getting a jury this morning. He guesses that the rain scared off a lot of potential jurors."

While Angela was speaking, Sean was pleasantly surprised to see his lovely bride of one day less than one full month enter the courtroom. As Jo walked slowly toward the bench, Sean sensed that something was very, very wrong with her. When Jo slowly approached the bench, Sean noticed that she looked like someone who had just experienced a major trauma. By the time that Jo was standing right in front of the bench, Angela and Jane were both staring at her silently. When Sean came around to her and put his arm around her, Jo just stood there motionless. When Sean asked Jo what was wrong, she struggled to speak. But, no intelligible words came out of her mouth, just sounds. Sean sensed that Jo was close to hysteria and did not want to break down in public.

Sean very carefully led Jo back to his office, followed by Angela, Jane and Miriam. When Sean and Jo reached the door to his office, Sean said, "Miriam, please hold my calls."

When Miriam waved a pink message slip at Sean and tried to say something to him, Sean glowered at her with a look that most Marine Drill Instructors only dream of developing. Once Jo was seated on his sofa, Sean closed his office door, none to gently.

Sitting very close to Jo, Sean asked in his softest, kindest voice, "Beautiful, what's wrong?" Jo stared at him, biting her lip while tears started pouring down her cheeks.

Sean asked, "Is it your family?" Jo shook her head.

Sean asked, "Are you sick?" Jo shook her head again. Being frustrated by his inability to communicate with Jo, Sean asked, "If I give you a legal pad and a pen, will you write down what's wrong?"

Jo nodded. A minute later, Jo wrote on the legal pad, in a very unsteady hand:

I'M ON PAID ADMINISTRATIVE LEAVE UNTIL THE

HEADHUNTERS ARE DONE WITH ME!

HELP ME!!!!!

While Sean didn't know too much about law enforcement procedures, he did know that if a cop was placed on paid administrative leave, the accusation was probably either not too serious, or not too credible. Still, he hadn't the foggiest idea what Jo could have been accused of doing. Sean let

Jo cry until she had managed to work it out of her system. Finally, Sean summoned the courage to ask her, "What happened?"

Jo stopped crying. Very slowly, she reached into her purse and pulled out a copy of the second section of that day's edition of the *Bugle*. Jo pointed to Winfred K. Rudd's column, which read:

SPECIAL RULES FOR SPECIAL PEOPLE

If you or me, or anyone else that we know, stood to inherit fifty million dollars if our spouse died, and if our spouse died under very mysterious circumstances early one morning when our whereabouts were unknown, what would happen? We'd probably get to learn a lot about the so-called Criminal Justice system, wouldn't we? At a minimum, we'd be grilled by the toughest, meanest homicide detectives that they could find, right? If we couldn't come up with a good alibi, we'd probably get hauled before a grand jury, indicted and arrested, wouldn't we? Of course, any regular Joe or Jane would.

But, if a judge is the person under suspicion, different rules seem to apply. In March of last year, Judge Sean Riley's wife died while he was allegedly out of town. The next year, his financial report shows him being $50,000,000.00 better off than he was when his late wife, Cheryl, was still alive. Has anything happened to him? Not a blessed thing has happened to him.

But wait, the story gets more interesting. Not long after his wife was dead and buried and her death was swept under the rug, Judge Riley started showing up at fancy restaurants with a stunning brunette, a female sergeant from the sheriff's department, who just happened to have been a supervisor at the very same precinct that investigated Mrs. Riley's death.

Sound suspicious to you? It does to me. But wait, the story gets even more interesting. A year after the late Mrs. Riley was laid to rest, there is now a new Mrs. Riley, the stunning brunette, who before she married Judge Riley, was known as Sergeant Jolene Scruggs. Well, now she is Lieutenant Jolene Riley, having been promoted to the personal staff of the sheriff, himself. Really interesting, huh?

It gets better. Before Sergeant Scruggs became Lieutenant Riley, she seemed to live pretty high on the hog for a lowly sergeant. She drove a brand new SUV, with no debt on it. She lived in a swanky house near the Southern University campus, which had no debt on it. Since Judge Riley teaches part-time at the S.U. School of Law several times a week, he was just a few blocks away from the future Mrs. Riley's plush pad, far away from prying eyes.

I guess that nothing will happen, though, because as we know, in Ransom County, *there are special rules for special people.*

Jo dried her eyes while she watched Sean read and then reread the column. Jo noticed that Sean was showing no obvious sign of emotion as he read, except that he had loosened his necktie and opened his collar. After looking at Jo for several minutes in silence, Sean leaned over to her, took her hands in his and said, "Beautiful, do you love me?" Jo somehow managed to rasp her assent.

Sean then asked, "Do you trust me?"

Jo responded, "With my life and my soul, I trust you completely."

Sean said, "Back on that awful day in August last year when you stopped those bank robbers, you were following your instincts, weren't you?"

Jo said, "I didn't have the time to think. I went on instinct—plain and simple."

Sean said, "As much as I'd like the opportunity to think this through, we don't have the luxury of being able to do that. Plus, I'm right in the middle of it, so my objectivity is shot. My darling, will you trust my instincts here?"

Jo smiled just a hint of a smile and said, "Of course, I trust your instincts. But remember, Rudd gets the choice of weapon."

Jo had said just the right thing. Both of them started laughing as they tried to picture Sean dressed in Regency clothing out on a foggy moor, preparing to duel. Sean said, "That's Plan B."

Sean rose and asked Jo, "Diet or regular?"

After Jo said that she probably needed some sugar with her caffeine, Sean picked up his telephone and punched in a two-digit number. A moment later, Jo heard Sean say, "Laura, if you'd be so kind, Jo needs a Coke and her husband needs a Diet Coke pronto."

A moment later, they heard a rap on Sean's chamber door. After Sean admitted Laura and shut the door behind her, he took the cold drinks from her and said, "Laura, thanks for bringing us the drinks. I used them as a cover to let you in here. Do you know what's going on?"

Laura said, "Bubba told us all about it. It seems as if the Rudd column was **the** topic of conversation over at the jury assembly ready room this morning."

Sean reached into his wallet and pulled out a very wrinkled piece of yellow writing paper. He handed it to Laura and said, "I need to talk to Justice Brown. The top number is his home number. The next one down is his cell phone. The number after that is his fiancé's home number. The last one is her cell phone. When you get him on the line, transfer the call to me in here. If you can't reach him at any of those numbers, let me know. I might have another way of reaching him."

As Laura was about to leave his office, Sean said, "Tell Miriam that it's safe to bring me all of my messages by now. And tell her that I'm not mad at her." A very nervous Miriam approached Sean's office. When she entered the office, Sean said, "I'll bet the first call that you had on voice mail when you came in this morning was from Bob Griswold, right?" Miriam nodded apprehensively.

After reviewing the messages, Sean said to Miriam, "If anyone else calls, tell them that I probably won't be available to speak to them until tomorrow, but that you'll give me my messages as soon as I am available."

Putting a stack of message slips aside, Sean said, "I'll return these calls today." Handing Miriam the rest of the message slips, Sean told her, "Please call these people back and tell them that I'll return their calls as soon as I can, maybe tomorrow."

Pausing for a second, Sean said to Miriam, "The next few days are going to be really busy for you. If you can't keep up with the calls, you've got my permission to draft Jane, Laura and Bubba to help you. If Bubba starts complaining, tell him that if he won't help, I'll pay Shirley to help. That should keep him awake long enough to help you."

As Miriam left, Jo realized that Miriam probably loved Sean, too, as did Laura. Somehow, Jo was reassured by this realization. As Jo was thinking, Sean took off his robe and put his suit coat back on. As he reemerged from his closet, Laura buzzed and said, "Justice Brown on line two."

After a very brief conversation, in which Sam Brown told Sean that he'd been expecting the call since he'd seen the column, Sam agreed to meet with Jo and Sean at his new office in Smithville. He agreed with Sean that since Bob Griswold was a licensed attorney, his presence would be very useful in analyzing the situation. Sam agreed to invite Griswold to the meeting. So, they planned to meet in Smithville around 1100 hours.

After Jo and Sean left his chambers, Angela, Bubba, Jane, Laura and Miriam all agreed that if this was how the week was starting, it was going to be one long week!

Chapter Thirteen

Sean wouldn't let Jo get behind the wheel of her SUV until he was satisfied that she would able to drive safely back to their place, where they would leave her vehicle. As they headed home, Sean devoted most of his time and energy to watching his driving and watching how Jo drove.

When they reached the house, Jo went inside to change and put on fresh makeup. Sean waited outside in his F-150 while the rain continued. During his wait, two things happened that brought cheer to a very upset and uncertain Sean. The first cheery thing was Miriam's call on his cell phone.

"I hate to bother you, but I thought that this might be important. Dean Churchill called to express his full support. He said that if there is anything he can do to help, please let him know. He made me promise to tell you that if you've got some time this afternoon, he'll make himself available to talk to you."

After thanking Miriam for calling him, Sean asked her how many messages he had waiting for him. Miriam said, "I've taken over one hundred. Bubba, Jane and Laura have taken more. When you come in, you're going to be busy returning calls." After thanking Miriam and telling her to thank Bubba, Jane and Laura for him, Sean sat in his truck in silence while waiting for Jo.

The second thing that boosted Sean's spirits was unexpected. Sean started crying. After a minute, he realized that his tears were tears of gratitude. Obviously, he hadn't been deserted in his time of trial. He knew that God always loved him. In addition, Sean knew that Jo loved him. He knew that the Twins and his cats all still loved him. His office staff, particularly Laura, was behind him. His old friend and mentor, Sam Brown, and his friend and consultant, Bob Griswold, were with him, as well. But, the best news was that Dean Churchill was with him, too. Sean had always respected and admired the dean. Having Dean Churchill's support meant a lot to Sean.

While Sean sat in his F-150, the rain began to slowly subside. Off in the distance, Sean saw a very small patch of blue sky beginning to emerge. As he waited, Sean saw rays of sunlight in the distance. Very slowly, the clouds began to blow away, and light and warmth began to conquer the gloom and doom that just a few minutes before had surrounded him. As the sun slowly returned, Sean was gripped with a feeling that somehow, the day's troubles would be vanquished. As he waited for Jo, Sean said a *Pater Noster*.

A few minutes later, Jo appeared, wearing a red-checked blouse, designer blue jeans and a pair of white sandals that he'd never noticed her wearing before. Her hair was pulled back in a ponytail. She had reapplied her makeup. Jo looked perky and upbeat—Central Casting's idea of a happy farm wife. She looked more stunning than usual.

After Sean helped Jo into the truck, they started down the road toward Smithville. As they drove, Jo broke the ice by saying, "Precious, I'm guessin' that we're gonna be Sam's first guests at his new office. I'm pretty sure that we're gonna be his first clients, too. So, I brought a house-warmin' present."

Jo opened her purse and produced their joint checkbook. After they both laughed, Sean said, "Jo, I see that you understand lawyers!"

In spite of everything, both of them had kept their wits about them and maintained their sense of humor. Sean felt confident. As they drove along, the mental image of John Wayne in *True Grit* popped into his mind. By God, he was ready to take on the forces of darkness. He had no idea whether he would win or lose, but he was sure that when the fight was over, not all of the blood on the floor would be his.

As they passed the large, white sign painted with "Welcome to Smithville," Jo asked, "Precious, why are you smiling?"

Sean said, "Promise that you won't tell our doctor friends this. Every year, when I begin my Legal History class, I put up on the overhead screen an image of an English doctor from the 13th century. I tell the class that back then, the professional ancestors of our medical colleagues were busy putting leaches on the behinds of their patients, pulling teeth and cutting hair."

Jo giggled. Sean continued by saying, "Then, I give them a chance to see what our professional ancestors were doing. I show them a film clip from an early movie version of *Ivanhoe*. Are you familiar with it?"

When Jo asked if *Ivanhoe* was one of those knights in armor movies, Sean nodded his head and added, "I show them the scene where Rebecca was condemned to death after a rigged trial. When her sentence was pronounced, she was informed that she had the right to have her case decided by combat if any knight there would be her champion. None of the assembled knights moved a muscle. As the time for a champion to come forward was drawing to a close, she cried out for a champion."

Noticing that he had Jo's full attention, Sean went on with the story, "None of the knights responded. Just as time was about to run out, there was dead silence in the great hall where they were all assembled. At the last possible moment for a champion to come forward to save her, the silence was broken by the sound of a gauntlet being thrown down and sliding noisily on the wooden floor to the center of the room. A voice boomed from the edge of the room, announcing that Wilfred of Ivanhoe would take up her cause."

Jo interrupted Sean by remarking, "Wow! What happens?"

Sean continued, "Rebecca's champion prevails. The false accuser dies in battle."

Looking at Jo, Sean said very earnestly, "I always tell my students that if you enter a courtroom to represent someone, in their eyes, you are their champion. Act like it and never forget it!"

Jo, being confused by Sean's reference to the Middle Ages as retold by Sir Walter Scott, asked, "What does that have to do with us?"

Sean, frustrated at Jo's inability to see what was obvious to him, said, "I'm sure that we'll be able to get ourselves cleared in a trial, which is the modern version of the jousting field."

Jo said nothing, keeping her doubts to herself. She trusted Sean's analysis of the situation, even if she didn't understand what he wanted to do exactly. For Jo, the main thing was that Sean was showing signs of confidence. This made her feel confident in return.

****

When Jo and Sean arrived at the address that they had been given, they weren't sure if they were at the right place. It was the old Smithville Bank Building, which was a dark brown, pre-World War II building. As soon as they pulled into the parking lot, Sarah walked toward them carrying a large sign, similar to those that real estate agents put in front of houses.

When Sean rolled down the window, Sarah said, "Sorry, the temporary sign was just delivered a few minutes ago. Park around back. Sam and Bob are up there already."

Sean and Jo drove around to the back of the building while Sarah posted the sign on the bank's front lawn. When they reached the back of the building, they saw a door with a handmade sign next to it, which read:

BROWN & RITTER
Attorneys at Law

The door opened to a hallway leading to an elevator, which took them to the second floor. When the elevator door opened, Sam and Bob greeted them warmly. After the greetings were over, Sam led them to a conference room. He said, "You're lucky that you needed me today instead of last week. The conference room furniture was delivered late last Friday. If y'all would've come here Friday, we would've had to sit on the floor."

After Jo and Sean took their places at the table, Sam started off by saying, "Bob and I talked about how to handle the mechanics of your representation. Sean, since you and Bob have a preexisting attorney-client relationship, anything you say to him, arguably, would be privileged. But, since he also performs non-legal services for you, it could be challenged. So, if you and Jo are agreeable, I propose that you and Jo hire me as your counsel. I'll retain Bob to provide me with technical public relations advice. So, as my agent, both you and Jo can talk freely with him. Agreed?"

After they agreed, Sam asked Jo and Sean each for a dollar bill. Sam said that these two dollars were the first fees earned by the new law firm and that he and Tom were going to frame the bills. Then, Sam handed Jo and Sean an engagement agreement. After they signed it, Sam had Bob sign the agreement that they had drafted earlier. Once these formalities were over, Jo asked Sam, "Can we sue the *University City Bugle* and Rudd?"

Sam said, "Sure, but it won't solve your immediate problem."

Jo looked askance at Sam, who said, "Jo, in this state, we have a statute called the London Libel Law. It says that we have to give a newspaper a written demand to publish a retraction before we can sue. If they don't retract the offending statement within thirty days, then we can sue. Since today is September 11th, by the time that they'd have to respond, after filing some dilatory pleas, the election would have come and gone. I'll be glad to send both Rudd and the *Bugle* a letter to start the clock running, but I doubt that you'll get much out of pursuing them. Besides, there are a couple of technical problems that you'd have to overcome, which would make recovery real difficult."

Jo inquired, "Technical difficulties? Like what?"

Sam looked at Sean and said, "I'm guessin' that on your honeymoon, you didn't talk about *New York Times v. Sullivan*, did you?"

After Bob, Sam and Sean all chuckled, Sam continued, "Back years ago, the Big Nine in D.C. decided to let the media be able to take cheap shots at public figures and get away with it. So, they came up with a ruling that makes it darn near impossible for a public figure to sue over any sort of nasty story, true or not."

Jo said, "Sean's a public figure, I understand that. But, what about me?"

Sam shook his head and said, "The cases say that public employees are public figures to the extent that their activities affect the performance of their duties. The cases have applied that definition to public school teachers and city water department employees. We can do some research, but I'm not very confident that we can get around that problem."

At this time, Sarah entered the conference room. She said that in a few minutes, she'd take their orders for lunch. She handed them copies of the menu from a local Chinese restaurant that delivered. She asked if, in the meantime, anyone wanted anything to drink.

After Sarah returned with their libations, Sam continued, "Jo, you've got another problem with filing suit. What are your damages?"

"I'm on administrative leave from the department!" Jo told him.

Sam asked, "Paid leave?"

Jo replied, "Sure."

Sam smiled and said, "You don't have any economic damages yet."

Changing the subject slightly, Sam said, "Tell me what happened at work after the article came out."

Jo, after pausing for a second, said, "Around 0815, the sheriff walked into my office. He looked like his best friend had just run off with his wife and his dog in his pickup truck."

Bob Griswold, who hadn't said much until then, said, "Jo, I'm not surprised. The sheriff sees you as one of the rising stars in the department. When he retires in a few years, he wouldn't be at all unhappy if you succeeded him. I'll bet the column really hit him in the gut."

Jo, not knowing what to say to Bob's kind words, continued with her story. "After I read the article, we went over it line by line. We laughed at some of the obviously stupid things that Rudd wrote. We both knew that I couldn't have had anything to do with the investigation of Cheryl's death since the department doesn't have jurisdiction."

Sean interrupted by saying, "I don't understand. Why wouldn't your department have jurisdiction?"

Sam stepped in, saying, "Sean, back when I was a rookie prosecutor, some unhappy litigant in a rural county tried to take his revenge on a judge who'd ruled against him in some case by shootin' out the windows of the judge's home. Fortunately, nuthin' happened to anyone in the house. But, for some reason, no one was ever arrested. The judge's wife's mother was a sorority sister of the governor's wife, so the governor called a special session of the legislature to address the issue of threats and acts of violence directed toward state officials and their families. An obscure law was passed, givin' the state police exclusive jurisdiction in crimes of violence directed toward state officials and their families."

Sam asked Jo, "What else happened with you and the sheriff?"

Jo said, "I told the sheriff that Sean and I met last March, a year after Cheryl died. When I told him that we were introduced by Kyra and Max Townsend of the D.A.'s office, he wrote down their names and smiled."

Sam asked, "What else happened?"

Jo told Sam, "The sheriff wanted to know if what Rudd said about my financial condition was true. I told him that it was. He looked sour when I said that. Then, I told him about my late first husband leavin' me a bunch of money in trust. Next, he asked me a bunch of very specific questions."

Sam asked, "What did he ask and what did he say or do in response?"

Jo replied, "He asked when and where Abe and I were married. When I told him, he wrote it down. Then, he asked me if I could verify the existence of the trust. I told him the name of my trust officer and gave the sheriff the trust officer's telephone number. When he asked me if I would be willin' to give the department access to my trust records without a subpoena, I told him that I would. A moment later, the sheriff asked me to phone my trust officer. I did and asked what I needed to do to let the department have access to my trust records. The trust officer faxed me a release form, which I signed and faxed back to him."

Sam asked, "Anythin' else happen?"

Jo started to get red-eyed when she resumed speaking, "The sheriff looked really sad when he said this to me. He said if I had any other position in the department, he would let me stay on the job, pendin' the verification of the facts that I had just told him. We both agreed that I couldn't be dealin' with the media while a storm was ragin' about me and my husband. The sheriff asked me if I'd prefer to be temporarily reassigned or put on paid administrative leave until things calmed down. I asked for the leave. He told me that if I was cleared, no matter what was happenin' with Sean, I could come back to work. I hope that he meant it."

Bob Griswold intervened at this point by saying, "Jo, I guess that you don't know this about Sheriff Walker. But, he and his wife had a daughter, who looked a lot like you, and had she lived, she would be about your age now. Talking to you today just about broke the sheriff's heart. I know, because he called me right after he spoke to you. He asked me to tell you what he couldn't say himself. He doesn't believe a thing that Rudd wrote about either one of you. But, there isn't anything he can do about Sean since the whole matter of Cheryl's death is out of his jurisdiction. But, I know this, once he verifies what you told him, you'll be back to work."

Jo started crying at this news. The sheriff's respect was as important to her as Dean Churchill's respect was to Sean. She was so glad to hear that the sheriff didn't believe Rudd's foul lies.

Sarah then took their lunch orders, which gave Jo a chance to calm down a little bit. When the discussion resumed, Jo asked, "If we can't clear Sean's name before the election, what are we gonna do?"

Looking at Sean, Sam asked, "Sean, are you sure that you're up to livin' with this feisty young lady?"

When Sean said, "Some days, I'm not at all sure," Jo shot Sean a very disapproving look.

Sam said, "Jo, I said a moment ago that you're feisty because you jumped to a conclusion. Did I say that I couldn't help you two?"

Jo shook her head. Sam smiled very sweetly and said, "All I told you was that I couldn't file a libel suit and clear y'all before the election. I didn't say that I couldn't help. I think that I can help you."

Sam asked, "Sean, since you teach Legal History, what do you remember about the origin of the office of the coroner?"

Sean replied, "If I remember correctly what Professor Maitland wrote, the coroner was originally supposed to be a check on the power of the reeves of the shires, who quite early on were notoriously corrupt. The coroner's original job was to convene an inquest if the remains of a dead person were found. The coroner's jury was supposed to determine if the person died from natural causes, an Act of God, misadventure, suicide or from the hand of another, either lawfully or unlawfully. The coroner's job was just to determine the identity of the deceased and the cause of death. He didn't have any criminal enforcement power. But, obviously, if the coroner found a death to be at the hand of another, pressure would be placed on local officials to investigate, arrest and prosecute the person responsible."

Sam asked, "Jo, did you know that you married a walkin' encyclopedia of useless legal facts?"

Jo smiled and said, "That's part of his charm. Besides, a man with his mind in the fourteenth century probably won't be wastin' his time lookin' at other women."

Sam said, "Jo, you're every bit as smart as you're feisty and lovely. Sean's a lucky man to have you. Anyway, when we became a state, coroners were part of our system of government. By the late 1950's, the job had become an anachronism since pathologists could easily do a better job. So, in 1959, the constitution was amended to abolish the job as an elected office in every county. But, a compromise was needed to get the amendment through the legislature so the amendment, as it was submitted to the voters, read that all powers to conduct inquests were placed in the attorney general. After the amendment was passed, the next session, the legislature passed a statute settin' forth the procedures to be followed in inquests. The first opinion that I was assigned to write when I joined our Supreme Court had to deal with a mandamus action brought against the AG for not appointin' a coroner when requested. My opinion held that the duty was ministerial in nature and granted the mandamus. I've checked the cases and my opinion is still the only opinion on the subject. The statute is still the same."

Sean asked, "How would this inquest help me?"

Sam smiled and said, "It will give you just what you need—a public forum to clear your name before the election."

Bob Griswold smiled and said, "We talked about it before you two arrived. It's your only clear shot at putting this to bed before the election. If you can get a ruling in your favor, I can use this controversy to your advantage—big time."

Sean asked, "Bob, you think you can actually bail me out of this mess politically. How can you do that?"

Bob smiled and said, "I'm working on that right now. Can we meet here on Saturday morning around 10:30? By then, my plans will have crystallized enough to present them to you. You're gonna love it! Rudd and Greene are gonna feel like they were just run over by a garbage truck."

Jo and Sean looked at each other and smiled. The normally gloomy Griswold's sudden enthusiasm was something that they both appreciated seeing, even if they had doubts about what he was saying. Bob added an afterthought, "Sean, from now on, if you get any calls from anyone who thinks that you have been mistreated, please ask them to call my office. I need to start compiling a database for our counterstroke."

After a moment, Sean looked at Sam and asked, "Sam, what do we have to do to get an inquest?"

Sam explained, "The statute requires the AG to appoint a licensed medical doctor, board certified in pathology and a resident of this state, to be the coroner at the inquest once a request for coroner is received. The AG has only ten days to comply once the request is received. Requesting the inquest is a piece of cake. The statute has the form of the request written in it."

Sean asked, "Who can make the request?"

Sam said, "Any five or more persons resident in the county, who would be eligible to register to vote, may make the request."

"What happens after the AG receives the request and appoints the coroner?" Sean wanted to know.

Sam told him, "Once the request has been received and the coroner appointed, the coroner must hold a preliminary hearin' within fourteen calendar days. At the preliminary hearin', each of the requestin' parties, plus the district attorney for that county and any other interested persons as defined by the statute to be close family members and companies with insurance on the decedent's life, are to submit a list of persons, things and documents to be subpoenaed. The actual inquest is to begin not later than fourteen days after the preliminary hearin'. At the hearin', the coroner, either directly or through his attorney, the people who requested the inquest and interested persons—again either directly or through counsel—may interrogate the witnesses. Procedure, beyond that, is pretty loose."

Sean looked outside and saw that the sun was now shining brightly. He smiled. Tom Ritter stuck his head through the conference room door.

Sam asked, "Did you get it?"

Smiling, Tom said, "Now, we're officially lawyers in private practice. We've got stationery." After Sam looked approvingly at the letterhead, he introduced Tom to Jo and Bob.

Sarah then appeared at the doorway and announced that lunch had arrived. While they ate, Sam brought Tom up to date on what had happened. Tom thought Sam's approach was excellent.

As they ate, Sean said, "Just out of curiosity, who do you suggest that we ask to sign the request forms?"

Sam pointed to the couple and said, "You're one and Jo is two."

When Sean asked Sam if his daughters could be three and four, Sam said, "Bob and I were talkin' about that before y'all arrived. His guess is that the media, not knowin' what else to do, might hound the other three people. So, unless we really get desperate, let's find some different people."

Sean asked, "What sort of people would you recommend?"

Bob suggested that the best choices would be mature adults, who knew Sean well. He further suggested that the signatories be well regarded in the community and the sort of people who wouldn't be intimidated if a camera crew showed up at their front door. He suggested that they stayed away from people in law enforcement, lawyers and Sean's employees.

Sean thought for a second and said, "I'm sure that Father Wilson will do it." Right after he finished his statement, Sean called Father Wilson on his cell phone and asked him. When Sean received a positive response, he let Sarah make the arrangement to come by the rectory that afternoon and obtain and notarize his signature on the required form.

A second later, Sean looked at Jo and asked if it would be okay with her if he approached Daphne and her husband to join in the request. When Jo nodded her head, Sean picked up his cell phone. Before he could dial, Sam asked, "Is there somethin' about your relationship with this Daphne that I ought to know about?"

Sean said, "We're friends. A long time ago, we were more than that."

With a skeptical tone of voice, Sam inquired, "How long ago?"

Sean managed to get a laugh from everyone present when he said, "The end of Richard Nixon's first term as President."

On cell, Daphne not only agreed to sign the request form, but volunteered her husband, as well. Daphne and Sarah arranged a time for Sarah to come by and obtain and notarize the signatures of Daphne and her husband.

Thinking ahead, Sean asked Sarah if she would give him an extra request form to take with him to the law school. He suspected that one or more of his colleagues might volunteer to help.

As the meal wrapped up, Sean's cell phone went off. Miriam was on the other end, telling him that a lady named Professor Rodriguez had called and said that if he needed a lawyer, she was available and to call her. Sean informed the group of the call. Then, he asked Sam, "How many lawyers are we going to have at the inquest?"

Sam replied, "The more the merrier. If Isabel wants to sign on, I'd recommend that you sign her up. She's smart as a whip, tenacious and very, very passionate. Besides, that way, Jo wouldn't be the only woman sittin' with us at counsel's table. The women on the jury would notice that favorably."

Sean called Isabel on his cell phone. After bending his ear for ten minutes about the horrid thing that had befallen him, Sean stopped her cold by saying, "Isabel, remember what Socrates asked Crito? He asked him if he would have preferred that Socrates had been condemned justly. Let's be thankful that I've been wrongly accused!"

Very quickly, Sean said to Isabel, "I'm meeting with my lead counsel right now. He's someone that you know, retired Justice Sam Brown. Let me put him on the line."

Sean was amazed at the part of their conversation that he heard. They sounded like old friends. Several minutes later, Sam ended the call by saying, "Tom, Sarah and I will look forward to seeing you here at three."

Right at 1300 hours, Sean and Jo were preparing to leave the offices of Brown and Ritter. As they stood up, Sam said, "We'll mail the retraction demand letters to Rudd and the *Bugle* from the downtown U.C. post office tonight. Sometime this week, I've got to go to Capitol City to sign some forms for my pension. As soon as I've got five or more inquest request forms in hand, I'll leave directly and mail the request to the AG from the downtown Capitol City post office. That way he'll get it within a few hours."

When Jo and Sean stood to leave, Sarah asked, "Sam, do you think our guests would be offended if we asked them to stay over just long enough to sign and notarize their request forms?" Grinning, Sarah said to Jo, "Lucy told me a long time ago that lawyers need to have non-lawyers around them to handle small details that are too minor for them to contemplate."

Bob, Sam, Sean and Tom all agreed that it was too true. Lawyers do tend to get so engrossed in their work that they tend to forget small things. At this time, Jo pulled the checkbook out of her purse and said, "I've got a little over $10,000.00 in my checkin' account. Will that be enough for a retainer?"

Sam looked at Tom, who looked back at Sam. Since neither one of them had ever been in private practice before, neither had any experience asking for fees. Sean broke the ice by saying, "Jo, write a check for $5,000.00. When they need more, they know where we live."

****

When Sean and Jo left the offices of Brown and Ritter, both instinctively grabbed their cell phones and checked their messages. Sean looked at Jo and said, "I'll return my calls from my office on campus. Did you have any exciting calls?"

Jo nodded her head and said, "Darla just called to say that there's a mob of reporters all up and down County 191 waitin' for us. What do you want to do?"

Sean smiled and said, "Let's go visit our neighbors."

When Sean said *neighbors*, he was playing a bit fast and loose with the term. Sean's fifteen acres were carved out of a six hundred acre tract of land, the residue of which was owned by Jared and Alice Lesniak. Sean's property was bordered on the east by County 191. But, the Lesniak property bordered his property on the other three sides. So, technically speaking, Sean and Jo had a neighboring couple, rather than multiple sets of neighbors.

Sean and Jo drove the long way to see the Lesniaks. Driving three miles west of County 191 on an asphalt road, they picked up a gravel road that ran parallel to County 191. They drove north until they hit the old, glorified former cow path that would take them east again, right to the front gate of the Lesniak property.

When they arrived at the Lesniak farm, the Lesniaks were busy in the barn. When they heard Sean's truck drive up, they dropped what they were doing and came up to greet them.

Jared arrived at the truck first and said, "Sean, Alice and me was wundrin' when y'all were gonna come by to see us about them reporters camped out in front of y'all's place."

Sean asked Jared if he knew when the camera crews appeared. Jared, after scratching his head for a second, said, "I reckon around 11:30."

Sean looked at Jo and said, "We just missed them."

Alice said, "Anythin' we can do for y'all, just ask."

Sean asked, "Could we go in and out of our place from your pasture?"

"Sure thing. Anythin' else we can do?"

Sean smiled and said, "Pray that this blows away soon."

Jared and Alice both smiled and said that they would pray. Then, Alice drove up with them to show Sean where the gate to the pasture was located. Sean drove right up to the barbed wire fence and let Jo out. Jo walked very carefully around the truck to the fence since sandals and pastures weren't exactly made for each other. Somehow, despite her sandals, Jo nimbly climbed the fence and started to walk toward home, carrying her purse over her shoulder.

As Sean and Alice drove back toward the barn, Alice turned to Sean and said, "I can see in your eyes how worried y'are about Jo. Relax! She's a country girl. Somehow, she'll survive. We always seem to be able to make it through the bad times. Tonight, when you get near our place, call us. With all of them reporters around, we're gonna have to lock our front gate when it gets dark. We wouldn't want one of them citified fools gettin' gored by a bull, would we?"

They both laughed. Alice continued by saying, "Tonight when you drive in, I'll give you a spare key to the gate. No tellin' how long them fools 're gonna be camped out there."

As Sean drove away, he figured that he had better drive to campus on a road parallel to County 191 since the last thing he wanted to do was to tip his hand to that howling pack of mongrels. As he drove off, he remembered two things that Jo had said to him when they drove up to meet her family over the Memorial Day weekend. The first thing was that country people are generally very nice, warm, generous people. He'd always thought that. As he got further away from the Lesniak farm, he also remembered Jo saying, "No matter what you do, no matter how hard you try, dairy farms always stink."

* * * * * * * * * * * *

When Sean arrived on campus, he felt safe. First thing that he did was to say hello to Pamela, the dean's secretary. When he told her that the dean had asked to see him, she looked at the dean's schedule and suggested that he come by right at three. Since it was now 1410 hours, Sean went to his office. When he opened the door to the office, he was surprised to see a volume of a multi-volume treatise on tort law on his desk. A large bookmark jutted from the top of the volume. When Sean opened it at the marked page, there was a section entitled, "Libel of Public Officials and Persons after *NYT v. Sullivan.*" Next to the bookmark, Sean found a handwritten note on perfumed, feminine stationery:

Dear Sean,

I hope that this helps. If you need anything else, just ask me.

Beth

Sean was touched by Beth's kindness.

He somehow managed to return all of the messages on the pink message pads in his pocket within thirty minutes. Actually, most of the calls were almost the same. Just about every caller told him that Rudd was a #^&*=&# on his best days and that the caller didn't believe Sean could have ever killed anyone, much less his wife. All of the sympathetic callers offered to help. Sean thanked each one of them and asked them to call Griswold.

The messages on Sean's cell phone voice mail were a different matter. These were primarily personal calls. The callers were very angry. The worst voice mail message that Sean listened to was from Pat, who was in tears. Sean quickly returned her call and got her voice mail. Sean left Pat a message, asking her to call him this evening after class. Then, he called Mo.

She sounded a little better, but not too much. He told her about his call to Pat. When she asked if it would be okay if she and Pat came by, he had to tell her that it wouldn't be a good idea because of the media. Mo suggested lunch on Wednesday. Sean agreed and they arranged the details. Mo promised to tell Pat about it, and then she told Sean to hang in there.

At precisely 1459 hours, Sean appeared at Dean Churchill's office. Pam arose and led Sean to the dean's office. As she rose, Sean thought that, except for Jo, Pam was the loveliest woman he'd ever seen. Talking to Pam always made him feel better when he was having a bad day.

As Sean entered Dean's Churchill's office, it took him a few seconds to adjust to the carpeting. The carpeting in the dean's office was incredibly plush. Walking on carpet that thick made Sean think of the traditional artistic conception of the people in heaven walking on fluffy clouds.

As Sean approached his desk, the dean rose. As had happened many times before, when Dean Avery Steed Churchill stood up, Sean always had the feeling that if a Hollywood studio was casting the roll of law school dean, they'd pick him just purely on appearances since the man embodied Hollywood's image of a mature, dignified, male WASP authority figure. Being six-foot-six, Dean Churchill towered over most other men. His thin, tan, healthy athletic appearance, his full head of gray hair and his bespoke Saville Row suits and shirts always made him look imposing. When Dean Churchill spoke, his deep bass voice and his upper-class English diction completed the image of grand authority. Sean had long suspected that if God the Father took human form, he'd look and sound like Dean Churchill.

After shaking hands with Sean, the dean asked Sean to sit. Dean Churchill came right to the point, offering Sean his help. Sean, being prepared, said, "There is something that you could do for me. I'm requesting that the attorney general appoint a coroner to conduct an inquest."

When Sean finished speaking, he handed Dean Churchill the request form. After reviewing the form, Dean Churchill asked if coroner's inquests were still done on this side of the pond. Sean smiled and produced a copy of Justice Brown's opinion in the case that dealt with the matter.

When Sean said that he was pretty comfortable that he could get an inquest going quickly, the dean smiled and said, "Sam Brown is a good man. He's from the class of '63, I think. Anyway, if Sam's heading up the show, I'll be glad to sign on. Who else is on board?"

Dean Churchill did not recognize Tom Ritter's name. But, he smiled when he heard that Isabel Rodriguez had signed on, too. Putting on his reading glasses, the dean looked at the request form. Then, he buzzed Pam to come into the office with her notary seal. When Pam walked into the office, Sean couldn't help but notice what really fine legs she had. As she leaned over the dean's desk to notarize his signature, Sean smelled her perfume. As Pam left a few seconds later, Sean found himself hoping that Mrs. Churchill didn't die under mysterious circumstances. If he was being crucified for getting involved with Jo months after Cheryl's death, imagine what an evil-minded person could come up with under these circumstances about the dean.

As Dean Churchill walked Sean to the door of his office, he handed Sean the signed, notarized form in an envelope. At the door, Sean said, "The AG will give you notice of the first hearing date. You have the right to appear in person and examine witnesses yourself or retain counsel."

After pausing for a second, the dean said, "Sean, if you don't mind, I'd like to be at those hearings. Leave Brown's numbers with Pam. I'll call him to see if there is anything I can do to help prepare the case."

At Pam's desk, Sean said to her, "Dean Churchill asked me to give you telephone numbers for Sam Brown. The dean may want to call him in the next day or so."

Sean bent over Pam's desk and wrote out Sam Brown's various numbers on a piece of paper. As he straightened up, Pam batted her baby browns at him and said, "Judge, that newspaper article was trashy. Is there anything that I can do to help you?"

Sean said that there was and asked her to call Griswold's office. He wrote down Griswold's number for her. As he was leaving the office, he heard Pam on the telephone saying, "I'd like to sign up to help Judge Riley."

Sean smiled as he walked back to his office. Then, he called Sam to let him know that Dean Churchill had signed on. He made arrangements for Sarah to come by the classroom to pick up the request form.

As Sean got ready for class, it dawned on him that tonight's class might be a trifle awkward for the students. Sean suspected that when he was a law student, if he had only had two classes with a professor who was trashed as badly as Sean had been today, he probably would have felt very uncomfortable. As he walked to class, Sean wondered what he should do.

When Sean entered the classroom, he felt as if all of the students were staring at him. Sean, putting his years on the bench to good use, maintained his calmest demeanor. After looking around the room for a bit, he finally spoke, "Last month, when my bride and I were on our honeymoon, we visited Virginia City, Nevada. One of the things that we saw there was the desk where Sam Clemens, who adopted the pen name of Mark Twain, began his literary career writing for a paper called, *The Territorial Enterprise*. Although Twain eventually moved away from journalism and became what we today call a freelance writer, he brought away from his time as journalist a number of choice comments, one of which is particularly relevant today. Twain used to talk about a man that he had known in his youth. He said that the poor man had been kicked in the head by a mule as a boy. Ever since then, the poor man hadn't been right quite right, believing everything that he read in the newspapers."

The class roared in laughter. After that, their demeanors returned to normal—for law students.

Just as the break after the second hour was about to begin, Sarah slipped into the back of the classroom. All eyes turned toward her. Sean couldn't blame the students, particularly the male students. Sarah looked lovely. But, the strangest thing was that Sarah didn't look like she normally did. She was all dressed up, wearing a navy suit with a very expensive looking blouse and a strand of pearls. When Sean handed Sarah the envelope from Dean Churchill, Sarah said, "I'm dressed today as the secretary of the two most prominent lawyers in Smithville. How do I look?"

Sean smiled, as Sarah pirouetted to give him a full 360° view.

Sean winked at her when he said, "You look better in shorts, but you look fine under the circumstances."

Sarah laughed. Then, she told him, "I'm on my way home. I've already got the forms from Fr. Wilson and that English lady doctor and her husband. Sam will mail the requests off to the AG tomorrow morning from the main post office when he drives in to Capitol City."

Sean smiled and fought off the urge to cry. Then, he said, "Thank you. I really appreciate it."

Sarah smiled back and said, "Sam hid it pretty well today, but he was awful angry when he read that column. I think that he might be a bigger fan of yours than I am, if that's possible."

Sean thanked Sarah again and as she turned to leave, she said, "Be strong for Jo. She needs you."

The rest of the class was uneventful—mercifully! When class was over, Sean ran into Pam, who was chatting with one of the male students. She said, "Judge, your wife called. She asked me to tell you that everything is okay at home. But, you should call her before you come home, because she needs to tell you something."

After delivering the message, Pam walked away with one of the male law students. From their body language, Sean guessed that they were in love. Sean was pleased to see that in the midst of the cold sterility of a law school, love could be found.

When Sean returned Jo's call, all she said was that he didn't have to worry about the reporters any more. When Sean asked why, Jo giggled and told him he'd figure it out when he came home. Jo also added that when he came home, he'd be real glad that he'd married a farmer's daughter.

✴✴✴✴✴✴✴✴✴✴✴✴

When Sean drove down County 191, near his home, he noticed that the embankment of Flatboat River across the road from his house was blocked off by saw horses, bearing signs from the office of the County Department of Public Works. When he got just a little closer, he started to smell something rank. As he drove even closer, the smell became very intense. When he rolled down his window to press his access card against the card reader, he thought that he was going to gag. Somehow, he was able to pull in to his property. Once he made it past the gate, he saw the source of the odor. There was a huge pile of manure off to his left. He quickly drove past it and toward home.

When Sean entered the house, he noticed that the place was full of burning, scented candles. When Jo appeared, he noticed that she was wearing a silk robe that came down halfway to her knees. Jo was beaming. She had soup and a sandwich ready for Sean.

As Sean ate, Jo asked, "Precious, you didn't notice any reporters, did you?"

Sean said, "I didn't. I noticed something else. What did you do now?"

Jo smiled and said, "I improvised. I adapted. I overcame." After watching Sean for a second, Jo continued sweetly, "After you left early this afternoon, I realized that I had nuthin' to do for the rest of the day. So, I decided to play with that nice, expensive weddin' present you got for your country girl bride. I got on it and decided that since we're gonna plant flowers by the driveway and put trees down by the stone fence, I might as well begin to prepare the land."

Sean said, "How do you do that?"

Jo, now beaming, said, "Well, since we can't plant until the spring, all we can do is plow the ground and then prepare the soil by puttin' down some fertilizer. So, I started to plow up the area by the gate and driveway where the flowerbed will be. You know, I love that little Deere™ tractor you got me. The reporters must have liked it too, 'cause they kept pointin' their cameras at me."

Sean asked, with some trepidation, "What were you wearing?"

Jo smiled and said, "If those cameras weren't there, I would've worn a bikini. But, since they were there, I wore a baseball cap, sunglasses, a State t-shirt and shorts."

Jo continued, "About the time that I'd finished plowin' the area by the gate, I had one of my brainstorms. So, I drove my tractor up to the house and called the Lesniaks. We were in luck. Once a week, they haul off their excess manure and sell it to a company that sells fertilizer for gardeners. Jared had just loaded up the dump truck and was about to go off with it when I called. So, I offered to buy the load from him if he'd drop it off."

Sean asked, "How did he get through the mob?"

Jo smiled and said, "We lucked out again. The reporters and the camera crews had been blockin' the road, so about the time that I was on the phone with Jared, a couple of deputies started ticketin' vehicles on the embankment where vehicles were illegally parked. So, they had to move their vehicles. When Jared's truck appeared, the deputies cleared the way. After he dumped his load of manure, the reporters and camera crews headed for the high cotton and haven't been seen since. Tomorrow, I'm gonna start movin' the manure around, after I finish my plowin'. What I'm gonna do is start movin' the manure to the farthest areas first. I figure by the weekend, most of it will be gone from the gate. Of course, by then I'm sure that the camera crews and the reporters will be someplace else."

As Sean led Jo away from the table, he said, "Jo, you done good—real good. I'll bet you need a bath right about now."

Jo just smiled, as she and Sean headed for their large tub.

Chapter Fourteen

Jo planned Wednesday evening to take their minds off of their troubles. When Sean arrived at home, she greeted him at the front door in a long, pale-blue, nearly translucent negligee. She had her hair up the way that Sean liked it best. Jo was wearing high-heeled sandals. Her finger and toe nails were the same color as her bright red lipstick. Jo was wearing a generous amount of Chanel No. 19. Frank Sinatra on CD provided the music for the evening.

Quickly shedding his suit coat and tie, Sean decanted the bottle of Hungarian red wine that he'd bought on the way home. While he was filling their glasses, Jo asked how his day had been.

Sean replied, "It was **very** interesting. Bubba called me on my way downtown and told me that there were camera crews and reporters camped out in the hallway leading to the courtroom. I parked my truck a few blocks away from the courthouse and walked around back to the service entrance of the building. Bubba got maintenance to let me ride up on the service elevator. The varmints didn't see me come in."

Jo asked, "Did they go away?"

Sean shook his head and said, "They were hanging around the hallway making pests of themselves. The people coming in to probate wills were having a problem getting to court, so Bubba went out and talked to them about good manners and respect for the rights of others."

Jo smiled and guessed, "That didn't work, did it?"

Sean replied, "In a strange way, it did. Right after that, Bubba recited the section of the Criminal Code that makes obstructing access to a public building, or any portion thereof, a Class B misdemeanor. They backed off and let the litigants and their lawyers enter and leave the courtroom without obstruction."

After sipping some of his wine, Sean continued, "Once the hearings were over, I returned my telephone calls. A few of the calls were from cranks, but most of them were from friends, supporters and well-wishers. I thanked them and asked them to call Bob."

After Jo served the *vichyssoise*, Sean continued, "I met the Twins for lunch on campus. I was surprised to learn that they had gone to visit Griswold after class yesterday. Bob encouraged them when they asked about organizing a student group to work on my campaign. The group is going to have a booth on the main quadrangle to recruit campaign workers."

Then, Sean added, "The strangest thing happened. As I explained to them what we'll be doing to clear my name, Pat became really interested, particularly in all of the procedural aspects of an inquest. When we were done eating, Pat surprised us with an interesting question. She asked me, if she wanted to go to law school after she graduated, did I think that she could get in?"

Jo asked, "What did you say?"

"Nothing! I didn't get a chance. As soon as Pat was done asking the question, Mo told her that law school wasn't like medical school where you need prerequisite courses to get in. Pat was pleasantly surprised."

Sean said that he thought they were showing a lot of maturity by wanting to do something constructive.

Over their salads, Sean told Jo that Bob Griswold had called with both good and bad news. Before Jo could say anything, Sean said, "The bad news was that my opponent, Tom Greene, has started running television ads. The good news was that Bob said Greene's just wasting his money running them this early, which was fine by both of us."

When Jo inquired what the ads were like, Sean indicated they were generic, proclaiming that Tom Greene, candidate for probate judge, is a man of character. Sean said that Griswold told him the ads were rather amateurishly done. As they discussed the theory of political advertising, Jo served the entrée, London Broil, with creamed peas and rice pilaf. While they ate, Sean recounted that by the end of the afternoon, he had finally returned all of his accumulated telephone message calls. Then, just as he had been ready to try to slip out of his chambers, Sam called to say that the letters were sent out by certified mail before lunch. Jo was very glad to learn that the wheels of justice had begun to turn.

After complimenting Jo on her cooking, Sean said, "Just as soon as I hung up the phone with Sam, Bob called. He was really upbeat, which isn't at all normal for Bob. He told me that his office had logged over three hundred calls this week—so far—from supporters. When I asked him why he was so cheery, he said that I'd find out on Saturday. Then, he surprised me by asking if you and I would be free to go out of town in the afternoon of the 19th and probably not get back until the 23rd. When I told him that you were certainly free right now and that I could see about getting a visiting judge and could reset my Thursday evening class, he told me to do it and call him back as soon as possible. If the sheriff calls you back to duty, will you be able to get away?"

Jo replied that in the unlikely event that she ever heard from the sheriff again, she still had months of comp time available to be used, if she needed it.

After the dishes were cleared away, they retired to the living room. As they enjoyed the peace and quiet, Sean asked Jo about her day. Jo said, "All mornin', I used the bucket attachment on my little tractor to spread manure. Around lunch time, I decided that I'd had as much fun as I could stand for one day, so I came back up here and skinny dipped for a bit before I came inside and had lunch. After lunch, I took a long bath and then started cookin'."

Jo continued, "That was pretty much it, except that Alice Lesniak returned my call invitin' her and Jared to swim with us on Saturday night." Jo then mentioned something that Sean hadn't expected at all, "Right around the time that I was fixin' to start the London Broil, Julie Sharpe called."

Sean, not looking very happy at the name of a media person, scowled. Jo further explained, "She said that she wanted to see me someplace where no one would know her. Julie said that she wasn't gonna ask me anythin' and that our conversation would be *off the record*. She said that she had some information that might be helpful. I was skeptical, but when Julie let me pick the place and said that I could search her for a wire, I decided to chance it. We're gonna have lunch at the Chinese place in Smithville."

Sean's only comment was that Jo should be real careful. While promising Sean that she would be very careful, Jo lit candles to set the mood for the rest of the evening.

✳✳✳✳✳✳✳✳✳✳✳✳

Jack's Chinese Garden™ was a very busy place during the lunch hour since it was the only restaurant in town that didn't serve its entrées on a toasted bun garnished with French fries. Smithville was getting large enough to support another restaurant, but so far Jack's was the only non-fast food restaurant in town.

Jo arrived early to grab a table at the back. Slipping the waitress a twenty, Jo told the waitress that she was waiting for a tall, blonde woman about fifty, named Julie. The waitress, a pretty, little redhead, said that she would keep her eyes peeled for a tall, blonde named Julie.

At the appointed time, Julie Sharpe arrived and was brought to Jo's table by the grinning little redhead. Julie looked like a Hollywood film queen trying to look conspicuously inconspicuous, wearing huge, green sunglasses and a scarf wrapped around her blonde mane. Julie, a stunning, leggy blonde, would have been noticed whatever she wore. The over-done disguise made her stand out all the more.

After the waitress took their orders, Julie got down to business quickly. First thing that Julie did was to empty her purse on the table, saying, "No recorder. If you want to go into the powder room to search me, I'm ready."

Jo's response was, "They make microphones so small nowadays, if I was gonna search you for a wire, I'd have to do a full-body cavity search. Since the powder room isn't big enough for that, I'll just have to trust you."

Julie continued by saying, "Thanks for trustin' me. After the week you've had, I wasn't sure that you'd talk to anyone connected with the *University City Bugle*. Can I have your promise that what I tell you won't be attributed back to me?"

After Jo agreed, Julie told her tale, "These days, I'm seein' a nice man very regularly. Since I work on weekends, we normally get together on Monday nights, which is always the slow night of the week for parties and entertainin'. This last Monday evenin', he and I were at a table way in the rear of The Palm Tree by the back entrance. As my date and I were talkin', I saw the hostess come around and sneak a group of people in from the outside to a private room. From what I could tell, they were havin' a good time back there with lots of caviar, champagne and lobster."

Jo, looking a bit confused and wondering if Julie had a point to make, asked, "Would I know any of the people there?"

Julie replied, "I know that you'd know Mrs. McReynolds. When she came in, her escort was someone that I suspect you know by name— Winfred K. Rudd."

Julie now had Jo's complete attention. She continued, "There were four other couples there that I didn't recognize. So, I asked the waiters to find out who was dinin' with Mrs. McR. and Rudd. Fifty dollars later, one of the waiters told me that one of the men was a politician named Tom Greene, who had come with his wife."

Jo sat at the table in stunned silence for a minute. When lunch came, Jo recovered enough to thank Julie for sharing this information with her. Then, Jo asked, "Julie, why are tellin' me this?"

Julie replied, "Jo, as I drove here today, I asked myself the same thin'. The best I can explain it is that I like you and Sean. I dislike sleazy, egomaniacal, pseudo-journalists like Rudd. I despise dishonest politicians like Greene. I'm absolutely revolted by women like Cynthia McReynolds. The only thin' more revoltin' than her is the thought of what I'm sure Cindy and Winnie were doin' together after their party."

Jo asked, "Why did you say that?"

Julie shot back, "I wasn't bein' catty. They both had **the look** and were hangin' onto each other like teenagers in heat."

The rest of the meal passed uneventfully. When it was over, Julie asked, "If my gentleman friend wanted to contribute to Sean's campaign, who would he contact?"

After Jo told Julie to contact Griswold, Jo hugged Julie goodbye. As soon as the blonde had left the restaurant, leaving her usual cloud of perfume in her wake, Jo fired up her cell phone. Jo called Griswold first and then Sean, who promised to relay the information to Sam. Jo made a note to herself to add Julie to her Christmas card list.

****

While Jo was returning home to her tractor and manure pile, Sean encountered something equally as smelly. Bill Morrow had just dropped by unannounced for a visit. Sean smelled a rat the moment that Morrow entered the room. After a few minutes of small talk, Morrow came to the point, saying, "Sean, we think that it would be best for both you and the party if you file to have your name removed from the ballot. This way, you can devote your full energies to clearing yourself."

Morrow equivocated when Sean asked him to define "we." Eventually, Morrow repeated his request for emphasis. Sean stared at Morrow as if he was a lab specimen under a microscope. Morrow, not taking the hint, babbled on and on about how the mythical "we" thought that the party would be best served if Sean's name was off the ballot.

After several minutes of Morrow's repetitious prater, Sean picked up the telephone and asked Miriam if she would be so kind as to escort his guest to the door. When Miriam arrived, Morrow stayed in his chair. Sean bade him farewell and walked out of the room. Several minutes later, Miriam interrupted Sean and Bubba in the empty courtroom, telling them that Morrow had just left in a very unhappy frame of mind.

When Sean returned to his desk, he started to feel the walls closing in on him. Just as he started seeing the world as a very dark, evil place, Miriam announced that the presiding judge had called while he was in with Morrow and that he would have a visiting judge to cover for him next week.

Sean, hoping that something would help cheer him up, called Griswold. Griswold was in great spirits, telling Sean that now that he knew Sean and Jo would be available next week, the plan—whatever it was—was just about in place.

While Sean was talking to Griswold, Jo was riding her John Deere tractor. When her cell phone went off, Jo put the tractor in neutral and walked away from the noise of its engine. Jo was anxious to take the call, which was from the number used by Helen, the sheriff's secretary.

Jo relaxed once she heard Helen's friendly voice. Helen said that she was calling because the sheriff was having trouble finding a file and needed to know where to look. Jo, for once being as obtuse as Sean, told Helen that the file was probably filed alphabetically, right where it should be. Helen told Jo that the sheriff had said it would be okay to tell Jo that everyone in the office missed her and hoped she was doing okay.

Jo told her that she was doing well. When she told Helen about how the manure had driven the reporters away, Helen laughed and told her that the sheriff would get a real kick out of the story. Helen added that the sheriff would be relieved to hear she was doing all right. Then, Helen told her something that she probably shouldn't have.

Helen whispered, "This mornin', the sheriff sent someone to Capitol City to your bank. When the deputy returned with a thick envelope, the sheriff spent two hours holed up in his office reviewin' the papers. When he came out, he was smilin'. He asked me to copy the file and carry it to Internal Affairs."

Jo wasn't entirely sure, but that sounded like good news. Helen closed by saying, "Keep your chin up. I think that somehow, somethin' good will come of this."

After the call, Jo felt better. She also no longer felt abandoned. She wasn't sure exactly why, but she had a feeling that things would work out for her and Sean. Jo believed that good—more often than not—wins out over evil. While not as overtly religious as Sean, Jo felt God's presence with her very strongly. Deep in her soul, Jo knew that things were happening as they were supposed to happen.

★★★★★★★★★★★★

On Friday night, Jo and Sean were both exhausted. After dinner was over and the dishwasher was loaded and running, they sat on the sofa together and talked. When Jo asked Sean if he had had doubts over the past week, Sean told her something that he'd never mentioned before. Sean said, "My dad saw combat in World War II, so I grew up knowing that if there was a war, I'd follow in his footsteps. Four years of military school convinced me that my future lay in the military. So, when the Army rejected me for the last two years of R.O.T.C. because of my eyesight, I felt that I'd let both my dad and my country down. When I talked to my dad about it, he said something that I'll always remember. He told me, *Remember, not every patriot wears a uniform or carries a rifle.*"

Jo looked confused. Sensing that he wasn't getting through to her, Sean tried a different tack, saying, "Jo, when a military person goes to war, he or she is fighting for everything that makes their country unique—its people, its way of life, its language, its culture and its social institutions. Obviously, if a country were to lose a war, those things might be destroyed, right?"

Jo agreed. So, Sean continued by saying, "In our system, the question of who is going to make and enforce the rules that all of us are supposed to live by is answered by elections. Sometimes, elections can be nasty, vicious and untruthful. If men and women of courage and honor fail to seek office, those lacking character will win by default, damaging the country. Or, as Edmund Burke once wrote, *When bad men combine, the good must associate; else they will fall one by one, an unpitied sacrifice in a contemptible struggle.*"

Sean continued, "My duty is clear. I must fight to keep sleaze from winning. I might lose. But, unless I'm willing to let the unprincipled win without a struggle, I must fight with the weapons on hand, like a soldier on the battlefield."

Jo said, "Precious, one of the things that I first admired about you is your willingness to stand up for what you believe in."

Sean smiled and said, "Blame that on a long-dead Cavalier named Richard Lovelace. Having been imprisoned for doing his duty, he wrote to his lady that:

"I could not love thee, dear, so much,

Loved I not honor more.""

Lovelace's words caused both of them to tear up, but neither was willing to surrender to the urge to cry. Changing the topic to the near future at hand, Jo asked, "Do you have any idea what Griswold has planned for us next week?"

Sean shrugged his shoulders and said simply, "I don't know what he's got going, but whatever it is, he's really pumped up about it. When I spoke to him today, all he said was *Judo.* Does that mean anything to you?"

Jo replied, "From what I learned about it in the academy, in judo you take your opponent's strength and turn it to your advantage."

Sean laughed and said, "That makes sense. I guess we'll find out tomorrow."

Serious conversation ended when two lovely, little, furry ladies jumped up on the sofa and demanded attention. Feeling a bit guilty about being preoccupied with human things all week to the exclusion of Law and Equity, Jo and Sean gave the two furry ladies lots and lots of attention. When the kitties were happy again, they led the way to bed, with Jo and Sean obediently following their lead.

✱✱✱✱✱✱✱✱✱✱✱✱

Sean and Jo arrived early at Sam's office on Saturday, eagerly awaiting word of Bob's secret plan. When the elevator door opened, their nostrils were assaulted by a strong, noxious smell. **FRESH PAINT!** signs were all over the lobby, which was also full of boxes of law books. Tom Ritter saw them as entered and guided them carefully to the conference room, which was a sea of tranquility compared to the rest of the place. Once they were seated, Sam and Bob joined them. While Bob plugged cables into his laptop, Sam said, "I've got some news for y'all."

Jo quickly inquired, "What kind of news?"

Sam, his eyes twinkling, said, "It depends on your answer to this question: Did either or both of you, either individually or acting in concert with others, cause the death of Cheryl Riley?"

Sean and Jo both replied in unison, "**NO!**"

Now smiling from ear to ear, Sam said, "Then, I have **great** news." He passed a fax to Sean and Jo. The cover page of the fax bore the seal of the attorney general and was marked, "**RELEASE DATE: September 18, 2000**." Sean quickly scanned the three pages, the last two of which were of an official document entitled, "Notice of Appointment of Coroner."

When Sean finished reading, he jumped up and yelled very loudly, "Thank you, God!" Then, Sean reached around and hugged Jo and planted a big, wet kiss on her lips. After that, he gave Bob, Sam and Tom high fives.

Jo, not knowing what was going on, asked, "Precious, what it is?"

Sean said, exuberantly, "The Bloodhound is on the case!"

Before Jo could say anything, Sam intervened, "Jo, I'm gonna guess that you've never heard the name of Rufus T. Hill, have you?"

When Jo shook her head, Sam said, "Rufus is probably the best person in the entire country to be the coroner in this inquest. Plus, he's so colorful that he'll get us great press coverage. Hill is also one of the most famous lawyers in this state."

After taking a breath, Sam took over by saying, "When he was a boy, his father gave him a set of Sherlock Holmes for his twelfth birthday. He was so swept up by Conan Doyle that he grew up to become a nationally famous forensic pathologist. When Hill turned forty, he abandoned science to go to law school. After he passed the bar, he served as an assistant DA over in Queen City. Hill garnered a reputation there for always goin' after the truth, no matter how obscurely hidden. That's how he got his nickname, *Blood Hound*. After a few years, he became a criminal district court judge. After two terms, he retired and hung out a shingle. He mostly hires himself out to handle cross-examinations of doctors. He has written books and articles galore on the interface of law and medical science. He also puts on seminars for lawyers on how to deal with doctors and seminars for doctors on how to deal with lawyers. Despite his bein' in his seventies, he can run circles around younger lawyers and doctors. But, for our purposes, the best thin' about his appointment is that he is as colorful as they get. He's a big man with a boomin' voice and a totally unruly mop of white hair. In warm weather, he always wears perfectly tailored, white linen suits with a rose in the lapel. Wherever he is, the media is there, thick as flies on manure."

Jo said, "Don't mention flies and manure right now, please!"

After the laughter ended, Sean asked, "Sam, how did you manage to get the Blood Hound appointed?"

Sam smiled and said, "Sean, as much as I'd like to tell you that I pulled strings, I've gotta confess that I didn't. As you recall in my cover letter, I referenced the statutory language that the coroner be a board certified pathologist, licensed in this state. That's a pretty small universe to pick from. When I requested that the coroner be someone with extensive experience in Forensic Pathology and the conduct of hearin's, that was like a road map to the Blood Hound's office door."

After Jo and Sean both thanked Sam for his wisdom, everyone turned to Bob, who had the overhead projector fired up and ready to go. Bob said, "I hope you like my plan, because I've put my heart and soul into it."

Tom hit the lights and Bob began his presentation. "Let me first say that Sam was dead-on to think Sean's problem is more political than legal. I'll let Sam get you your inquest to clear your name. My strategy is purely political and public relations."

The first screen of the presentation that Bob put up contained the old axiom, "Write what you want about me, just spell my name right!" Bob said that as long as the story played, Sean's name was getting better and better known every day. Since Sean hadn't been charged with anything, by election day, all that would remain of the publicity would be an increased public awareness of the name. Bob indicated that right now, they were at Stage I, which blended in with and overlapped Stage II.

Stage II, Bob said, involved recruiting people to be on the campaign's email and mailing lists. Bob then went to the next screen, which showed the portions of the electorate that had been targeted:

- Lawyers
- Doctors
- College Students
- Law Students
- Business People
- Insurance Professionals
- Law Enforcement
- Personal Friends

Bob said that they already had enough names to ensure a big crowd for their event in Stage III. He continued, "In the meantime, we're going to lay low until the inquest is over and your name is cleared. Let them waste their money on useless ads in September and early October."

Then, Bob punched another button and a screen came up that only said, "Stage IV."

Jo asked, "What is it?"

Bob said, "We are going to get a crowd together at the Ransom County Fairground for a big, big campaign rally on Saturday, October 28th, which is the Saturday ten days before the election. At this rally, we're going to use our **SECRET WEAPON** for the first time."

When Jo asked, "What's our Secret Weapon?" Bob smiled and said, "Haven't you been curious about why I want your calendars free for Wednesday through Saturday of next week? Here's why!"

Bob flashed the next screen, and Jo was rendered speechless. Sean's jaw dropped. When Bob explained exactly what the photo represented, Sean stood up and said, "Bob, they say that there is a thin line between genius and madness. I need a minute to talk to Jo about which side of the line she thinks you're on." Sean and Jo went out to the lobby to talk. Their team back in the conference room only heard bits and snatches of the conversation.

> SEAN: Could we do that in public in front of hundreds of
>
> strangers?
>
> JO: We've done it before in public, haven't we?
>
> SEAN: What if it doesn't work? We'll be laughed at.
>
> JO: Sean, what's more important, your dignity or fightin'
>
> back?

Finally, after a few minutes of softer conversation, Bob, Sam and Tom heard what sounded like kissing and giggling. When Sean came back in the room, he was grinning. He said, "The most important phrase in a married man's life is *Yes, dear*! Momma thinks that we can do it, so we'll do it."

Bob looked relieved. After a minute, he continued, "The final step in my plan will go into effect during the rally. So, by Monday of the next week, everyone in Ransom County will know your side of the story."

After giving them the rest of the details for how he was going to implement the final stage of the plan, Bob said, "I've got a cost estimate for distribution." Sean looked at it and handed it to Jo.

When Jo nodded, Sean said, "I'm okay with the cost. Send me the bill if the campaign account can't cover it."

Then, Bob handed Jo and Sean a manila folder. While they reviewed its contents, Bob said, "You two are going to be busy, aren't you?"

After Jo and Sean nodded, Bob said, "There's one other thing. We are going to operate in complete secrecy. So, no one is going to know where you are. Agreed?"

After Jo and Sean nodded in agreement, Bob said, "The limo will arrive at Sam's house at 1830 hours **sharp**. Make sure that you and your stuff are all hidden out of sight before it gets there. Sarah and I will both be there beforehand. We'll take the limo to the general aviation section of the airport. No one will know that we're gone for a day or so. After we arrive in Houston, we'll stay at a hotel out by Intercontinental Airport. Next morning, Sarah will rent a car in her name, and we'll be off to the Texas Hill Country. Any questions?"

When Sean and Jo asked how they would be able to get messages if there was a communications blackout, Sam suggested that they give their families and offices the number to Sean's satellite phone, with the understanding that they would probably be unavailable for most of the time.

Sean said, "I've got to know, Bob. Did you think this up all on your own?"

Sam interjected, "Last Monday, before y'all got here, Bob and I were kickin' 'round the politics of the situation while Sarah was in the room. She's the one who showed us the digital photo. That started Bob and me goin'. You can see where we wound up. It took a few days to get it all set up, but I'm sure that we're gonna knock 'em dead!"

Bob and Tom nodded in strong agreement.

****

On Sunday evening, Sean and Jo discussed their trip. Jo said to Sean, "Precious, for a citified, Yankee lawyer, you're really okay. Most judges wouldn't even consider doin' anythin' this crazy."

Sean said, "Remember, there were two people in that picture!"

Looking Sean directly in the eye, Jo said, "Precious, you aren't bored with your little, barefoot, country girl wife are you?"

Sean said, "Beautiful, my guess is that as long as we're together, neither one of us will ever be bored."

Jo said, "Considerin' what's happened in the first month or so that we've been married, I couldn't argue with you, even if I wanted to."

****

Sean, after the week that they had just endured, surprised his staff by coming in to the office in a bright and cheery mood on Monday the 18th of September. His staff rightly surmised that he was looking forward to his days off.

Just before lunch, Bob told him that the AG's announcement of the appointment of a coroner to conduct an inquest had broken mid-morning. Bob had already received telephone calls from the local television outlets for the major channels, as well as calls from several cable news channels, asking if a statement would be forthcoming. Bob wanted Sean's input. Sean deferred to Bob, who said that he thought a statement would be an excellent idea.

Right before Sean resumed the bench, Bob called to let Sean know that the media had lapped up the statement like kittens at a bowl of cream.

Several of the outlets had asked Bob to email a jpeg of Sean's photo, which Bob had just done.

****

On the way back home from class that evening, Sean called Bob to see how the story had broken. Bob said, "All four of the local affiliates of the major networks, as well as Fox News, MSNBC™ and CNN Headline News, have run coroner's inquest stories. The stories were all almost identical, focusing more on what an inquest is than on any specifics. Most of the broadcasts used my line that you are invoking your rights as a citizen to clear your good name of the false charges leveled against you."

Laughing, Sean asked, "If the *Bugle* carries the story at all, want to bet whether they use that line?"

Bob surprised Sean when he said, "Sean, don't fall into the trap of thinking that everyone in the media thinks the same way about a story. In my experience, media people are just like everyone else, they don't always agree with each other. In most newspapers, the reporters hate the columnists, the reporters and columnists hate the editors, and the reporters, columnists and editors all hate the publisher. Let's see what happens tomorrow with the report that's printed in the *Bugle*."

****

When Sean arrived home at 1730 hours on Tuesday, Mo and Pat were already at the house helping Jo load their bags into their vehicles. After promising his furry, little friends that Pat and Mo would come by every night to see them and feed them, Sean slipped out to the waiting vehicles, which were parked far away from any prying eyes. Sean and Jo each squeezed down low, so that they wouldn't be visible in the back seat of the car that Maureen drove. Pat, driving the SUV, followed right behind. After a thoroughly unpleasant drive to Sam's house, Jo and Sean were glad to be able to leave their hiding places and stand up straight again.

After saying their farewells to the Twins, Sean and Jo went into the house to wait for the limousine with Sarah and Bob. While they were waiting, Bob pulled out the news story from that morning's *Bugle*. Sean and Jo agreed with Bob that despite their misgivings, the story displayed no bias one way or another, just recounted the facts that Judge and Lieutenant Riley and several other people had petitioned the AG to appoint a coroner to conduct an inquest into the death of the late Cheryl Riley. The rest of the story was taken up with quotations from a law professor at State and a lawyer who talked about how rare a coroner's inquest was in these days of forensic science. Bob said that the story was a good first step, because guilty people rarely ask for investigations.

The flight to Houston Intercontinental Airport was uneventful. After take off, Bob went over—again—the plans for their three and a half days in Texas. Halfway to Houston, Sean asked Bob if he had thought that Sean would buy into his wild and crazy plan. Bob said he had no doubt that Sean would go along with the plan, because it was so illogical that it would work. That actually made it logical. Sarah and Jo laughed at this notion, but agreed with Bob.

Sean, growing serious for a second, said, "When I was driving in this morning, I asked myself why I was going on this trip—which could make me a laughing stock if it backfires. I came up with the same reason that Bob did. But, after a while, I started to warm up to the whole crazy idea. I couldn't figure why I was going to be dropping a pile of my own money to finance a plan that is so unlike me. I was puzzled until the time that I got home. Then, reality hit me. Despite all my years of schooling and all my years of working in the cold, logical world of law, I am the son of a lady of French ancestry, who was both a writer and an artist. I guess deep down, this plan must appeal to something that my mother planted in my brain when I was small. I had the strangest feeling that my mother was with me, telling me that since I was her son, I'd not only do it, but do it very well. I can't explain it further."

On their final approach into Houston, Bob told his companions that he'd never been to Texas before. He asked if any of them had ever been there. Jo and Sean indicated that neither of them had. Sarah told them about the many times that Tommy had played at the Houston Rodeo. She had warm memories of Houston, speaking well of the people, if not the climate.

When Bob asked, "Sarah, is everyone in Texas that warm and friendly?"

Sarah replied, "Pretty much, except in Dallas." They all laughed.

Chapter Fifteen

Peering out the peephole into the Media Center, Jo said, "Sheriff, I can't believe how many reporters and cameramen we've got waitin' on us."

Sheriff Walker responded obliquely, "Griswold correctly suspected today's conference would attract more coverage than usual."

Sean was going to watch the conference in the sheriff's personal office with Bubba, on the sheriff's monitor, because Sean's presence at the conference would distract from its purpose—clearing Jo's name.

As Sheriff Walker and Jo prepared to face the howling mob, Sean rushed to Jo, kissed her on the cheek and said, "Break a leg!" Jo giggled at Sean's remark, while the sheriff looked a trifle confused.

Jo smiled at the sheriff and said "We've learned quite a lot of new thin's recently."

The closed-circuit television in Sheriff Walker's office did not show just how tightly packed the hot, sticky Media Center was that morning. The glare from the lights was painfully bright. The air was full of the sounds of grumbling reporters. When the sheriff and Jo appeared on camera, Bubba glanced at his watch and said very slowly, "Judge, I reckon that them reporters don't have too many press conferences this early in the mornin'."

Sean agreed while watching the monitor very closely. After what seemed like an awfully long time, Sheriff Walker strode to the podium, stared at the assembled media types just long enough to establish that he was in charge and intoned deeply, "On September 11th, two weeks ago today, a column by Warren K. Rudd in the University City Bugle impugned the integrity of both Lieutenant Jolene Scruggs and this department. After conductin' a thorough investigation of the allegations raised by Rudd's article, I have concluded that there is not one shred of evidence to support the implications of misconduct made by Mr. Rudd. As I reviewed the report that will be distributed to you at the end of this conference, I remembered somethin' from my time in the Army. Back then, the worst job was shovelin' dirt into latrines when it was time to leave an area. The more dirt that was shoveled into the latrine, the viler the smell became. Rudd's allegations make me think of a very ripe latrine at Fort Riley, Kansas in the middle of an August heat wave."

After giving the comment enough time to sicken the reporters, the sheriff turned to Jo and said, "As of this mornin', Lieutenant Riley is returned to duty." Then, turning to three very large, very mean looking deputies that the sheriff had pulled in from the jail for this duty, he said, "This conference is concluded. In a moment, these deputies will distribute copies of the report, which is quite detailed."

As the sheriff turned to leave, a female reporter yelled loudly, "Should we expect indictments in this case this week?"

Normally, the sheriff would have just walked away and ignored the comment. But, too much had happened over the last fortnight for the sheriff to let her remark pass unchallenged. Sheriff Walker returned to the podium and said, "Ma'am, you'll have to ask the District Attorney what he plans to do about Mr. Rudd."

The sheriff and Jo slowly exited the Media Center amidst shouts of, "Sheriff! Sheriff Walker! What charges are being pursued against Warren K. Rudd?"

When Sheriff Walker returned to his office, he looked at Jo, Sean and Bubba and said, "The district attorney may never speak to me again! I'll bet those fools spread the word that Rudd's gonna be indicted!"

Turning to Sean and Bubba, the sheriff said, "Judge, I've got a lot of work piled up for your wife, so if you don't mind, I'm gonna let you go back to your chambers now."

Turning next to Bubba, Sheriff Walker inquired, "Deputy, do you think that you can get Judge Riley back to his chambers unnoticed?" Bubba promised that he could. So, Sean, after kissing a now smiling and relaxed Jo, retreated down a secure stairway, away from the howling media mob.

****

Since the press conference had been so early in the morning, Sean arrived back in his chambers half an hour before he was to take the bench. Although he had piles of orders to review and sign, Sean decided to read the *Bugle* to see what was going on. Except for Rudd's column, all was quiet. Rudd's column was an attack on Judge Sean Riley for attempting to suppress the public's **right to know** by closing a guardianship hearing last week. Rudd said that Judge Riley must have a desire to return to the Court of the Star Chamber, which the British Crown had used to torment American colonists before the Revolution.

When Sean reached Griswold on the phone, Griswold was already on top of the situation. Bob told Sean that Dean Churchill had already called and told him that the editor of the *Bugle* was going to let the dean write an op-ed piece for Wednesday's edition of the newspaper, explaining the statute that authorized closed hearings in guardianship hearings. Sean told Bob he was glad that he and Dean Churchill were on his side.

After rooting around in the law library for a bit, Sean called Pam and said, "Pam, this is Dean Churchill's research assistant. I'm going to email you a few citations that the dean might find helpful in his writing."

After Pam expressed her concern about how Sean was being unfairly treated, Sean said, "Pam, thanks for your concern. Remember, the game isn't over until the last out. When they count the votes on Election Night, I'll have my say."

****

The rest of Sean's Monday passed peacefully, unmolested by politics, until half an hour before Sean was due to leave for class, when he received a draft of Dean Churchill's op-ed piece in his email. Dean Churchill had put the citations to good use.

The piece began by pointing out that Rudd's assertion that the Court of Star Chamber was used by the British Crown in the 18th century to harass the inhabitants of the American colonies was totally erroneous since that infamous court had been abolished by an act of Parliament in July, 1641. The dean used that obvious error as an opening to attack the rest of Rudd's article, illustrating point by point that Rudd had no earthly idea what he was writing about. The next to the last point in the dean's piece was that judges are not free to make up the law as they go along, which was what Judge Riley had done. Dean Churchill suggested that if Rudd had problems with the law, he should go to the legislature and try to have the law changed. The dean's final paragraph rammed the point home, suggesting that before Rudd tried to get the law changed, he should acquaint himself with a library and get his facts straight. He intimated that if Rudd petitioned the legislature with as few facts to support him as he had currently, Rudd would be laughed out of Capitol City.

Sean emailed Dean Churchill to tell him that the op-ed piece was perfect and that he was very grateful for his support.

****

Sean and Jo had found the cryptic nature of Sam's invitation to dine on Monday evening after Sean's class a little odd. But, since they had both put in a very long day, they were glad to have someone feed them. Once the dishes were cleared, Sam and Sarah joined Sean and Jo out on the back porch.

After giving them a little background, Sam said, "Last Tuesday, after the story about the coroner's inquest broke, I received a call from a woman lawyer who—so Bob tells me—signed on very early to support you. She told me that she and her husband wanted to meet with me, but they were afraid that they were bein' watched and their telephone lines tapped. Before I could say anythin', she said that she was callin' from a pay phone at the airport."

Sean interrupted Sam by asking, "Who called?"

Sam continued, "Her name is Kim Brownlee McReynolds." Sam now had their full attention. "She told me that she and her husband would like to meet where they wouldn't be noticed. I suggested Lucy's place on Sunday afternoon, knowin that someone followin' her would have problems tryin' to slip into the resort without registerin' and payin'. Besides, tryin' to find someone on a crowded beach is hard to do inconspicuously. "

After pausing for dramatic effect, Sam continued, "To make life a little more interestin', I suggested that she borrow a friend's car for the trip to Lucy's. Early on Sunday mornin', she and her husband met her secretary and her secretary's husband at her office and exchanged cars in her closed parkin' lot. The switch worked. Just to make it good, her secretary and her husband drove toward the coast for a while with the idiot followin' them."

After they all laughed, Sam said, "The cloak and dagger was worth it. Kim and her husband really did have a story to tell."

Sam handed Sean and Jo photocopies of several documents. After they had looked at them, Sam continued, "I've got the originals hidden away in a safe deposit box. These documents may create a legal earthquake."

Sean added, "Jo, in the days to come, Sheriff Walker's remark to the reporters today may seem prophetic."

They all laughed again. Then, Sam returned to his narrative, saying, "When Kim and her husband arrived at the resort, she was carryin' a wicker tote sack. When Sarah and I joined them down by the lake, I had Sarah carry one, too. After the transfer of the documents, I slipped them into Sarah's sack. I don't think that anyone noticed since Sarah was in and out of her wicker tote sack quite a bit. To make it look good, we stayed awhile in the sun. Sarah and Covin'ton went for a swim while Kim and I guarded the bag. When they came back, Kim and I went for a swim while Sarah and Covin'ton guarded the bag. After that, we went our separate ways."

Sam added, "I forgot to tell you. Kim and Covin'ton both send their regards." Then, Sam looked at Sarah and asked, "How far along would you say that she was?"

Sarah said, "I'd guess about three months."

****

On the way home from Sam's place, Jo said, "Precious, I guess that you were right about Kim sendin' out strong sexual vibes. If you'd taken her to the Spring Fling, you'd be campaignin' with a visibly pregnant wife."

After Sean said that while he was fond of Kim, he was better off with Jo, Sean asked, "Beautiful, do you have anything to tell me?"

Jo smiled and said, "Not yet! But, the evenin' is still young!"

****

Tuesday night, September 26th, Jo and Sean had planned a night at home alone. Except for their two furry companions, they were all alone, but their evening was not peaceful. The closed door, preliminary hearing of the inquest had been held that morning. From what Sam had told Sean, the entire proceeding took less than an hour. After the hearing was over, Rufus T. Hill held a short press conference to announce that the inquest would begin on Tuesday, October 9th.

Sam said that Rufus had been in fine form and had charmed the reporters. Apparently, the legendary charm of Rufus T. Hill had worked its magic on the producers of the television news reports, as well, because all four of the local affiliates of the major networks carried a story about the inquest in their noon newscasts.

Shortly after lunch, Griswold had called, saying that he received so many calls from media outlets and reporters that he suggested they hold a press conference at four that afternoon.

The conference, held later in the day, was very short. Sean had read from a prepared statement, explaining in simple terms why the inquest had been sought and that he looked forward to it, so he could clear his name. When the reporters tried to delay Sean's departure with shouted questions, Sean ignored them and returned to the courthouse. Bob told him that the conference had gone well.

Tuesday night, Jo and Sean were snowed under with telephone calls from family, personal friends and well-wishers. Since Fox News, MSNBC and CNN, as well as the traditional four major networks, had all picked up the story, they received quite a few calls and emails wishing them well.

Just before they retired for the evening, Maggie Anderson reached Jo. Her life had been affected by the inquest, too. After the call ended, Jo told Sean, "Right before the end of her shift, Sheriff Walker asked Maggie to come to his office. Maggie was surprised and flattered when the sheriff told her that she was gonna be in charge of the security detail for the inquest.

Maggie was even more surprised when the sheriff told her that since this might be the only time on his watch that Ransom County was gonna be in the national news spotlight, he wanted everythin' done right. The sheriff gave her free rein to pick the people to serve under her. Maggie picked four very large—but diplomatic—male deputies to handle the mob in the hallways. Inside the courtroom, Bubba's gonna be the coroner's bailiff. For additional courtroom deputies, Maggie picked the other four of our group from the party at Plum Lake. Darla and Karen will be dealin' with the reporters and camera crews. Ashley and Stacy will back up Bubba. Just to make the whole event a bit more telegenic, the sheriff agreed to her request that all the deputies will be in their dress uniforms."

Noticing a look of confusion on Sean's face, Jo said, "Precious, have you ever noticed that when I'm in my dress uniform, it's cut way tight at the chest? Have you noticed that when female deputies wear our service uniforms, we wear pants, but in our dress uniforms, we wear skirts?"

Smiling, Sean said, "I get it. Darla and Karen will have the male reporters under their thumbs by mid-morning on the first day."

Half an hour later, Jo, Sean, Equity and Law were all curled up together, dreaming peacefully.

* * * * * * * * * * * *

Sean enjoyed reading the Wednesday, September 27th edition of the *Bugle* for a change. Below the fold on page one of the first section, there was a news story about the preliminary hearing. Several lawyers were quoted in the story, explaining the history and mechanics of the coroner's inquest. Professor Rodriguez was quoted as saying that she believed a public hearing would give her friend and colleague, Judge Sean Riley, an opportunity to put to rest any questions that might exist about the death of his late wife, Cheryl. The coverage played the story right down the middle, setting the stage for the inquest. Later in the day, Sean noticed that Matt Drudge had picked up the story.

Sean enjoyed seeing Dean Churchill's op-ed piece. He wondered if Rudd enjoyed being told, in effect, that he really had no idea what he was talking about. Sean suspected that management at the *Bugle* was telling Rudd something by publishing Dean Churchill's op-ed piece.

* * * * * * * * * * * *

The next week was very peaceful. For the first time in over two weeks, Jo and Sean had a chance to lead a normal life. Since local judicial races are low interest races, judicial candidates, unlike candidates for higher offices, spend relatively little time campaigning. Incumbent judges continue hearing their dockets and lawyer candidates practice law. Jo and Sean enjoyed their time together, free of interference from the outside world. They found great comfort in the mundane things of ordinary life—work, going to church, shopping, swimming, jogging and just being together. For seven glorious days, Sean and Jo were reminded of what normal life was like.

✳✳✳✳✳✳✳✳✳✳✳✳

Their tranquility ended on the evening of Wednesday, October 3rd, when Sean arrived at the studio where the judicial candidates' joint television commercial was to be filmed. At first, he was unsure of what to expect. He found out soon enough.

As Sean walked into the studio, carrying his robe over his arm, Bill Morrow pounced on him like a cat on a mouse, saying, "Judge, we need to talk."

Taking Sean aside, Morrow told Sean that he was going to be excluded from the commercial. Morrow handed Sean a refund check. Although Sean had a very strong desire to smash Morrow in the mouth, he took the check and walked off angrily.

As Sean headed out the door, he ran into Bob Griswold, who was walking in with Ransom County's newest district court judge, a leggy blonde named Sally MacPherson. As Sean recalled, Sally had been a colleague of Max and Kyra. Both had spoken highly of her, particularly Kyra.

Sean told Bob that he had just been thrown out of the commercial by Bill Morrow. After listening to Sean vent, Bob looked very sternly at Sean and told him to calm down and wait for his call in his truck. Sally volunteered to walk with Sean and keep him company. As they walked, Sally had a few choice words about Morrow to share with Sean. As Sally spoke, he remembered Max telling him that Sally was every bit as outspoken as Kyra. After listening to Sally, Sean agreed with Max.

As Sean and Sally waited by his F-150, Sean debated calling Jo and then decided against it, not wanting to upset her. He and Sally passed the time, sharing Kyra stories. After what seemed like an eon, Sean's cell phone went off. Griswold asked Sally and him to come to the front door of the studio. Griswold said that he wasn't sure what was going to happen, but it would be interesting.

By the time that Sally and Sean had walked around to the front of the building from the parking lot in back, a crowd of almost a dozen judges, all carrying their robes, was milling about. When the crowd saw Sean, they let out a loud cheer.

When Sean and Sally reached their colleagues, one of them, an older, gray-haired judge, named Deakins, said, "Morrow is in there pleading with the few remaining judges and candidates to stay."

When Sean and Sally both asked what happened, the older judge said, "When Griswold walked in the door, he called for his candidates to gather 'round him. When he told us what Morrow had tried to do to you, a bunch of us walked out."

As soon as the older judge stopped speaking, Sally remarked that the rest of the judges and candidates seemed to be heading out the door of the studio, as well. A few paces behind them, Griswold and Morrow followed. Morrow was shouting and gesturing wildly at a smiling Griswold. All the judges and candidates stopped to watch Morrow.

One of the criminal court judges said, "Please God, let Morrow take a poke at Griswold." They all laughed, knowing that if Morrow swung first, the much larger Griswold would be allowed to hit back. Until then, Sean hadn't realized that Morrow was so universally detested.

Seconds later, Judge Deakins said very loudly, so everyone—including Griswold and Morrow—could hear him, "I'm too damn old to be standin' 'round watchin' people argue, unless I'm gettin' paid for it. Judges, I propose that we all go over to The Palm Tree to discuss options for filmin' **our** TV commercial."

Winking at Sean, Judge Deakins added, "Since Riley's rich, he's gonna pick up the tab."

As soon as Judge Deakins had stopped speaking, Morrow yelled, "Judge Riley, will you lead your colleagues back into the studio, so that we can finish shooting this commercial with **all** of you in it?"

After the cheering and hooting stopped, a happy group of judges returned to the studio, smiling totally artificial smiles at Bill Morrow.

Later that night, as Sean recounted the story to Jo, she said laughingly, "I guess that Morrow isn't gonna ask me to run for the legislature again."

Sean said, "I wouldn't be too sure about that. He likes his job. Right now, I think he senses that he needs to mend a lot of fences."

As they retired for the evening, Jo said, "Now that I've had a bit of time to think about it, maybe our time in Texas wasn't such a big gamble."

Sean grabbed Jo around the waist and whispered in her ear, "Remember, *Good Will Win in the End.*" That night, an embattled judicial candidate, a peace officer and two cats all slept soundly.

****

Knowing from experience just how traumatic a birthday ending with a zero can be for a woman, Sean took no chances concerning Jo's thirtieth birthday on Friday, October 5th. It wasn't until right before they arrived at their destination that Sean told Jo exactly where they would be that night. Jo was very pleasantly surprised to learn that Sean had booked the penthouse suite at the Hilltop Inn™ in Capitol City, an internationally known hotel and resort that catered to the rich and famous. Jo had heard about the inn, but had never been there.

At dinner that evening, Sean surprised Jo with two birthday presents. The first present was a custom-designed pin, made of gold and shaped in the outline of a heart, containing the letters J and S intertwined within the heart. The pin was accented with small sapphires. Jo was overwhelmed at the beauty and thoughtfulness of the gift.

When Jo finished telling Sean what a good job she must be doing in training him, Sean reached into his suit coat and produced a small piece of paper—a photocopy of some other document. The paper was a form letter, indicating that a poem submitted by one Sean Riley had been accepted for publication by a poetry journal. Before Jo could say anything, Sean produced still another paper from his pocket. Jo looked at that piece of paper for several minutes before handing the paper back to Sean. The candlelight of the restaurant could not hide Jo's tears.

Jo said, "Precious, if I remember rightly, the poem's a sonnet, right?" Sean acknowledged that it was and asked if sonnets always made her cry.

Jo said, "It's really beautiful. How did you come up with the title, *My Love is like a Mixed Metaphor*?"

Sean said, "The first weekend after we got back from our honeymoon, you and I were talking about something minor after coming in from swimming. You were quite naked. As you walked by me, I noticed that you walked with the grace of a cat. Then, I remembered what you said at Lucy's, when you described yourself as looking like a cheetah. After a second, I realized that I couldn't describe you as a cheetah, because they have yellow eyes. After thinking about it for a bit, it dawned on me that you cannot be described adequately with just one metaphor. I hope you like what I came up with."

Jo said, "How could I not like bein' described as havin' the physical grace and beauty of a cheetah, eyes the color of the sea, the strength of steel, the warmth of a roarin' campfire on the prairie on a night in December and the gentleness of a mother nursin' her child? Precious, if you really believe all of those things about me, you're a fool. Please don't ever change!"

By the time the meal was over, both Sean and Jo had the same plan for the rest of the evening.

****

The next morning, after the sun woke them, Jo asked Sean what he thought about the previous evening. Looking at both Jo and the vista from their penthouse suite, Sean said simply, "Magnificent view!"

Over breakfast, Jo surprised Sean by saying, "Precious, Kyra told me that after Cheryl died, you went into yourself and were hard to reach emotionally. She guessed that you were very depressed. Precious, ever since the Rudd column came out, I've been watchin' you real close to make sure that you don't slip away from me. In case you haven't noticed, I've been real friendly to keep you with me. I suspect that next week is gonna be real painful for you. When we're in court, if you feel one of your black moods comin' on, just look over and tap me on the arm, the leg, my watch or even my table or chair three times. When I do the three taps back, that'll be our signal that you aren't alone, 'cause I'm with you. My taps will also mean that as soon as we get home, I'll give you as much attention as you'll need to make you feel better. Deal?"

For a minute, Sean sat very quietly and just stared at Jo. The awkward silence ended when Sean tapped his water goblet three times with his knife. Just as Jo was starting to feel relieved, Sean asked Jo in his most serious tone of voice, "Beautiful, who gets to decide how much and what kind of attention I'll need when we get home?"

Jo replied, "Management."

Sean's words, "Yes, dear!" sounded very meek and docile. However, the smile on his face said something different to Jo. The kiss that Sean planted on her hand a second later told her that Sean understood that as painful as the inquest would be, he would not be alone.

****

Later that day, when Sean and Jo arrived at the offices of Brown & Ritter to discuss the last-minute plans for the inquest on Tuesday, they walked in holding hands and gazing in each other's eyes. Bob, Dean Churchill, Isabel,

Pam, Sam, Sarah and Tom were pleasantly surprised at the good spirits of the embattled pair.

The meeting itself was uneventful. The order of witnesses for the hearing was designed to allow the facts to be told in chronological sequence. Since the inquest was not an adversarial proceeding, the lawyers would have relatively little to do because the witnesses, guided by questions from the coroner, would be allowed to give their testimony in narrative form. Afterward, each lawyer would be allowed to ask questions. To avoid being repetitive, they all agreed that only one lawyer from their team would ask questions of any one witness. Each lawyer was very comfortable with his or her assignment of witnesses. As the meeting was ending, Sean asked Dean Churchill what Pam's role would be in the hearing.

Pam smiled and said, "Since Dean Churchill signed off on the application to protect the honor and good name of the school, I've been authorized to be his paralegal at the inquest. In English, that means I take notes for him."

After everyone present had a good laugh, Sam said, "Since Kyra and Max are down as witnesses, the DA is going to use special counsel. They've hired a lawyer named J.T. Downin'. You know him?"

Sean said, "I heard Max mention him once. Back in the early sixties, he was a hot shot in the DA's office. He left to join a P.I. firm around the end of that decade. He made a pile of money and retired a few years later. From what I've heard, he mostly just plays golf. I don't think that he's been in a courtroom in years."

Sam said, "I think that the DA is sendin' us a message." After discussing J.T. Downing a while longer, Sam mentioned to Sean and Jo that the *Bugle*'s lawyers wanted an extension of one week after the coroner's report was made public for the newspaper to issue a retraction. Sean agreed that was a reasonable request and told Sam to give it to them.

Chatting for a few minutes more, the meeting broke up right after Sean told everyone that their contributions were appreciated more than they would ever know. Several minutes later, Jo and Sean departed, holding hands.

After Jo and Sean left, Sarah asked Sam, "Are we going to be like that in a few months?"

Sam said the right thing when he told Sarah, "No! Worse! Much worse!"

Chapter Sixteen

Before the inquest began, Sean and Jo took a bit of good-natured ribbing from Sam. Sean was wearing a navy-blue suit, white shirt and dark-blue tie with big, white polka dots. Jo was wearing a navy-blue dress with little, white polka dots and a medium strand of pearls. Whatever else they may have been, Jo and Sean were color coordinated.

At precisely 0900 hours on Tuesday, October 11, 2000, Rufus T. Hill, a.k.a. the Blood Hound, called the inquest to order. His booming voice practically shook the courtroom. The cameramen and the photographers had a field day. How often did they get to work with a mountain of a man with a mop of white hair, wearing a white-linen suit with a red rose in his lapel? The Blood Hound was a dream come true for people who made their livings presenting vivid visual images. Truth be known, the Blood Hound didn't mind the attention at all.

Addressing those at the counsel tables, the Blood Hound asked if there were any preliminary matters to be addressed before the jury was picked. Sam Brown rose and inquired as to the appropriate form of address for a coroner.

The Blood Hound replied, "Last weekend, my wife and I were watchin' an old English picture show set in a remote fishin' village in England around the time of Edward VII, in which the key scene was a coroner's inquest. I noticed that everyone called the coroner in that movie, *Your Worship*. My lovely bride suggested to me that that particular term of address should remain across the pond. Reluctantly, I must concur. So, address me as Mr. Coroner or as you would any other judge—to his face."

After the laughter stopped, the Blood Hound continued, "Speakin' of etiquette, I have a bit of a problem, as well. Lookin' out at counsel, I notice a retired justice of our illustrious Supreme Court, a current judge, a law school dean, a law school professor and a lieutenant. How would y'all prefer to be addressed?"

Sam indicated that since this was an inquest, not a trial per se, he would prefer to be addressed as "Justice Brown." Isabel indicated that "Professor" would suit her perfectly. Sean said that "Judge Riley" would be fine with him. Jo said "Lieutenant Riley." Dean Churchill indicated that "Dean Churchill" would suffice for him. JT Downing surprised everyone by showing signs of life and advising the Blood Hound that he was a retired colonel in the Army reserves and since everyone else was using a title, he would prefer to be addressed as "Colonel."

Looking at Tom Ritter, the Blood Hound asked if he had any preferences. Tom, not missing a beat, rose and said, "Judge, since I'm the junior partner to a living legend—or so I'm told—I'm not allowed to have any preferences."

After the laughter subsided, the Blood Hound looked at Pam, smiled sweetly and said, "What would you like to be called?"

Rising, Pam said, "I'm not a lawyer, so Ms. Longstreet will be fine."

The Blood Hound replied, "So noted!" After indicating that he would try to honor those requests, the Blood Hound turned to the throng of reporters and spectators, and announced, "In the preliminary hearin', counsel agreed that since this was not a contested case with someone bringin' an action against someone else, we could dispense with the usual rigmarole of pickin' a jury and submit a questionnaire to potential jurors instead. We've already screened out jurors who thought they might have a problem."

Then, turning to Bubba, he said, "Please bring in the panelists."

A moment later, twenty-four very confused people entered the room and were asked to stand before the bench. The Blood Hound said, "A few minutes ago, each of you answered a questionnaire identical to this one. Has anythin' happened to make any of you change your minds about any of your answers?"

When no one said anything in reply, the Blood Hound swore in the panel and asked them to be seated. After Bubba and Darla escorted the jurors to their seats, the Blood Hound gave the jurors a welcoming talk, explaining the origins of the office of coroner, its history and what the jurors were expected to do in this inquest. After taking several housekeeping questions from the jurors, the Blood Hound declared a short recess.

At 1015 hours, the first witness, Deputy Morrissey, took the stand. Having been sworn, the Blood Hound asked him to tell what he knew about Cheryl's death. He said that he was on patrol on the day shift the morning of Cheryl's death, March 9, 1999. Driving down County 191 at approximately 0730 hours, he came across a spot just beyond a hill where there were skid marks and a missing guardrail at the far side of the embankment. Deputy Morrissey indicated that he called the matter in to dispatch for a traffic investigator. While waiting for the investigator, he taped off the area.

When Tom Ritter asked him if he knew Judge Riley, Deputy Morrissey indicated in the negative. When Tom asked him if he knew anything of Lieutenant Riley, he said, "She was a supervisor on the night shift back then. I worked days, so I never had any dealings with her."

When Tom Ritter asked him if Lieutenant Riley had ever contacted him about the death of Cheryl Riley, he said that she had not. Considering that Deputy Morrissey looked like Central Casting's image of a very nervous, young, farm boy, trying to make a good impression on a bunch of city slickers, Tom asked no additional questions.

At 1035 hours, Sergeant Gregory of the Ransom County Sheriff's Department's Traffic Investigation Division was called to the stand. Sergeant Gregory had about two inches of height, twenty-five pounds of weight and thirty years more experience on Deputy Morrissey. He testified that when he arrived on the scene, he dismissed Deputy Morrissey. Sergeant Gregory indicated that based on his thirty years of law enforcement experience, the last twenty-four of which had been in accident investigation, it appeared to him that a vehicle had skidded off of County 191, through the guardrail and into Flatboat River. He said that he then called for a boat and a dive team.

Sergeant Gregory testified that when the boat arrived, it searched the area with a magnetometer. When the magnetometer indicated the presence of a metallic object in the water large enough to be a motor vehicle, a diver was ordered into the water.

Sergeant Gregory testified that when the diver surfaced, he reported there was a late model Mercedes on the river floor, containing what appeared to be the corpse of one person. Gregory went on to testify that when the diver reported that the vehicle appeared to have official state plates, he followed established procedure and immediately called the State Police Headquarters in Capitol City to send out an investigator. After saying that no other action was taken until the State Police investigator arrived, other than attaching a buoy to the vehicle and videotaping the vehicle underwater, Sergeant Gregory was dismissed.

Following a short recess, testimony resumed at 1115 hours with Sergeant Reed, the diver. Sergeant Reed repeated what Sergeant Gregory had said about finding the Mercedes on the bed of Flatboat River near where the guardrail was missing. He testified that after attaching a buoy to the vehicle, he dove with an underwater video camera to record the scene.

After the Blood Hound asked Bubba to dim the lights, the videotape was played. As soon as the lights went down and the tape went on, Sean and Jo each grabbed each other's hand very tightly, fearing that some grisly scene would appear. Actually, the tape was somewhat of a non-event. Even with the external lights that the diver had used—even close up—the water was too murky to make out much, except that the vehicle was tilted about thirty degrees to port and wedged into a sandbank. The license plate was visible, but very little else.

Sergeant Reed indicated that after the completion of the dive, he and Sergeant Gregory waited until the State Police investigator arrived. He and Sergeant Gregory assisted with the removal of the vehicle from Flatboat River onto a barge. He indicated that once the vehicle was on the barge, he and his team were dismissed.

The inquest then recessed for lunch. As soon as the Blood Hound left the bench, Sean called Miriam on his cell phone to put in their lunch orders at Joe's Diner.

****

The lunchtime conversation was quite light at first since everyone in their group—which included everyone at the counsel's table, except for JT Downing—was unsure about Sean's mood. Sean amazed them with his calmness. When lunch ended, Jo and Sean stayed behind in his office.

As soon as the door to Sean's office closed, Jo threw her arms around him and kissed him passionately. Sean held Jo tightly. After a minute, he said, "The pathologist will come up this afternoon. If I can make it through his testimony, I'll be okay. How are you doing?"

Jo answered truthfully, "I'm very worried about you."

Sean looked into Jo's big blue eyes and said, "I've got you on one side of me and Sam on the other. For litigants, that is as good as it gets. Stay with me, please. We need each other."

Jo kissed Sean very passionately and said from her heart, "Always."

****

At precisely 1330 hours, the inquest resumed with the testimony of the accident investigator for the State Police, Sergeant Conrad Ernest. Sergeant Ernest's narrative indicated that he arrived on the scene at 1038 hours on Tuesday, 9 March, 1999. He testified that he took charge of the recovery of the Mercedes from Flatboat River and supervised its transport to the State Police Headquarters in Capitol City. He also thoroughly photographed the scene of the apparent accident. He then described in detail his analysis of the vehicle once it was in his workshop.

Watching the jurors start to nod off, the Blood Hound asked Sergeant Ernest if he had brought a copy of his report. When Ernest produced the report, the Blood Hound had it marked as an exhibit and admitted into evidence.

After asking the appropriate questions to qualify him as an expert witness, the Blood Hound announced that Sergeant Ernest was deemed to be an expert in accident reconstruction. When asked if he would summarize his report, Ernest gave the following testimony:

1. The subject vehicle appeared to have been in excellent working condition prior to the time of the incident.

2. From the skid marks in the embankment, his opinion was that the subject vehicle was traveling too fast for conditions, appearing to have been traveling at forty-five miles per hour, which was ten miles per hour over the posted limit. His opinion was that, in light of the conditions on the morning in question, a safe rate of speed would have been no more than fifteen miles per hour.

3. At the place where the vehicle left the embankment, there was a deep depression at the spot where the left side of the vehicle had been. This led the vehicle to travel not parallel to the surface of the water, but at a forty-five degree angle to the left, which was exacerbated by the weight of the driver of the vehicle. The vehicle also entered the surface of the water at a twenty-degree angle forward.

4. The force of the vehicle hitting the surface of the water caused the air bags to deploy.

5. The vehicle sank rapidly, settling on the driver's

     side on a sandbar.

After Sergeant Ernst finished his narrative, Dean Churchill rose and asked in his deep voice, "Sergeant, did your investigation unearth anything that would raise a suspicion in your mind that this was something other than an accident?"

Sergeant Ernst looked at Dean Churchill for a moment, studying him carefully. Finally, he broke his silence by saying, "Based on the physical evidence I have described, I have no reason at all to think that the Mercedes entered the water as the result of anything other than an accident. Now, I wasn't there, so I only can go on what I have been able to learn from the physical evidence. But, I can find no reason to even suspect that anything other than an accident was the cause of the Mercedes being in Flatboat River that day."

Dean Churchill rested. The report of Sergeant Ernest, along with its pages and pages of photographs and diagrams, was published to the jury, who seemed to be alert again.

After a fifteen-minute recess, testimony resumed at 1422 hours. The next witness called was the pathologist, Dr. Ernesto Garcia. As soon as his name was called, Jo noticed that Sean tapped her legal pad three times. Jo tapped back three times very quickly.

Dr. Garcia was quickly qualified as an expert witness in the areas of Medicine, Pathology and Forensic Pathology, having a very long resume. He had worked as a forensic pathologist for a number of years in Los Angeles until he accepted a professorship at the Medical School at State.

After his CV was admitted and published to the jury, the Blood Hound asked Dr. Garcia if he had conducted the autopsy on the remains of the lady found in the Mercedes. When he replied that he had, the Blood Hound asked, "Doctor, did you determine that the decedent was Cheryl Riley?"

Dr. Garcia said, "Yes, I did. The face, features and age of the decedent matched perfectly with the driver's license in her purse. Following procedure, her fingerprints were also run. The Automated Fingerprint Identification Systems, known commonly as *AFIS*, confirmed that the victim of the accident was Cheryl Riley, a resident of Ransom County."

The Blood Hound then asked the pathologist if he had brought a copy of his report along with him. The copy of the report, with its gruesome autopsy photographs, was quickly admitted into evidence and published to the jury. When asked, Dr. Garcia summarized his findings as follows:

1. Immediately prior to the time of her death, Cheryl Riley was in excellent health for a woman in her late forties.

2. There was no evidence to suggest that at the time of the accident she was in any way physically or mentally impaired. Her blood showed no evidence of any drugs or other chemicals, except caffeine, consistent with drinking one or two cups of coffee shortly before the time of death.

3. The cause of the death was drowning.

4. The decedent's hands showed signs of bruising, consistent with attempting to smash open the passenger side window of her vehicle. This was also consistent with scratches on the interior glass of the passenger-side front window.

Professor Rodriguez asked Dr. Garcia, "Doctor, is there any evidence that would support a conclusion that the decedent died from anything other than accidental causes?"

He replied emphatically, "No, there is not!"

Another twenty-minute recess was declared. Jo and Sean slipped out one of the back doors into the freight elevator. As they rode down the elevator to Sean's floor, Sean held onto Jo's hand very tightly. When they reached the security of his office, Sean went into his bathroom and took two aspirin tablets. After grabbing some bottled water, Sean told Jo that he was going to make it. The worst was over. Jo said, "Precious, you're doin' a lot better than I thought you would. How come?"

Sean replied, "Because hI didn't have to see the autopsy pictures. I've seen other autopsy pictures, and they're never pretty. I wasn't sure if I could handle seeing shots of Cheryl cut up and dissected like a laboratory animal."

Looking relieved, Sean looked at his watch and said, "I guess we ought to think about beginning to go back upstairs."

Laughing, Jo said, "Think a lady might be allowed to visit the little girl's room?"

Sean said, "Thanks for reminding me. You go first."

As they prepared themselves to return to their ordeal, Sean surprised Jo by asking her, "Beautiful, how are you holding up?" Jo told him that she was okay since he was doing so well. Several minutes later, Sean and Jo amazed everyone at counsel's table with their calm.

At 1540 hours, the Blood Hound called the last witness for the day, Lieutenant Hiram Lee, who had been the detective in charge of the overall investigation of Cheryl's death. He was about forty-five. His reddish hair, twinkling blue eyes and wide grin made him seem likeable from the first moment that anyone saw him. After describing his methodology and his research, he stated his conclusions:

1. Cheryl Riley's death had all the earmarks of a vehicular mishap. There was no evidence at all to suggest that her death was the result of foul play. After reading the pathologist's report and the report of the accident investigator, he had concluded that Cheryl Riley did not die from foul play.

2. The only other possible cause of death other than accident left to be investigated was suicide. After interviewing her husband, Judge Sean Riley, several friends, Kyra and Max Townsend, a number of professional associates, her pastor and her hairdresser, he concluded that there was no evidence to suggest suicide. In addition, Cheryl

Riley did not fit the profile of a potential suicide. She was in good health, happily married and had two daughters that she cared about. Further, she was professionally successful. She had no addictions or psychological problems. And, most importantly, she was an active churchgoer in a religion that forbids suicide. Finally, suicide by driving a motor vehicle into a body of water is rarely the act of a female suicide victim. Drunken or drugged men are much more likely to commit suicide that way than women.

When Lieutenant Lee was finished with the summary of his report— the full copy of which had been previously marked, admitted into evidence and published to the jury—Dean Churchill rose and said, "Lieutenant Lee, in light of the hour, I promise to be brief. In your professional opinion, is it possible that Cheryl Riley died as the result of the unlawful conduct of one or more persons?"

Lieutenant Lee's response was equally as brief, "Sir, anythin' is **possible**. But, in light of the evidence developed in this case by the diver, the accident investigator, the pathologist and myself, I'd say that the likelihood of Cheryl Riley havin' died as the result of any unlawful conduct—other than her own speedin'—is as great as the likelihood that she was abducted and murdered by space aliens. In other words, such a possibility is too remote to waste our time talkin' about."

After Lieutenant Lee was dismissed, the inquest was recessed until 0900 hours the next day.

****

Once Sean and Jo arrived home, Jo surprised Sean. She made him put on his workout clothes and jog three miles around the property with her. After they finished jogging, she ordered him to her heavy punching bag that hung from a beam inside the garage. After tightening his gloves, Jo said in her best DI style, "Yankee Boy, I want one hundred good sets of one-two punches."

Since Jo was doing the counting, she disallowed quite a few of his early sets of punches. By the time Jo finally counted to one hundred, Sean's biceps, triceps, shoulders and pecs all felt like they were on fire.

Jo cooked while Sean showered. After eating, Jo let Sean retire to the living room to read for a few minutes. Once he was done with his mail, Jo made Sean undress and lie face down on the bed. Before Sean could protest that he was too tired for sex, Jo applied lotion to his body and began slowly massaging the glycogen out of his aching muscles. By the time Jo had worked her fingers down to the small of his back, Sean was sound asleep. Jo covered him and let him sleep. A few minutes later, Jo undressed and crawled into bed with Sean, feeling cheated that she hadn't had a chance to fully relax him.

Sean's physical exhaustion allowed him to sink into a very deep sleep. Sometime after 0300 hours, Sean had the dream to end all dreams. The dream started off with something that had really happened to him. Sean dreamt that he was back in his old parish church, when he was twelve. It was Holy Saturday night, the vigil of Easter. Sean remembered that while the fire was lit, the water blessed and the Litany of the Saints sung, the church was still quite dark. And the phrases, "Ora pro nobis!" and "Orate pro nobis!" echoed throughout the dark, Gothic-style church.

Next, came one of the most sublime moments of his life, as the celebrant of the Mass, a young priest with flaming red hair and the sweetest baritone this side of heaven intoned the first few words of the Gloria. The Lenten gloom was banished by the lights slowly, but surely, brightening the entire church while the magnificent bells of the church, silent for forty days, began to peal joyfully. This was one of the happiest moments of his life.

After the Gloria ended, Sean found himself as an adult, seated at a table in the Horizon Club while the maitre d' brought two women to his table. The room was bright and sunny. From a distance, the women appeared to be well dressed in early 1940's styles, resembling ladies at Rick's in *Casablanca*. Their hats obscured their faces as they approached.

When the ladies reached his table, Sean rose and kissed each of them on the cheek, which was the least he could do to greet his mother and first wife. After the waiter took their orders, Sean's mother broke the ice by asking Sean how she looked. Sean, replying honestly, said, "Voluptuous." Once he realized what he had just said, Sean blushed, much to the amusement of his companions.

His mother said, "Dear, you're old enough now to recognize that I always was a red-haired beauty, blessed with ample curves. Why do you think your father married me?"

Not wanting to go there, Sean asked, "How is dad?"

"Very happy that you didn't go to medical school. The way the practice of medicine has degenerated into a bureaucratic mess, he's so glad you ignored his advice and went to law school. He finally admitted the other day that you were wiser than he was about your career choice."

After all three of them laughed at his father's stubbornness, Cheryl asked, "Do you know why I'm here?"

Sean said, "I'm not entirely sure, but I think we're finally going to say goodbye to each other properly, which we never had a chance to do."

Chuckling, Cheryl said, "Is that why I brought your mother along?"

Sean answered, "Yes. Saying goodbye has always been painful for you. You wanted moral support."

Cheryl said, "You've only been married to Jolene for two months and already she's managed to develop something in you that I never could, a sensitivity and understanding of women. I'm impressed."

Patting Cheryl's hand, Marie said, "Dear, don't be too hard on yourself! I left you a diamond in the rough. You did a fine job of civilizing him. If you had had a bit more time, you would have finished the job."

After thanking Marie, Cheryl asked, "How is living with Jo going?"

Looking a bit confused, Sean said, "We haven't had the easiest month or so. Rudd's column made our second month of marriage rather painful."

Cheryl insisted, "That wasn't what I was asking and you know it!"

Sean, knowing that he couldn't get around this one, answered, "She's different. Besides the obvious physical differences between the two of you, she's a lot more emotional than you were. She throws herself completely into everything. Whatever she does, she does with reckless abandon. You were always more cautious and restrained."

Looking at both of them, Sean asked, "Is there anything special that prompted your visit now?"

Cheryl looked at Sean and asked, "What do you think?"

Feeling confused, Sean said, "I'm guessing that after the inquest is done, I'll be able to let you go and give myself fully to Jo."

Cheryl said, "You're getting warm. Think about today! You did something different. What was it?"

After a very long time, Sean blurted out, "After lunch, alone in my office, when Jo asked me how I was doing, I told her and then asked about her. I was much more worried about her than about myself!"

As soon as Sean finished his last statement, his two guests rose and kissed him on his cheeks. His mother said, "Congratulations! You've made it! You're grown up now. You don't need a wife as a mother substitute anymore."

Cheryl asked, "Now, can you figure out why we're here today?"

After pausing for a second, Sean said, "If I don't need to be taken care of any more, my guess is that I've got to take better care of Jo."

Cheryl looked at his mother and said, "Marie, you did raise him right, after all!"

Sean's mother said, "You love Jo, but you've held back a part of yourself. You've told yourself that it's because of Cheryl, but it really wasn't. Sean, what's the one thing that you're a snob about?"

Looking very embarrassed, Sean said, "I've never been a snob about money, education or social standing—only intelligence."

Cheryl said, "Sean, I hate to break it to you, but in due course, you're going to learn that Jo is probably the brightest person you've ever met. She's certainly smarter than you."

Marie asked, "Sean, do you know why you've been paired with Jo?"

After pausing for a second, Sean said, "If I've finally grown up, it must be something for Jo's benefit. Right?"

Marie smiled at Sean and replied, "I **did** raise you properly. Have you figured out what you can give her that most men never could?"

After pausing for a while, Sean said, "Confidence?"

Marie said, "Cheryl, you've got to claim some credit here. You really polished this diamond very well."

After Cheryl graciously refused to accept credit for Sean's growth, Marie continued, "Sean, you're an authority figure. You're a well-read intellectual—a professor, no less—in addition to being a judge. Plus, even though you're not much of a traveler, you've been to Europe and understand something of the history of the world. Plus, in Jo's eyes, you represent old money. While we know that you don't really qualify as old money, in Jo's eyes, you're close enough to the world of the McReynolds family. Jo needs your urbanity, your wisdom and your approval if she is going to reach her full potential. You need to nurture her as patiently as Cheryl and I nurtured you."

Before Sean could respond, Marie said, "Sean, speaking of sleep, you need to return to your bed. Your bride needs you."

As Marie and Cheryl stood up, Sean said, "Is there anything else that you can tell me about the future?"

Marie, making a coquettish pout, said, "I can tell you several things. You are going to have a long life and a successful career. Jo will not compete with you directly. But in her career, she will become a superstar if you develop her talents properly. And your son will outshine you both."

As his companions started to walk away, Sean said, "When will I have a son?"

Cheryl turned, put her hand on her hip, which she had thrust out suggestively, winked at him and said, "Roughly nine months from now, sailor! Enjoy!" Then, she blew him a kiss and was gone. Marie waved at him, and then she disappeared as well.

When Sean awoke from the dream, the digital clock indicated it was 0430 hours. He was wide awake. His heart was racing. His body was soaked with sweat. He could tell from her movements that Jo was near wakefulness. As Sean listened to Jo's breathing, an idea popped into his head. Very slowly, Sean left the bed, threw on a robe and grabbed two large towels from the linen closet. Then, he went out to the pool, set the towels down by the edge of the pool and turned on the pool heater. A minute later, Sean was back inside the house, brewing a pot of coffee. Once the coffee was ready, Jo awoke to breakfast in bed.

After breakfast, Sean suggested that she might like to start the day by taking a dip in their now warm swimming pool. When Jo said that the idea sounded good to her, Sean surprised Jo by pulling back the covers and carrying his unclad bride in his arms to the pool, which was now throwing off a small fogbank in the cool night air.

After playing in the pool for a while, Jo swam to one of the sides of the pool, near a jet of warmed water. Sean joined her. As Sean and Jo floated at the edge of the pool, Sean said, "Beautiful, I had one strange dream last night."

"Precious, do you want to tell me about it?" asked Jo.

Sean silently swam to the shallow end of the pool, exited, toweled off and turned off the heater. Then, Sean said, "I'll tell you about it later. Let's go back into the house."

Jo asked, "Will you carry me back to the bedroom?" Sean obeyed joyfully.

****

When Sean and Jo arrived at the inquest, they both glowed, full of good spirits. The men at counsel's table were all amazed. Isabel, Pam and Sarah—who had joined Sam today—gave each other knowing looks.

Sean and Jo were again color coordinated. This time, they were wearing earth tones. Sean was in a khaki summer suit, white shirt and a Royal Tank Regiment necktie[12]. Jo was wearing a light-weight, brown-tweed suit, honey-colored blouse and the pin that Sean had given her for her birthday. Jo wore shoes with low heels, so she wouldn't have to worry about her balance when she went up to testify. Wanting to look like the simple, farm girl she once was, Jo wore nude hose and only a touch of lipstick. With no makeup, her freckles were quite visible. Jo looked both beautiful and wholesome.

The Blood Hound called the inquest to order at 0900. The first witness for the day was Laura, who testified about picking up Sean at the airport after his recusal hearing in Queen City had ended. Laura testified that the word about Cheryl's death reached Sean's chambers right after his flight from Queen City had taken off. So, as an old friend, she drew the unenviable task of telling him that his wife was dead.

Laura broke down in tears several times as she described how Sean reacted very emotionally to the news of Cheryl's death, but struggled to regain his wits enough to be able to plan on how to break the news to the Twins. None of the lawyers asked Laura a thing since her testimony showed that Sean had loved Cheryl and the news of her death was a devastating surprise to him.

Kyra and Max Townsend were the next two witnesses. As usual, Max was called to testify first, so Kyra could have the last word. Both of them testified to Sean's deep grief over Cheryl's death, his loss of interest in life and about his blind date with Jo. Max testified that before the date, Sean looked as nervous as a green Marine about to assault a hostile beach. Kyra said she was surprised that Sean actually showed up for the first date and was proud of the effort he made to be sociable. Both testified they never observed anything that would lead them to conclude Sean or Jolene had ever met before. Kyra emphasized that Maggie Anderson was the person who introduced Jo to Kyra with an eye toward arranging a blind date for Jo. Kyra closed her testimony by saying that neither Sean nor Jolene had wanted to go on the blind date and that it was almost a miracle that they went out again.

The Blood Hound recessed the inquest at 1025 for fifteen minutes. After the recess was over, the Blood Hound called Lieutenant Jolene Scruggs Riley to the stand. Once she had been sworn and testified as to her name, rank and employer, the Blood Hound asked her, "Lieutenant, what is your connection to this matter?"

Jo replied, "I'm married to Cheryl Riley's widower, Judge Sean Riley."

"Lieutenant, do you know anything about the death of Cheryl Riley?"

Jo replied, "No, sir!"

After passing the witness, Professor Rodriguez rose and asked Jo a few biographical questions, making certain the jury heard that Jo's father was a retired Marine Colonel decorated with the Medal of Honor and her mother was a retired Navy nurse. Professor Rodriguez also asked Jo questions about growing up on a farm, graduating from State, going through the academy and her various assignments within the sheriff's department. Professor Rodriguez's questions about the bank robbery and her decoration for valor embarrassed Jo. After asking a few questions about Jo's current assignment, Professor Rodriguez asked her, "Where is the patrol station nearest to where Mrs. Riley's car entered Flatboat River?"

After Jo answered the question, Professor Rodriguez asked, "On March 9, 1999, were you assigned to that patrol station?" Jo replied that she was.

Professor Rodriguez then asked, "Were you involved in investigating the death of Cheryl Riley?"

Jo said, "No, Ma'am."

Professor Rodriguez inquired further, "Did you attempt in any way to either contact or influence the actions of Deputy Morrissey, Sergeant Gregory, Sergeant Reed, Sergeant Conrad Ernst, Dr. Ernesto Garcia, Lieutenant Hiram Lee or anyone else with respect to the investigation of the death of Cheryl Riley?"

"No, Ma'am," responded Jo.

Professor Rodriguez, seeing the jury was following along with Jo very closely, asked Jo, "Did you know Cheryl Riley?"

"No, Ma'am."

Changing her approach slightly, Professor Rodriguez asked Jo, "Lieutenant, when did you first learn of Cheryl Riley's death?"

Jo straightened to her full height and, after pausing for a second, said with great determination, "A few days before I met Judge Riley."

"Lieutenant, when did you first meet Judge Riley?"

"March 31st of this year!" proclaimed Jo.

In her best sarcastic tone, Professor Rodriguez asked, "Why do you expect the members of this jury to believe that you first met Judge Riley a year after his wife died?"

As she was speaking, Professor Rodriguez pointed to the jury. Jo, following her lead, answered the question while looking squarely at the jury panel. Jo said, "I expect the jury to believe what I say because that's the truth!"

The Blood Hound declared a short recess, mostly because he noticed a few of the jurors had wet eyes and probably needed some time to recover from the intensity of Jo's testimony.

At 1136 hours, the Blood Hound called Judge Sean Riley to the stand. After ascertaining the name of the witness, the Blood Hound's first question to Sean was, "Judge Riley, how long were you married to Cheryl Riley?"

Sean replied, "Almost a quarter century."

"Judge Riley, do you know anything about the death of Cheryl Riley?"

Sean replied softly, "No, sir!"

After the Blood Hound passed the witness, Dean Churchill rose and asked Sean a few biographical questions. Quite abruptly, Dean Churchill changed the topic and asked, "Judge, why are we here today?"

Sean said, "We are here today because my wife, Lieutenant Jolene Riley, and I want our good names back."

Sean didn't notice it, but the jurors were nodding their heads in agreement with him, except for those who were crying. Had Sean relaxed long enough to notice, he would have seen that at counsel's table, Pam was crying along with Jo.

In the first row of spectators, Sarah was crying. Near Sarah, Daphne was giving him a very Winston Churchillian "V for victory" sign. Had Sean looked at the crowd, he would have wondered who was answering the phones in his office, because most of his staff was there at the inquest, along with the staffs of the other courts, as well as many of his judicial colleagues.

Up in the balcony, most of his current students, as well as many of his students from years past, were present. The current students must not have noticed or cared that quite a few of the law faculty were there, observing them skipping class. There weren't many dry eyes up in the balcony either. Sandra Cobb was crying on the shoulder of her very pregnant cousin, Lucy Travis, who was also crying.

At this exact moment, there were many, many deep emotions in the inquest room. On any other day of his career, Dean Avery Steed Churchill would have quit right then and there. But that day, for some reason, something compelled him to go for the brass ring, to go for the gold—to win. He did not consciously realize it, but Dean Churchill was responding to the most primal of lawyerly instincts.

Deep in the soul of every lawyer who has spent his or her career toiling in law libraries and offices, lives an advocate crying to be set free. Although Dean Churchill had spent his career as a securities lawyer and as an academic, inside him there lay dormant a **trial lawyer**. This was his moment. Dean Churchill, being as casual as a securities lawyer in a bespoke Saville Row suit could be, turned to Sean and said, "Judge Riley, I'm sure everyone here noticed that yesterday you looked very uncomfortable. Yet today, you seem very relaxed and poised. How do you account for the change in your demeanor?"

Now that Dean Churchill had thrown him a slow-hanging verbal curveball, Sean swung for the proverbial bleachers when he said, "Yesterday, I was very bothered and upset listening to the details of my late wife's death."

Looking away from Dean Churchill and directly at the jurors, Sean added, "Today, we're past the gruesome details. Today, Jo and I have had a chance to say our piece. I feel better just knowing that the truth has finally been unshackled."

"Judge, is there any other reason why you are relaxed **today**?"

Sean, after glancing at his inquisitor, looked squarely at the jury and said, "As a lawyer, a judge and a law school professor, I have a deep love and respect for our legal institutions. While not always perfect, I know that in the vast majority of cases, they work very well. I have faith that in our legal system, truth eventually will prevail over falsehood; and that in the long run, the good triumphs over the bad."

Dean Churchill concluded his examination. JT Downing thought about asking a question or two, but in light of the pandemonium that had just begun, thought better of it.

The Blood Hound declared a recess until 1400 hours. As soon as the Blood Hound was off the bench and the jurors gone from the jury box, the audience in both the mezzanine and the ground floor started to applaud. Not wanting to disappoint their supporters, Jo and Sean stood together and waved. The applause, polite though it was, was too loud for the peaceful precincts of the courthouse. Maggie quickly hustled Sean, Jo and the other members of Team Riley to the freight elevator.

At precisely 1400 hours, the inquest resumed. The Blood Hound asked Bubba to call the next witness, one Winfred K. Rudd. As the name was called, a murmur began in the audience. When Rudd appeared a moment later, giggles were heard. Because most of those present in the courtroom only knew what Rudd looked like from the twenty-year-old image that appeared at the top of his weekly column, his current appearance was a bit of a shock. Since that photo was taken, Rudd had lost all of his hair, gained sixty pounds and acquired a very red tint to his face and head. The handsome, virile-appearing, crusading columnist, alas, was no more, having succumbed to the ravages of time and Demon Rum.

After Rudd was sworn in and asked his name by the Blood Hound, Sam Brown addressed the bench, "If it may please the court, since I subpoenaed this witness, may I conduct the initial examination?"

The Blood Hound, knowing that something big was about to happen, assented to Sam's request. Sam approached Rudd with a marked copy of his September 11th column and asked him to identify it. After the witness identified the exhibit, it was admitted into evidence.

Then, Sam asked Rudd to read his column into the record. Rudd did so with difficulty, even with his reading glasses on. As he read, his voice was shrill and cracked several times. When Rudd finally finished reading his column, Sam asked that the column be published to the jury.

Sam then asked that a copy of the sheriff's department report detailing the allegations raised against Jo be admitted into evidence. When the copy of the report was admitted, Sam asked that it be published to the jury, which it was.

After pausing for a second and pacing back and forth as if he was distracted, Sam suddenly turned and asked Rudd, "Mr. Rudd, in your column of September 11th, you alleged that the late Cheryl Riley died under **very mysterious circumstances**, if I recall your phrasin' correctly. Now Mr. Rudd, did you make that up or did you have information that would lead you to that conclusion?"

Looking very disgusted, Rudd said, "I certainly did not make it up. I had information to support that contention."

Smiling, Sam said, "Mr. Rudd, when a lawyer uses the term, *personal knowledge*, he means information obtained through one's senses—information that was either seen, heard, felt, smelled or tasted. Usin' that definition and that definition alone, at the time that you wrote your September 11th column, did you possess personal knowledge concernin' the death of Cheryl Riley?"

After waiting for a moment, Winfred K. Rudd indicated he had no personal knowledge concerning the death of Cheryl Riley.

Pausing to let those words sink into the brains of the jurors, Sam then inquired, "Did you acquire some of your information concernin' the death of Cheryl Riley from one or more other persons?"

Before Rudd could answer, a lawyer popped up in the audience and identified himself as Henley Grimes, counsel for Mr. Rudd, and asked if he might approach the bench. When counsel reached the bench, Mr. Grimes indicated that he was present to protect the rights of his client under the First Amendment. When asked by the Blood Hound if he was making an objection now, Grimes said that it looked like he soon would be. The Blood Hound gave Grimes permission to find a spot at counsel's table.

Sam repeated the unanswered question, which Rudd answered in the affirmative. Sam then approached Sarah, who handed him a document. Wasting no time, Sam offered the document into evidence as an **official record**. When presented with the document, Rudd identified the it as a certified copy of an assumed name certificate that he had filed with the county clerk, authorizing him to conduct business under the company name of Media Consultants of Ransom County.

After thanking Mr. Rudd for his cooperation so far, Sam looked around the room for a second, and then asked Rudd very calmly, "Mr. Rudd, did you ever receive anythin' of economic value from any of your sources for the September 11th column, either prior to, durin' or subsequent to writin' your September 11th column?"

Rudd shot back, "I don't understand what you mean by *economic value.*"

Sam said, "Fair enough. Let me rephrase my question. Did any of your sources for your September 11th story pay you money—either by cash or by check, either in your own name or in an assumed name?"

Rudd was silent for an awfully long time. The silence was broken when Mr. Grimes rose to invoke his client's right to protect the identity of his sources, protected under the freedom of the press clauses contained in both the federal and state constitutions.

Sam addressed the court, "Your Honor, learned counsel must have misunderstood my question. I wasn't inquirin' into the identity of his sources, just whether he received payments from any of those sources."

The Blood Hound overruled the objection and told Mr. Rudd he should answer the question. Before Rudd, who was now sweating profusely, could answer, Mr. Grimes rose and informed the Blood Hound that he was hereby invoking his client's right to refuse to answer the question based upon his privilege against self-incrimination.

The crowd began to get loud and unruly. The photographers snapped and snapped, and the red eyes of the video cameras all focused on a very uncomfortable Winfred K. Rudd. After a moment, the Blood Hound banged his gavel as a signal to the bailiffs to take action.

Once the bailiffs succeeded in calming down the throng, Sam asked, "Mr. Grimes, if I ask your client if he traveled outside of the country with any of his sources for his September 11th column, would you invoke his right against self-incrimination again?"

Grimes indicated that he would so advise his client. Sam said, somewhat disappointedly, "Well, I guess that I'd better move on to somethin' else. Mr. Grimes, if I ask your client if he ever engaged in sexual relations with one or more of his sources for the September 11th column, would you invoke his right against self-incrimination again?"

Grimes indicated that he would invoke that privilege on his client's behalf if that question were asked. Noticing that the jury was paying rapt attention to his every move, Sam motioned to Sarah. A moment later, when Sarah handed Sean a quart-sized, plastic freezer bag, every eye in the huge room was on the bag. After having the court reporter place a sticker on the freezer bag, Sam asked Rudd if he would identify the endorsement on the back of the check in the freezer bag.

A now totally defeated Winfred K. Rudd indicated that the signature below the rubber stamped name, **Media Consultants of Ransom County**, was in fact his.

Sam asked permission of the coroner that a photocopy of the exhibit be retained in the records of the proceeding in lieu of the original document. When the Blood Hound agreed, Sam asked if the High Sheriff of Ransom County, who was sitting in the audience, could be called forward to take custody of the original exhibit. Once the Blood Hound agreed, Sheriff Walker was called forward.

As the sheriff strode toward the bench, his gaze was riveted upon Winfred K. Rudd, who was now looking blankly into space. When he reached the bench, Sheriff Walker took possession of the evidence and assured the Blood Hound that he would put his best detectives onto this investigation immediately. As the sheriff passed by the counsel tables, Jo observed the hint of a smile on the sheriff's face.

After the sheriff had exited the courtroom, Sam asked the Blood Hound if he could address several housekeeping matters. The first one was a request to publish the copies of the check —front and back —to the jury.

After that request was granted, Sam addressed the Blood Hound and said that he had one other request to make. Motioning to Bubba, who had produced a large cardboard box approximately three feet by six feet in size, Tom and Pam helped Sam remove two very large blowups of the check from the box. When Sam asked if he might offer these blowups of the check to assist the jury, no objection was made and the Blood Hound allowed it. Pam and Tom thoughtfully placed the blowups on easels, near enough to the jury box so that no one could miss seeing the front and back of the $500,000.00 check from Cynthia McReynolds to Media Consultants of Ransom County.

After Sam announced he was finished, the Blood Hound indicated he would charge the jury after a thirty-minute recess. This long recess served a very beneficial purpose. It allowed all the media types there to examine the blowup of the check and marvel over the stupidity of Winfred K. Rudd and Cynthia McReynolds. As they walked out of the courtroom, Sean whispered to Jo that within two hours, Winfred K. Rudd's career would be over.

At 1615, the Blood Hound charged the jury and told them to take their time, be thorough and let the bailiffs know if they had any questions or needed anything.

* * * * * * * * * * * *

That evening, Sean and Jo grabbed some take-out ribs on their way home. After the meal, they were both too exhausted to do much of anything, so they sat on the sofa and played with Law and Equity. As they sat quietly, Sean broke the silence by saying, "I had the strangest dream last night. This morning, I only could remember part of it. In it, I had lunch with my mother and Cheryl—both aged about forty."

Jo surprised Sean when she asked what they were wearing. Sean said, "My mother was wearing a pale-green suit and one of those 1940's hats—it matched her suit. Cheryl was wearing a white suit and a big hat with a pale-blue ribbon around the crown. Why did you ask that?"

"Precious, I've had a lot of experience with dreams. From what you've told me about what they were wearin', I'm gonna guess that it wasn't a sad dream. Am I right?"

"Yes, my beautiful, insightful Jo, you're absolutely right. The strangest part of the dream was that they talked about you and said awfully nice things about you."

A smiling Jo replied, "Sean, you sound surprised at that. Why?"

"I'm not sure. When I saw the two of them together, I sort of expected that I was in trouble, I guess." Jo giggled.

Sean inquired, "Jo, do you think that you know me well enough to answer a couple of questions about your time at State?"

"As my husband and lover, Precious, I'll answer whatever you ask."

"How did you do on your SATs?"

"Sean Riley, that's a really personal question. But, I guess that considerin' we have a somewhat more than casual relationship, I guess I can tell you. I don't remember the exact scores, but I was in the top one percentile in both Verbal and Math."

"How were your grades at State?"

Plopping her bare feet in Sean's lap, Jo said, "I might be persuaded to tell you that with a little bribery." Several minutes later, Jo purred, "I graduated Magna cum Laude. Why are you askin' me these fool questions?"

Looking a little embarrassed, Sean finally said, "In the dream, Cheryl told me that you're a lot smarter than I am."

Jo, struggling hard not to laugh, gently put her right foot up against Sean's cheek and said, "You just figured that out now?"

Sean, looking a little embarrassed, asked, "Why did you play the dumb ol' country girl with me?"

Jo, now sitting up straight, looked Sean in the eye and said, "The country girl part wasn't an act. The dumb part was only part act and part real. I found school borin', so I never learned how to act like an intellectual. When I met you, I knew from the gitgo that you actually learned all that stuff in school and remember it. I'll never pass for an intellectual, no matter how hard I work at it. I'm just not the type."

Sean, looking a bit skeptical, asked, "Anything else?"

"Precious, when I met you, I was scared that you wouldn't like me, you bein' a judge, a professor and a man who's been to Europe. So, I played my strongest suit. You didn't seem to mind it too much, did you?"

"I certainly didn't. If I can change the topic a bit, after the election is over, do you think you could take a Friday and Monday off for a long weekend?"

"I think so. Where do you want to go?"

Sean replied, "Where do **you** want to go?"

"I've always wanted to see the Grand Canyon," said Jo.

Sean took the idea a step further, "I'll check with my travel agent and see about getting a visiting judge for that Friday and Monday after the election." Jo liked that idea a lot.

"Jo, do you have a passport?" asked Sean.

"No, why?" inquired Jo.

Sean explained, "You'll need it when we go to Europe. It probably won't be until next summer at the earliest, but go ahead and get one after the election. They're good for years and years."

"Precious, did that dream do somethin' to you? Somethin' that you haven't told me about?" asked Jo.

Sitting up straight, Sean said, "The dream made me realize how important we are to each other. I'm awfully sorry that I've been preoccupied with the campaign. I promise that from now on, no matter what happens, I'm not going to pull away from you."

A very happy Jo led Sean to bed. Law and Equity raced ahead of them.

Chapter Seventeen

The morning of Thursday, October 11th was one of the slowest of Sean's life. Since he hadn't known how long the inquest was going to be, his docket was empty. Sean tried to read, but his nerves kept getting the better of him. After attempting to read the same paragraph in a law review article for the fourth time, Sean realized that it was hopeless. He looked out the window for a while.

Mercifully, Jo sent an email asking if he had heard anything. He replied that her email was the most exciting thing that had happened to him all morning, but had hopes for their lunch at Joe's Diner.

Sean surfed the net for a few minutes. He almost called Sam's cell phone, but he thought better of it. His rational mind—what was left of it— told him that if and when something happened, Sam would call him. Sean looked out the window some more. Finally, he sent Jo an email reminding her to see if she could take off the Friday and Monday after the election to go to the Grand Canyon.

Laura came in and chatted about nothing of consequence. Sean was glad to have something to do and someone to talk to. Unfortunately, Laura was as anxious as he was, so they just made each other more nervous. After Laura left, Sean looked at the clock on his credenza. It was only 1000 hours and he was a basket case already.

Sean's chambers were as quiet as an undiscovered tomb. Laura tried to pour through some accountings. Miriam was so concerned that she was actually quiet. Since Bubba was attending to the inquest jury, he wasn't available to enliven things. Jane was off for the day, preparing for her wedding.

Around 1030 hours, Sean's pacing back and forth in his office was interrupted by Angela, who brought him several files. She also brought Sean a homemade peach pie. Angela, after insisting that Sean was about to waste away, practically twisted his arm to get him to have a slice. Had Sean had an appetite, he would have noticed that Angela's peach pie was something to dream about. After trying to rouse Sean's spirits, Angela left the files and the pie with Sean.

A little after eleven, Sean received an email from the presiding judge authorizing a visiting judge for the Friday and Monday after the election. Sean forwarded a copy of that email to Laura and Jo. A few minutes later, Jo responded, indicating that she wouldn't have any trouble getting those two days off. Jo suggested an early lunch because she was starving.

Sean managed to kill some time by calling his travel agent and outlining what they wanted to do. She promised to call back after lunch. Sean told her to take her time.

****

At lunch, Jo and Sean didn't say much. They held hands and looked into the other's eyes. Anyone seeing them together would have thought that they were acting like fourteen-year-olds. They were and didn't care. They were sheltering each other from reality.

At around 1230 hours, Sean and Jo decided that they might as well go back to their offices, not wanting to hog a table at Joe's during the lunch hour. As they walked along, Sean's cell phone went off. It was Sam. The inquest jurors had just finished their deliberations and notified the Blood Hound that they had reached a verdict. The Blood Hound sent them to lunch and announced that the verdict would be made public at 1400 hours.

Reversing direction, Sean and Jo turned toward the courthouse, hoping that they could slip in the back way before the camera crews caught them. As they walked, Jo called her office to let them know what had happened and where she would be.

Sean and Jo spent most of the next hour in his office with the door closed. Sean gave Jo a really intense shoulder massage and foot rub. The activity and physical contact helped both of them relax a bit.

When Sean and Jo arrived at the top floor of the courthouse, they were unfazed by the crowd of reporters and camera people. They walked into the courtroom calmly—appearing to be totally unconcerned about anything. It was all an act, but a very effective one.

After the Blood Hound called the inquest to order, the foreman of the jury indicated the jury had reached a verdict. Bubba was directed to deliver the verdict from the foreman to the Blood Hound. As Bubba walked past the counsel table, Sean noticed that Bubba was holding the form oddly, separating his index finger from the rest of his fingers as he carried it. Sean wrote Jo a note that said one word: **UNANIMOUS**. Jo wasn't sure if that was a positive thing, but since Sean appeared to be visibly relaxed as he slipped her the note, she hoped he was right.

The Blood Hound reviewed the short form silently, as the tension in the room intensified. After what seemed like an awfully long time, the Blood Hound read the verdict out loud very slowly, allowing every word to carry its full weight. The verdict was simply, "We, the jury, find that on or about March 9, 1999, Cheryl Riley died as the result of mishap or misadventure."

The Blood Hound indicated the verdict was unanimous. He turned toward the jurors and verified that it was unanimous. It was. The Blood Hound received the jury's verdict and concurred in it. He indicated that his final report would be ready for distribution in a day or so. Then, looking squarely at the cameras, Rufus T. Hill, a.k.a. the Blood Hound, intoned in his deepest and most solemn voice, "There's not one bit of evidence that would lead any sane, honest human bein' to any conclusion other than that the late Cheryl Riley died as a result of a traffic accident. To my way of thinkin', anyone who says otherwise is either a fool or a knave. Judge and Lieutenant Riley, I'm so sorry that you had to undergo this ordeal to clear your names. But, they're now **cleared**."

Then, looking at the jury, the Blood Hound thanked the jurors for their service and told them that when he adjourned the inquest, they would be free to go. Looking around the room with a practiced, theatrical flair, the Blood Hound inquired if there were any other matters pending.

Bubba rose and said **very** slowly, "Well Judge, a number of the jurors asked me to ask you if'n it'd be okay for them to talk to Judge and Lieutenant Riley after they're dismissed."

The Blood Hound replied, "Of course, they may. Seein' no additional matters are pendin', this inquest is adjourned."

As soon as the Blood Hound finished speaking, a loud cheer filled the room. Stacey and Ashley blocked the bar leading to the front of the courtroom, allowing Bubba to guide the jurors to Sean and Jo in order. As cameras clicked and whirred, twenty-four people—all good and true—one at a time came up to shake hands, hug and in some cases kiss Sean and Jo. A bystander—who did not know what had just transpired—could have easily concluded that Sean and Jo were long-lost relatives of the jurors.

After the jurors had filed past, a horde of well-wishers approached Sean and Jo to offer their congratulations. By the time they finished with Sean and Jo, Sean realized it was time for him to leave for class.

As Sean prepared to leave, Jo, looking at her wristwatch said to Sean, "Precious, you don't have time to take a cab today. Please take the keys to my SUV. I'm gonna stay awhile and chat with our team. Pam and Dean Churchill will give me a ride to the law school, and I'll meet you there."

Sean agreed and hurried off to class.

＊＊＊＊＊＊＊＊＊＊＊＊

307

When Sean arrived at class, he guessed from the looks on the faces of the students that something was up. Sean noticed many of his colleagues standing at the back of the room. Before he could say anything, he heard a loud male voice say, "We'll start at three. One. Two. Three."

Sean was overwhelmed when everyone in the room stood and sang, *For He's a Jolly Good Fellow*. It took every bit of Sean's strength of character to not break down in tears. When the quick party ended, Sean somehow mustered up the strength to begin class.

Amazingly, he made it through the first and second hour of class okay. At the beginning of the third hour, Sean was interrupted by Dean Churchill and Pam, carrying a large white cake. Dean Churchill said that Sean should keep teaching while he, Pam and Jo cut and distributed pieces of the cake to the students. After the cake was handed out, Pam and Dean Churchill left, but Jo took a seat in the back of the room and watched the class very intently. Jo was very well behaved until class was over. As soon as class ended, however, Jo practically dragged Sean out to the SUV to take them both home.

****

As Sean and Jo drove downtown on the morning of Monday, October 16th, Sean said, "The one good thing about this messy, nasty campaign is that it has given us a great chance to work together. How have I been to work with?"

"Precious, you have been a joy to work with. You've tried so hard to please me. I haven't a doubt at all that people will still be talkin' 'bout how great we were together fifty years from now."

Sean suspected that Jo was exercising her God-given right as a Southerner to exaggerate. Nonetheless, Jo's praise made the beautiful, sunny morning seem even better. As they drove along, Sean turned on the radio and found the area's most popular country station. After listening to one song, they heard Sean's campaign ad for the first time. The announcer, whose voice commanded the authority of Dean Churchill while retaining its distinctively country flavor, simply invited everyone to the Ransom County Fairgrounds on the afternoon of October 28th to an old-time, political rally for Judge Sean Riley. Musical entertainment would be provided by Cowboy Jimmy Wharton, who would show his new, never-seen-before music video.

When the ad was over, the DJ said, "Can you imagine that? Cowboy Jimmy Wharton is gonna make his first public appearance in five years right here in Ransom County! I'm sure gonna be there and suspect that y'all will too. Our next song is a favorite, *Good Will Win in the End*, recorded by the late Tommy Breen and his wife, Sarah, who lives right here in Ransom County. Not too many folks know this, but Cowboy Jimmy Wharton was in the band for the recordin'."

As soon as the DJ quit talking, Jo had Griswold on her cell phone telling him, "Bob, we heard the ad. It sounds even better than it did in the studio. How did you get the DJ to give the rally an extra plug?"

Putting her cell on speaker, Sean and Jo heard Bob say, "I sent the CDs of the ads on Friday to radio stations all over the county. When they played them to check their length and quality, I started gettin' calls like you wouldn't believe from country and mainstream entertainment media. I don't know if you realize it, but you two are now mini-celebs. Every country station in the area is getting requests to play *Good Will Win in the End* every two hours from six in the morning to midnight. The student volunteers have been magnificent makin' those requests."

After Jo told Bob that they had just heard it, Bob said, "I suspect that between now and Election Day, you are going to hear it a lot." All three of them, even normally serious Bob, laughed at that.

As Sean and Jo neared their destination, Jo broke the silence by saying, "If I hadn't been so pushy, we wouldn't be in this situation, would we?"

Sean, not sure what Jo was really talking about, asked, "You mean the nasty campaign?"

Jo said, "If I hadn't been such a flirt, we could have waited to get married until after the election. It's my fault."

Sean replied, "You are not responsible for our being in this situation. Tom Greene, Cynthia McReynolds and Warren K. Rudd are not subject to your control. So, don't blame yourself. Besides, I seriously doubt that I would have made it through this campaign without you."

When Sean parked the SUV in the lot, Jo surprised him by reaching over and planting a big, wet, lipstick-smearing kiss on his lips. As Jo corrected the damage to her hair, lipstick and makeup, she told Sean she had been bothered by this nagging fear that her impulsiveness had hurt him. Jo looked very relieved to hear Sean say that she wasn't the person to blame. Jo lit up when he said that impulsiveness was a big part of her charm. They parted company in good spirits.

****

When Sean walked into his chambers, Miriam jumped up and said loudly, "Did you see it?" When Sean asked Miriam what she was talking about, she replied, "The *University City Bugle* endorsed you. You gotta read it!"

A minute later, Sean was at his desk, taking his copy of the *Bugle* out of his briefcase when Jo called, babbling more excitedly than Miriam. Sean was able to calm Jo down just enough to find out that she had already read the morning's edition of the *Bugle*. Jo said that in place of Rudd's column, there was a long piece by the publisher of the paper and that on the editorial page they had endorsed Sean glowingly. After telling Jo that he loved her and hanging up the phone, Sean looked at his watch and realized that he might have enough time to look at the *Bugle* before he had to be out on the bench, if everyone would leave him alone. It was not to be. In the space of five minutes, Sean received congratulatory telephone calls from Sam, Kim, Max, Griswold, Father Wilson, Pam, Kyra, Daphne and the Twins. As Sean scurried to take the bench, Laura gave him a big thumbs-up signal and Bubba smiled one big smile.

So, it wasn't until mid-morning that Sean finally had a chance to lock himself in his office, sit down and actually read what everyone had told him about. Sean was glad he had the time to read slowly. Looking at the editorial page first, he noticed the endorsement. It said, very matter-of-factly, that Judge Sean Riley had always shown himself to be very dedicated to the law, a legal scholar, a judge of exceedingly fine judicial temperament and a dedicated public servant. The endorsement then said, "With great pleasure, we endorse Judge Sean Riley for reelection without hesitation, reservation or qualification." Sean, while glad to have the endorsement, wondered if it was a case of too little, too late.

Sean had a different reaction when he read the column by the publisher.

We Really Messed Up This Time

By Timothy Jamieson, Publisher

The column by Warren K. Rudd, published in this newspaper on September 11th of this year, concerning Judge Sean Riley and his wife, Lieutenant Jolene Riley, is hereby retracted in its entirety. The entire family of the *University City Bugle*, from its highest-ranking staff to its trainees and interns, hereby apologizes to Judge and Lieutenant Riley for the totally unjustified and unwarranted distress, pain and humiliation that Warren K. Rudd's September 11th column inflicted upon them.

There have been two changes over the last few days here at the *University City Bugle*. The first change is that Warren K. Rudd no longer writes for this paper. The second change is that Julie Sharpe, who, until today, wrote the society column, has been appointed editor of this paper. Ms. Sharpe, prior to coming home to University City to be our society editor, had a long and distinguished career working for major newspapers in Los Angeles and Washington, D.C. Her broad experience and her high journalistic standards are what we need as we try to reclaim this newspaper's reputation.

The Rudd imbroglio, unfortunately, reflects a problem with American journalism today. Before the Watergate scandal, journalists saw their jobs as reporting the news. Since Watergate, journalists have seen themselves as a priestly class, whose mission is to uncover scandal—at any cost—making sure that they get a book and movie deal for themselves in the process.

There are two problems with this way of looking at the world. The first is that major governmental scandals are rare. While public officials sometimes break the law and more often do stupid things, most in government are hard-working people, who try to do the right thing. Consequently, journalists, who always assume that if something goes wrong there must be a sinister reason for it, have a decidedly biased viewpoint. Reporting events filtered through a conspiratorial prism presents a distorted view of reality.

The other problem with the post-Watergate mentality is that it has alienated the media from the rest of society. It has created an US vs. THEM approach, in which the US **knows** that we are smarter and more virtuous than the THEY could ever hope to be. Besides distorting the news, this arrogant, supercilious attitude has had a very corrupting influence on the news media. Since media types **know** that we are truly superior to the rest of the human race, there is a belief that the normal rules of conduct that govern mere mortals need not bother us. The Rudd imbroglio is one illustration of the results of this foolish attitude. I hope that the changes announced today will in some small way return journalism at this newspaper to its true calling—reporting the news accurately, fairly and honestly.

Sean sat in silence for a moment after he finished reading the column. After a while, he realized that Timothy Jamieson had done something unique. He told the whole truth. The *Bugle* could have just published a retraction and an apology and been done with it. For some reason, Jamieson took the opportunity to say what he probably wanted to say for a long time. Sean realized that Timothy Jamieson was one of the rarest of people, a man to be admired and respected for his honesty and intellectual courage.

Sean thought about calling Griswold, but realized that by now, Bob was already busily arranging to make sure that every voter in Ransom County received a copy of the column. Sean emailed Jo and thanked her for giving him the good news. Sean also suggested lunch at The Palm Tree. Jo readily agreed, making his morning one of the best he had had in some time.

* * * * * * * * * * * *

Sean was amazed at how many people the Horizon Club's main dining room could hold once the usual dining tables and chairs had been moved elsewhere and folding chairs placed in their stead. This Meet the Candidates Night, sponsored by the local League of Women Voters on Wednesday, October 18th, would be Sean's only face-to-face encounter with Tom Greene. Because of the number of judicial and non-judicial candidates invited to speak, each candidate's remarks would be limited to three minutes. When Sean had first told Jo about the three-minute time limit, her response had been an incredulous, "Are they crazy? How can anyone say enough in three minutes for anyone to tell whether they're qualified?"

Sean had agreed wholeheartedly with Jo, and then enlisted her help getting him ready for the speech. Sean had practiced the speech so many times that he was sure both he and Jo could both recite it backwards in their sleep. Although he felt a bit edgy, Sean also felt ready and eager to take on the forces of darkness and despair since he knew his speech as well as anyone could ever know anything.

Since the candidates would be called to speak based on ballot position, Sean and Jo knew they had a long wait in store for them because Sean's race was the last one on the ballot. As they waited, Sean held Jo's hand. Turning to look at her, Sean noticed that Jo looked absolutely radiant. Her profile was a thing of great beauty. Her brown hair, which now fell way past her shoulders, contrasted very well with the blue of her dress, which was exactly the same color as her eyes. Jo was a study in blue and brown that night.

As they waited, Jo whispered to Sean, "CG?" Once Sean nodded, Jo slipped her shoes off and rubbed her feet back and forth on the carpeting. "CG" was short for "country girl," which meant barefoot. While Jo rubbed her feet in obvious relief from being out of her high heels, Sean thought that despite having gone to college in a big city and having worked in urban law enforcement for almost a decade, Jo was still a freckled-faced country girl at heart—unassuming, honest, passionate and loyal. Sean prayed that she would never change. Sean knew he was lucky beyond belief to have Jo

Rory R. Olsen

sitting next to him. For a few tranquil moments, Sean was no longer a candidate—just another man in love.

Sadly, Sean's moments of peace and blissful admiration of his new bride were disturbed by a tap on the shoulder by one of the host committee. After a big, wet kiss from Jo, Sean followed his hostess to the area behind the platform.

When he arrived, the lady in charge—a tall, gray-haired woman wearing a large name badge that read "**Thelma**"—told him that there would be two more sets of candidates before he and Tom Greene were up. When Sean asked Thelma to point out Tom Greene, she smiled and said, "He hasn't checked in. I'll let you know when he arrives."

Sean was confused. Where was Thomas A. Greene? When the final candidate scheduled to speak before Sean was introduced, a member of the host committee brought a tall, thin, red-haired, young man—certainly not a day over twenty-six—to meet Sean. The young man appeared hostile and flustered. After refusing to shake Sean's hand, he said to Thelma, "I'm Todd Williams. I'm here tonight on behalf of Mr. Greene, who was detained in Capitol City on a pressing legal matter."

Sean said, "Ma'am, I believe the rules that were distributed to the candidates weeks ago indicated that each candidate was to appear in person. Substitute speakers would only be allowed for the gravest of reasons by permission of the host committee, upon written request filed at least seventy-two hours in advance. Has the host committee given this young man permission to speak?"

Thelma, who so far had appeared to be totally unflappable, looked very confused for a second. Then, she caught the eye of the organization's president, a lady named Grace, who listened to Thelma and said, "Judge Riley, you'll be speaking by yourself this evenin'." Before Todd Williams could speak, Grace flashed the young man a warning look that implied that if he dared to raise his voice in protest, she would turn him into a pillar of salt. As young Todd Williams left the staging area, Grace escorted Sean to the main stage and introduced him.

As soon as Sean's name was mentioned, something unexpected happened. First, just a few people rose to their feet and started clapping. Then, a few more rose and joined the ovation. Then, within the course of a few seconds, almost everyone in the room was standing and clapping. Sean had no idea what to say or do. So, Sean did what judges have done since the time of Henry II, he just stood there with a poker face, totally masking his true feelings, which were three parts of euphoria mixed with one part of gratitude and one part of relief.

Once the audience had retaken their seats and order returned to the room, Sean's introduction was completed. Sean surveyed the room before he began to speak. As he scanned the room, he noticed quite a few familiar faces tucked into the crowd. He saw Shirley sitting with Bubba, who looked uncomfortable in his suit. Sean noticed a gaggle of ladies from the courthouse. Miriam and Laura were seated near the front. Sarah and Tom were on the aisle, near the front, sitting with Daphne, Pam, Dean Churchill and Isabel. On the far right side of the room, as Sean continued to scan the audience, he saw Jo's friends from the party at Plum Lake. Seated next to the ladies from Plum Lake and their escorts, Sean observed Kim and Covey.

Abandoning his planned speech, Sean said, "Madame President, members and guests of the League of Women Voters, thank you for coming out tonight to listen to the candidates speak. Your presence here tonight speaks well of your interest in good government. Since my opponent was unable to join us, I will depart from my prepared text and keep my remarks brief."

Sean knew that he would get a favorable response to that line, so he waited until the cheers had died down and continued by saying, "I have over nine years of experience as a probate judge. My opponent has no judicial experience of any kind. I practiced in this area of law before I took the bench. My opponent has no known experience in the area. I have taught Probate Law for many years. My opponent has no comparable experience. I have drafted changes to the Probate Code, which our state legislature has passed into law. My opponent has no such experience. In short, I am the only qualified candidate in the race. Please remember to tell your friends and neighbors that between now and November 7th. And remember that when you vote. Thank you."

Sean's remarks must have touched the audience, because he received a standing ovation.

After the meeting ended, Sean spent thirty minutes with Jo at his side, shaking hands and thanking his many, many enthusiastic supporters—most of whom he'd never met before—for their support. Sean noticed something previously absent from his campaign—a sense of victory.

****

Thursday evening, after class, Jo and Sean discussed the last twenty-four hours over salad and whole-wheat lasagna. Jo was very glad to hear Bob's analysis that the inquest and the *Bugle*'s endorsement had dissipated any lingering problems Sean might have had with the urban female vote. Jo, not having Sean's experience in politics, wanted to know why that would be the case.

Sean replied, "Beautiful, the scenario that Rudd suggested in his column, was straight out of a bad made-for-TV movie. Middle-aged man murders middle-aged wife, so he can take up with a beautiful, younger woman."

Jo's response was, "Oh! I never looked at it from that viewpoint."

Sean said, "Country women are our other difficult demographic. We'll make our effort in a few days to win them back, won't we?"

Jo smiled and said, "Practice! Practice! Practice!" Sean nodded his head in agreement.

The rest of the evening's conversation dealt with the question of where had Tom Greene been the night before. Jo indicated that she had heard Greene was either served with a grand jury subpoena or was arrested. Sean was skeptical that either happened because it had only been a week since the inquest concluded. Sean said that he had heard those same rumors from Bubba, plus Angela had told him that she heard Greene had had a nervous breakdown. Jo agreed with Sean that the courthouse rumor mill was wrong most of the time, so they should just stick to their game plan.

Later that evening, as they prepared for bed, Sean said to Jo, "Beautiful, I'm sorry that we haven't really had a normal time to adjust to married life. I promise that after the election—win or lose—I'm going to devote myself to you."

Jo surprised Sean when she said, "Precious, while we haven't had the most pleasant time since we returned from our honeymoon, that hasn't been all bad. Because of the grief we've gone through, we've gotten to know each other in ways that few couples ever do. We've seen each other in really awful situations and have learned how well we both deal with adversity. You've really needed me and I've really needed you. I consider these bad times a blessin' from God since we've really learned how much we need and depend on each other."

Sean, choking back a tear, nodded his head and said, "You are far wiser than your young years. I love you."

Chapter Eighteen

"Jo, is Sean always this danged nervous?" Cowboy Jimmy Wharton asked.

Jo laughed and said, "You should have seen him on our blind date. When we were introduced, I half-expected him to run out the back door, right after he shook my hand."

The band laughed loudly. Then, Cowboy Jimmy asked, "Sean, you afraid of girls?"

Sean, knowing that everyone was looking at him, paused for a second, and then said, "I'm not afraid of the opposite sex by any means. But, I do have a healthy respect for them, particularly young and very beautiful women, just like I have for wild animals, firearms and explosives. That's how I managed to live to age fifty."

Cowboy Jimmy and the band howled. They might have laughed into the next month if Sarah hadn't come up to Sean and planted a very ostentatious kiss on his cheek, and then said, "Sean, you need to share some of your wisdom with Sam."

After the laughter died down, Cowboy Jimmy suggested that they have lunch. Everyone concurred, even the very nervous Sean. As they ate, Sarah asked Cowboy Jimmy to tell everyone the story about how he took up music as a second career.

Cowboy Jimmy was glad to tell his story. He began with, "When I was a boy, all I ever wanted to do was be a cowboy. Since I growed up in the Texas Panhandle, that wasn't very unusual. After I left the service, I worked on a ranch. Just for the fun of it, one day, me 'n a bunch of buddies tried our luck at a local rodeo. None of us did any good, 'cept for me. Next thin' I knowed, I was drivin' all over the place, chasin' the rodeo. I done pretty good at it. Bein' young and foolish, I enjoyed the pretty ladies and the parties and thought that it would never end."

"One year, at the big Houston Rodeo," Jimmy continued, "I had the pleasure of meetin' Sarah and Tommy Breen. Somebody must've told Tommy that I spent a lot of my spare time entertainin' the ladies with my guitar. So, Tommy asked me to play and sing somethin' with him. To my utter amazement, Tommy told me that if'n I ever got tired of gettin' all busted up, I should give him a call about joinin' his band. I was flattered, but didn't think twice about it until a year later when I was in traction in a hospital in Amarillo. Layin' there, I remembered what Tommy had said and called him. I got his answerin' service and figured that I'd never hear from him. A few days later, when Tommy and Sarah showed up at the hospital, I dang nearly cried."

Jimmy went on, "Anyway, a few months later, I was pickin' guitar in his band. Tommy was a right good teacher. Everythin' that I know about music and the music business, I learned from Tommy. When Tommy and Sarah started to slow down, Tommy opened all the right doors for me, so I could go solo. Everythin' that I am today, I owe to Tommy and Sarah. So, when Sarah called me askin' me to help some friends of hers, my reply was, *Whatever you want, I'll do it*! That's why me and the band 're here."

After finishing the last of his barbeque, Cowboy Jimmy added, "Course, once I met you and Jo, I was glad to do it. I hate what they tried to do to you two. Y'all are nice people and deserve a lot better than that."

****

Fifteen minutes before the rally was set to begin, backstage at the Ransom County Fairgrounds, Cowboy Jimmy and his band were all running around making last-minute preparations. The scene was organized chaos. Sean and Jo sat off to one corner with Sam and Sarah, Max and Kyra, Lucy and Ralph, the Twins and Bob and Roxanne Griswold.

Flipping his cell phone closed, Bob said to the group, "Our volunteers outside just checked in. The crowd is so large that the overflow parking lot is now almost completely full. The deputies are going to have to let people start parking on the side of the road. Sean, I'm so glad that we ordered those extra screens and speakers. You'll be playing to a really full house."

Sean's only comment was, "Thanks, I think?" Turning to Jo, Sean said without conviction, "If you're going to make a fool of yourself, might as well have a big crowd see it!"

Jo's reply was, "Precious, think before you answer this. Have I ever embarrassed you in public? Have you ever been embarrassed in public when I was there?"

After pausing for a few seconds, Sean, forgetting their wedding reception, replied, "In all honesty, No! Occasionally, you talked me into doing things that I was a little hesitant about doing, but I've never been embarrassed in public with you at my side. Thanks for reminding me."

At 1410 hours, Sam appeared on stage and announced that the rally would begin in exactly five minutes, so everyone should find a seat, or at least a comfortable place to stand.

Five minutes later, Sam appeared again on stage and introduced Cowboy Jimmy Wharton and his band. The crowd went wild with enthusiastic shouting, yelling, clapping and foot stomping. Cowboy Jimmy and his band played a medley of his old hits for about forty minutes. When the medley was completed, Jimmy moved to the front of the stage and told the crowd, "For a while now, I've toyed with the idea of doin' a music video to go with a song I wrote. Little more than a month ago, my dear friend, Sarah Breen [Applause!] introduced me to two fine people, Sean and Jo Riley, who offered to help me out with my video. Since they live here in Ransom County, I figured I should show it here first. I hope you like it. It's called, *The Ballad of Whit and Jane*."

While Cowboy Jimmy had been speaking, a large video screen was lowered into place at the back of the stage, behind and above where the band sat. The lights on the stage dimmed. Then, the first image appeared, showing the title of the video. After the title had been on screen for a few seconds, the next image appeared—that of Sean dressed as an Old West lawman, circa 1875, walking down a dusty street, looking like John Wayne in *Rio Bravo*. Accompanying the image, Cowboy Jimmy sang, telling the story of a hard-working, honest lawman, lonely because he had no lady to share his life. Many in the audience started to notice that the video was made like an old-time, silent movie. After pausing for a few seconds on the image of Sean looking into the distance, the scene changed.

In the next scene, Sean's character, Whit, was introduced to Jo's character, Jane, the town's new school teacher, at an ice cream social. When Jo appeared on camera, the audience went wild with applause and cheers. Jo was costumed as an Old West schoolmarm. In silent-movie fashion, Jo's eyes were made up heavily. And she was wearing very long false eyelashes. In the video, as Cowboy Jimmy sang of the couple's love at first sight, the camera focused on Jo's long, fluttering eye lashes and her freckles.

Very quickly, the next image to appear on screen was that of the couple leaving the church on their wedding day and driving off on a buckboard. As the buckboard drove into the distance, the camera focused on their smiling faces. Country Jimmy's accompanying music was happy and upbeat.

The next image was that of Whit in his office, ashen faced, reading a telegram. The telegram said that a killer, Billy Longly, apprehended by Whit years ago, had been pardoned and released from prison. The telegram advised that he was expected to arrive in town that day on the 2:10 train with a gang of five. As the scene unfolded, Country Jimmy's voice and music conveyed the danger that this presented to Whit.

In the scene that followed, Whit helped Jane onto a buckboard. Whit told Jane that she should hide out with some of his friends at their ranch until the trouble was over. The camera then focused on Jane, Jo's character, crying very heavily as she left town on the buckboard. The accompanying music was funereal in pace and somber in tone.

The camera then cut to Whit staring down the track. In the distance, a wisp of smoke was barely visible. Over Whit's shoulder, a clock showed the time to be several minutes after two. Then, the camera cut to Whit sitting alone outside the deserted railroad station. The camera then showed the completely empty streets of the town. Nothing was moving, except for a bit of tumbleweed.

The next scene was shot of Whit. His face showed a look of grim determination. The clock displayed the time to be eight minutes past two. Behind Whit, a plume of dust became more and more visible over his shoulder. Whit, peering forward, failed to notice the plume.

Then, the camera cut to a view of the railroad track. As the engine of the train became quite visible on the screen, the camera very quickly panned to the action going on behind Whit. Quite suddenly, a multitude of men on horseback had appeared at the station to aid Whit. Just as the train was about to reach the station, the camera cut to a shot of Whit swearing in his new deputies—all armed to the teeth. The camera then showed Billy Longly about to leave the train, and then stopping and telling his men to stay on board when he saw Whit and his armed deputies.

As the train departed with Billy and his gang still on board, one of the new deputies turned to Whit and said in silent-movie fashion, "Whit, when Jane reached our place and told us about your trouble, we weren't 'bout to let you face them varmints alone. We're your friends and neighbors."

The video ended with a shot of a totally entranced Whit, walking down the street with his arm around Jane's waist while Jimmy ended the ballad happily. Jane, of course, in classic silent-movie fashion, fluttered her eyelashes for all she was worth. In the last shot, the scene went from tintotype to modern color. The blue of Jo's eyes filled the screen.

When "THE END" flashed across the screen, the audience went wild, cheering and applauding for a good five minutes. As the applause started to die down, Cowboy Jimmy said, "Now that you've seen them on the big screen, let's see how they look in person. I give you Jo and Sean Riley."

Sean and Jo appeared on stage to tumultuous applause. They were dressed perfectly for the event. Sean was wearing a long-sleeved, blue denim shirt, tan chinos and a shiny pair of brown dress boots. Jo had her hair tied back behind her head. She was wearing a red and white checked blouse, a long, denim skirt and brown dress boots. After taking a few bows, they waved to the crowd, making the applause grow even louder.

When the applause finally died down, Cowboy Jimmy took center stage for a second, saying, "Let's hear from the man of the hour, Judge Sean Riley."

The crowd cheered again. As the cheering continued, Cowboy Jimmy and Jo moved off the center of the stage. Sean, feeling incredibly energized, said, "Since this is supposed to be a political rally and since I'm the only person on stage running for office," then looking back at the band, Sean ad libbed, "but not necessarily the only person on stage running for something, I guess I ought to say something political." The audience loved the ad lib. As he spoke, the volunteers started handing out his campaign literature.

Sean continued, "I've had the pleasure of serving the people of Ransom County as a Probate Judge for a little more than nine years. I'm seeking another term. Some people don't like that idea. Instead of challenging my record, they've resorted to telling tall tales about me and my wife, Jo. But, the truth is now out. I'm the only qualified candidate in the race. When you go to vote on November 7th, please remember to vote for me."

Sean paused for a second. When he received the sign from Bob Griswold that the campaign materials were being distributed, Sean continued, "This campaign has been hard on me. But, the campaign has been even harder on my lovely wife, Jo." Jo's name brought another round of applause. Sean noticed that Maggie, Darla, Karen, Stacey and Ashley were in the front of the crowd and were acting as de facto cheerleaders.

As the applause at Jo's name wound down, Jo appeared back on center stage, carrying her own microphone. As Sean started to speak, Jo, in her deepest drawl said, "Precious, these people don't want to hear you talk all afternoon. Why don't you just get it over with and tell 'em that the worst part of the campaign was me havin' to put up with you?" That line brought the house down.

After the laughter stopped, Jo, now being serious, said, "Sean's right. We have been through some awfully tough times. But, we always knew that we'd make our way through them somehow, just like Whit and Jane did in Cowboy Jimmy's video, because we have faith in God and faith in our friends and neighbors, the good people of Ransom County. When Sean and I were datin', we found a song that had a special meanin' for us, a song about a couple who had to endure troubles not of their own makin'. The song was first recorded by the late Tommy Breen and his wife, our friend, Sarah Breen. With Sarah's permission, we'd now like to sing it for y'all."

A moment later, the band, which had quietly made its way back on stage, began to play *Good Will Win in the End*. Sean sang the first verse. While he was singing, the camera projected his image on the smaller screens all around the fairgrounds, as well as on the screen hanging above the band. Sean's singing, his fears notwithstanding, was flawless. When it was time to sing the first chorus, Jo and Sean stood close together, their gazes firmly fixed on each other. They radiated their love back and forth. No one who saw their faces on the big screen could doubt that for a second.

When Jo sang the second verse, a hush fell over the crowd. They knew that they were hearing something very special since Jo had the voice of an angel with a very deep drawl. Jo and Sean sang back and forth. After the sixth and final verse was over, they began to sing the final chorus. The chemistry between them was magical. As they sang, they truly were totally lost in each other's gaze.

When the last note was sung, Jo had the presence of mind to remember to say, "We've recorded this song. If you'd like a copy, you can download it at Reelectsean.com. We'll also have copies available for sale after the rally at the tables in the back."

A few seconds later, Cowboy Jimmy appeared on stage and said, "If you aren't reelected, come see me. Y'all can take country music by storm."

A moment later, Cowboy Jimmy introduced the final number of the afternoon, a rousing spiritual, which was perfect to end the rally. Cowboy Jimmy joined Sean and Jo onstage.

Just as they were about to sing, Sarah stepped forward, saying, "I haven't appeared on stage since about the time that Jo was a gleam in her father's eyes. It's been too long." The crowd roared its approval.

After that final number, Sean, Jo, Sarah and Cowboy Jimmy all thanked the audience. That ended the rally.

As soon as the curtain came down, the Twins rushed on stage to hug Sean and Jo. Sam and Sarah, Bob and Roxanne and Kyra and Max all told them both that they had been big hits. After thanking them, Sean and Jo expressed their deepest thanks to Cowboy Jimmy and the band, as well as the technicians who made the entire rally work. Then, Sean and Jo worked the crowd for several hours until there was no one left.

When they were finally done, Bob Griswold caught them. Bob told them that starting tomorrow, their one-minute TV ad would saturate the local TV market. Bob indicated that because he bought the time in the middle of September, he was able to keep from being pushed aside by the Bush and the Gore campaigns. Bob said that all of the local country stations would receive on Monday morning, by hand delivery, a CD of their performance of *Good Will Win in the End.* Bob said that their army of volunteers would keep the requests coming.

Bob smiled when he said, "Since the TV ad uses *Good Will Win in the End* as its theme music, by the time the election is over, just about everyone in Ransom County will have that melody etched into their brains. You were great on stage today, but the audio that we recorded in Texas in Cowboy Jimmy's personal studio is better quality. I'm really glad that we took the time in between video shots to record it."

As Bob and Roxanne were about to leave, Bob added, "I wouldn't be at all surprised if you see yourselves tonight and tomorrow on local news. I know that all four local channels had crews here. If the local TV channels want to interview you on their only morning talk shows, will you be available?"

Sean and Jo laughed at the thought, but said that they would be available.

✼✼✼✼✼✼✼✼✼✼✼✼

Surprisingly, the plane back home left La Guardia exactly on time. Once the plane had reached its cruising altitude, Jo looked at Sean and asked, "CG?"

Sean smiled and said "Of course. But, considering the price of those shoes, don't lose them!"

While Jo kicked off her shoes and made herself comfortable, Sean opened his laptop computer. Looking at Sean, Jo asked, "Precious, have you caught up your journal?"

"Jo, since the rally eight days ago, I really haven't had the time or inclination to make my entries. Will you help me remember what happened this past week?"

"Precious, I'm not sure that my memory is any better than yours, now that I'm thirty. But, I'll try. I guess the week started off on Sunday afternoon, when Bob called us when we were out at the pool."

Sean nodded his head and started typing while saying out loud, "I was pleasantly surprised when he told us that he had gotten us booked on the early morning show on the Fox affiliate. I was shocked when he told us that we needed to be there at 0500 hours for a pre-interview and to get made up."

Jo replied, "I'm glad we went to bed early Sunday night. Jan, the hostess of the show was awful nice. I couldn't figure out why she kept lobbin' softball questions at us until after the show, when she told us that she and

Julie Sharpe had been college roommates. Do you think I'll look that good when I'm her age?"

Sean smiled and said, "Better." Before Jo could say anything, Sean added, "Getting up at four in the morning has got to take a toll on anyone's appearance. I promise you that I'll make sure you spend enough time in bed."

After Jo gently kicked him with her unshod foot, Sean said, "Monday night, I'll never forget. I never expected my Probate I class to show up in blue jeans and cowboy hats. I certainly never expected them to sing the chorus of *Good Will Win in the End* as well as they did at the beginning of class. They really had fun with that."

Jo said, "You should have seen the look on your face after class on Monday, when I told you that we were due to be at the ABC affiliate at 0445 for the pre-interview and makeup. Luckily, they didn't make us sing. The video that they shot on Saturday looked real good, didn't it?"

"Definitely! I was really surprised when someone brought in a video of the interview and played it at Rotary on Tuesday. I noticed that all that makeup didn't hide your girl-next-door good looks at all."

Jo giggled, and then said, "Precious, Wednesday was the real killer. How we managed to make it to both the NBC and CBS affiliates in one mornin' is a miracle to me. I don't remember too much about those interviews."

Sean agreed, "Jo, I don't either. Fortunately, we looked good, wholesome and energetic when we played the shows back on TiVO. Bob said that those were our two best local interviews."

Jo said, "Weren't we lucky that the Founders' Day Ball, the big event on the university's social calendar, was Wednesday night. Precious, I was amazed that you were so upbeat and animated that night. How did you manage it?"

"Sleep deprivation, mostly. Did you have a good time?" asked Sean

Jo replied, "How could I have avoided it? You, Sam and Dean Churchill kept me, Sarah and Mrs. Churchill laughin' throughout the meal. Mrs. Churchill's English, isn't she?"

Sean smiled and said, "Indeed. She and Daphne knew each other as students. Small world, isn't it?"

Quite rapidly, Jo's expression changed. She added, "I made a real effort that night to not let Mrs. McReynolds and her bad manners bother me. Have you ever seen anybody just sit there and stare at someone else like that?"

Sensing a chance to get Jo off of this obviously unpleasant topic, Sean said, "No. My commitment hearings never last that long."

It worked. Jo's laughter got her back in a happy mood. Sean typed for a minute. When he stopped typing, he asked Jo, "What was your reaction when I called you Thursday afternoon with Bob's big news?"

Jo said, "If I hadn't known you well enough to be able to tell from the tone of your voice that you were serious, I never would've believed you. I was just about speechless when you told me that Sean Hannity wanted to interview us in New York City on Friday night."

"Beautiful, what was Sheriff Walker's reaction when you told him that you needed to leave early on Friday to catch the plane to La Guardia to be on Hannity and Colmes?"

"Precious, all he said was, *See if you can get E.D. to send me an autographed picture.* Is she your favorite, too?"

Sean wisely replied, "I prefer brunettes. But, she is my favorite TV blonde."

After typing for a minute, Sean inquired, "What did you think of being on Hannity and Colmes?"

Jo replied, "I could tell that Hannity and Colmes—both of 'em—were used to interviewin' heavy hitters. They were well prepared and asked sharp, crisp questions. I loved the way that you handled the question that Colmes hit you with. What was it? *Don't you think that singing a country song on stage is a bit undignified for a judge?* I loved your reply, *Alan, anyone who has ever run for office can tell you that representative democracy is by its very nature undignified. Only autocratic governments are able to maintain the façade of dignity at all times. An occasional loss of a bit of dignity is a small price to pay for having an elected government.* Wow!"

"Beautiful, I didn't see that one coming at all. I'm glad that I didn't totally blabber. Could you believe that he came back and asked me if country music was appropriate for a serious campaign?"

Now smiling from ear to ear, Jo said, "I nearly fell out of my chair when you said, *Country music deals with the pains and joys of life that everyone faces. Only people with emotional problems and snobs can't understand it.* How'd you think of that?"

"When he asked me the question, I felt like a batter seeing a fast ball coming right down the middle of the plate. I had to do it. How come you were only asked softball questions?"

A giggling Jo said, "I think that it had somethin' to do with the fact that Alan interviewed you and Sean interviewed me. He really spent a lot of time talkin' about my law enforcement record, didn't he?"

"Off the air, what did you think of Sean and Alan?" asked Sean.

Jo responded, "Alan is younger and nicer in person than he appears on camera. About his partner, knowing my weakness for men named *Sean*, all I better say is that I'm surprised Mrs. Hannity lets him out of her sight."

Sean asked, "How come you let me out of your sight?"

Jo replied, "I've never known you to have a death wish. New York has got that crazy Sullivan Law, so I'll bet that Mrs. Hannity isn't as well armed as I am."

Sean wisely resumed typing. After several minutes, he asked, "Jo, what did you think of the rest of the trip?"

"Precious, I think that you saved yourself a bunch of money by stuffin' me with food after the show. What time did you wake up?"

Sean said, "I guess it was near ten in the morning. Weren't you glad that I had the presence of mind to order us a good breakfast from room service?"

"Precious, I was very appreciative of **everythin'** you did for me on the trip. I can't believe how much I spent at Bergdorf Goodman.™"

"Jo, I wasn't totally surprised. When I was in law school, one of my classmates went to New York City to interview with a Wall Street law firm. They put him up in a little room that wasn't much bigger than a walk-in closet. He was shocked to find out that the rent on that room for one night was almost as much as his monthly rent for a much bigger apartment in University City. No matter how much we paid for your gown, I can guarantee that you'll be the loveliest woman at the victory party on Tuesday evening."

Jo shook her head and said, "I doubt that! But, I'll probably be the most expensively dressed woman there, unless Mrs. McReynolds decides to come and celebrate your victory. Between the electric-blue evening gown and the matching shoes, I know that I'll get some envious looks and probably cause some husbands some awkward moments afterwards."

"Jo, I'm sorry that we didn't have time to do much sight-seeing. Want to fly back sometime and see all the sights that we missed?"

"Precious, I'd love to see all the sights that we didn't have a chance to see. But, while I'm sure that I'll love the view from the World Trade Center and I'll be overwhelmed by the architecture and the art in the museums, I doubt that anythin' there could surpass St. Pat's. The cathedral was absolutely awe inspirin'. I'm glad that we went to the first Mass on Sunday. The effect of the sunlight as it began to come slowly through the stained glass windows as the sun rose, is somethin' I'll always remember. Thank you for gettin' me up early and makin' me walk the two blocks from the Waldorf-Astoria. It was worth the sacrifice."

"Jo, after the horrible two months that we've both lived through, I'm glad the opportunity came our way to get away for a couple of days. You know, I may be the only person in the history of the world who spent two relaxing days on the island of Manhattan."

"Precious, are you worried about the election?"

"Not really. I've done everything that you and I and Bob and Sam could think up to win. If I lose after giving it my all, there won't be any shame in that. If I lose, I'll go back to teaching and practicing law. That isn't exactly what's bothering me. Just like that night in Reno right before we came back home from our honeymoon, I have this vague, undefined feeling that there's something dangerous in the air. It just hit me now."

Chapter Nineteen

Sean and Jo rose early on Election Day, November 7, 2000. The air was unusually warm and sticky. The skies were gray and foreboding. The weather forecast told them what they already sensed—a big electrical storm was about to hit the area.

Law and Equity were both very jumpy that morning, sitting on top of the sofa, which was their refuge in times of nasty weather. Not being cats, Jo and Sean had to leave the safe, dry shelter of their home and face the day. Jo had her new gown in a hanging bag, also carrying a small suitcase for her jewelry, hair curlers, makeup and a host of other grooming and wardrobe aids for the evening's victory celebration. Sean wore his London Fog™ raincoat and packed an extra umbrella in his truck.

Leaving home earlier than usual, they stopped off at their polling place to vote before heading downtown. The parking lot at the fire station was unusually crowded. After running the gantlet of campaign workers attempting to hand out push cards, Jo and Sean entered the polling place.

Having stood in line for a few minutes, they eventually reached the registration tables. Sean was pleased and Jo was surprised when one of the poll workers started to hum the chorus of *Good Will Win in the End* before being shushed by the Election Judge.

After voting, they ran into a couple in the parking lot—complete strangers—who told them that they were certainly going to vote for Sean. The couple said that they weren't sure about which way to vote until the big rally. They said that seeing Jo and Sean on stage convinced them that Sean must be a good man, considering how much he and Jo were in love. Sean and Jo thanked them both and then headed downtown.

Notwithstanding the flashes of lightning and the thunderclaps in the distance, Jo and Sean were in a good mood. After talking about the many people who had told them that the rally convinced them to vote for Sean, Jo remarked, "Precious, you're awfully relaxed. How come?"

Sean surprised Jo when he said, "I realized this morning that tomorrow morning, win or lose, I won't hurt any more when I wake up."

After digesting Sean's comment for a minute, Jo asked, "Has it really been that bad for you?"

Sean answered, "Every day since the Rudd column appeared, when I wake up, I've had this feeling of fear in the pit of my stomach. Whatever happens today, I know that tomorrow, I won't have that awful feeling anymore."

Jo didn't say anything in response. Sean, sensing what was bothering her, said, "Beautiful, I didn't say anything to you because I didn't want to upset you. Besides, as a man grows up, he realizes that there are some things that happen in life that his mother, girlfriend or wife can't make better. You had your own problems. I'm sorry if I've hurt your feelings."

Jo smiled and said, "I never realized until right now that cops and lawyers have loneliness in common. Both groups keep to themselves too much. After the inquest was over and I was ridin' back with Dean Churchill and Pam, he said that one of the things law students are told is that *Lawyers have no friends in the courtroom*. That's like what I learned in the academy when one of our instructors told us that when on patrol, *Remember, 'cept for your radio and your piece, you're all alone out there*! I understand all too well! I can't blame you for actin' like a lawyer any more than you could blame me for actin' like a cop."

As Sean's F-150 neared downtown, the rain began to fall. By the time Sean let Jo off at the front door of the Sheriff's Department Headquarters Building, the rain was falling steadily, accompanied by lightning and thunder. Sean sensed that the day would not be dull.

****

After work, Jo met Sean at his chambers. Taking over his private bathroom, Jo got herself ready for the evening while talking to Sean. Neither one of them had had a dull day.

Jo had held a press briefing after lunch about the arrest of an armed fugitive from a convenience store robbery after a high-speed chase. Being a slow news day, the reporters asked her a lot more questions than usual— some of them downright silly. After a while, Jo figured out that the reporters were giving her a hard time as an expression of affection since reporters, like cops and lawyers, always present a hard, cynical façade to the world. Once the briefing was over, four of the reporters asked to see her in her office—off the record.

Jo told Sean, "Precious, I couldn't believe it. They each had one of our CDs. They asked me to autograph the liners of their jewel cases. What was even stranger was that all four of them said they had voted for you, even though you were a Republican." Sean appreciated their votes, but was shocked to hear how openly the reporters had disclosed their Democratic bias.

Sean's day had been very interesting, also. In the morning, he had refereed two discovery disputes. In each case, both lawyers had acted badly.

Sean had to translate—slowly and painfully—the discovery requests into English, rule on the objections and then force the other lawyer to agree on the record to comply by a certain time and date to those portions of the requests that Sean had allowed.

After Rotary, Sean had heard an objection to the legal fees of a personal representative's lawyer. The hearing was a farce. The objectors could point to nothing specifically objectionable in the fee statements, arguing instead that taken together the fees were too high. Considering that the estate was quite large and had numerous parcels of raw land to be sold, the objection didn't hold much water. What made the hearing farcical was that the fees being paid to the lawyer of the objecting party were substantially more than the fees being objected to by that party. Sean denied the objection.

When Jo finally finished her preparations for the evening, Sean told her that it had been worth the wait. Jo looked stunning in her electric-blue gown. While the gown did not show very much skin—except for Jo's bare shoulders—the gown hung on Jo in such a manner as to accent her curves in a most appealing way. Jo reminded Sean that the sales person had described the gown as being "a corset dress, which would hug her curves with a flirtatious flair." Sean agreed with the description. Jo's matching Italian-made, sling-back, satin shoes completed the ensemble.

Wearing a gray suit, solid red tie, white shirt with gold cuff links and black wing tips, Sean looked as dull as a pigeon next to a peacock. The differences in their wardrobes notwithstanding, arm in arm, Jo and Sean prepared to meet their fate at the University City Country Club.

****

The drive to the University City Country Club was laborious, the rainstorm slowing traffic to a crawl. The bright lights over the portico of the main building were welcoming beacons to Jo and Sean on that dark, wet evening, offering them a chance to escape the gloom that had taken over University City and all of Ransom County.

The Grand Ballroom of the country club was configured differently from the last time Jo and Sean had been there. What had been the dance floor for the Spring Fling in May was now filled with a set of large screens, each screen having its own projector connected to a laptop computer. Each laptop had cables attaching it to the Internet and was attended by a college-aged person. Seeing the profusion of computers, projectors and screens, Jo sensibly asked, "Precious, why are there so many of them?"

Sean replied, "Election reporting has gone hi-tech. Tonight, every half an hour or so, they'll release updated numbers. Since the statewide candidates will get their numbers from the secretary of state's computers, I'm sure that a few of these screens will show statewide results. The rest of the screens will show Ransom County results. My race is at the bottom of the ballot, so my guess is that the results in my race will probably be on the screen located on the end."

Most of the crowd that evening was to be found at the opposite side of the Grand Ballroom, where a number of large screen televisions were broadcasting the national election results. Sean and Jo spent the next hour or so mingling with their many friends and supporters in this part of the ballroom. The most enthusiastic of these was Bill Morrow, who babbled on and on about what a great comeback Sean had made from near political oblivion. Sean held onto Jo's right hand tightly, not wanting her to be able to slug Morrow in the mouth, which Sean well knew was what she really wanted to do. Morrow seemed surprised when Jo replied to his inquiry about her running for the legislature in 2002, by saying "Not unless Hell freezes over first."

Not knowing the meaning of the word "No!" Morrow exited after telling Jo that once the stress and excitement of Election Night 2000 had worn off, he'd really like to visit with her again to discuss the matter. Jo said nothing in return.

Almost everyone that Sean knew politically was at Victory Party 2000, except for Bob and Roxanne Griswold. At 1925 hours, Roxanne appeared. Sean and Jo both noticed that Roxanne looked really lovely, her green dress highlighting her blonde mane to excellent effect. Roxanne was also showing a lot of very shapely leg. Sean was somewhat surprised that he had never noticed before just how beautiful Roxanne was.

Roxanne told Jo and Sean that Bob had sent her to baby-sit them since Bob was sure that Sean was driving Jo crazy by now. Jo thanked Bob for his thoughtfulness and inquired where Bob was hiding out. Roxanne speed dialed Bob on her cell phone and handed it to a surprised Jo. After chatting with Bob for a bit, a smiling Jo handed the cell phone back to Roxanne a minute later.

Whispering in Sean's ear, Jo told Sean, "Bob said that there's about a three-minute time lag between when the updated numbers are known at the clerk's office and when they hit the Internet. He told me to tell you that shortly the count of the absentee ballots will be posted. He said that you're up 52-48%."

A minute later, Bill Morrow announced from the microphone on center stage that local results were due momentarily. The crowd slowly moved toward the big screens. When the screens lit up, Sean noticed that statewide the ticket was doing quite well. Locally, everyone seemed to be doing better than he was in the absentee balloting. Sean told Jo, "I'd rather be up by four points than down four."

Taking a table near the big screen television showing Fox News, Sean and Jo waited with Roxanne, Sam and Sarah, Kyra and Max and Laura and her husband, Dr. Rizzoto. Sarah told them that Lucy and Ralph had decided that since Lucy was more than eight months along, it might not be real smart to tempt fate by driving around on a dark, stormy night. Everyone agreed that she was wise, particularly Laura's husband, who opined that Lucy would be better off going into labor at home than in the Grand Ballroom.

Sean was glad to be surrounded by friends that evening. For about forty-five minutes, he paid no heed to anything or anyone except those sitting with him.

Near 2030 hours, Roxanne said, "Bob told me that I should remind you that you'll probably slip below 50% in the next update, which will include mostly ballots from traditionally Democratic areas." As soon as Roxanne had finished speaking, her cell phone went off. After talking to Bob for a second, Roxanne hung up and said, "Sean, you've gotten Bob confused. When they post the new local totals in a minute or so, every one of our countywide candidates will—as expected—drop below 50%, except for you. Bob can't explain it, but he's glad that it happened."

Five minutes later, Sean was standing by the big screens, taking a lot of good-natured teasing from the other judicial candidates since he was leading them all at the moment. Roxanne's theory was that their musical media blitz had worked better than expected. Sean, not wanting to look a gift horse in the mouth, just smiled.

Around 2100 hours, the mood in the Grand Ballroom turned sour, when the networks—traditional and cable—began to award Florida to Vice-President Gore. No one at Sean's table said anything for a long time until finally Max said, "Cheer up! Gore won't be as bad as Clinton. Besides, his wife's a lot better looking!" Although everyone agreed with Max's assessment, it didn't do much to cheer up the group.

Fortunately for Sean and Jo, around 2110 hours, Roxanne's cell phone went off again. After talking to Bob for a second, Roxanne ended her call and said to Sean and Jo, "Your baby-sitter is now off duty. You don't need her anymore."

Jo asked, "You sure 'bout that?"

Roxanne replied, "I've got to pick up Bob now, so I can gloat! He didn't believe me when I predicted just how big a win you'd have. He just admitted it to my great joy! Bye, kids! Enjoy your victory!" Roxanne then departed, leaving a table of confused people in her wake.

At 2130 hours, Bill Morrow announced that a new set of local numbers would be posted momentarily. As expected, all the Republican countywide candidates went back into the plus fifty percent range. Sean was now leading the pack at 58% of the vote. Since it looked like both the county and the statewide races were going Republican, the party began to wind down, most of the party-goers wanting to go home and hope against hope that somehow Governor Bush would pull off two miracles by winning both New Mexico and Oregon. Jo and Sean decided to wait it out there in the Grand Ballroom of the University City Country Club with their friends.

At 2210, Sean's cell phone went off. Griswold, sounding a lot happier and looser than Sean had ever heard him before, asked, "Sean, where are you?"

When Sean said, "Sitting right here with Jo and a bunch of our friends in the Grand Ballroom of the University City Country Club," Bob said, "Sean, you're going to drive me to the poor house. Roxanne offered me double or nothing on whether you had gone home yet. I lose." Before Bob hung up, Sean managed to wheedle out of him that the original bet was for roundtrip airfare to New York City, so that Roxanne could spend a day of shopping at Bergdorf Goodman and Tiffany & Company. By doubling the bet, Bob was going to have to go along with her and carry her bags, as well as spring for a night in the Waldorf-Astoria and a dinner for two at a place of her choosing. The ladies at the table thought that Bob was a good sport.

At 2248, another batch of local totals was posted. With 96% of the precincts reporting, Sean Riley was leading the pack with 62% of the vote. After calling the Twins with the good news, Sean and Jo decided that it was time to go home to celebrate with Law and Equity.

* * * * * * * * * * * *

While waiting for their truck to be brought around by the valet parkers, Jo and Sean both noticed that the rainstorm was gone. The sky was clearing. The moon and the stars were visible again. There was a very mild breeze blowing from the south, keeping the air temperature pleasantly warm. The night was almost as lovely as Jo.

Once Sean's F-150 had cleared the city and was heading on the interstate toward County 191, Jo said, "Precious, we've been sorta busy recently, so I haven't had a good time to ask you this before now. Do you think that I'd be a good lawyer?"

Sean, knowing full well that Jo was a source of endless surprises, said, "Yes. Why do you ask?"

Jo replied, "I've been bored on the job for a while. I didn't realize it when I did it, but puttin' in for sergeant was the stupidest thing I've ever done. Once you've got rank, you stop bein' a cop and become a paper shuffler. I'm bored!"

Sean, attempting to be as diplomatic as he could, said, "Jo, lawyers have been known to shuffle papers occasionally. Have you thought about that?"

Jo's reply caught Sean off guard, "Precious, from what I can tell, lawyers aren't bureaucrats. When they do paperwork, it's for a reason."

Sean, not wanting to dampen Jo's enthusiasm, asked, "When did you start thinking about this?"

Jo said, "After we started gettin' serious, I started to wonder if I could fit into your world, so I took the L.S.A.T. exam late last spring."

When Sean asked how she did on the test, Jo said, "They must've made a big mistake with my test paper, because I came out at the top of the heap."

Jo was very pleasantly surprised when Sean responded, "I'm not in the least bit surprised by that. I guessed on our blind date that you had a good deal of verbal intelligence."

A now intrigued Jo asked, "How'd you figure that out?"

Sean replied, "You used words very well. That's characteristic of verbally adept, intelligent people. I sensed right away that you were sharp. Have you applied to law school yet?"

Jo said, "Remember after the inquest, Dean Churchill and Pam gave me a ride to campus? I was so impressed with how you lawyers handled our problem and presented the evidence at the inquest that I asked him about applyin' to law school. When I told him my L.S.A.T. scores, Dean Churchill very strongly suggested that I apply. I took him up on it and completed the application the Friday before the rally. I asked for early consideration, so I'll hear around January 15th, not that I'm worried about it after what Dean Churchill told me. Just to cover my bets, I'm also gonna to apply to State, but I'd rather go to S.U., seein' what a great job they did with you and Sam."

After pausing for a second, Jo said, "But, there's a complication. I'm pregnant."

Sean calmly asked, "When are you due?"

Jo replied, "The doctor figures the date of conception at the end of September, so add nine months. Aren't you surprised?"

Sean replied, "Not really! You've been watching your diet for a few weeks. When you turned down a bottle of wine at dinner after our interview with Hannity and Colmes, I started to suspect strongly that you were pregnant. I figured that you'd tell me after the election."

"Precious, can I handle motherhood and law school?" Jo asked.

Sean replied, "Going to law school is no different than having a job. Could you handle motherhood and a job?"

Jo replied indirectly, "I have one last thing to tell you. Daddy wants to retire. He and Momma are sellin' the farm to my brothers. They were thinkin' about movin' up here and buyin' a place near Lucy's. Would that be okay with you?"

Sean didn't have a problem at all. Sean got along well with his in-laws. Having Jo's mother around would definitely give Jo a lot of flexibility with childcare. Sean told Jo that that would be a capital idea.

As Sean's F-150 pulled up to the gate at the edge of their home, Jo asked Sean, "Will you help me prepare for class? I know that there will be a lot of serious intellectual types in law school. I'd like to read some books to help me prepare, so I don't make a complete fool of myself."

As they pulled up the driveway, Sean said, "Beautiful, I'm sure that the law school still sends out a reading list to incoming students. I'll see if I can get you a copy of this list on Thursday. If you don't mind, I'd love to help you."

After parking his truck in the garage, Sean went around to Jo's side and helped her down. As they started to leave the garage, Jo said, "Precious, don't leave your coat in the truck. It might be cold tomorrow mornin'."

Bowing to Jo's common sense, Sean grabbed his London Fog and carried it over his shoulder. As they walked through the covered breezeway separating the garage from the house, Jo and Sean were as happy as they could be, holding hands as they walked toward the back door of the house. When they were approximately a dozen feet from the house, destiny took a hand. Their solitude was interrupted when a loud, shrill voice commanded, **"Don't move and put your hands up!"**

Cynthia McReynolds, clad in black from her neck to her Nikes,™ stepped out of the shadows, holding a small, shiny revolver pointed at them.

In a split second, something both wonderful and awesome occurred, irrevocably changing the lives of the four persons present in the breezeway on that dark, November night. Sean Patrick Riley—analytical, emotionally detached, passive and pedantic—without a bit of hesitation or contemplation—charged Mrs. McReynolds. While waving his raincoat over his head, he screamed the only war cry that he knew, a sound that was the last that many Federal troops had heard during the Recent Unpleasantness: **Woh--who--ey! Who--ey! Who--ey! Woh--who--ey! Who--ey!**[13]

Mrs. McReynolds froze, half-thinking that she was seeing a fiend from Hell, a thought that would have given great pleasure to Sean's distant ancestor, Brian Boru.

When Sean was about three feet away from his assailant, he snapped his London Fog at her head and lowered his right shoulder, slamming into her unprotected mid-section. Mrs. McReynolds hit the door with a very loud thud, dropping the revolver from her hand as she fell.

Three minutes later, a very dazed Cynthia McReynolds lay on the patio decking on her stomach, her hands cuffed behind her, while Jo called on the satellite phone for a patrol car to pick up her prisoner.

When Jo finished her call, Cynthia McReynolds was privileged to overhear Sean and Jo's first real argument. While it took Jo about five minutes to let Sean know exactly how she felt in terms that any Old Corps Marine D.I. would have appreciated, the gist of her complaint was that Sean Riley was a fool, who had risked his life unnecessarily.

When Jo ran out of steam—finally—Sean said very calmly, "Beautiful, may I speak briefly in my own defense?"

Jo, still catching her breath, snapped, "Make it quick, Yankee Boy!"

Sean said, "I have three points to my defense. Point One, I love you. Point Two, you are pregnant with our child. I didn't want bullets flying around you and our baby. Point Three, the type of revolver that Mrs. McReynolds was carrying is very familiar to me. When I was a boy, my father taught me how to shoot one just like it. Most people don't know this, but besides making the famous one-shot weapon, Colonel Deringer also made a five-shot revolver."

Jo interrupted Sean's discourse by saying, "Sean, you're babblin' again."

Sean tried to apologize. "Sorry dear, I'm nervous."

"I'll bet you're nervous. You just charged a woman pointin' a loaded gun right at your heart! Aren't you a little **late** with the adrenalin rush?"

Taking a deep breath, Sean said, "What I 'm trying to tell you is that Colonel Deringer's revolver is single action. You can't fire it unless the hammer is pulled all the way back. I could see from where I was standing that Mrs. McReynolds hadn't cocked the hammer. I did what I did to redirect her attention away from cocking the hammer. It worked, didn't it?"

Jo would have said something smart in reply, but at that exact point in time, two patrol cars—one from the sheriff's department and one from the state police—arrived at the gate to their property.

****

A while later, having delivered Mrs. McReynolds into the custody of the other deputies and having taken care of the paperwork, Jo joined Sean, Law and Equity in the house. Law was sitting on Sean's lap and Equity was sitting behind him on the top of his chair. When Jo spoke to Sean, he didn't reply. He just sat in his chair, staring at Fox News. When Jo checked to see if he was okay, Sean just nodded his head and pointed to the TV. Turning up the volume, a very pleased Jo and Sean both heard a **very tired** Brit Hume say that Fox News just declared Governor Bush the winner in Florida. Florida was now colored red on the big map on their television screen.

After the shock of the sudden reversal in the presidential race had worn off, Sean asked Jo, "What did you charge her with?"

Sean was more than a bit surprised when he heard Jo say, "Precious, I sent her to the county mental health facility for an evaluation. Let's hold off on chargin' her until we see if they want to keep her."

Sean asked, "Why didn't you throw the book at her?"

Jo replied, "All I could've charged her with were two Class B misdemeanors—criminal trespass and reckless conduct. If this was her first offense, she'd probably get a year's probation, a hundred hours of community service, anger management classes and a big fine. That won't do much to discourage her from either doin' the job right next time, or even worse, hirin' a hit man to come after us or our family. It struck me that the best thing I could do for everyone involved—includin' her—would be to get her head examined. You have to wonder if anyone who points a firearm not ready to shoot at two armed people isn't really suicidal."

Sean nodded his head, silently noting the mature, reasoned approach that Jo had just taken to resolve this difficult situation.

Jo added, "When the patrol car drove off, Mrs. McReynolds was screamin' her head off and tryin' to kick out the back window. I'm sure that she'll really impress the shrinks when she arrives in that condition."

****

Half an hour later, having played with Law and Equity enough to calm down, Jo and Sean were in their bedroom, preparing for bed. As Jo undressed, she asked, "What **were** you thinkin' when you charged her?"

A very embarrassed Sean said, "As soon as I saw her revolver with the hammer uncocked, I just knew that she wasn't ready to shoot. After that, I didn't think. I just acted to protect you and the baby."

Jo said, as uxoriously as she could, "Cut that stuff out! I don't want to be a two-time widow any time soon, okay?" Sean meekly nodded.

Sean did not realize it, but for the first time since Cheryl died, he was not detached from life. The emotional barrier that had separated him from the rest of the human race had come crashing down like the Berlin Wall.

Fifteen minutes later, Jo, Sean, Law and Equity were curled up together. Law and Equity purred very loudly. Judge Sean Patrick Riley fell into a deep, contented sleep, surrounded by three females who loved him dearly. Sean was at peace with the universe. Lieutenant Jolene Lee Scruggs Goldberg Riley slept even better than Sean, because she had finally found her place in this world.

Epilogue

The doctors at the county psychiatric facility filed papers to have Cynthia McReynolds involuntarily committed to a mental hospital. As luck would have it, the case was assigned to Judge Sean Riley, who rapidly recused himself and requested that a visiting judge hear the case. No trial was ever held because Cynthia McReynolds chose not to contest the matter, against the advice of her team of high-priced lawyers. She spent sixty-two days in a private psychiatric hospital in the mountains.

While Cynthia McReynolds was in the hospital, a grand jury began looking into her financial dealings with Winfred K. Rudd. No indictment was obtained, largely because Winfred K. Rudd produced certified official documents showing that he and Cynthia McReynolds had been secretly, but lawfully, married in a small island nation in the Caribbean the preceding summer, prior to the date of the check.

Thomas A. Greene moved to Coastal City and bought a thirty-five foot sailboat, took up blue-water sailing and retired from both law and politics. He won a number of offshore races and began to write for sailing magazines.

Covington McReynolds threatened to file suit to have his mother removed as a trustee of his trust, based upon her alleged mental incapacity to serve as a trustee. Rather than have her personal problems spread about in the media, Cynthia McReynolds resigned as trustee of Covington's trust.

After she was released from the hospital, Cynthia McReynolds Rudd moved to Malibu with her new husband. A few months later, Warren K. Rudd's novel was released to critical acclaim. It stayed on the bestseller list of the New York Times for thirty-two weeks. The novel was a thriller about how a corrupt judge attempted to silence a crusading newspaper man through illegally committing the wife of the newspaper man to a ghastly mental hospital.

The novel was made into a full-length motion picture starring a tall, thin, handsome English actor, aged forty-five, who spoke with a crisp Oxbridge accent and sported a full head of dark hair. The leading lady in the film was played by a charming, curvaceous, dark-eyed, thirty-year-old actress from Brazil. Despite glowing reviews that described the film as "...a serious, insightful look into the trials and tribulations of a crusading journalist, who fights every day to protect our First Amendment rights from corrupt government officials...." the film bombed at the box office.

End Notes

1. Southern University is a private university located in Southern State. Southern State could be any one of the states of the Confederacy, save for Virginia, Florida and Arkansas. Both the university and the state are partly fictional and partly a composite of a number of schools and states. Most of Southern University's law school classes are held during the day. But, certain electives, taught by practitioners, are held in the late afternoon or at night as a convenience to their instructors. These tend to be the most popular classes, which fill up very quickly.

2. State University, also known as "State" is located in Capitol City. Capitol City is approximately thirty miles east of University City.

3. Jolene was really 5'11". Not knowing that Sean was 6'2", Jolene had worn shoes with low heels.

4. Sean didn't know it, but the good taste that Jolene's wardrobe displayed was largely Kyra's since they had spent Wednesday and Thursday evenings shopping at Capitol City's most expensive shops to get Jolene ready for tonight.

5. The term, "jury view" can be misleading. In its usual use, the term refers to a situation where jurors physically go to view a place. In a bench trial, where the judge is the fact finder and there is no jury impaneled, the viewing of a place by the judge would still be called a "jury view." So, it is possible to have a "jury view" even when there is no jury to view anything.

6. When the post-Reconstruction constitution for Southern State was drafted in the 1870s, each county was given a county attorney, who was made the county's chief legal officer for all matters except felony prosecutions. Back then, felonies were handled by judges who rode circuit in multi-county districts. A district attorney would handle felonies for that circuit. By the 1920s, each county in the state had acquired enough population to have at least one district court in each county, so the division of labor between the two offices made no sense. State constitutions being very difficult to change, this inefficient arrangement continues to the present day— except that shortly after World War II, district attorneys were given full responsibility for all criminal cases. Since mental health commitments are civil matters, the county attorney, not the district

attorney, had responsibility for prosecuting those matters for the state.

7. The term "voir dire" means to speak the truth. In the South and Midwest, it is pronounced as voy (rhyming with boy) dire (which rhyming with tire). In the rest of the country, the term is pronounced "vwa dear." Since the term is of Anglo-French origin, it is anyone's guess how it was originally pronounced.

8. "Clear and convincing" is the legal standard between the civil standard of a "preponderance of the evidence" (more likely than not) and the criminal standard of "beyond a reasonable doubt."

9. A grouping of adult house cats is properly called a "clowder." Since the cats treat Sean like a large, somewhat stupid cat, from the feline standpoint, this clowder has three members.

10. Unfortunately, "If it ain't broke, don't fix it!" doesn't translate well into church Latin. Had it, there would not have been a *Vatican II.*

11. Southern University was founded by substantial donations from three very wealthy men, known collectively as *The Founders.*

12. The primary color of the necktie is a coffee color. There are also small stripes of cote d' emerald green and new red.

13. A recording of the Rebel Yell made by a Confederate War veteran can be found at: http://www.26nc.org/History/RebelYell/main.htm. Historians believe that Confederate forces in different theaters of action used several alternate versions of the yell. Alternate versions may be found at: http://members.aol.com/h4texas/yell.htm.

About the Author

Rory R. Olsen was born and raised in the Midwest. His bride of more than thirty years, Trish, grew up in East Texas. They met when Rory was a student at Duke University School of Law.

Rory and Trish have lived in Houston, Texas since 1980. They have one daughter, who is a C.P.A. in Dallas. They also have two cats.

Rory practiced probate and estate planning law for eighteen years before becoming the Judge of Probate Court Number Three, Harris County, Texas in 1999.

Rory may be reached by e-mail at: author@pobox.com. His website is: http://www.goodwillwonintheend.com/.

Printed in the United States
57692LVS00001B/85-204